Frost Prisms

(The Broken Prism, Volume 5)

V. St. Clair

Asher,

This is the last letter I will ever send you.

That you would even give me such an ultimatum shows that you have turned against me. You, who I always counted as a friend, who I trusted beyond all others, and now it has come to this? I will not turn back from the road I'm on—the road to true greatness. I have discovered new depths of magic that you could never even fathom.

I am content to leave you to your own path, out of respect for the friendship we once shared. But if you are determined to die for your betrayal, then so be it. I will meet you in battle, and I will prove that you are still—and forevermore—the weaker of the two of us, as you have always known in your heart, even at Mizzenwald.

There are no prizes for second-best, old friend.

A. Frost

1
A Fair Exchange

"Aleric?"

Asher's voice was so soft that for a moment Hayden could convince himself that he had misheard, or that the Prism Master was playing some horrible joke on him, or that he was still stuck in the schism going insane after all...

The man Hayden knew as Hunter was standing upright now, still looking a little disoriented from the effect of moving from the realm of anti-magic back to this one. His eyes focused on Asher in that moment, taking in the red metallic Mastery robes and the details of his face.

His expression transformed from confusion to delight in the span of a heartbeat, and he grinned when he said, "Who did you steal Mastery robes off of, Ash? That's one way to get women, I suppose..."

For a horrible moment the tableau was frozen like that: Hunter grinning, Asher still staring at him in silent terror, and Hayden standing in the no-man's land between the two.

Then the moment ended.

"Hayden, get away from him," Asher found his voice at last, motioning Hayden towards him without taking his eyes off of his old friend.

Hayden was still too stunned to move.

He's wrong—Asher has to be wrong. There's no way that Hunter can be the Dark Prism...that he could be my father. My father's been dead for years, ever since the day he showed up at my mother's house...

A little voice in his head pointed out that the Dark Prism's body had never been found after the explosion.

Neither was my mother's—they were both vaporized in the blast.

With the force of the explosion, it would have been easy for a schism to open up. Maybe his father had been propelled into it before the magical backlash in the area could incinerate him.

A schism would still be open there if that was the case...

But he knew that wasn't necessarily true; he had seen schisms snap open and shut within the span of a second as a result of powerful magic being used.

He's tall and broad-shouldered and has blond hair; he doesn't look anything like me!

Everyone had always agreed he had his mother's hair and eye color, but there was something similar about the shape of their faces, now that he was looking for it....He had felt a sense of familiarity with the man from the moment they met that was hard to explain. He had chalked it up to being lost and half-nuts inside of the other realm, but maybe...

It can't be true!

While he was still struggling with the insane possibility that the man who had just rescued him from the schism was actually his infamous father, Asher said, "Hayden—*come here*," a bit more emphatically, drawing a prism slowly from his belt.

In the moment it took Hayden to shake himself from his stupor and realize that—if this *was* the Dark Prism—he was standing right in front of the man, Aleric Frost seemed to snap out of his joyful mood and grabbed Hayden roughly by the shoulder, pulling him closer.

"Leave it or the boy dies," Aleric commanded with his powerful voice, one strong arm wrapped around Hayden's torso, holding him in front of his body like a shield as he drew a knife and pressed it lightly against Hayden's throat. Hayden had seen him fight monsters with that knife only hours ago in the defense of his life, and now he was threatening to end him with it.

Asher froze with his hand halfway to his circlet, expression stony.

"Leave Hayden out of this," he said calmly, with the air of one who was trying to soothe a wild animal.

"Toss me that prism or I'll cut his throat," Aleric returned coldly, pressing the knife a little deeper into Hayden's flesh for emphasis, until he could feel a trickle of blood oozing down his neck. Hayden tried not to swallow, for fear that the motion would cause him to cut his own throat on accident.

"That boy is your son," Asher pointed out, expression still scarily neutral, though Hayden could tell he was doing some fast thinking; he could almost see the thoughts spinning around his mentor's brain as the man weighed his options.

This is the best chance Asher will ever have to defeat him, Hayden realized abruptly. *My father doesn't have any prisms on him right now and he's just come through the schism—he's still a little dazed, possibly vulnerable while his Source recovers from the shock...*

That was when he knew that he was going to die.

Asher had to kill the Dark Prism right here, right now, or there might never be another chance when he could get the upper hand in battle. And where was Hayden? Standing directly in the line of fire because he was too slow on the uptake to move when Asher first instructed him to.

"And you think that matters?" Aleric answered his former best friend's question with icy indifference. "Give me the prism or the boy dies."

"Don't do it," Hayden interjected, speaking for the first time and causing the Dark Prism's grip on him to tighten painfully.

"Shut up, Hayden," his mentor informed him without taking his eyes off of Aleric. After another moment of consideration he said, "Let the boy go."

Hayden could hear the derision in his father's voice and guessed that he was smirking.

"You always were weak, Asher. We could have remained friends, if not for that little character flaw."

"Funny, I was thinking the exact same thing about you," the Prism Master responded coolly.

Their attention was momentarily diverted from the question of Hayden's mortality by a small, dark-purple dragonling that was gliding towards them from the castle, casting shadows over the grass as he flew closer.

Cinder, Hayden realized with a pang of understanding.

Cinder had been his father's familiar before he disappeared five years ago. Now the dragonling alit gracefully onto his master's shoulder as though he'd never been gone, the shadow of his wings falling over Hayden's face.

It was that, more than anything, that convinced Hayden that his father was truly alive and standing right behind him with a knife pressed against his throat. Cinder was reclusive by nature, and only liked Hayden because he carried his father's blood. He would never perch on a stranger's shoulder like this.

"I tire of waiting for you to decide whether the boy's life is worth more to you than my death," Aleric informed Master Asher. "You have three seconds to decide whether this boy is more valuable to you than your vengeance, and then I'll make the decision for you."

Asher tossed him the prism before he could even begin counting, and Aleric caught it with the hand that was holding the knife. In one fluid motion, Hayden was shoved forward, hard, so that he stumbled and fell to his knees in the grass. He saw Asher snatch another prism from his pocket and bring it up in front of his eye, not bothering with the eyepiece, and Hayden flattened himself against the ground to avoid getting caught in the crossfire. Before the Prism Master could successfully get a spell off, he lowered the prism and said, "Damn—he's already gone."

Hayden turned his head and confirmed this. They were alone on the lawn right now; Cinder and his father were nowhere to be seen.

Asher helped him to his feet, which felt surprisingly wobbly and unsteady at the moment, like they didn't want to hold his weight anymore. Hayden narrowed his gaze at the Prism Master and said, "You let him get away," without inflection.

"I did," he admitted with a frown. "You look like you've been through the wringer, but unless you think you're bleeding internally, your injuries will have to wait until we've had a chance to inform the others about this new development."

Hayden wasn't quite ready to change the subject yet, and as the two of them began walking back towards the castle he said, "You could have killed him. You'll never have a better chance at finding him weaponless and defenseless than you did just now, and you let him get away."

"That's probably true," Asher allowed, slowing his pace to match Hayden's limping gait, even though it was obvious that he wanted to sprint inside as fast as he could to warn the other Masters.

"Then why didn't you take your chance?"

Asher gave him a funny look and said, "Do you really have to ask? I would have had to go through you to get to him, and if my magic didn't kill you, he certainly would have before I could stop him. There was only one way to get you out alive and I took it."

Hayden swallowed a lump of emotion and didn't bother asking the next obvious question: *you think my life is more important than all the people he's going to kill now that he's free?*

The answer was obvious, or he'd be a corpse on the back lawns right now. He was thankful to be alive, but not sure if Asher had made the best choice for the Nine Lands.

If anyone finds out he let the Dark Prism go free, he'll be murdered by the Council for sure.

Hayden opened his mouth to say, "Thank you," but the words never quite made it out. Instead, they walked in silence across the back lawns until they were at the entrance of the castle.

He realized that classes must still be in session or else there would be more people in the hallways. As it was, they passed no one as they walked through the corridors, which was at least one bit of good luck, because Hayden really didn't want to deal with his gawking peers right now. They made it all the way to the Prism Master's office without encountering anyone else, and Asher motioned Hayden inside and said, "I'll be back in a minute. Don't open the door for any reason."

And with that he shut and locked the door with them both inside, grabbed his Mastery Charm, and vanished.

Momentarily alone and safe, Hayden felt the full weight of his weariness settle over him, and he slumped over in Asher's most comfortable chair and rested his head on the desk in front of him. His nose was pressed against their most recent research notes, and for a few seconds Hayden simply stared at the streaks of blue and green beneath his eyes that he had drawn only days ago; it felt like much more time had passed since he did that work.

He closed his eyes in an attempt to ward off the throbbing in his head, without any real effect. Dimly, he wondered why Asher had locked him in the office and told him not to open the door for anyone.

Surely he doesn't think I'm going to be attacked here...not so soon, at least.

Hayden found it extremely unlikely that his father would come back to storm the castle in search of him—especially as he had let Hayden go free only minutes ago, but Asher obviously wasn't taking any chances with his safety right now.

His teeth were chattering obnoxiously, and try as he might, Hayden couldn't stop the unwanted movement. He wasn't sure why they were being so uncooperative; he wasn't even cold, but now that he thought about it, his entire body seemed to be racked with shudders at odd moments.

*Cyclical convulsions, symptomatic of a level-three state of shock. Administer warm blankets and fluids until symptoms subside...*Mistress Razelle's voice came to him then, from one of their Healing classes years ago.

The sound of rustling papers prevented him from dozing off, and he snapped his head upright in time to see Master Willow materialize into the office, the motion causing some of the loose papers on Asher's desk to cascade to the floor.

"Hayden—you're back," the Master of Wands looked surprised to see him there, but before he could say anything more than that, Masters Kilgore, Sark, and Laurren appeared. As they each looked at each other and then at Hayden, even more Masters materialized in the office: Razelle, Graus, Reede, Dirqua, Potts—the Master of Herbalism, and finally, Asher himself.

The office was hardly large enough to contain them all, which was the first comment out of Master Sark's mouth as he stumbled into Graus in an attempt to put his back to the wall.

"You mind telling us why we had to abandon our classes to cram into your office like sardines?" he snapped at Asher.

The Prism Master was in no mood for sarcasm—which might be a first, now that Hayden considered it—and opened his mouth to explain, only to be cut off by Kilgore, who caught sight of Hayden and said, "Frost! You made it back in one piece!"

This brought the attention of the other nine Masters to him as well, and Hayden nodded wearily and said, "The schism is closed."

There was a collective clamor of approving noises at this news, though Sark said, "While that's excellent to hear, I still don't see why we had to stop teaching just to celebrate…"

"Don't celebrate just yet," Hayden mumbled, though somehow everyone in the room seemed to hear him perfectly. A few of the Masters now looked confused, and Hayden had no intention of being the one to break the terrible news to them that their number one enemy was back in action because of him.

Thankfully, Master Asher did it for him.

"Aleric's alive," he blurted out before anyone else could interrupt again. "He was inside the other realm all this time, and he crossed back through with Hayden and escaped from the grounds not five minutes ago."

You could have heard a pin drop in that cramped office.

After an uncomfortably long silence, it was Reede who said, "Please tell me that this is a terribly distasteful joke you two are playing on us," to his colleague.

"Afraid not," Asher sighed. "I saw him with my own eyes—spoke to him, briefly. As everyone is keen on reminding me, I was the man's best friend for most of our lives, so if anyone would recognize him after a five year hiatus, it would be me."

Another horrible pause, while the others digested this information in silence. Hayden was surprised that none of them were gaspers or shouters—there was usually one in any given group of people.

Finally Master Willow said, "Where is Aleric now? You said he's left the grounds..."

Asher shook his head.

"He caught me off-guard and took one of my prisms. I have no idea where he went to, but if he's been stuck in the other realm for five years then he'll probably need time to set up base again and reestablish his magic."

So that was to be the official story: Asher was surprised by the Dark Prism's unexpected appearance and got overpowered. Hayden committed it to memory so he wouldn't be the one to say otherwise.

"Does the Council know?" Willow prodded.

"No, not yet," Asher replied.

"Someone needs to tell them immediately, or we'll be brought up on charges for withholding information," Master Dirqua pointed out pragmatically.

"As soon as Hayden tells us—succinctly—how in the world he happened to bring the Dark Prism back through the schism with him, we will inform the Council," Laurren responded, weighing Hayden with those strange, blue-purple eyes.

Once more, everyone turned to him, waiting for an explanation. Trying to ignore his throbbing headache, he gave the best overview he could manage right now and hoped it was enough.

"I have no idea how long we'd been in the other realm before I met up with him. Harold was already dead, and Tanner and I were attacked by hyenas after we cleared the swamp. Tanner died saving me, but there was still one hyena left. That's when Hun—when my father showed up. He finished off the hyena and said he saw the flash bomb I'd set off in the swamp, and came to investigate. He told me his name was Hunter and offered to help me find the schism aperture, once I told him what I was doing."

"And you didn't recognize him on sight?" Master Sark seemed unable to interject at this point.

"I'd never seen him before, other than the time he blew up my house, but I don't have most of my memories from that time. It's not like I look exactly like him or anything, and I was well on my way to losing my mind by the time I met him, so I wasn't at my mental peak anyway."

The others frowned at this and Master Kilgore made an impatient motion with one hand to wave him on.

"Anyway, we traveled together for the rest of the way. He kept me talking because it helped keep my mind focused, so I ended up telling him my entire life's story, including all the stuff about him…"

"This doesn't make any sense," Reede interrupted. "If Aleric spent five years inside the other realm he should be a slobbering pile of drool by now. Hayden has the worst Foci the world has probably ever seen and he barely lasted two days in there."

Wow, I was only gone for two days? It felt like a week had elapsed inside the schism.

"He's obviously found a way to use magic inside of the other realm, probably with that accursed Black Prism of his," Sark scowled. "He duped Hayden long enough to get free of the schism and then showed his true colors."

"I don't think that's true…" Hayden interjected softly. "I mean, I don't think he was pretending not to know who I was. He was much stronger than me and much better at surviving—he could have just taken my prism from me and followed the ley lines for himself. Heck, I *gave* him the void-prism to hang onto because I was afraid I'd lose my mind and accidentally use it too early," he explained to general astonishment. "He didn't seem to understand magic at all; I had to tell him how Foci and Sources work, and what prisms even were. I don't claim to know him very well, but surely he can't be that good of an actor, especially when there was just no reason for it."

A few of the Masters frowned thoughtfully in the silence that followed this.

"And he didn't show any signs of recognition when you were sharing your life story with him? You said you told him about his own role in how you came to be at Mizzenwald..." Master Kilgore prodded gently.

"He just looked like it was an interesting story—not like it was familiar at all. I don't know why, but I think for some reason he really didn't remember any of that until we left the schism. Even once we made it out, it took him a couple minutes to remember who he was."

"Hayden's right," Asher interjected at this point. "When he caught sight of me he initially thought we were still friends. He asked me who I'd stolen Mastery robes off of."

"That still doesn't make sense," Master Potts persisted. "The other realm should distort anyone who crosses through with open Foci, and since we've established that Aleric probably wasn't using magic to protect himself inside the other realm, he should have been as affected as Hayden was by it."

"Should he?" Master Laurren asked quietly, capturing everyone's attention in that subtle way of his. "He was already suffering under massive distortion effects from his own work with broken prisms. We really have no idea what happens to someone who crosses realms under those circumstances. If it drives a sane person crazy, mightn't it force a crazy person sane?"

Hayden's mouth wasn't the only one to drop open at that mind-blowing possibility. Master Asher had spent over a decade trying to find a cure for mental distortion; was there another way to go about it involving schisms? Admittedly, forcing someone to live in that horrible realm for the rest of their lives in order to remain sane was hardly ideal, but maybe it was a start...

"If he was suddenly cured of his mental issues, then why didn't he remember who he was?" Master Sark persisted, though he looked floored by the very thought of a sane Aleric Frost.

Laurren shrugged and said, "I have no idea. Maybe after suffering from the distortion for ten years, when he was suddenly free of it inside the other realm he lost his memory?"

"I think it's something like that," Hayden spoke again, recalling his own recent experience. "Towards the end, when it got really bad, I couldn't remember who people were anymore. I forgot about all of you, all of my friends, and even who I was and what the void-prism was for. At first it was terribly painful, but towards the end I started to get used to it, like my brain was rebuilding itself around the effects. Maybe he did the same thing, only he had a lot longer to build a new life for himself..."

Now most of the others were giving him concerned, pensive looks. Master Reede actually asked if he felt he was still suffering from the effect of being inside the other realm for so long, and Hayden shook his head.

"No, I started to get better as soon as I came back through the schism, but it took me a couple minutes to orient myself. It took him even longer, which I didn't really understand until I learned who he was, but maybe it's because he was in the other realm for such a long time—so there was more to sort through to get back to normal; well, normal for him anyway."

"That seems as likely as anything," Master Graus agreed slowly. "If he had to rebuild himself inside the other realm and didn't have any of the people or places he knew to help him along, it makes sense that he would have started from scratch and given himself an entirely new identity."

"I asked him how long he'd been in that realm and he said for as long as he could remember. At the time I just thought that meant he was born there, but in hindsight I feel pretty stupid for missing it."

He rested his forehead in his hands and sighed.

"I can't believe I unleashed the Dark Prism on the world again, especially when he was doing just fine for himself in the other realm. Every time I try to do something good, something even worse happens in the aftermath."

That was, sadly, true. Last year he'd fought in a war to save his friends, which led to the schisms opening in the first place. Now he'd gone into the schism to close it and protect his friends at Mizzenwald, only to reincarnate the greatest magical threat the Nine Lands had seen in a century.

I should stop trying to do good things before I get us all killed.

No one really said anything in response to that, which only confirmed that they too were blaming him for bringing the Dark Prism back to life. He kept his face turned down and his eyes closed as Master Willow said, "I'll inform the Council. We need to beef up our defenses around the school significantly in order to prevent him from reappearing here at will."

"We don't know what sort of magic he has at his disposal since he acquired the Black Prism," Sark pointed out. "Nothing we do may be able to keep him out if he's determined to get into Mizzenwald."

"No, but we can still try," Kilgore grumbled. "We haven't been idle for the last five years and he has; we may yet have some new tricks up our sleeves that he isn't prepared for."

Hayden listened to all of this with his eyes shut. Eventually he heard the flutter of papers around Asher's office being blown off of their piles, and knew that the other Masters were disappearing to go do whatever task they had been assigned in fortifying the school. When he opened his eyes, only Master Asher remained.

For a moment they stared at each other in silence. Hayden wished his mentor didn't have such a sad, sympathetic look on his face, because it just made his chest hurt.

"Cinder left with him," he pointed out, mostly to break the silence.

"He was always Aleric's familiar. He will stick with him until the end." Asher nodded.

"I'll miss him," Hayden said glumly. "I'm sure Bonk will too." Frowning, he added, "Does this mean he and Bonk will be enemies if they see each other again?"

Asher looked unhappy when he said, "If you find yourself fighting your father, then yes, I expect so."

For some reason that made Hayden even sadder than the thought of loosing the Dark Prism on the world. Bonk and Cinder had been friends for as long as Hayden had been at Mizzenwald, and they would be forced to fight each other just because of a battle between their masters.

Another moment of silence passed between them before Asher said, "So, what did you think of the Aleric Frost—Hunter, that you met in the other realm?"

Hayden frowned and said, "I liked him—and I was jealous of him, though I'm not sure if it was because my mind was turning on me or if I would have felt that way no matter what. He was everything I'm not: tall, stupidly handsome, self-confident, naturally charming…"

He sighed and continued. "I was glad for his help and I would have died without him, but I still felt like the loser little kid who was tagging along—even though it was my mission in the first place and he was nothing but nice to me."

"Aleric did have that effect on the people around him," Asher said with a sympathetic smile. "It was a side-effect of being his friend, though I was probably just as cocksure as him so it didn't bother me at the time. It took the magical community by surprise when the boy who seemed to have it all morphed into the Dark Prism."

"I'm still trying to reconcile the two different versions of him in my head," Hayden admitted. "I can't believe he was ready to slit my throat not two minutes after carrying me on his back through the schism to save my life. You'd think that the fact that I'm his son would have counted for something, especially after I shared my life story with him…"

Master Asher shook his head.

"Becoming the Dark Prism removed the last of the humanity from him; you don't matter to him any more than I or anyone else at this point."

Very quietly, so softly that he wasn't sure if his mentor even heard it, Hayden whispered, "He said any father would be proud to have me as a son."

Saying it out loud made his heart hurt. The man he had known as Hunter had listened to all of the struggles he'd overcome in the last five years with great interest, and had told him that he was brave and worthy of admiration.

Asher rested a gentle hand on his shoulder and said, "So he would have been, if he had been the father you deserved." He sighed and retracted his hand.

"The fact that he was willing to kill me without hesitation as soon as we came through the opening sort of suggests that he didn't show up at my mother's house five years ago to recruit me as an ally," Hayden transitioned to a less painful subject.

"I'm not sure we can say that just yet," Asher countered mildly. "He may have wanted to assess your strengths and see if you would be an asset to him, or he might have just been curious about you. Either way, Aleric now prizes himself more than anything, and since he thought I was going to kill him when he came through the schism, he would have willingly sacrificed anyone to prevent that from happening, even if he was otherwise interested in keeping you around."

Hayden frowned thoughtfully.

"How long do you think it'll take before he's ready to start terrorizing the world again?"

His mentor shrugged and said, "I have no idea. A few weeks, at the earliest, while he recovers his strength and gets the lay of the land. He'll also need time to refortify his defenses at the Frost estate—assuming he decides to return there. After that, who knows?"

Hayden was old enough to remember the way the world was the last time the Dark Prism was strong. Mages were impossible to find, as they all attempted to lie low and avoid the attention of Aleric Frost. This was largely responsible for the boom in the monster population that the Nine Lands was still attempting to recover from. Even non-magic people lived in fear of their towns being the next to burn, their friends being murdered, their houses being ravaged by monsters they weren't equipped to fight off.

We can't go back to that.

Hayden didn't really see a way to prevent it though, short of getting rid of his father once and for all, but unless they got phenomenally lucky and a schism opened up in the Dark Prism's bedroom one night, they would have no choice but to start sending mages to fight him again.

There's no way I'll be able to avoid that. Calahan will make sure that I get sent to battle my father to the death, no matter what.

Which meant that Hayden was probably going to die soon. He was too emotionally exhausted to be fearful just now, though the idea did raise a new question for him.

"What do you think the Council is going to do once Master Willow finishes telling them?"

Asher made an ugly face and said, "Nothing pleasant, I'm sure." Then he continued, "In the immediate future, they'll spread word far and wide of your father's return so that people aren't caught by surprise and have a chance to prepare themselves. Most towns will probably implement curfews again and open up the old underground shelters to hide in if Aleric shows up."

"What I really meant was, what do you think they'll do to *me* for being the one to bring him back into the Nine Lands? Do you think there's any chance at all of them believing I didn't do it on purpose?"

The expression on his mentor's face was not encouraging.

"Some of them may believe you, but Cal won't be one of them, and unfortunately this is a perfect way to discredit you and attempt to make you a villain now that he's gotten you to close the schism for him. Remember, he's acutely aware of the fact that you have more hero status than the entire Council combined, and that you could use that public support to get him ousted from his position."

Hayden remembered that conversation from before he went into the schism, and how he had threatened to get Calahan fired if he made it out alive. It seemed like a long time ago.

"But now that I'm the boy who resurrected the Dark Prism, I'm going to lose all my adoring fans?" Hayden asked with a bite of sarcasm.

"You may," Asher answered seriously. "Which is no small thing, even though you scoff at it. It will take every friend and ally you have to get you out from under whatever horrible fate Calahan plans for you."

"What do you think he'll try to do? Arrest me? Put me back in lead Binders?" The latter made Hayden more fearful than the former, as he had already had to wear the uncomfortable, heavy metal bracelets for two years and had no desire to repeat the experience.

Master Asher looked troubled when he said, "I wish I could tell you how the man will act, but he's become more and more of a loose cannon where you're concerned. The pressure to deal with the sudden return of mage-kind's worst enemy will either delay his plans to tear you down long enough to send the glorious hero to deal with his evil father, or else it will expedite them."

"Well that's reassuring," Hayden groaned, massaging his temples.

"We need to get you to the infirmary so you can rest while there's time. The Council we be on us soon enough, and you'll need your strength." Asher motioned him towards the door, unlocking it so that they could exit and leading him down the hall.

Unfortunately, since all the Masters had abandoned their posts during the middle of class, students were milling around in the hallways or relaxing on the lawns, so plenty of people saw Hayden walk past with the Prism Master. A few people called out to him excitedly, congratulating him on his successful return and deducing that this meant the schism had been closed for good. Hayden ignored the chatter and pushed his way through the crowds to keep pace with Asher.

He was just outside the door to the infirmary when he spotted Tess at the other end of the hall. At first her eyes widened at the sight of him, and then her features transformed as the shock of seeing him alive turned to joy. She took a tentative step towards him and smiled, but he shook his head and turned away, trudging behind Master Asher into the safety and quiet of the infirmary. He couldn't stand to face Tess right now, to be the one who turned her joy to misery when she heard that her mother's killer was back.

He laid down in the same bed he typically used whenever he was holed up in the infirmary, while Asher tore around the room like time was running out, pulling elixirs from the cabinets seemingly at random and stacking them on Hayden's bedside table.

It's sad that I spend enough time here to have a favorite bed.

Asher threw a few bundles of rolled bandages at him and Hayden fumbled them and had to get out of bed and retrieve them from their various places on the floor.

"Why the rush?" he asked grumpily, head still throbbing as he crawled back into bed and reclined against the pillows, trying not to feel bad for getting the white sheets all dirty.

"Sorry, but there are things that need to be done quickly and not a lot of time in which to do them," his mentor apologized without looking at him, still pulling a few last minute supplies for him and dumping them in Hayden's lap. "I'll leave these with you and be off. Try and get some rest."

"You're going? I don't even know how much of these elixirs I'm supposed to take. Remember, I'm failing the subject this year..."

"Tess will help you—and Laraby, if I'm not mistaken."

Hayden frowned and said, "I don't want to see them right now, especially Tess. How can I face her after what I've done?"

Asher finally turned to look at him properly and said, "You don't have the luxury of shutting out your friends until you feel better this time. Unless we can outsmart Calahan and his supporters, this might be the last chance you have to see your friends for a very long time."

Hayden gulped, and before he could think of an appropriate response to that gloomy prediction, Master Asher had swept from the room and closed the door behind him.

Alone with his thoughts was not where Hayden wanted to be right now, so he dedicated himself to the task of getting cleaned up and bandaged. He filled a bucket with warm, soapy water and washed everything he could reach, peeling off the remnants of his clothing and depositing them directly into the trash can. Once he was finally as clean as he was going to get, he applied burn paste and aloe wherever it seemed necessary and wrapped the areas carefully with bandages, donning a clean robe he found in Mistress Razelle's supply closet. He climbed into bed—one that wasn't covered in grime, and was just about to close his eyes and try to relax when the door to the infirmary opened.

There were Tess and Zane, as expected. They somehow managed to look hopeful and grim at the same time when they approached.

"Well, I think it's safe to say that no one was really sure you'd make it back in one piece," Zane greeted him, approaching the bed and pulling up a spare chair. "But once again, you've proven everyone wrong and managed to be a total beast."

He was smiling at Hayden, but he obviously knew that something was wrong, because the smile was edged with worry.

Tess was silent, watching him carefully as she sat down beside Zane and began sorting through the elixirs on the end table, metering out some of each for Hayden without asking any questions.

"I'd hold off on the praise if I were you," Hayden sighed, utterly weary.

Zane pursed his lips and said, "Why is that? Tess said you looked like death warmed over, but everyone's talking about how the schism is closed now so things can't be all that bad..." he seemed to reconsider as a new idea struck him. "Hang on—you're not still crazy, are you?"

Hayden shook his head gently. "Not anymore, no." He drank whatever Tess handed him, not even asking what each thing was for but simply trusting her. He began to feel better almost immediately—physically, at least.

"Whoa," Zane leaned back in surprise. "You mean you actually *did* lose your mind for a while?" When Hayden nodded his friend grimaced and said, "What was it like?"

"Weird," Hayden answered truthfully. "I couldn't tell which thoughts were mine and which were the distortion, and eventually I forgot everything and everyone I knew. If not for Hu—the help I had, I would never have made it back." It was still hard to think of Hunter as the Dark Prism.

Zane raised an eyebrow and said, "You mean those two normals you brought with you actually managed to pull their weight? Good for them!" He grinned in surprise.

"No—I mean, yes, Tanner and Harold both pulled their weight...I was actually the useless one most of the time." He sighed. "But no, it wasn't them who saved me in the end."

"What are you talking about?" Zane looked confused. "You three were the only ones who went into the schism—who else would have been there to help you? Unless...you didn't find one of the old expedition teams, did you?"

He looked around the infirmary as though expecting to see Delauria and her companions sitting in the next bed.

"No, I never saw any sign of the other groups in there." Hayden sighed, preparing himself to get the worst part over with. "I met someone else in the other plane, someone who had been living there for years. He was the one who helped me at the end, when I was too far gone to help myself, and he carried me out of the schism on his back before I could get sealed inside while battling monsters."

"Wow," Zane whistled, impressed. "Where's this random hero who saved the day and made sure you got back home? I'd like to shake the hand of anyone who can survive a schism for years on their own."

Hayden frowned and said, "I doubt you'll be able to. He's probably off plotting to kill me and take over the world again."

Now both Tess and Zane looked confused. For the first time since she entered the room, the former spoke.

"What are you talking about?"

Hayden's heart hurt as he met her eyes.

"It's my father, Tess. I accidentally brought my father back from the other realm."

A terrible moment of silence followed this, during which Hayden's two friends stared at him like they couldn't even process the words that had just come out of his mouth.

"You—*what?*" Zane recovered first, looking incredulous.

"I found my father inside the other realm; he must have gotten blasted there the day my house exploded." He rubbed his eyes with the palms of his hands. "I guess I shouldn't be surprised that the magical explosion was bad enough to open a schism—actually, I'm more amazed that it closed itself before anyone else noticed it was there, given how bad the blast was."

Zane was shaking his head slowly.

"Hayden, you must still be a little nuts if you think there's any way you encountered the Dark Prism inside of a schism and brought him back into our world with you. It just...it doesn't make sense..."

"The story of my life," Hayden sighed. "Sadly, no, I'm not still crazy. I met my father on the other side—though I had no idea who he was and neither did he. If he had known, he probably wouldn't have saved my life and brought me back here. The Masters think he was driven sane in there, since he was already crazy going in, and that he built a new identity for himself when he forgot who he was. Unfortunately, he got his memory back when he came through the schism with me. He nearly slit my throat in the back lawns, but he left me and escaped instead."

"That can't be true," Zane insisted, no trace of humor on his face now.

"The Masters stayed around long enough to pump me for information, and then they went to do whatever it is they do to secure Mizzenwald and notify the Council of Mages that Aleric Frost is back in action."

His friends stared at him in silence for a long moment. Compelled to break it before it spiraled horribly, Hayden blurted out, "I'm sorry," to Tess.

She raised an eyebrow at him and said, "Whatever for?"

"Uh..." he started, "you know, for bringing my evil dad back with me on accident. I'm sure your father is going to hate me forever now, after all the Dark Prism cost the two of you the last time he was around."

Tess scowled and said, "It wasn't your fault, Hayden. No one knew he was inside the other realm, and if he really did save your life and bring you back here then…well, then I guess I can't be angry about it."

"You say that now," Hayden grumbled. "But wait until he starts killing again…"

"As long as you're around, there's still hope." She gave him a small smile that Hayden didn't feel he deserved. "You're the only one who's ever beaten him before, and that was before you even knew you had magic."

Hayden was about to open his mouth and tell her that she really shouldn't put so much faith in him, because he still had no idea what happened on that day at his mother's house, and after meeting his father and seeing how good the man was at virtually every task he set his mind to, he wasn't at all sure he could take him in a fight.

Zane prevented him from voicing any of his concern by saying, "Tess is right. You did it before and you can do it again. I've seen you work your way out of every horrible situation you've been thrown into in the last four years. Your father should have killed you while he had the chance, because you're going to end him once and for all this time around."

Hayden had absolutely no idea what to say in the face of his friends' absolute belief in him, so he said nothing at all.

"Get some rest," Tess said soothingly, resting her hand on his. "We'll be here when you wake up."

"Thanks," Hayden mumbled sleepily, yawning and closing his eyes, desperate to block out the world for a little while, to hide somewhere safe and recover.

Soon there won't be anywhere that's safe for me.

2
A Pile of Problems

True to their word, Tess and Zane were still sitting slumped in their chairs when Hayden opened his eyes. They were having a whispered conversation, but had broken off for the same reason that Hayden had snapped awake all of a sudden: the loud thump of something heavy slamming against the outside of the infirmary door.

"What was that?" Hayden mumbled, rubbing sleep from his eyes and sitting upright.

Zane and Tess looked at him in surprise and the former said, "No idea, but it startled me so badly I nearly jumped out of my skin. Sounded like a giant sack of potatoes hitting the door."

"It must have been someone banging on the door as they went by," Tess scowled. "Practical jokers. I wish they hadn't woken you up, because you need the rest."

"No, it's okay, I'm feeling a lot better already," Hayden assured her, stretching his arms and legs to limber them back up. His muscles were sore, but thanks to all the elixirs and salves, that was about the worst of it right now. "How long have I been asleep?"

"Less than two hours," Zane informed him.

"What were you all talking about while I was out?"

"Just what we think the Council of Mages is going to do now that they know about your father being back in town," Zane explained.

"Ah, I see. The Masters couldn't seem to decide whether I'd be arrested or praised and sent off to fight him," Hayden said without enthusiasm. "I'm personally hoping that someone else takes care of my father while I'm in prison, at which point the Masters will think of some cagey way to get me out of there and life will be good again."

Zane snorted in dry amusement.

"I don't think you'll get that lucky. Everyone is counting on you to be stronger than your old man—again. No way will they let you rot in a jail cell while he's on the loose."

Hayden frowned.

"I don't have magic that he doesn't, and I'm certainly not faster at casting than him. Asher always stomps me in duels, and my father managed to beat *him* the first time around like it was nothing."

"But time has passed since then," Tess insisted gently. "You don't know how good of a fighter Master Asher was five years ago, just how good he is now. And your father has been out of practice for just as long, so maybe things won't be as bad as they were the first time."

Another loud thump hit the other side of the infirmary door, causing them all to jump in unison.

"What in the world is going on out there?" Zane grumbled. "Some kind of party in the corridor?"

"No idea," Hayden answered without interest. "And anyway, he may be out of practice, but he still knows spells that I will never be able to learn, courtesy of the Black Prism."

"But everyone says you have the most Source power they've ever seen—maybe even more than your father," Zane countered mildly. "If that's true, then you at least have more raw power than him, which gives you an advantage."

"That's true..." Hayden admitted slowly.

Hayden opened his mouth to say something else, but for the third time they were startled by the sound of something slamming against the other side of the infirmary door.

"That tears it," Zane stood up so rapidly that his chair was shoved backwards and toppled over behind him. "I'm going to punch whatever idiot keeps banging on the door to a sickroom."

Zane stomped over to the door and tugged it open with righteous fury on his face, but his expression immediately changed as he said, "Oh—hi, sir...uh, what's going on?"

"Sorry to bother you with all the noise," Master Asher's voice answered, sounding unusually strained—as though he was lifting something heavy while he spoke. "But since you're here, do you mind grabbing his legs and helping me?"

Intrigued and alarmed, Hayden got out of bed and hurried to see what was going on, Tess in tow. They both stopped right behind Zane, gaping at the sight of the Prism Master attempting to drag an unconscious body away from them.

"Any day now," Asher snapped. "I need to be ready in case more of them show up, and I don't want their bodies littering the hallways and scaring off all the other students."

Still looking stunned, Zane hurried to lift the unknown man's legs and assist with carrying him towards an unused classroom.

"You mind telling me why you're knocking out—I *hope* he's only knocked out—strangers in the hallway?" Hayden asked curiously, following along with Tess at his side, both of them shielding the body from view of anyone who happened to walk by.

"He's alive—they all are," Asher explained curtly, still straining from the effort of hauling the slightly-overweight mage into the empty classroom, where he dropped the body unceremoniously besides two others.

Examining them more closely, Hayden noted that they were all mages—two men both slightly older than Asher, and a woman who looked a couple years younger. Judging by the equipment on their belts, the first man was a Powders major, the second a Conjury one, and the woman was carrying mostly wands.

"Uh, I usually try not to question the weird things you do," Hayden began uncertainly, "but I have to draw the line at hauling unconscious mages around the school. What in the world is going on here?"

Asher spared him an unreadable glance as he chivvied them back out of the room and withdrew a prism to magically lock the door behind them.

"Willow sent word that the Council reacted quite predictably to the news that Aleric has returned—which is to say, they went nuts." He sighed and motioned for them to precede him into the infirmary. "He asked me to watch out for attempts to take you from Mizzenwald against your will, which is what I've been doing for the past couple hours. As you can see, his concern turned out to be valid; these three showed up practically on top of each other. It's all I can do to knock one out before the next arrives."

Aghast, Tess blurted out, "Those mages were sent by the Council to kidnap Hayden?"

Asher shut and sealed the door to the infirmary with them inside, adding a few more protective spells of some sort to the door for good measure. In his stunned state, the only one Hayden recognized on sight was a Ward of Warning, to let them know if magic was being used on the other side of the door.

"I'm not sure whether it was a Council decision, or if Calahan—or one of the other half-cracked members with a grudge against you—made that call on their own." He frowned at them all. "All I know is that when strangers sneak into the school and start looking for you, it's my job to make sure they don't reach you."

"Why is Calahan—or whoever—trying to abduct me?" Hayden asked as calmly as possible, sitting on the edge of his bed.

"I expect they're trying to take advantage of the chaos to get control of you quickly. If they have you in their custody, they control what happens from then on. Once they get you into the Crystal Tower it will be nearly impossible to get you back out again," Asher answered grimly. "As long as we can keep you here, we have some leverage against them."

"You make it sound like a war," Tess offered quietly. "Like Mizzenwald is going to be against the Council of Mages soon, fighting for control of Hayden."

"That's more or less where this thing is headed," Asher confirmed heavily. "On the bright side, they won't try to blow up the school with him still inside of it—not unless they go completely insane, and not even Calahan is that nuts yet. And this place is designed to be a fortress, so short of blowing the place up, it will be nearly impossible to penetrate Mizzenwald's defenses."

Hayden frowned at this unexpected turn.

"What happens if they get their hands on me?"

"Nothing good for you, that's for sure." He began ticking options off of his fingers. "They'll either put you on trial or they won't. If they do, they can convict you of willfully bringing Aleric back—which comes with a death sentence, or unintentionally bringing him back—which comes with its own realm of unpleasant options: a simple prison sentence, having your Foci destroyed, lead Binders, being sent to fight him to the death before you're remotely prepared to take him on…just to name a few. If they don't even bother trying you then they can simply vanish you from the face of the earth and register you as missing."

Hayden and Zane both grimaced in unison.

"I can't stay here forever though," the former said slowly. "The school year is almost over and we've got the Dark Prism on the loose thanks to me, whether I intended it or not. I can't just spend the rest of my life hiding out, taking classes while other people fight battles over me, and my father runs around killing people on a whim and experimenting with dark magic."

"I know that, and we'll think of something," Asher assured him. "But we need a little time to get our thoughts together and work out a plan with the others. We can't do that if the Council snatches you away from us and locks you in a cell right at the outset."

Hayden tilted his head to concede the point, little though he liked it.

"Now, if you'll excuse me, I need to go stand guard some more." Asher stopped his pacing of the room and went back to the door. "Stay in here until one of us Masters come to get you. If someone you don't recognize manages to get past me and the protections on this room, fight like your life depends on it—because it probably does."

On that extremely ominous note, he left the three of them alone once more, locking the door of the infirmary behind him when he left.

"Well, this is a disaster," Hayden stated simply.

"Tell me about it," Zane grimaced. "The Dark Prism is on the loose and the Council of Mages is going to waste their time battling over you instead of fighting him."

"Maybe someone will be able to talk some sense into them soon and focus their attention on the real problem," Tess volunteered, though she didn't sound terribly optimistic about their chances.

"Sure, the Council members have been nothing but sensible, in my experience with them," Hayden smirked, eliciting a dark laugh from his friends.

It took another hour before Master Willow came to get them from the infirmary, disabling the wards carefully from the outside. He didn't look terribly surprised to find the three of them with their weapons of choice pointed at him when he opened the door, simply raising an eyebrow and saying, "Hello. It's good to see that you three appreciate the gravity of the situation."

They lowered their weapons and got to their feet.

"Is it safe to come out now?" Hayden asked tentatively. "That classroom isn't stuffed full of unconscious mages, is it?"

Master Willow raised an eyebrow and said, "Unconscious mages?" like this was the first he was hearing about it.

"Uh, yeah," Zane confirmed. "I had to help carry a guy's feet for Master Asher. We were taking bets on how many bodies would be heaped up in the room by now, at the rate they were coming in earlier."

The Master of Wands lifted both eyebrows in unison, the only display of how alarmed he was at the news of his students carrying unconscious strangers around the school.

Does nothing surprise that man? Hayden wondered idly.

"Well, I suppose we should begin with that," Willow said calmly. "Lead the way, please."

They set off down the hallway, Hayden feeling silly in his borrowed robe. He made a mental note to get some fresh clothing as soon as he was permitted to leave the infirmary for good.

They stopped outside of the magically-sealed door and Zane said, "I think Master Asher put up wards to keep people out, so I would be careful about touching that door if I were you…"

"Thank you, Laraby," The Master of Wands spared him a look and then drew a laurel wand, casting silently at the door after a moment of thought.

The others were so entranced with watching him work that they didn't hear Master Asher approach until he was directly behind them.

"Want help?" he asked his colleague, startling Hayden and his friends so badly that they jumped, though Willow barely twitched.

"That would be nice," the Master of Wands replied smoothly, stepping aside as his colleague lowered a violet prism into place and began working.

In less than a minute, Asher had the door open. For a long moment Willow stood there in silence, staring at the three prone figures on the classroom floor. Then he turned to Master Asher, calm as can be and said, "I thought I told you to slow them down, not incapacitate them."

"You weren't really specific as to how I might slow down intruders that were looking for Hayden," the Prism Master answered smoothly. "Also, I would like to point out that I have followed your instructions exactly: they are moving very slowly at present."

Willow spared him a glacial look and then rubbed his temples as though allaying a headache.

"I'm getting too old for this," he muttered wearily, removing his hands from his face and straightening up.

"You want me to wake them up and apologize?" Asher offered casually.

"Best not, since the damage is already done and they'll only complicate things. When the others return from their assignments we'll figure out a place to drop them off before waking them up."

"If you're certain," Asher sighed like it was a real shame. "Some people's dispositions improve greatly by being unconscious."

Master Willow let out a quiet chuckle of agreement before closing the door on the three mages once more, as though to lock away the problem for another time.

"Am I free to leave the infirmary, or should I plan on staying the night there?" Hayden asked during a lull in the conversation.

The two Masters exchanged a glance and then Asher said, "I suppose you're free to go. Most of the others have returned to the school, and the Council surely knows that we've intercepted their people by now. With my colleagues back, I doubt they'll be quick to send more kidnappers."

"Think you can at least hold off my enemies long enough for me to put some clothes on?" Hayden gestured at the infirmary robe he still wore.

Master Willow gave him a flat stare and said, "I daresay we can," in his driest tone.

"Thanks," Hayden turned to his friends and added, "see you all in a bit."

He walked off before anyone could answer, looking forward to having a few minutes alone with his thoughts. He hadn't really been alone—and conscious—since he returned from the schism with his father in tow.

Unfortunately, with classes cancelled due to the Masters' unplanned absence from the school, there were plenty of people walking around the corridors as Hayden strode purposefully towards the pentagonal foyer. People gawked at him openly as he walked past in a robe, many of them calling out to him, shouting praises for successfully closing the schism for good, or bursting into tumultuous applause. Hayden couldn't really decide how he should react to all the attention: it seemed churlish not to wave or smile or something, but it also felt wrong to bask in the praise, knowing that few of these people would be so pleased if they knew who he brought back from the other realm with him.

The different emotions warred for dominance of his face, which resulted in a half-smile, half-grimace that probably just made it look like he had to use the bathroom. Annoyed, he sped up his pace so that he was nearly jogging by the time he hit the main stairwell that led up to the dormitories.

He hurried down the third-floor hallway, blowing past the common area without slowing down at the sound of more cheers in his general direction, finally finding refuge inside the room he shared with Zane, Tamon, and Conner, though all three were elsewhere at the moment.

Bonk paced back and forth in front of the doorway, as though guarding the entrance for him, while Hayden shucked off his robe and donned fresh clothing, slipping his Focus-correctors back onto each wrist.

After dressing, Hayden sat down at his desk and rested his chin on his folded hands, staring absently out the window and trying to collect his thoughts. The view from his room showed the eastern side of the castle, with the stables and Torin's cabin visible below. The pen full of animals who were destined to become familiars was partially obscured by the log cabin, and Hayden watched a few monkeys swing around the little wooden posts that marked the boundaries of the pen. He found himself remembering the time that he had entered the pen in search of a familiar and ended up with Bonk, back in his first year.

I didn't know anything about magic back then. I thought my life was difficult; I was an idiot.

It felt like such a long time ago. What he wouldn't give to have things be simple again, with nothing to worry about except for people disliking him for being the son of a dead villain. He hadn't appreciated how uncomplicated things were back then, despite the difficulty of making friends in a new place where people were inclined to be suspicious of him.

Now all I have to worry about is trying to stop the monster I accidentally unleashed on the world for a second time—after narrowly being killed inside an alternate plane of reality— while hiding from the ten most powerful mages on the continent, who are all screaming for my head at the moment.

Should be simple.

He had no idea how long he sat there, staring out the window and watching the sun set. Occasionally he glanced down at the homework on his desk, sketching a few alignments idly in the margins with colored pencil while he let his thoughts wander.

I don't even know if I'm going to be able to finish the last few weeks of school this year.

It seemed trivial to be worry about his education right now, but he couldn't help but rue the lost opportunity. He just wanted to take his final exams and move on to the next level in all his classes, but he knew he wouldn't be able to abide hiding out at Mizzenwald forever, playing at school while the world at large was plunged into chaos. Even if he was permitted to remain here by the Council of Mages, he wouldn't be able to live with himself for not doing his part to stop his father—or die trying.

With a sigh, he got up and rubbed his eyes tiredly, wincing because his back hurt from sitting for so long. He turned to find Bonk still watching the door for him.

"Come on, let's go get some dinner," he said to his familiar, who perked up immediately at the promise of food.

Now that Hayden thought about it, they had probably missed dinner entirely, but surely he could talk someone in the kitchens into making him up a plate. He and Bonk left the dormitory and were walking past the fifth-year common area when Zane called out to him from inside, saying, "In here."

Pausing at the threshold, Hayden was surprised to see that the common area was much fuller than usual. Zane, Tess, Conner, and Tamon were waiting for him inside, along with what looked like half the students in their year, all crammed into the space around the fireplace or lining the walls. Oliver was leaning against the wall nearest the door, chatting quietly with his brother; both boys looked up as Hayden entered the room.

"I hope that's for me," Hayden pointed to a plate of cold-cuts and cheese that was sitting in front of the fire. "I was just headed to the kitchen to beg some scraps."

"I thought you might be hungry," Tess smiled lightly, gesturing to the food.

Hayden took the only open seat, a high-backed red velvet armchair directly in front of the fireplace—though it was turned around to face the rest of the room so that it felt like a throne.

Apparently this is question-and-answer time.

He settled down in the chair and watched Bonk hop gleefully into the flames, rolling around amongst the burnt logs and using them to scratch his back while Hayden took a few bites of food and tossed some ham to him in the fire. It was a little eerie how quiet everyone was while they stared at him.

After a minute or two the silence became unbearable, and Hayden set down his mostly-full plate of food and said, "So, I assume there was some kind of announcement at dinner?"

Conner nodded, looking pale and rattled.

"The Masters said the Dark Prism is back—that you saw him inside the schism and didn't know who he was, and that he came back with you."

The collective room seemed to hold their breath as Hayden nodded.

"Yeah, that's more or less what happened."

He waited for one of the Trouts to begin hurling accusations at him, insisting that he dragged his father back into their world on purpose, but to his mild surprise they both remained silent and watchful. Lorn's doughy face looked young and frightened.

"What happens now?" a girl Hayden had never spoken to before asked from the back of the room, looking hesitant.

Toying idly with a piece of turkey, Hayden said, "Now I try to figure out a way to stop him before he wrecks the world again. If anyone has any ideas, feel free to send them my way," he added with a smile that was anything but amused.

"So you really didn't bring him back on purpose?" a boy named Richard from his Elixirs class asked softly.

The silence in the room thickened into something oppressive. Meeting Richard's gaze unblinkingly, Hayden said, "I never met my father until the day he killed my mother, and I didn't even remember what he looked like. All he's ever given me is two years in lead-Binders, a lot of negative attention I never wanted, and the chance to live in Merina's finest orphanage. What do *you* think?"

Richard relented and said, "The Masters said it wasn't your fault, but people will talk."

"If by 'people' you mean the Council of Mages, then yes, they already are." He sighed and nibbled on a piece of cheese, contemplating what Master Asher had told him about needing all the allies he could get. His brain kicked into gear and he began planning.

"I don't intend to sit here at school while he roams the countryside, slaughtering people wholesale—not for any longer than necessary to come up with a good plan of attack, at least. People say I've got the strongest Source they've ever seen—stronger than his. It's hard to say what kind of shape he's in now, but if that's still true, then I've probably got the best chance of anyone at going up against him, and I've got Bonk on my side to help out."

Though my father will have Cinder...

"What do you need us to do?" Conner asked heavily.

"Huh?" Hayden looked up in surprise.

"We all know you're the real deal," Tamon piped up. "You're the best hope we've got, and we want to help. Tell us what we can do."

Hayden frowned thoughtfully as he considered this unexpected boon, glancing briefly at Tess and Zane, who had both remained silent so far.

Finally, he answered, "Right now I need time, and I need information. The Council is already trying to take me from Mizzenwald so they can keep me under their thumb, either to arrest me or throw me up against my father before I'm ready—or to use me as bait for all I know." There were a few gasps at this. "The Masters are trying to watch my back right now, but they've got a lot to do to get us ready to fight, and they can't see everything. If you should encounter strangers roaming the school, looking for me, do me a favor and send them off in the wrong direction."

There were a few chuckles at that.

"I also need information. A lot of you have parents and siblings who are part of the magical community in Junir—and even a few in the other lands. I expect my father to return to the Frost estate at some point to set up base again, but I need to know if he goes somewhere else, or what he's doing. If you all can tap your resources and get me anything on what he's working on, it will go a long way towards helping me plan. And of course, if anyone happens to have a brilliant idea for overpowering one of the fastest, strongest magic-users of the century, feel free to let me know."

That earned a few dark snickers from the assembled group.

"Also..." Hayden added, suddenly hesitant. "If you all could just do me the simple favor of believing that I didn't bring my father back to this realm on purpose, I would appreciate it. It may seem like a small thing, but just knowing that there are people who believe me would be a huge relief."

"Of course we believe you," Tamon scoffed, as though the very thought of the alternative was ridiculous. "You don't have anything to gain from the Dark Prism coming back, and everything to lose."

Hayden smiled humorlessly and said, "Be a dear and tell that to the Council of Mages, will you?"

He couldn't resist the urge to glance at the Trouts as he said this. Lorn looked mulish, but Oliver's expression was carefully neutral.

"So..." Conner began, looking timid. "What was he *like?*"

"My father?" Hayden asked with a raised eyebrow, frowning at the memory. "He was actually kind of awesome," he admitted to general astonishment. "He clearly didn't remember anything about his life before getting knocked into the other realm, and he saved my life about a dozen times before we made it back to Mizzenwald. I watched him wrestle schism-monsters bare-handed without breaking a sweat, not that that's particularly good news right now."

His peers continued peppering him with questions for as long as he was willing to answer them. By the time he finished the plate of food his friends had brought for him, he was getting tired and thought it would probably be a good idea to get a full night's rest before facing whatever horrors tomorrow had in store.

Mercifully, the assembled group began leaving the common area ahead of him when he begged for an end to the questioning, and most of them still seemed to respect and like him at the end of it. Acting on sudden inspiration, Hayden waved his friends on without him and cornered Oliver and Lorn before they could slip out of the room.

"Not so fast," he blocked their path. "I need a favor."

3
A Sympathetic Link

"I believe it's *you* who owes *our* family a favor, if memory serves me correctly," Oliver pointed out casually. "We did help you reacquire your estate at the beginning of the year."

"I remember it clearly, and I know I'm still in your debt—but I can hardly return the favor if I'm dead or in prison," Hayden explained patiently.

Oliver shrugged to concede the point and said, "I'm listening."

Lorn was being uncharacteristically silent, perhaps waiting to see whether Hayden's request was going to be impertinent before opening hostilities.

"The Council of Mages is my biggest immediate problem," Hayden stated bluntly.

Which is pretty impressive, given that the most infamous murderer of the century is running free again.

Oliver frowned and said, "If you're thinking I can persuade them that you're a wholesome young man who's tragically misunderstood then you're wasting your breath. I imagine Calahan isn't going to rest until he has you publicly discredited and your image destroyed; he was already plotting out ways to bring you low on the off-chance you survived the schism."

"I know Cal's a lost cause, but some of the others on the Council might not be, and you have their ear."

"Not really," Oliver answered blandly. "I'm not the ruling member of my House, nor am I on the Council."

"But your mother is," Hayden countered flatly.

"So you want our mom to go out on a limb for you again, and never mind the cost to her career," Lorn snapped hotly.

"I'm not asking her to preach my virtues to the Council, but she is one of the savviest people I know. Don't tell me there's nothing she can do to slow her colleagues down or divert them away from me and onto the real problem. Heck, they probably wouldn't even realize she was manipulating them she's so crafty."

Oliver smirked.

"I'll see what I can do. No promises."

"That's all I'm asking," Hayden assured him, relieved that he didn't have to stand here all night trying to convince Oliver to have a word with his mother on his behalf. If he'd asked either Trout for a favor during his first year at Mizzenwald he'd probably have gotten punched in the face.

A testament to how far our relationship has progressed since then, he thought ruefully.

"Frost," Oliver called out to Hayden when he had nearly rounded the corner. Hayden stopped at the threshold without turning. Oliver seemed to wrestle internally with his question for a few moments before finally asking, "Do you think you're stronger than him—honestly? Can you win?"

Hayden closed his eyes and reflected on all the things he had seen his father do before he realized that the man he'd known as Hunter was also the Dark Prism. He'd defeated schism-monsters for five years with nothing but his bare hands and homemade weapons, was an expert rock climber, and carried Hayden out of the schism on his back while fending off a dragon. All of that, without a drop of magic.

"Honestly? I have no idea," Hayden admitted. "Probably not. But I have to try."

Oliver didn't seem to have anything to say to that, and Hayden walked back to his room alone.

It came as no surprise that classes were cancelled the following day. With the threat of the Dark Prism and the Council of Mages looming over them, the Masters of Mizzenwald had better things to do than teach. It was close enough to the end of the year that some students had already returned home, terrified at the thought of staying in a place that might soon be attacked by the most evil mage in the Nine Lands. Popular opinion was that Hayden's father would be returning for him any day now, as soon as he established a base of operations and tuned up his powers.

"Can't blame them for thinking it," Zane offered mildly as they watched Master Reede drawing translocation circles in the front courtyard to send home anyone who didn't want to remain at school. "All anyone knows is that the last thing your crazy dad did before disappearing for five years was show up at your mother's house demanding to see you. Makes sense that he might go back to whatever his original purpose was once he gets set up again."

Hayden shrugged, not able to disagree with his friend's logic.

"Wish I knew what he wanted from me back then."

"Shame you didn't know who he was when you were in the schism together or you could've asked him," Zane added, watching another small group of people vanish from the main courtyard. "I actually think I could draw those translocation circles now if I tried," he switched subjects abruptly.

"Even if I had asked him, he wouldn't have been able to answer," Hayden frowned. "That's the whole problem—he didn't know who he was either. This would be a lot simpler if I *had* known he was the Dark Prism; I would have just left him in the other realm. And why wouldn't you be able to draw those translocation circles? You're a Conjury major..."

Zane shrugged.

"But you said you only made it out of there because your old man carried you out on his back. So if he stayed behind then you would have been stuck too." He scowled at the thought. "And anyway, I know I'm a Conjury major, but it's not like you could use all your crazy, quadruple-inverted, kajillion-alignment spells when

Frost Prisms

you first walked in the door here. I was just harkening back to my first year, and of how proud I was when I mastered the single crosshatch. It's weird being on this side of things."

Hayden rolled his eyes.

"I didn't say I wish I was stuck in the schism-world with my father, just that it would make things simpler out here. And a quadruple-inversion would just make things look normal, since you can only invert something once..." he grinned.

"You know what I mean," Zane made a face at him.

"I know. And it does feel strange being mastery students, when I remember not even knowing what the five major arcana were on my first day here." Hayden grimaced at the memory. "I kept mentally calling Powders 'piles of sand' until someone told me what it was actually called."

Zane snorted so loudly it sounded painful.

Hayden was unsurprised by the whispers and stares that trailed in his wake in the following days. In fact, he was so accustomed to it by now that the attention didn't even bother him. He was more surprised at breakfast one day when the Masters announced that school would be continuing on as normal, with one small adjustment.

"As you all know, final exams were not scheduled to occur for another three weeks," Master Willow explained to the assembled students before classes started. "Due to the pressing demands on our time, and the threat of the Dark Prism, we have advanced that timeline significantly. As a result, your exams will begin tomorrow."

He stopped speaking against a torrent of protests and exclamations throughout the room, people panicking over the reduced studying time. Hayden just couldn't believe there were people who cared more about their exam grades than the threat of his father.

Wait until he starts killing again; I'm sure their priorities will change once that happens.

He frowned at the dark thought and turned back to his bacon and eggs, offering his leftovers to Bonk, who gulped them down enthusiastically.

When the room quieted down once more, the Master of Wands continued. "A revised schedule will be handed out in your third-period lessons today. I realize that many of you were counting on the extra time to prepare, but with the situation our land is in right now, we need to end the school year early so that we may better assist the Council of Mages with addressing this new threat. If the danger isn't neutralized soon, we will likely cancel the next term as well."

More muttering broke out at the idea of not being able to return to Mizzenwald. Hayden frowned and ignored the renewed glances in his direction from all of his peers. He supposed he could see the Masters' logic in not reopening the school; collecting magically-gifted children in one convenient place might just provoke the Dark Prism to attack the school for a fresh supply of victims anytime he was feeling bored. Still, the thought of possibly never returning here was horrible enough on its own.

He knew he should be focusing in his lessons, as his teachers were now rapidly trying to review exam material with them, but Hayden's mind kept drifting to darker matters instead.

I wonder where my father is right now.

Would he already be back at his childhood home—the place that Hayden had fought to get control of so recently? Was he already beginning to plan his next campaign of terror, or was he still adjusting to the sudden return of his memories and powers? Did he still have his memories from the day he blew up Hayden's first home, and if so, would he ever circle back to visit Hayden for whatever it was he wanted that day?

The only class he paid attention to that day was Prisms, and that was only because Master Asher made it impossible to slack off. For one, Hayden was still the only student in the mastery-level class, so it would have been a bit obvious if he was asleep on his feet, but Asher had also decided to stuff his head full of new material rather than reviewing for exams.

"Focus, Hayden. That's the second time I've had to repeat an alignment for you," the Prism Master chided, somewhat snappishly.

"I'm trying, but that's about the twentieth new complex, compounded alignment you've thrown at me in the last hour, and it's a little hard to absorb so much information so quickly."

Asher frowned and said, "There is no time for a casual learning environment, not anymore."

Rubbing his eyes tiredly, Hayden mumbled, "Everyone else is just reviewing for exams. I'm getting a year's worth of prism lessons from you in a single day."

"Exams are useless to you and you know it," Asher snapped with uncharacteristic annoyance. "Do you really think Aleric is going to care if you got question thirteen right on your finals when he's snuffing the life out of you?"

Hayden grimaced at the mental image.

"No, of course not, but I can only absorb information so quickly. Snapping at me for being slow isn't going to make me any faster."

Asher sighed and leaned back in his chair, making a visible effort to unclench his muscles and relax.

"I know, but time really is of the essence for you. We have no idea where Aleric is or what he is doing, but at some point you're going to have to go up against him in battle. Ideally, you would have about fifteen of us alongside you, but your father would hardly let himself get caught against such bad odds. I have no idea what spells his Black Prism is capable of, which puts you at an enormous disadvantage; the only thing I *can* do to try and keep you alive is to cram every alignment that might be even vaguely useful down your throat before you meet him."

"That one for trimming toenails seemed a little far-fetched," Hayden commented with a faint smile.

"Though if I survive my encounter with him I'll never have to search for nail-clippers again."

Asher snorted in weary amusement and leaned forward once more, gesturing to the hand-held chalk board that sat on the desk between them, currently marked up with the most recent alignment.

"Do we need to review Cloning again, or do you have it?"

Rather than answer, Hayden lowered his eyepiece and looked through his clear prism, holding a violet one in front of him to compound. He located the alignment quickly and cast the spell immediately, wincing and touching his head as it took hold. Compounding mastery-level prisms was difficult enough that it still gave him a headache to do it, though Asher said this would improve with practice.

An exact copy of himself stepped away from his body and stood there looking bored. It was eerie sitting next to himself—the copy looked very solid.

"Good, now make it do something more than stand around looking vacant," Asher prompted without complimenting his achievement.

Guess we're past the stage where he tells me what a good job I'm doing.

"How?" Hayden asked uncertainly. The clone-Hayden mirrored his confused expression.

Do I really look that stupid when I'm asking a question?

"The magic is still active for as long as the clone exists—you should feel it slowly pulling through your Foci," Asher explained. "Seek out the magical connection between your Source and the clone—find it and command it."

Hayden almost made a sarcastic comment about how much he loved vague instructions, but didn't think it would be well received just now. Instead he closed his eyes and tried to look inside himself, feeling out the threads of magic that were open between his mind and the prisms. It wasn't as hard as he thought it would be, and soon he discovered the link to the clone; it felt almost like holding the strings of a puppet.

Tap Asher on the shoulder, he commanded mentally, opening his eyes.

The clone obeyed, though he jabbed the Prism Master a little harder than Hayden had intended—or maybe he was subliminally taking out his frustration on his mentor. Asher looked mildly amused, though he massaged the spot on his shoulder with one hand.

Let's up the stakes.

Hayden mentally commanded the clone to use one of its prisms. The clone obeyed, drawing its clear prism rapidly and casting at Asher, who tensed but made no move to draw his own weapon. It was immediately apparent why, as the spell went straight through him with no visible effect.

"Clever, but impossible." Asher gave him an approving nod. "The clone is nothing more than a shadow of magic—solid as it may appear. Nothing about it—including its weapons—are real, so its magic is useless."

"It was worth a try," Hayden shrugged.

"I would have been disappointed if you hadn't thought of it," his mentor confirmed.

After a thoughtful pause, Hayden asked, "Would it work if I handed it one of my actual prisms?"

Asher tilted his head and considered the question seriously for a moment before answering.

"It shouldn't. Copies have no magic of their own, they are simply a reflection of your own power. But still, best to be sure. Go ahead and try it."

Hayden handed the copy of himself what was left of his clear prism and had it cast Light, mostly because it was the most innocuous array he could think of off the top of his head—in case the magic actually worked.

But no, Asher had been correct. Even through a real instrument, the clone's magic was worthless.

"Too bad," Hayden frowned, reclaiming his prism and dismissing the clone. It vanished from existence between one blink and the next. "It would have been nice to make a few clones of myself, arm them to the teeth, and send them to fight my father on my behalf."

"Indeed," Asher exhaled heavily. "Still, you would have to be controlling all of them independently and at the same time, or most of them would just stand around uselessly, so it's not terribly practical at any rate."

"Guess not."

"Even being able to conjure one copy of yourself—or anything else—can be quite handy though, especially when trying to confuse the enemy," Asher put in bracingly. "It might buy the real you time to escape, if nothing else."

"That's true," Hayden allowed, frowning as the Prism Master wiped the chalkboard clean and began sketching a new alignment in different colors of chalk.

"Okay, onto the next one…"

By the time Hayden was freed from the Prism Master's clutches—the man insisted that things like 'eating dinner' were minutia that could be ignored for the sake of higher learning—it was nearly curfew. His roommates were still awake, studying for their finals tomorrow, but though Hayden hadn't even begun preparing for his exams, he was too tired to care.

"Did you just get free from Master Asher?" Zane asked in alarm, while Hayden threw himself heavily on top of his sheets, fully-clothed and covered in chalk dust.

"Yes. I think he just taught me every alignment in the known universe, though he swears there are thousands more out there. My brain might explode soon."

"Did you learn anything useful?" Conner set aside the stack of notes he'd been rereading with a tired yawn.

"Oh sure, plenty of it was useful. I just hope I can remember it all come tomorrow; we went through it way faster than I'm used to. He's also started teaching me how to translocate myself with prisms."

"Really?" his roommates exclaimed in unison. "Nice! Is it hard?"

Hayden rubbed his eyes and kicked off his shoes, letting them fall heavily to the floor.

"It's awful," he groaned. "The Masters make it look easy, but that's only because their Mastery Charms take most of the magical load for them. Trying to translocate without one involves a lot of different alignments being cast in the exact right order—without too much time between them—or you just end up sending one of your legs to a stinking bog."

"Speaking from personal experience?" Tamon asked with a raised eyebrow.

"Can you not smell the stink on my sodden left pant leg?" Hayden grumbled.

"I just assumed you were trying a new cologne," Zane laughed. "I was going to advise against it before you met up with Tess again, or she might leave you for someone with basic olfactory senses."

Hayden rolled his eyes, though from his position on the top bunk none of his roommates could see it.

"I was at it for almost an hour and I didn't successfully send myself anywhere even once—even with the wards around Mizzenwald that are supposed to make it easier. The closest I got was ripping my leg off, and after I stopped screaming long enough to see that I wasn't bleeding to death, Asher went to get it for me."

"Well, translocations are super-advanced magic," Conner pointed out fairly. "I'd be surprised if you mastered it in an hour, even as powerful as you are."

"Yeah, you're being too hard on yourself," Tamon added. "It just takes time."

"Time is the one thing I don't have, according to all of my teachers. They keep looking at me like they expect me to drop dead at any moment, even while they're giving me all this bolstering advice."

No one really knew what to say to that closing line, and an awkward silence filled the room. Hayden didn't mind because he was asleep within minutes; not even his smelly pant leg could keep him awake.

By some miracle, he was able to focus on his first two exams well enough to do himself justice, even with the constant threat of his evil father materializing into the classroom and killing him looming over his head. After two hours of disgorging every scrap of knowledge he had ever learned about Healing, he was more than ready for a lunch break.

Zane was complaining loudly about his Conjury exam when Hayden took his seat at their usual table.

"—can't believe I misread that crosshatch on question twelve! I thought it was an ink smear—I tried explaining to Reede afterwards, as soon as I'd realized my mistake, but he just laughed and told me to go to lunch."

"I doubt you're going to fail Conjury just because of one mistaken crosshatch," Conner said with a raised eyebrow at this gross overreaction.

"I know I'm not going to fail the class—but it could be the difference between qualifying for the mastery level and having to repeat the level-five. I'm still hoping to get one of his apprentice positions too, which means I have to beat out about twenty other people, and every mistake counts against me!" Zane snapped, looking slightly unhinged. Hayden made a mental note of how his friend looked when he was feeling particularly off-kilter, for future reference.

"Research isn't all it's cracked up to be," Hayden offered in consolation. "Sure, it'll be cool to actually discover something, but Asher and I have spent all year on one project and it still isn't done. Mostly I just spend hours every day banging my head against the wall, in between doing whatever menial chores Asher is too important to do himself."

"You said the two of you were close to a breakthrough on your project though," Tess pointed out mildly, watching idly as Bonk snuck a cherry off of her plate and devoured it in one bite—stem and all.

"Well, that's true..." Hayden allowed, before adding, "I doubt we're going to get the chance to finish it up anytime soon though, what with current events."

Tess frowned thoughtfully and opened her mouth to say something consoling, when the doors of the dining hall opened rather abruptly and loudly, startling everyone.

Hayden felt his stomach lurch at the sight of the three Council members who had just entered the dining hall, wearing the gold-and-black uniforms that signaled they were on official business. Hayden was only mildly relieved when he saw that Calahan wasn't among them.

Most of the Masters didn't look surprised by the sudden visit, and Hayden looked around wildly for some sign of what he was supposed to do, but for some reason no one would meet his eye—not even Asher, who was on the opposite side of the room, eating with a group of third-years. The three Council members were rapidly scanning the room, obviously searching for something. Their goal became apparent when one of them spotted Hayden and nudged his colleagues.

"Hayden Frost," the man called out to him from the threshold as the three of them moved closer. Hayden stood up without knowing what exactly he intended to do. "I have a warrant for your detainment, co-signed by the Chief Mage and the High Mayor. You are to come with us immediately to the Crystal Tower, where you will be formally charged in the case of the Dark Prisms's reappearance."

Most of the room fell silent when the Councilman started speaking, and still none of the Masters would meet Hayden's eye. Bonk had taken flight sometime in the last minute and was hovering in front of Hayden, flapping his wings gently to keep himself aloft. At first Hayden thought that his familiar was trying to act as a shield for him, but then—for the second time in his life—he heard Master Asher's voice magically amplified inside of his head.

Tell them to take a hike and grab hold of Bonk!

The Prism Master still wasn't looking at him, but Hayden could see the man glancing through a mastery-level blue prism almost lazily, compounding it with a violet one that he was holding in front of him on the pretext of examining it for dust.

There wasn't time to question Asher's instructions; the Councilmen were closing in on him fast.

Drawing himself up to full height, Hayden called out, "I have better things to do than play Calahan's stupid games. If he decides to get his head out of his butt and start hunting my father, then we'll talk." Then, not knowing what it would accomplish, he grabbed hold of Bonk.

Between one blink and the next, Hayden found himself in the formal dining hall of the Trout estate. Magdalene Trout and Master Kilgore, of all people, were there to greet him. Oliver's familiar, Slasher, was perched on the floor nearby, standing inside of a small conjury circle that had been drawn in chalk right on the plush carpet.

"What just happened?" Hayden blurted out dumbly, caught off-guard by the abrupt translocation.

"I see you are still fond of questioning the obvious," Mrs. Trout said in her typical curt manner. "You translocated away from Mizzenwald before my colleagues could bring you to the Crystal Tower to stand trial."

Hayden released Bonk, who was beginning to squirm in his grasp, and said, "But I don't know how to do translocation magic yet—not even inside Mizzenwald with the wards helping me." He frowned. "And I wasn't even looking through a prism or trying to think through the spell."

The Master of Elixirs chuckled and said, "We performed the magic for you. Magdalene told us when the Council got formal permission to move against you, so we were able to plan your extraction. Speaking of which, I must return to the school before I am missed."

Without explaining anything else to Hayden, Master Kilgore clasped his Mastery Charm and vanished from the Trout estate.

"I thought it was almost impossible to translocate someone from a different location without their assistance," Hayden continued questioning Mrs. Trout, for lack of anyone else to pester. "Or else my father could just vanish people at will and bring them to him from all over the world, without ever having to leave the house."

"It is extremely difficult, which is why we channeled the magic through Slasher and Bonk." She gestured to the familiars, who were now perched on opposite sides of a grand fireplace mantel like gargoyles. "Magical creatures of one family can form a sympathetic link between them with long-term proximity—"

"Yeah, I know about that," Hayden interrupted her. "It's why I knew Cinder was in trouble during my third year in the Forest of Illusions—because he and Bonk were close and Bonk started feeling his pain."

Thinking of Cinder was uncomfortable, given that they were probably now officially enemies.

"That link also enables us to channel some of the more difficult magic through them—especially as they're dragons, the most powerful of familiars," Magdalene continued, not looking upset by the interruption. "We weren't sure that Slasher and Bonk were close enough acquaintances for it to work, but it seems we got lucky."

Hayden frowned thoughtfully, his mind still racing to catch up with this new development.

"So why didn't the Masters warn me to run if they knew the Council was coming after me?" he asked after a minute of silence.

"They would have been dragged into this whole mess as well. The last thing we need are more people on trial at the Crystal Tower, and Calahan is unstable enough right now to press the issue."

"I thought the Masters were *already* in the middle of things, since they stopped those three mages from abducting me as soon as I came back through the schism."

Mrs. Trout shook her head.

"They were well within their rights to protect you at that time, as no formal charges had been laid against you, nor did Calahan have a Writ of Extraction. Now he does, so the situation has changed, and the Masters can't be seen helping you evade the Council."

Well, that explains why everyone was conveniently avoiding my eye when those three goons barged in to haul me to a jail cell.

He looked around at his surroundings again to convince himself that they were really there. At the beginning of the year he had wondered if he would ever see this place again; he never thought he'd be enjoying the hospitality of his former nemeses again so soon.

"Why am I here, of all places?"

Mrs. Trout gave him that look she used when she thought he was being particularly obtuse. He was surprised by the wave of nostalgia it evoked in him.

"You resisted arrest. You're officially on the run from the law," she pointed out casually, in the tone one might use when explaining the features of the dining room.

"Yes, I know, but why *here*?"

Magdalene's eyes lit with understanding and she graced him with a slightly mocking smile.

"Who would ever think to look for you here? It's a well-known fact that you and my children do not get along, and I am an upstanding member of the Council itself, so there is no reason for me to harbor a fugitive."

Calahan is a fool to underestimate this woman.

"Not that I don't appreciate it and all, but why did you agree to hide me here again? As you pointed out, you will get into a world of trouble if old Cal ever finds out that I was here…"

Mrs. Trout had such a haughty look on her face that for a moment the resemblance to Oliver was alarming.

"It would take more guts than Calahan possesses to get up the nerve to search *my* estate," she informed him coolly. "And unlike him—and some of his cronies—I am not shortsighted enough to risk the fate of the Nine Lands over a petty grudge. I'm convinced that if anyone stands a chance at defeating Aleric a second time around, it is you—the one who stopped him the first time he was powerful. You can hardly do that if you're locked away in the Crystal Tower, and believe me when I say that if Calahan ever gets you inside that place, you will never see the light of day again while he is in power."

Hayden shuddered at the thought.

"Not to sound like a nay-sayer, but people keep crediting me with beating my father when he showed up at my mother's house, like I deliberately blasted him into that schism. But honestly, I still don't remember what happened that day—I didn't even know I had magic, so I can't have overpowered him."

Mrs. Trout pursed her lips and said, "Just because you don't remember it, doesn't mean it didn't happen. You are currently our best hope, and so you are an integral part of our planning. At the very least, you're a part of Aleric's plans, and we must keep you from him for that reason alone."

Hayden tilted his head to concede the point. As long as people knew that he didn't have a solid game plan for besting his father in open combat, he didn't mind them going out of their way to help him.

"So," he said after another long minute of silence. "What do we do now?"

"See if you remember your way around well enough to find your old room. I need to be prepared for Calahan's summons when he gets news that you've eluded him."

"How angry do you think he'll be?" Hayden asked curiously.

A truly evil smile lit Magdalene Trout's face when she said, "He'll be apoplectic."

"Sometimes you frighten me," Hayden pointed out mildly.

"I'll take that as a compliment."

4
Allies

Hayden was excited to take part in his very first strategy meeting in the effort against the Dark Prism. It was late that night when Mrs. Trout returned home from wherever she spent her days and summoned him back to the formal dining room. Bonk squawked at the lateness of the hour and stubbornly refused to be dragged out of bed, but Hayden was wide awake at the prospect of doing something productive, especially after spending the day alone in his room with only his familiar for company.

When he arrived in the large dining room, Masters Kilgore, Willow, Lauren and Asher were already seated around the table, as well as Master Mandra from Valhalla and—to Hayden's utter disbelief—Kiresa, the Prism Master of Isenfall. Hayden's last memories of Master Kiresa were not pleasant; during his second year of school the man had lied to him, terrified him, and then nearly let him die during the penultimate round of the I.S.C.

He didn't realize he was standing there gape-mouthed until Kilgore said, "Take a seat and close your mouth before something flies into it."

Shaking off his shock, Hayden did as he was told and settled into a seat beside Master Mandra, across from Asher. Both men greeted him pleasantly enough, though the latter looked tired and careworn. Unfortunately, that wasn't a new look for Hayden's mentor these days.

"Frost," Master Kiresa greeted him with a smirk. It was the derisive note in his voice that prompted Hayden to respond with, "What are *you* doing here?"

"Normally, your unflattering disbelief would amuse me, but I'm far too tired for it right now," the Prism Master answered flatly.

"All of us want to stop Aleric before things get out of hand," Master Willow explained patiently, shooting a brief glance at Kiresa to accent the point. "No one wants to repeat the ten years in which the Dark Prism ran around, unchecked, doing as he pleased with the world and everyone in it."

Remembering his last interaction with the Prism Master of Isenfall, Hayden wasn't prepared to swear that was true, but knew better than to argue the point. If the Masters of Mizzenwald trusted him, that was good enough for him.

Hayden almost jumped out of his seat when the last two people entered the room and shut the large doors behind them. Oliver Trout he halfway expected, this being his mother's house and all, but the man beside him was another member of the Council of Mages. Hayden had mentally classified the entire Council as "the enemy" in his mind, with the exception of Magdalene, so seeing another member in their top secret meeting nearly made his heart leap out of his chest.

"Calm down," Oliver chided him, barely resisting the temptation to roll his eyes. "He's on our side."

"For now," Master Mandra muttered under his breath, just loud enough for Hayden to hear. Under the cover of everyone getting up to shake hands with the newcomers he added, "Laris wants Calahan's job as much as Magdalene. They've both been gently feeding his fears and leading him to ruin in the hopes he will be deposed. When that happens, I expect Laris and Magdalene's alliance to fall apart quite rapidly, as they battle over who will replace him."

Hayden raised his eyebrows to show he appreciated the whispered explanation, though he privately thought that anyone who put themselves against Magdalene Trout was a fool.

"Let's get started," their host called everyone to attention, taking her seat at the head of the table. There must have been some planned order to this meeting that Hayden wasn't aware of, because Master Willow immediately began.

"Your colleagues are still tearing apart the school in search of Hayden, stone-by-stone," he addressed Magdalene Trout. "We're slowing them down as much as possible, but they'll likely satisfy themselves that Hayden isn't hiding there by tomorrow morning."

"Keep them looking as long as you can," she answered with a curt nod. "Time is of the essence."

"Kirius can run them around in circles for a while longer," Master Laurren opined gently, his purple-blue eyes and soft tone giving him an otherworldly aura. "It's well-known that he dislikes Hayden, so he's been casually fanning their suspicions that Hayden wouldn't leave Mizzenwald without Tess and Zane at his side."

Magdalene opened her mouth to answer but Hayden managed to beat her to it by interjecting, "Why do we want those three Council members tearing apart Mizzenwald in search of me?"

Laris, the Council member sitting beside Oliver, said, "The three people that Calahan sent after you were not chosen at random; they're his greatest allies in the Council. The longer we can keep them from returning back to him, the better, especially as we have a meeting first thing in the morning, and it will be much easier to manipulate Calahan without his saner allies present."

For a moment Hayden almost felt sorry for the Chief Mage. True, he had never liked the man much, but even his closest circle of advisors were trying to drive him to ruin.

Small wonder the man has become paranoid; he can't trust anyone.

"And how does driving Cal nuts make things better, aside from furthering your own political agendas?" Hayden asked boldly, ignoring the slight wince from Master Willow, who was always more diplomatic in his accusations.

Laris pursed his lips in annoyance but Magdalene answered readily.

"Calahan will never side with you. Even without us goading him to folly, he sees you as too much of a threat to his rule. He knows he has made an enemy of you, and he has been regretting that ever since the day you met, but knows it is too late to win your support at this juncture. Now he has no choice but to destroy you before you can destroy him—or so he believes. The sooner we can get him to commit a large enough mistake and remove him from his position, the better for you."

She looked like she was getting ready to change topics and continue the meeting as scheduled, but Hayden interrupted once more, knowing that he was pushing his luck but not caring.

"And where *are* Tess and Zane?"

Asher raised an eyebrow at him and said, "At Mizzenwald, preparing for the second day of final exams. Why?"

"Laurren said the Council members don't think I'd leave school without Zane and Tess. You don't expect me to believe they're just going to leave them wandering around free, do you? They're going to be stalking them to see if my friends will lead them to me."

Kilgore chuckled at Laris's raised eyebrows and said, "Told you the boy's not dumb." He turned to Hayden. "As soon as term ends they're going to be tailed relentlessly. Reede has already instructed them to return home and act naturally until one of us comes to get them; we need to make sure they're free of magical traces before we can risk bringing them to you."

Hayden knew that his friends would probably be going crazy having to go home for the winter without knowing what was happening with him, but as long as they didn't run amok of the Council of Mages they should be safe, which was better than the alternative.

"Do they know where I am, or do they think I just disappeared in the middle of lunch and fell off the edge of the world?"

"They haven't been told where you are, in case Calahan can trump up an excuse to have them magically interrogated, but they've been subtly informed that you're alright."

Hayden nodded. It seemed like the best he could hope for right now.

Not giving him the opportunity to interrupt again, Magdalene said, "Laris and I are doing all we can to exert pressure against Calahan without our hand being seen in it, and if we can get him to strip Hayden of his Medal of Heroism that will go a long way toward turning the public against him."

"We'll have to time it carefully," Mandra interjected. "We can't begin floating the information that Hayden is being wrongfully defamed and is working to form a coalition against the Dark Prism too early, or Calahan will be able to back down in time to save himself. Conversely, if we wait too long, Hayden's reputation will be too tarnished for us to recover it."

"There is a critical point at which we must put Hayden forth as a maligned hero, but we have not yet reached it," Magdalene agreed curtly. "He needs to be stripped of his honors, and we need Calahan to publicly turn against him. Then we will be ready to act."

It felt really bizarre to have all of these people talking about when to deploy him, like he was a chess piece waiting to be moved around the board. Frowning, Hayden said, "You all are very flippant when it comes to deciding how much disgrace you'll *allow* me to bear before doing anything about it. I wonder if you'd be so casual with your own lives and reputations."

Master Kiresa rolled his eyes and said, "The poor boy is feeling misused." Then, as an aside to Oliver, he whispered, "I told them he wouldn't have the grit for this," loudly enough for the entire table to hear.

Slamming his hands onto the table and standing up, Hayden barked, "The only thing I've seen *you* excel at is bullying people half your age. Can you even use your prisms, or do they just decorate your belt?"

Kiresa drew a prism so quickly it was like he was waiting for Hayden to provoke him all this time. Face purpling with anger, he held it in front of his eye without bothering with the circlet and cast at Hayden, who didn't even have time to identify the spell being used against him.

Bracing for impact, he was shocked when Kiresa was thrown backwards, knocking over his chair and crashing to the floor in a tangled heap of limbs, while nothing of consequence happened to Hayden. The reason for his good fortune became apparent when he turned his head and saw Master Asher—who always had a prism equipped in his circlet—with the eyepiece pulled down in front of his left eye.

Despite the unpleasantness of the situation, Hayden couldn't help but ask, "Reflect?" of his mentor.

"I thought he should get a taste of his own magic," Asher answered back languidly, glaring at his counterpart, who was getting to his feet and looking furious. "You should learn to control your temper, Kiresa—or are you so unsure of yourself that you'll allow a few harsh words from a teenager to unhinge you?"

It was hard to say who hated the other more. The look Kiresa gave Master Asher was venomous enough to cause nightmares, but the latter didn't look remotely bothered by it.

A few of the others had stood up as well during the chaos, and Willow was now trying to get control of the situation by saying, "Let's all sit back down. We don't have time for petty squabbling amongst ourselves or else Aleric has already won."

Something about the Master of Wands was inherently soothing, and everyone followed his directions, even Kiresa. Hayden wished he knew how Master Willow managed that kind of power, but maybe it was just a gift.

"He can't hide behind your robes for much longer," Kiresa said coldly to Asher. "If he isn't prepared to risk his precious reputation for this, then we are wasting our time here."

Nettled, Hayden said, "I'm not afraid to risk myself for this, but stop acting like I'm your damn mascot."

"That's exactly what you are," Laurren interjected softly, resting his chin on his folded hands and leveling his gaze at Hayden. "You are the mascot for the fight against Aleric—something we didn't have last time but sorely needed. People need something to rally behind, something to believe in, and you are ideally suited to the task."

Hayden frowned at that but said nothing, feeling the momentary surge of anger drain out of him. He felt tired and hollow in its wake.

"Any news on Aleric's whereabouts?" Master Willow turned back to Magdalene Trout as though there had been no interruption whatsoever.

She frowned and drummed her fingers lightly on the table as she said, "Nothing helpful." Hayden could tell that this was a considerable thorn in her side right now, as she rarely fidgeted. "Preliminary reports have him setting up at his old estate—well, legally it is Hayden's estate at the moment."

"I doubt he'll see that as an impediment," Hayden interjected with a wry smile, and Magdalene tilted her head slightly in acknowledgement. "And here I just got control of the place," he sighed. "I've only gotten to visit it once on my own since winning my suit against the Council, and now we're going to have to search it for booby-traps all over again once he's gone."

Several of the others lifted their eyebrows at the bold assumption that they would defeat the Dark Prism a second time and he would get his house back. Hayden was simply being optimistic because he didn't think that anyone would appreciate pessimism at this point. There was no choice but to go forward, and openly casting doubt on his abilities was hardly going to make things any better.

"Yes, well, we do know that while he's setting up his old base, he's spending a lot of time away from it, but none of our numerous contacts have been able to figure out where he's going or what he's doing," Magdalene continued glumly. "It's not like we're able to get anyone close enough to place a magical trace on him—and even if we did, he'd surely know about it immediately and use that infernal Black Prism to unravel it."

"He has to turn up eventually," Asher stated pragmatically. "He's hardly going to become a hermit and remain inside the Frost estate for the rest of his life; he wouldn't be such a threat if that were the case. Like last time, he'll eventually need to move into the open and we'll get a sense for what his goals are."

There was a collective shudder around the table as they imagined what kind of horror that might entail. Hayden was hoping they could stop him before it got to that point.

"No one has asked the important question yet, so I'll take the initiative," Master Kiresa said bluntly, shooting Hayden a brief glance before focusing on Asher. "Is the boy actually skillful enough to take down his father, or is he truly only a mascot to our movement?"

Total silence followed his question for almost a full minute, while everyone looked at Asher and Asher in turn stared at Kiresa. Finally he said, "I doubt Hayden will be alone when it comes down to it. The rest of us aren't going to shove him into a closed room with Aleric, wish him luck, and wait outside to greet the victor."

"I realize that," Kiresa answered in a level tone, "but you're avoiding the question. If push comes to shove, and Aleric manages to isolate the boy from us, *can* he win?"

Hayden's mentor shrugged and said, "You're asking me to predict the future, a tricky business at best. There are too many random factors to take into consideration—Aleric could sneeze at the wrong time and lose for all we know. Added to the fact that I have no idea what level Aleric's skill is at since the last time we battled, almost six years ago…"

"We realize that you haven't kept in touch with the Dark Prism in recent years," Laris interrupted, though he looked like he wasn't sure he really believed his own words. "But based on what you *do* remember of his talents, what do you think?"

Another moment of silence, and then Kiresa snapped in annoyance, "*Well?* Can he overpower his father or not?"

After another contemplative moment, Asher replied.

"Honestly, I'm not sure. In terms of raw power— yes, I believe Hayden is stronger than Aleric. I've been gauging his Source power for years, and I have yet to find the limits of it. The more practiced he becomes with magic, the more fully he is able to draw on his Source, and I expect that to continue for some time before he reaches the absolute extent of his power."

Hayden was a little surprised to learn that his mentor had been trying to analyze him this way for years, though he supposed he shouldn't be. The others looked mildly cheered by this testimonial to his skills.

"Raw power—while important—is not everything," Master Mandra pressed gently. "What about speed of casting?"

Asher frowned.

"Aleric has him there," he admitted truthfully. "Hayden has taken enormous strides to improve, and he has come a long way, but unless Aleric got rusty during his five-year hiatus, he will be at least twice as fast as Hayden."

Hayden thought this was actually good news, since when he began his one-on-one combat lessons with Master Asher two years ago, he was estimated at five times slower than the Prism Master, who was still slower than Aleric Frost. The others didn't look wholly pleased with his enormous amount of improvement in such a short time though, and he couldn't entirely blame them. Being half as fast as the Dark Prism would still likely get him killed.

"Endurance?" Willow prompted gently, not commenting on the issue of speed.

Asher made a wavering motion with one hand.

"I'm not sure. Hayden has more endurance than anyone I've ever seen—and it increases as he gets more practiced tapping into his Source directly, so I'm inclined to give that one to him."

"Then why the uncertainty?" Kilgore put in curiously.

"Honestly, I haven't seen anyone challenge Aleric sufficiently to really test his endurance, not since he started messing with broken prisms. At the very least though, I believe we could call them evenly matched on that front."

"And force of will?" Magdalene prompted.

"Another tricky one, though I might give it to Aleric," Asher admitted. "Hayden can drum up an impressive amount of willpower, but typically only when he—or someone he cares about—is on the very brink of annihilation. Aleric is all willpower, all the time, and alarmingly self-disciplined."

Hayden felt like it was necessary to interject at this point. "To be fair, I and everyone I care about *will* likely be on the brink of annihilation when we're fighting him, so that should help."

Asher frowned. "Even then, he may still have you trumped on willpower."

"Hmm, two out of four isn't terribly reassuring," Magdalene pursed her lips, "though admittedly better than most others could manage." She tilted her head to Hayden in acknowledgement.

"Are you sure you aren't overstating his abilities?" Kiresa asked bluntly. "If you hadn't insisted on sheltering him all these years, he might be further along in his studies by now, but even so—"

"Test him for yourself, if you'd like," Asher cut his counterpart off, quite rudely, before another argument could ensue.

"Oh, I intend to," Kiresa smiled nastily.

Great, something else to look forward to, Hayden thought joylessly. *This day just gets better and better.*

"For what my opinion is worth, I've seen him in action for years now, and Master Asher's not overestimating his power or endurance," Oliver, of all people, interjected on his behalf. "His major flaw is that he sometimes chokes under pressure, but after everything that's happened in the last couple years he's probably gotten better about that too."

"Thanks, I think," Hayden said quietly.

"How is he with the other arcana?" Laris pressed on during the silence that followed this. "Ever since Aleric went dark he has almost exclusively relied on prisms."

"And why not?" Kilgore scowled. "With that blasted Black Prism of his never depleting, what need does he have of secondary instruments?"

"Yes, but that is an advantage that Hayden does not share," Magdalene intoned mildly. "He'll need every weapon he can get—we all will, in the event of a prolonged battle."

Master Willow said, "He has always had a good mind for Wands, which are probably his second most-powerful weapon," without prompting. "Dirqua has reported similar success with Charms, where his Source power gives him an obvious advantage over others."

"We should load him up with the most powerful charms we can get our hands on before engaging Aleric."

"But we'll have to make sure not to bog him down so much that his charms are consuming all of his Source strength and fatiguing him," Kilgore countered. "He'll need enough power left over to perform magic."

The image of himself weighted down with dozens of charms, wands, and other magical weaponry so that he could barely walk, let alone fight, filled Hayden's head and he suppressed a chuckle, despite the grim context. He would take what small amusement life had to offer, these days.

"Even with all of that, I don't like our odds," Master Mandra spoke up, fidgeting with his thumbs on top of the table. "We're all in agreement that Hayden is likely the only one who can overpower him in a straight-out battle, and even that is uncertain. We're going to have to attack him on so many fronts at once that he simply can't overwhelm us all, and hope that one of us can break through the standing spells he has sensing magic and protecting his person."

"Aleric is not a god, nor is he invincible," Asher pointed out softly, staring down at his hands in contemplation. "It's true that he is incredibly fast, skillful, and has spells that we aren't even aware of, but in the end he is just a man. He is not omnipotent, and he can be beaten."

A thoughtful silence followed this. Hayden found himself heartened by the Prism Master's words, since it was easy to forget that his father was only human during these discussions.

"Let's leave it at that for the night," Magdalene rose to her feet, and perforce, everyone else followed suit. "We will reconvene here four nights from now, to give a status update on our various pursuits. Hopefully by then we'll have made headway, either with Calahan, or with locating the Dark Prism and tracking his activities."

Maybe we'll all get lucky and he'll have a heart attack or something, Hayden wished privately.

The others mumbled various levels of agreement to this plan, and began vanishing from the room, clasping their Mastery Charms as they went. Hayden just realized that he and Oliver were the only ones in the entire group that lacked Mastery Charms, and of how odd it felt to be a part of something all of these important mages were working on.

Asher stayed behind when most of the others left and said, "I'll walk you to your room," to Hayden.

Half expecting this, Hayden nodded and led the way out of the formal dining room. He was a little surprised when his mentor seemed to know exactly where they were going, following the turns along their path without hesitation.

"How do you know your way around the Trout estate so well?" he asked curiously when passed the library.

"It's not my first visit," Asher answered simply.

"Well, I figured that much, but you seem to know your way around the house pretty well. The only reason I don't get lost is because I lived here for five weeks last year."

Asher gave him a wry smile and said, "I'm actually quite well-connected, you know, despite the hit my reputation took after Aleric lost his marbles. Oh sure, people shun me in public or mock me openly about the association, because popular opinion says it's a bad thing to associate with me, but privately, there are few people I am not connected to."

"And that doesn't bother you?" Hayden asked with raised eyebrows. "It would drive me nuts if people were horrible to me in public but then wanted to be buddies in private."

Asher smiled again.

"Actually I find it quite useful. Few people know how well-connected I truly am, or how many people owe me favors, which makes it very easy to surprise them and appear more enigmatic and powerful than I actually am. It pays to be underestimated by people—especially my enemies."

Hayden considered the idea for a moment and then grinned.

"To be fair, sir, you're pretty enigmatic all on your own. I don't think I've ever been able to predict what you'll say or do, and at this point, nothing would surprise me."

"I take that as the highest of compliments," Asher said with amused dignity. "Now, there's something I wanted to warn you about—though perhaps you got a sense for it during the meeting," he changed the subject abruptly, the smile dropping off of his face.

"Oh yeah?" Hayden prompted tiredly.

"You're going to be getting a crash course in magic—even more than you already have been with me," he amended, acknowledging Hayden's look of horror. "We're all going to be working with you individually as much as possible to bulk up your magic in all aspects, because we need you as good as you can be before we tackle Aleric."

Hayden's mind was overcome with the image of the entire group of them lunging at the Dark Prism and piling on top of him until nothing stuck out but his feet. Sometimes he cursed his vivid imagination.

"Even Kiresa?"

"Even him," Asher nodded. "And I know that neither of us are particularly fond of the man, but as much as it pains me to say it, he *is* adept at prisms, so you should try to learn whatever you can from him. He'll doubtless have a different approach than me, but that is a good thing, as it will give you another perspective."

Hayden tried to think positively about the experience instead of focusing on how much pain he was going to be in, because he very much doubted that Master Kiresa was going to pull any punches during their lessons.

"Not that I mind getting some advanced learning, but why does everyone seem to think I'm the crux of this whole thing? I know everyone on our side wasn't here tonight—the other Masters at Mizzenwald, for instance—so we've got to have at least a dozen or two highly-skilled mages to send against him. If we all attack him at once, he won't be able to overcome our sheer numbers; like you said, he's only human, and he can only cast one spell at a time through his Black Prism—as far as we know."

Asher frowned, stopping outside of the door to Hayden's bedroom and meeting his gaze.

"Yes, but we tried that same tactic last time around, and he always managed to prevent himself from being cornered by more people than he could defeat in battle. It's also worth mentioning that he keeps a few spells permanently cast around himself, to heighten his perception and grant him basic protection—where others might use charms for the same purpose. Our plan is to force him into a large confrontation, but we have to be cognizant of the fact that he might break us into smaller groups and take us down." He hesitated briefly before continuing. "Popular opinion right now is that at some point, your father is going to come for you, which is the only bit of him that is predictable at this time, and therefore makes you the lynchpin of this entire thing."

Hayden raised one eyebrow and said, "Why is everyone so sure of that? He had me in his grips when we came out of the schism and he let me go."

"That was only because he was unarmed and needed to escape Mizzenwald before anyone else showed up to attack him. Once he's back on his feet, we believe that he will come after you for the same reason he tried to find you when you were ten."

"And that is...?"

Asher shrugged. "You know I don't know the answer to that. Either he's curious about your similarities to him—magically speaking, or he wants you to join his cause, or he wants to kill you personally for all I know. The point is, he clearly didn't get what he was after when he showed up at your mother's house and got blasted into that schism, and he probably knows you are the biggest threat to him right now, so it is likely that he will try and isolate you from everyone else to make you easier to take."

"Great, something else to have nightmares about," Hayden grimaced. "I guess it's a good thing I have all of you Masters of the arcana on hand to teach me everything you know before that happens."

Asher tilted his head at this, glancing at his chrono.

"I need to return to Mizzenwald. Now that the term is about over, we'll have more time to dedicate to preparing for a fight with Aleric, so you and I will see each other soon. In the meantime, do the best you can to learn whatever our allies are trying to teach you, keep Bonk with you as much as possible, and never go anywhere unarmed, even in this house."

"You think he'll come *here*?" Hayden made a face. He certainly hoped that the Dark Prism wouldn't come storming into the Trout estate in the dead of night to capture or kill him.

Great, my nightmares just got even scarier.

"We're doing all we can to make sure that no one knows you are here, but better safe than sorry. If Aleric grabs one of our allies and tortures him or her sufficiently, they may give away your location."

"It seems like every time we part ways, it's over some horribly depressing news like this," Hayden pointed out. "You never pull me aside to tell me a joke or offer me ice cream or anything."

Asher snorted in amusement.

"You're right, it does seem that way. My apologies. Once this is all over, I'll be sure to end all of our conversations with a bad joke or some sort of baked dessert. For now though, I must go."

Hayden nodded and watched the Prism Master take hold of his Mastery Charm, narrow his eyebrows in concentration, and vanish into thin air.

5
The Duel

Receiving one-on-one training from some of the greatest mages in the Nine Lands wasn't nearly as glamorous as Hayden might have imagined, if someone had told him years ago where he would be right now. It actually involved a lot more muttered swear words and healing elixirs than he might have guessed.

"Get up, Hayden," Master Willow said from somewhere nearby. "We only have a few more minutes together before I need to depart."

Great, then one of my other allies will take up the job of beating me to a pulp in your stead.

Groaning, Hayden spit out the mouthful of grass he'd recently acquired after landing face-down on the far side of the arena in the Trout's back yard.

And to think, just one year ago I was mildly envious that I'd never gotten to practice my magical weaponry out here with the Trouts.

He decided that he should really be more careful with his wishes, since they had a nasty way of coming true in ways he didn't expect.

Squinting against the sunlight, Hayden pulled himself to his feet and tried to quickly assess whether he'd broken any bones or was otherwise critically injured. Since he didn't see blood pouring out of his body and onto the neatly-trimmed lawn, he figured he was well enough to continue.

"You should have used your maple wand against me, not the laurel," Master Willow explained patiently, looking mostly unruffled from their most recent bout. The only visible evidence that he and Hayden had been dueling for the last hour was his torn pant leg and a bruise on one cheekbone.

"I used up my maple wand twenty minutes ago, or I might have tried it instead," Hayden grumbled, tired of getting whipped repeatedly by more skillful mages. It certainly didn't do wonders for his self-esteem, necessary though it was.

"I know. You're too liberal with the use of your combat wands—you go for the grand effect when a simpler spell will suffice," the Master of Wands chided him gently. "You wasted the entire wand with one spell. Had this been a challenge arena, you would have received bottom marks for your extravagance."

"I was trying to box you in with those stones, but the wand was consumed before I got the last one into place." Hayden pointed at the structure that stood mostly-formed off to their left. He had thought it was quite inventive to pull large slabs of rock from the earth itself to construct his prison—though right now it was more of a crude shelter since it was missing the fourth wall.

"Most impressive, yes. And did it never occur to you that instead of exerting that exorbitant amount of power, you might have just as easily used your maple wand to attempt to knock my own from my hand?" The Master gave him a flat stare. "I believe maple is excellent for disarming."

Hayden's mouth dropped open. He immediately felt like an idiot for not thinking of something so basic—something he had learned in his very first year of schooling.

"Uh, no, it didn't," he admitted, embarrassed.

"You're an excellent mage, and quite magically-powerful," Willow relented, lowering his own wand at last and moving forwards. "But you need to work on exhausting simple solutions before going for complex ones, or you will find yourself weaponless and overtired before your opponent has even broken a sweat."

Hayden frowned.

"It just seems like my father isn't going to be throwing out simple spells when I fight him," he explained. "I don't expect a duel with him to last very long, so I need to give it everything I've got while I still can; he's already smarter than me, faster than me, and has magic I will probably never understand or possess. He's going to go in with everything he's got."

"That just means that he will be blind to the obvious," Willow waved an airy hand. "Difficult casts take much longer to execute, especially if he is confining himself to only using prisms, because he'll need to trace alignments. If you are using simpler magic, not only will you conserve your resources, but it will help close the gap in speed between the two of you."

Hayden considered that in silence, wiping the sweat from his forehead with the back of his hand. Thanks to the climate control at the Trout estate, it didn't feel like winter at all, though he could have used some cool air right now.

"The time may come for you to throw out everything you've got," Willow continued into the silence. "All I am saying is, don't expend all your energy before you have to."

"Thanks, I hadn't thought of it like that," Hayden nodded, approaching a nearby bench and sitting heavily on it. He had one more appointment today, and almost no time to rest and prepare himself for it.

Master Laurren, who had been watching silently from the bench while he dueled Willow for the last hour, leaned over and said, "Not bad, Frost."

"Not good, either," Hayden countered lightly.

"Well, no, but for all that Willow looks like a little old man, he's quite the powerhouse. It could have been much worse for you if Asher hadn't been preparing you for the last several years."

Hayden lifted his eyebrows in acknowledgement.

"I thought you had him for a minute there, when you brought those rocks up out of the ground to cage him in. By the way, Magdalene will be furious if her lawn isn't put to rights before she gets home, you know that, right?"

Hayden groaned and nodded wearily.

"I'll fix it when I'm done with my last fight of the day—assuming I'm still alive and conscious," he amended.

"Oh, Kiresa knows better than to maim you too badly, even if he'd like to," Master Laurren said mildly.

"People keep telling me that, but I'll believe it when I see it."

Laurren just shrugged and said nothing. For a minute they sat there in silence—apparently the man had nothing better to do right now than watch him practice magic—and then Hayden was forcibly reminded that this was the first time he had gotten to speak to the Master of Abnormal Magic privately since before he went into the schism.

"Master Laurren," Hayden began softly, "do you remember the last thing you said to me before I went into the schism?"

The Master glanced sideways at him without turning his head.

"In the dining hall, yes? I was telling you about the vision I had…that you would come to a critical juncture at some point and that you needed to turn left or you would certainly die."

Hayden nodded.

"We came to a fork in the road inside the other realm, where the ley-lines split and went off in different directions. The way to the right looked clear, and the left side took us through a horrible swamp full of things that wanted to kill us."

"And you remembered my words and...went left anyway?" he guessed.

Hayden nodded again.

"Harold thought I was nuts, and he went haring off on the obvious path, where he immediately fell into the worst quicksand I've ever seen. Tanner and I went left after that, and we made it through the swamp, though Tanner was in bad shape. It was after that—"

"That you found Aleric?" Laurren guessed again, frowning thoughtfully.

"Well, yeah."

"So you're thinking that if you hadn't taken my advice, you would never have run into the Dark Prism, and we would not be here right now."

Hayden didn't bother stating the obvious.

"I'm not blaming you," he said quickly. "For all I know I'd be dead in that quicksand, or still stuck in the schism, or whatever. I just remember you saying that if I went left I might survive, and if I went right I would surely die. Did you know anything about my father being there when you told me that?"

Laurren shook his head.

"No, or I certainly would have advised you to leave him behind." He exhaled heavily. "I've been wondering if I was right to tell you as much as I did, since you returned with him in tow. I suppose I bear as much responsibility as anyone for your father's return."

"You're no more at fault than I am for bringing him back," Hayden assured him. "Who knew that my good friend Hunter would morph into my evil father as soon as we came back through the schism?"

"You know, I was a little surprised when Asher told me that Aleric caught him off guard upon returning and managed to steal one of his prisms," Laurren said lightly, staring straight ahead at nothing in particular.

"Oh?" Hayden ventured carefully, not sure what the man was getting at exactly, but refusing to betray Asher for saving his life. "Well, like I said, no one was really expecting the Dark Prism to pop up at Mizzenwald after everyone thought he was dead."

"Oh sure," Laurren agreed lightly. "But still, to rob Asher of one of his prisms, Aleric would have had to get very close to him, overpower him, and then translocate himself away from Mizzenwald. Asher has some of the fastest reflexes I've ever seen, so it's hard to imagine him being so paralyzed in the face of danger."

Uncomfortable, Hayden shrugged and said, "Well, that's what happened. I was there, so I would know."

Laurren finally turned those purple-blue eyes to him and said, very seriously, "Good. Make sure you never waver from that story for a minute, or things would go badly for your mentor."

He knows.

Hayden suppressed the urge to gulp guiltily and simply nodded in understanding. He supposed he shouldn't be so surprised that Laurren had figured it out; the man was eerily gifted in his own way, and was close friends with the Prism Master. It made Hayden wonder how many of the other Masters had figured out there was more to the story than they were hearing, and were simply keeping their silence out of respect for their colleague.

Before they could say anything else on the subject, Hayden's final combat instructor of the day arrived. The sight of Master Kiresa stalking towards him did nothing to brighten Hayden's mood, especially as the man was wearing his combat circlet.

Master Laurren got to his feet and prepared to depart.

"*Now* you leave?" Hayden asked incredulously. "The one person who might actually do me serious harm, and you're leaving me alone with him?"

Laurren spared him a glance and said, "Sink or swim, Hayden. Don't provoke the man into a rage if you aren't prepared for the consequences. Kiresa was right about that much, at least. Asher won't be there to intervene on your behalf forever."

And with that he walked off, pausing long enough to exchange greetings with the Prism Master of Isenfall before stepping carefully around the portion of the lawn Hayden had wrecked with his magic and leaving.

Kiresa and Hayden stared at each other for a long moment, the former looking almost contemplative.

"Frost," he said at last.

"Master Kiresa," Hayden returned, deciding that there was no point in opening hostilities any sooner than necessary.

"You look like hell."

Hayden shrugged and said, "I've been battling people all morning. You're my last match for the day."

"Don't expect me to go easy on you just because you're tired."

"I don't, sir." Hayden struggled to keep his tone respectful.

"Well, get into the marked combat area, and let's see what you can actually do, now that you don't have anyone to hide behind."

Hayden seethed internally but said nothing, clenching and unclenching his fists a few times to relieve his frustration. They would both find out soon enough whether Hayden was any good against another prism-user or not.

It seemed distinctly unfair of the Prism Master to wear a combat circlet when he knew that Hayden didn't have one, because it would lend him a speed advantage to not have to fumble around with the different prisms in his belt. Judging by the look on Kiresa's face, the man knew exactly what Hayden was thinking and was waiting to see if he would complain about it. Hayden refused to give him the satisfaction, simply equipping a fresh mastery-level clear prism and holding a violet one in his free hand.

"On the count of three," Kiresa informed him, tensing in preparation for the fight. "One...two..."

The Prism Master attacked on 'two', but Hayden had been prepared for trickery and activated one of the charms around his neck to shield him as he readied his own spell.

Pierce! Hayden found the alignment rapidly, aiming at the man's head in the hopes of ending the fight early; a migraine would do nicely to prevent Kiresa from casting effectively.

Unfortunately the Prism Master deflected the spell and twisted the prism in his eyepiece to a new alignment. A wave of heat washed over Hayden, and he managed to cast Water to drench himself just as his clothing caught fire.

Stun! Hayden tried next, casting while moving out of the line-of-fire. His aim was off, so he only hit the Master's right arm, but was pleased when it fell limply to his side. He followed with Break, aiming at Kiresa's prisms and hoping to disarm him, but his opponent recovered in time to block the attack, using a charm of his own to free his stunned arm simultaneously.

Kiresa compounded a clear and blue prism, and Hayden was suddenly caught in the middle of a vortex, the wind buffeting him into the air and slinging him around in dizzying circles, caught in the cyclone. Dirt flew into his eyes as he squinted into his own compounded prisms and stopped the wind entirely.

It was a powerful spell that consumed his prisms visibly, and Hayden only realized he had been turned upside down as he fell from the sky; he was barely able to turn in time to avoid landing on his head.

Kiresa attacked immediately, and Hayden threw out a barrier so strong that he heard the magic slam against it and bounce back upon its caster, who was forced to dodge his own attack. Hayden rolled quickly to his feet, ignoring his growing sense of fatigue and casting Clone on himself as fast as he could, over and over again.

Like a mirage, he was suddenly standing in the midst of a dozen perfect copies of himself, and Kiresa blinked and took a step backwards in surprise. Hayden reached within himself to find his tie to each of the copies, giving them all the command to spread out and attack Kiresa with their imaginary prisms, because there were way too many of them for Hayden to give them each individual commands.

His plan had the desired effect. Thirteen Haydens were now fanning out in all directions, forming a wide circle around the Prism Master and casting through their prisms at him. Since Kiresa didn't know which Hayden was the real one, he was forced to dodge all of the attacks, not knowing which would have actual magic behind it.

The Prism Master started casting Dispel upon the clones, which caused them to disappear one by one, while the real Hayden seized his opportunity, compounded his prisms, and cast Drain at Kiresa.

Unfortunately, Drain was a powerful enough spell that his opponent felt it coming and reacted instantly with Reflect, trying to force the spell back at the caster. Hayden was pleased to see the note of fear in Kiresa's eyes as their magic clashed, because Drain would pull the Source power right out of his Foci if he allowed himself to get hit. It would take all day for him to recover from the loss, a feeling Hayden remembered all too well from his second year of schooling.

The force of their wills collided as the magic got stuck halfway between them, pushing against some invisible midpoint and waiting for one of them to give way. Hayden channeled all of his willpower into the cast, pulling Source power from his charms and back into his core so that he could draw upon it—which left him virtually defenseless. Kiresa's eyes widened as clasped his Mastery Charm and used it to amplify his power.

Cheat all you want. We're matching Sources now, and I have the largest Source anyone has ever seen.

This was the one area that he knew he had the advantage over Kiresa—over anyone, probably even his father. Hayden felt his lips pull into a smile as he put the full weight of his Source power behind his cast and pushed with all his willpower. He felt the invisible melding point between them give way as Kiresa's magic was dispersed. The Prism Master was thrown backwards by the onslaught of Hayden's power as the magic was wrought from his body.

The Prism Master of Isenfall hit the ground with a soft *thump* and stirred feebly. As Hayden approached, he recognized the effects of a mage with an empty Source, who was trying furiously to keep himself conscious.

Standing over him and smirking, Hayden said, "Don't ever try to match Sources with me. Even with three-inch correctors on each of my arms, you will always lose."

He might have said more, but the Prism Master passed out at that point. It was only then that Hayden felt the full effect of how tired he was as well, slumping onto the ground and rubbing his eyes, only barely aware that his prisms had been fully expended during his last cast.

"Well, well," the voice of Magdalene Trout floated into his ears from somewhere nearby. "It seems that Asher wasn't just talking you up after all."

Hayden blinked open his eyes and forced his brain to re-engage. His hostess was standing beside Oliver, who was glancing around at the ruins of his back yard with a neutral expression on his face.

"How long were you two watching?" Hayden asked dumbly.

"Since Kiresa arrived," Magdalene answered smoothly. Hayden was just as glad that he hadn't realized he had an audience any sooner, because it might have thrown him off of his game.

He got to his feet and staggered into Oliver, who caught his arm in a pincer-like grip and steadied him.

"You look drained," he observed blandly.

"I am," Hayden replied with a yawn, too tired for sarcasm. "Do you two want to stand around chatting, or can I go take a nap?"

He didn't really wait for an answer before tugging his arm from Oliver's grasp and walking away. Belatedly, he remembered that he hadn't put the Trouts' lawn back in order from all the fighting, but he was too tired to deal with it right now and resolved to come back outside later. As it was, he barely managed to stay conscious for the walk to his bedroom, occasionally banging off of walls and nearly crushing Bonk as he collapsed heavily into bed with his shoes still on. His last, satisfied thought, was that at least he had wiped the smug grin off of Kiresa's face for a few days.

When he woke up, six hours later, he stretched his back and got to his feet, feeling refreshed and hungry. Deciding that business should come before pleasure, he motioned Bonk onto his shoulder and returned to the back lawns with the intention of fixing them up before going to seek food. To his pleasant surprise, they had already been put to rights by the time he got there, and he turned towards the kitchen instead. He was surprised by the sound of cutlery clinking together as he passed the large dining room, and stopped to consider that perhaps it was actually dinner time.

Pushing open the doors and stepping inside, he realized he was correct. Oliver was eating with Masters Asher, Reede, and Laurren. All four of them looked up at the sound of his arrival, and the latter motioned him over to join them.

"Good, you're awake. We were just discussing whether to send someone to check on you," he said by way of greeting. Oliver made some subtle gesture with his hand that obviously cued the housekeeping staff to bring dishes and food for Hayden.

"I didn't mean to sleep so long," Hayden responded, motioning for Bonk to hop off of his shoulder and settle into an empty chair beside him. "I also meant to fix the damage I did to your back yard," he said to Oliver, "but someone beat me to it."

"My mother and I took care of it after you stumbled off like a drunkard," he replied coolly.

The usual spread of different sized plates, bowls, and glasses were placed in front of Hayden by the deft hands of a staff member, who came back only moments later to load them up with the food from whatever course they were on right now. She even set out a small glass dish containing stewed bits of meat for Bonk, which he gobbled down gratefully.

"Where are Magdalene and Laris?" Hayden glanced around the room as though expecting to see them hiding nearby.

"They're still at work," Oliver remarked. "Not everyone gets the benefit of being able to sleep the day away after a few quick fights."

"*Quick fights?*" Hayden made a face at him. "You try dueling half our Masters for hours on end and tell me how good *you* feel afterwards. Speaking of which...how's Kiresa doing?"

Asher tried and failed to conceal a grin as he said, "He woke up eventually and hauled himself home. I'm surprised he declined the generous offer to join us for dinner tonight."

"I think that you repeatedly rubbing his face in it had something to do with that decision," Master Reede remarked dryly. "You shouldn't antagonize the man any more than necessary; little though you like him, he *is* an ally of ours."

Asher sighed and looked mildly repentant as he said, "I know, I know. So," he regarded Hayden with professional interest, "how did you find fighting him as compared to fighting me?"

Aware of the attention of the others, Hayden answered as diplomatically as possible.

"Well, he was more aggressive than you usually are, but his casting was a little slower. Even though he obviously knows more spells than I do, I managed to get him locked in a battle of wills, because I knew I could win if we were matching Source power directly."

Asher inclined his head and said, "I did try to warn him that you have more raw power than anyone I've seen, but I suppose it was a lesson he had to learn for himself." For a moment Hayden thought he was going to receive a compliment, but then Asher changed tracks abruptly and said, "Willow tells me you were wasteful with your wands during your duel with him. You know you can't afford that."

Not used to being publicly criticized by his mentor, Hayden pursed his lips and said, "I know—he pointed it out to me as soon as we were done dueling. I'll work on it."

The Prism Master seemed to accept him at his word and let the subject drop for the time being.

"Not that it matters terribly at the moment," Hayden spoke into the silence, "but how did I do on my final exams?"

It was Master Laurren who answered.

"Willow told me to lie to you if you asked about your exams; he thought the truth would only upset you and distract you from your lessons." His voice was so light that at first Hayden chuckled, thinking that the Master was joking with him. When none of the others cracked a smile he said, "Wait, I didn't actually do badly, did I?"

Reede shrugged and said, "Wil said that if he was going on exam results alone, he'd have to demote you to level-four wands. Not only did you botch half the exam, you even forgot how to spell 'cherry' at one point—it took him two pages to realize you weren't actually talking about 'sherry.'"

Hayden's mouth dropped open in horror as Oliver chuckled in amusement. Master Asher shrugged consolingly and said, "It's true that Kilgore thought you suffered a traumatic brain injury that you failed to report after grading your exam, but everyone realizes that you've had more important things on your mind recently. Forget about your classes for now and just focus on what matters; the rest can be sorted out once all of this is over."

Hayden was still trying not to die of shame over his poor performance in most of his subjects, while Oliver continued to laugh at his mix-up with cherry wands with a complete lack of sympathy.

"Are you all here for some kind of official business, or just mooching off of the free food?" Hayden turned his attention back on the Masters, his sarcasm getting the better of him because he was still embarrassed.

Reede leveled his gaze at him and said, "For your information, Frost, the rest of us continue on our assigned duties even when you're resting—including, sadly, making reports of our progress. Since this has become our unofficial base of operations, that means you'll be seeing a lot more of us."

Master Asher shrugged and said, "I'm just here for the food," earning a flat stare from his colleague.

Bonk had finished all of his portion and half of Hayden's by the time he turned back to his meal, and he chivvied the dragonling away and watched with ill-concealed delight as his familiar attempted to cadge food off everyone else's plates instead.

"Who's on your docket for dueling lessons tomorrow?" Master Laurren asked, after sacrificing his smashed peas to a relentless Bonk.

"Mandra, Kilgore, and you, sir," Hayden replied. "I'll need more materials before then though, since I used up all of my wands and prisms today." He admitted the last part reluctantly, wondering if he was about to receive another rebuke for his wastefulness of wands. Fortunately it appeared that the others considered him chastised enough for the time being, because no one brought it up again.

"One of us will drop supplies off tomorrow morning," Laurren waved a dismissive hand and got to his feet. "Since Bonk has cleared my plate for me, I'm going to call it a night and go relieve Kilgore at our post. Hayden, I'll see you tomorrow."

Hayden bid him farewell and watched the Master of Abnormal Magic leave, soon followed by the others as they finished their meals as well. It was just him and Oliver left in the dining room now; his host apparently had manners enough not to abandon him there, or maybe he just didn't trust Hayden alone with the good silverware.

"Where's Lorn?" Hayden asked as the two of them departed the formal dining room, making their way past the library and in the general direction of Hayden's guestroom.

Oliver arched an eyebrow at him and said, "Mother has decided that this is too dangerous a place for him to be, in the event that either Calahan or the Dark Prism catches us all here. He's spending the indeterminate future at our cousin's house in Wynir."

"Ouch, I'll bet he doesn't like that one bit," Hayden observed, recalling how little Lorn liked being excluded from the action in years past.

"No, he doesn't, but it's for the best." Oliver shrugged and turned down the hallway. "Keep training, Frost. I don't want to think that my family has put itself at risk for nothing."

Grimly, Hayden nodded and watched his erstwhile enemy walk away until he had disappeared from sight entirely. He wondered what Tess and Zane were doing right now, and if they had guessed where he was hiding out.

I'll see them again before it's time to fight my father. I know I will.

It was what he told himself before bed every night, because otherwise he might lose the nerve to do what had to be done. And tonight, just like every other night, he wasn't sure whether he believed it.

6
Aleric's Helping Hand

For the next three weeks, Hayden's life seemed to be on a repetitive loop: wake up, eat breakfast, duel a few Masters of the arcana, eat lunch, study magic in the library, eat dinner, go to bed. A few evenings a week were punctuated with meetings, which made things mildly more interesting, though there was rarely exciting news to report by any of the principal attendees. For once in his life, Hayden found himself jealous of Oliver Trout; at least he could leave the estate whenever he wanted to, and had businesses to run now that he had assumed control of some of his mother's work.

He was sitting in another one of their biweekly status meetings, twirling a laurel wand idly around the fingers of one hand while he listened to the others give updates.

"Calahan is getting close to the breaking point," Laris reported with ill-disguised delight. "He's officially stripped Hayden of all honors and awards, and he's almost prepared to declare him an enemy of the Nine Lands. As soon as that happens, we'll be ready to begin the counteroffensive and have him removed from office."

Master Willow was apparently not prepared to take his word for it because he raised an eyebrow and said, "Magdalene, do you concur?"

"Yes," Oliver's mother confirmed solemnly. She at least did a better job of appearing unhappy about tearing down one of her colleagues than Laris. "He's convinced that Hayden must be hiding out with his father, or he would have been found by now."

It felt odd to hear that he had officially had his medals and awards revoked, as though the events that earned them had been erased from history.

And yet, the Medal of Heroism and the Opalline Medallion are still laid out on the shelf in the guest bedroom. He can't really take them away from me until he finds me.

"The Nine Lands are a big place," Hayden pointed out mildly. "How can Calahan draw the conclusion that I must be hiding out with my father, just because his cronies haven't tracked me down anywhere else yet? I could be living in a cave in Osglen for all he knows."

Master Graus, who was typically quiet during these meetings, said, "He's got Wanted posters out for you all over the continent, right next to the ones of your father, offering up a hefty reward for anyone who provides information that leads to the capture of either of you."

"Oh," Hayden raised his eyebrows in surprise. "It's a sad commentary on my life that I just turned sixteen and this is the second time that I've appeared on

Wanted posters, alongside the most corrupt mage of the century, no less."

Asher half-smiled at the dry amusement in his tone.

"Since Calahan has made a big show of calling for you to come out in the open and meet with him to discuss tactics against your father, and obviously you haven't shown, it gave him the ammunition he needed to declare you must be working with him to destabilize the government."

Hayden rolled his eyes.

"If I *had* met with him like he wanted, he would have just locked me up in the Crystal Tower, told everyone I was using it as my base of operations while cooperating with the Council, and no one would ever hear from me again."

"That's an eerily close guess," Laris said, looking faintly impressed with his powers of deduction. "You must have spent more time in Calahan's company than I realized."

Hayden shrugged and said, "No, he's just not that hard to figure out once you get the measure of him."

A few moments of silence followed this, and then Magdalene said, "Wallis reported in the Council meeting this morning that he laid eyes on the Dark Prism." She turned to Hayden. "He claims that your father was at the outskirts of Locleth."

"Where's that?" Hayden asked with interest.

"I'm not surprised you haven't heard of it. Locleth is a very poor town in southern Sudir; the residents there are lucky if they can keep a fresh supply of water and a roof over their heads. Few mages would choose to settle there, for obvious reasons," Magdalene explained patiently.

"Then why on earth would my father be there?" Hayden wondered out loud. Surely the man wasn't vacationing in a place that didn't even have fresh water…

"We were hoping you could tell us," Laris piped up, leveling his gaze on Hayden, who frowned.

"For the tenth time, I don't know my father well enough to unravel all of his evil plans just because I'm related to him by blood," Hayden explained. "Nor did we discuss his nefarious goals while inside the schism together, as I was suffering from insanity at the time and didn't even know who he was until we left."

No one looked surprised to hear this, though Laris and Magdalene did look disappointed. The latter opened her mouth to speak, but was interrupted by the double doors of the dining room being pulled open by one of the staff. Magdalene raised her eyebrows at the tall, thin man who entered hurriedly and said, "I'm sorry to intrude, but you have a visitor in the entryway who demands to be seen."

Obviously caught off guard by the unexpected arrival, Mrs. Trout asked, "Who is it?"

"It is Mrs. Isla Strauss, and I directed her to the sitting room and had Liss offer her refreshments while she waits. She seems most flustered and anxious to speak with you."

"Isla?" Magdalene looked astounded. "I haven't seen her in years, and she chooses *now* to bring her silly problems to me?" she was clearly speaking more to herself than to anyone else.

"Should I send her away?" the man offered, taking a step backwards across the threshold.

"No," Magdalene decided at the last second. "Send her in, and I'll see what she wants," she sighed and addressed the others as the man left. "Isla and I used to be friends during school, but we grew apart after we left Mizzenwald. I can't imagine what she wants to see me for now, but it's best to have done with it." She looked at Hayden. "I would not count her as an ally in what we are doing, so you all need to hide before she comes in."

On cue, everyone at the table got up and began moving. Everyone with a Mastery Charm—which was everyone except for Hayden—gripped their Charm and cast a spell of invisibility upon themselves, standing silent and still along the walls where they wouldn't be in danger of getting run into by Isla Strauss. Hayden, not having the ability to vanish himself at will, was forced to duck behind the red velvet curtains that were pulled shut over the massive windows. He felt foolish flattening himself against the windows and trying to prevent the curtains from fluttering when he breathed, while everyone else simply used magic to conceal themselves.

Isla was ushered into the room about two minutes later, where she found Magdalene Trout waiting, apparently alone.

"I'm sorry to just barge in like this," she began before Mrs. Trout could open her mouth. "You know I wouldn't presume to just show up at someone's home uninvited, but I wasn't sure who else I should tell; the rest of the Council members are such old sticks, and I hate talking to them unless I absolutely have to."

Hayden could imagine Laris, who was standing hidden in the room near a tall potted plant, pursing his lips at this assessment.

"Calm down, Isla, you know I'm always happy to see a friend," Magdalene replied in a falsely pleasant tone that didn't really suit her, but it must not have seemed strange to her old friend, because Isla relaxed immediately. "I do admit that I was a little surprised to hear you came to see me this late in the evening…"

"I know it's late, and again, I'm sorry—but I didn't think it should wait until morning, and I still count you as one of my dearest friends, so I thought you should know what happened before anyone else."

"Please, sit down and tell me what's going on," Magdalene gestured her towards a chair, glancing casually around the room at the hidden mages, who she could obviously still see.

Stupid Mastery Charms, Hayden thought ruefully. *One day I'll have one of my own and then I won't have to stoop behind curtains anymore.*

Isla fussed around for a moment and then settled into a seat, fidgeting with her thumbs and bouncing lightly in her chair.

Does that woman never sit still? Hayden couldn't imagine how someone so bouncy and chatty could have ever been close friends with someone as self-contained as Magdalene Trout.

"It was *him*, Mags," Isla blurted out at last. "The one they call the Dark Prism."

Several of the Masters flinched noticeably, which Hayden only became aware of because it caused their invisibility spells to momentarily flicker out. Fortunately, Isla's attention was wholly focused on Mrs. Trout and she didn't notice the room full of hidden people. Hayden felt like a lead weight had settled into his stomach at the mention of his father.

"*What?*" Magdalene clasped her friend's hand, eyes wide with shock. "Do you mean to tell me that you've seen Aleric Frost? Where? When? Tell me everything," she commanded in her usual tone.

"I didn't just see him, Mags, I talked to him—he helped me."

Now Magdalene released her friend's hands and leaned backwards. "I think you must be confused. Few people who speak to Aleric Frost live to tell the tale these days, and he certainly hasn't proven himself to be a friend to mage-kind."

Isla shook her head and said, "I know it sounds crazy, but it was him, I swear it."

Pursing her lips, Magdalene said, "Explain."

"You know how I damaged my right Focus ten years ago in that stupid experiment in Powders? I haven't been able to cast magic through it at all since then, and the imbalance was even making it painful to channel magic through my left Focus…"

"I remember," Magdalene waved a hand to hurry her along. "What does that have to do with—"

"I was planting peas out in the garden today when he found me," she interrupted. "He just walked up the garden path around the side of the house like he was taking a stroll. Nearly gave me a heart attack, seeing him after all these years and after hearing all the stories about what he's done. I thought I was dead for sure."

Magdalene frowned and said, "You mean to tell me that you were gardening at home, and *Aleric Frost* just happened upon you in your backyard?"

"I told you, it sounds crazy, but it's what happened," Isla explained defensively. "Anyway, for a minute we just looked at each other—I was too scared to even move in case it set him off—but then he just introduced himself, calm as can be. He took my hands and looked at them like there was something interesting on them, and then he said, "Your Foci are badly damaged.""

Magdalene was watching her friend in silence, a look of utter shock on her face. Hayden understood how she felt; none of this made any sense, but he couldn't imagine why this woman would make things up for no reason.

"I told him I had broken the right one in an experiment gone wrong, years ago, and he asked if I wanted him to fix it for me."

"WHAT?" Magdalene practically stood up in her agitation, barely restraining herself at the last moment.

"I know, and I was terrified—I mean, there was his circlet just resting on his head with the Black Prism in it."

"You saw the Black Prism?" Magdalene interrupted, eyes wide. "How do you know? It would look like any other prism unless you were gifted in that area and happened to be looking through it."

"Well, yeah, but it was the only prism he had on him, and why would he only carry around one regular prism when the whole world is searching for him?" Isla shrugged. "Anyway, I said I didn't want to take part in dark magic, and he just smiled and said there was nothing dark about it. You wouldn't believe how normal and sane he seemed, Mags—I know that the posters all say he's mad and evil, but he seemed completely normal to me."

"Go on," Magdalene prompted softly, apparently beyond anything more complex right now.

"Well, it wasn't like I had a lot of choice—what am I going to do, fight the Dark Prism off when I can't even do magic properly?" she asked of no one. "Anyway, he looked through his prism, aimed at my hands, and…" she held up her hands as though presenting them as evidence. "He *fixed* them, Mags. He fixed my Foci."

Now Magdalene did stand up.

"I don't believe it," she said flatly. "Why would he fix your Foci? Aleric Frost has never been one to help others, nor would he just show up, fix your magic, and then leave. That's completely at odds with his personality: he doesn't go anywhere without a purpose."

For the first time, Isla looked flushed and indignant.

"I'm not lying! Here, let me borrow some powders and I'll show you." She held out her hand defiantly.

Looking skeptical, Magdalene reached into one of the slots on her robes and withdrew a pouch of magenta powder. Reflexively, Hayden held his breath to avoid sneezing, coughing, or vomiting—as he was wont to do all three in the presence of powders.

Isla took a pinch of the magenta powder and sifted it through her fingers for a moment as though savoring the effect. Then she snapped her fingers together so loudly that it seemed to echo around the room, and with a spark the powder ignited, coming together and transforming into a white, long-stemmed rose. Isla caught the flower in mid-air and held it lightly between two fingers, while Magdalene looked on in amazement.

"See? My Foci are perfectly balanced again; I don't even need correctors anymore." She smiled and passed the flower off to her friend.

"It just doesn't make sense," Magdalene said softly, staring at the undeniable proof in her hand. "Ever since he's taken this dark path of his, Aleric has never been one to help the needy. By all accounts, he shouldn't even take an interest in other human beings; he's too busy working on his own plans to even be cognizant of others unless he has a use for them."

Isla shrugged and said, "I know, and I wouldn't have thought it was possible either if it didn't just happen." A note of doubt was injected in her voice now as she said, "I know he was really bad before...but maybe he's different, now that he came out of the other realm? Maybe spending time there did something to help fix his mind..."

Magdalene got to her feet and seemed to make some internal decision.

"Thank you for telling me this, Isla. You can rest assured that I will relay this to the people who need to know and we will certainly take your testimony into account while making our decision about what to do next."

Isla continued to look slightly unsure.

"Are you going to lift the kill order on him, if it turns out he *is* better? Truly, he seemed perfectly normal to me, and with all the new magic he has probably discovered, he could make a lot of great contributions to mage-kind."

Magdalene's smile didn't reach her eyes, and Hayden thought there was something distinctly forced and angry about it, but she said, "If it turns out that he has recovered after his time in the other realm, then our position on him will certainly need to be revised."

Hayden noticed that she hadn't actually said they would rescind the kill order, a nice bit of weasel-wording there, but Isla seemed reassured, and left after another cup of tea and a couple biscuits.

When the staff reported that she had left the premises, all of the invisible people in the room popped back into view and Hayden came out from behind the curtains. Magdalene Trout was slumped forward in her chair at the table with her head in her hands, while the others reclaimed their seats.

"Impossible," Laris asserted amongst the general noise in the room. "She must be lying, or mistaken."

"Who would falsely identify themselves as Aleric Frost, when he is the most hated and feared man on the continent?" Master Graus pointed out lightly.

"I don't know, someone playing a bad joke," Laris waved a hand dismissively.

"Just how badly damaged *was* her right Focus before tonight?" Master Willow asked softly, prompting Magdalene to look up from her hands and rejoin the conversation.

"The right one was destroyed entirely—she couldn't get a drop of magic through it. Like she said, even her left was affected by the imbalance; magic would bunch up on the right side and then spill over through her left Focus in floods when the pressure became too great. She stopped using magic entirely, before her left Focus could be completely destroyed as well."

Hayden winced in sympathy at the thought of how unpleasant that sensation must be. Though severely warped, his Foci were still able to allow some magic to pass through them, and at least they were both equally damaged so he wasn't imbalanced.

"The fact that she was able to effortlessly use powders tonight implies that she was telling the truth," Master Willow continued heavily. "Unless you know anyone else who is capable of repairing damaged Foci?" he addressed Laris, who shook his head.

"No, of course not, but still..." he trailed off doubtfully. "You expect me to believe that the Dark Prism, of all people, just happened upon someone with damaged Foci at her home and was feeling magnanimous enough to cure her for no apparent reason? And then he just *left?*"

"I know, it sounds ridiculous, but she clearly wouldn't have made it back to us with this tale if he had attacked her, and the fact does remain that her magic works now where it didn't before," Graus countered evenly.

"Maybe he targeted her on purpose," Magdalene postulated, rejoining the conversation. "If he knew that her Foci were damaged, maybe he went there deliberately to fix them."

Everyone turned to stare at her.

"So now you're saying he's one of the good guys, roaming the countryside looking for the sick to cure?" Laris asked in disbelief, leaning away from her as though she were carrying something contagious.

"No, but it makes more sense than to just assume he was wandering around people's backyards in the hopes of finding someone worth chatting with." She ran her hands through her hair in frustration, the first time Hayden had seen such a loss of control from her.

"Maybe he really *has* become different since leaving the other realm," Master Kilgore, who had been silent so far, interjected. "Aside from a brief confrontation at Mizzenwald as soon as he crossed over, none of us have interacted with the man. Perhaps he just needed time to recover once he came back into our realm."

Everyone turned to Hayden at this point, apparently to get his opinion on how likely Master Kilgore's theory was. Hayden remembered the way his father smiled at Asher when he first laid eyes on him, how warmly he'd greeted his old friend. He also remembered the icy coldness in his father's voice as he held Hayden in front of him like a shield, pressing a knife to his throat and threatening to kill him. There was no love in that voice, no respect for human life; Hayden was nothing but a tool that would help him escape before Asher could kill him.

"If he's good now, that's a surprise to me," Hayden answered carefully, not wanting to lie and give the others false hope, but also determined not to get Asher put in jail for letting the Dark Prism escape. "It's not like we had a lengthy conversation before he escaped, but he sounded ruthless and cold and not at all interested in keeping me or anyone else alive."

The others frowned at this, and Master Willow turned to Asher, who had not rejoined them at the table, but was standing in front of the curtains that Hayden had only recently vacated, holding one side open and staring out the window.

"Asher, you've been silent thus far." *An oddity in and of itself,* was implied.

"Yes, Masters," Laris turned to him as well, "You knew the man better than anyone still living. To this day, you're probably the only person to survive a fight with Aleric, and you and Hayden were the only ones who saw him when he crossed through the schism at Mizzenwald. What do you think about all this?"

For a long moment Asher continued to stare out the window, keeping his back to the others at the table. Hayden wondered what was going through the man's mind, and if he was planning on answering, or if he was going to pretend he hadn't heard the questions directed his way. Finally, before Laris could open his mouth to reiterate his thoughts, the Prism Master turned around and joined them at the table.

"He hasn't changed," he stated quietly but firmly, briefly meeting Hayden's eyes. "I saw what he was when he came back into our realm; it is the same monster he had become before his disappearance."

"You seem very confident," Laris argued. "You could be mistaken."

"I am not mistaken," Asher countered easily. "I have no idea what game Aleric is playing right now, but he is no more stable now than he was on the day he disappeared."

Magdalene Trout frowned and said, "Normally I wouldn't argue with you on this, but the fact remains that he *did* help Isla…"

"More evidence that he is not himself," Asher explained. "Even at his best, Aleric was more arrogant than I ever was, and I am supremely conceited. He never had time for those weaker or dumber than him, and Isla Strauss is both. If he has given her so much as the time of day, it is only because it serves some purpose of his to do so."

That earned a stunned silence from the collective group as they digested that piece of information.

"What purpose would it serve for him to fix her Foci?" Kilgore changed tracks, accepting Asher's assertions without question.

"I have absolutely no idea," Asher replied without hesitation.

"We can't discount the fact that she says she carried on a normal conversation with the man," Magdalene pointed out. "He's supposed to be too corrupted and unstable to really interact with others, much less to pass himself off as sane."

"I don't know if that's really true," Master Willow disagreed lightly. "Even at his worst, he was perfectly capable of coordinating his movements, issuing threats, and speaking to whomever he pleased. The main issue is that it *pleased* him to take whatever he wanted to further his own corrupt magic, and he freely murdered anyone who he felt got in the way of that."

Magdalene tilted her head to concede the point.

"It's amazing that he's been able to keep his mind as functional as he has," Graus observed admiringly. "Most people go raving mad after a few months of working with corrupt magic, but he held together for over ten years—and appears to be doing just fine, even now."

"I did say that he had more stubborn willpower than any human being I've ever met," Asher added softly, with a glance at Hayden that seemed to say, *You'll never beat him on that front.*

"Maybe he's trying to deliberately confuse us," Hayden volunteered into the silence. "If he knew that Isla was Mrs. Trout's friend, he knew she would report to her as soon as he left, and that she would tell the Council—or us. He might want us to have this very argument, to divide us while we waste time arguing over whether he's good or bad, which leaves him unopposed—especially if we take the Wanted posters down at some point and the only person that is still being hunted by the Council is me."

The others were silent for almost a full minute, which forced Hayden to wonder whether his idea was ridiculously stupid and they were just trying to find a nice way of explaining it to him.

Finally, Master Graus said, "An interesting thought, Hayden. That *is* the sort of craftiness one might expect from Aleric Frost."

The others murmured various levels of agreement with his theory, which made Hayden feel like a real contributor to these meetings for a change, but he couldn't help but notice that Master Asher remained silent.

"What do you think?" he asked his mentor, who rubbed his eyes tiredly.

"It's as possible as anything, which isn't to say that I find it terribly likely. Aleric has never cared that the entire continent hates him. He hasn't cared that the Council of Mages has put a price on his head. He hasn't cared that we've sent countless mages to kill him—he's murdered them all and sent their heads back to us, gift-wrapped. He is absolutely confident in his abilities, in his Black Prism, and in the defenses he has in place around his base of operations—likely his estate. Why expend the effort to make us fight amongst ourselves and sow confusion, when he just doesn't *have* to?"

"By your account, he's invincible and we should just throw down our arms right now and accept defeat," Laris muttered mutinously.

Asher shook his head. "He is only invincible in his own mind. In fact he is just very, very skillful, and absolutely without morals. Still, the fact remains that he has never concerned himself with the opinions of others, and I don't see a reason for that to change now."

"This is obviously not a mystery we are going to solve tonight," Magdalene stood up, addressing the group collectively. "It's late, and many of us have early morning appointments tomorrow, so we should take what rest we can get. We'll meet again later in the week, and if anyone has any ideas or additional information, they should be presented then."

Everyone agreed and got up to take their leave. Hayden had never felt less tired in his life. This was the first real information they had gotten about his father's whereabouts or plans, and he had no desire to go to bed until he had unraveled the entire nefarious plot—and he believed Asher implicitly that his father had to be planning something unpleasant, even if it seemed helpful right now.

But he was forced to call it a night when the others left one-by-one, and he found himself alone with only Magdalene Trout in the dining room.

"Go to bed, Hayden. There's nothing more to be done tonight, and we'll all think more clearly in the morning."

"It's hard to imagine sleeping right now," he admitted. "I'll take some food scraps back to Bonk if you don't mind; he usually wakes up when I come to bed. Maybe some time alone will help me sort my thoughts and I'll get a brainwave."

"If you like." She shrugged as though she couldn't care less what he did with his free time—probably true. "I expect you to be fresh and bright-eyed for your training tomorrow, regardless of how late you stay awake tonight."

Hayden nodded and said, "You know me. There's nothing I like more than waking up at the crack of dawn to battle mages a dozen times more skillful than myself."

She chuckled wearily and left him alone. By now he knew his way around the Trout estate better than the Frost one, which seemed both ironic and horrible, and he made his way unerringly to the kitchen to request a late night snack for Bonk. One of the kitchen staff handed him a platter of shaved meat he couldn't readily identify the origin of, and Hayden thanked her and carried it back to his bedroom, where Bonk was awake and waiting eagerly for his return.

As soon as Hayden cleared the door the little dragon pounced on the platter of food, knocking it to the floor and descending on the scraps as though they might outrun him. Hayden sighed and left him to it, waiting for his familiar to finish devouring all the meat and licking the scraps off of the floor before picking up the empty platter and setting it carefully on the nightstand.

He laid back in bed and contemplated the meeting he had just departed, musing out loud to Bonk because it helped him think.

"It seems like Isla was telling the truth about meeting my father in her back yard, but it's just so weird to think of him fixing her Foci out of the goodness of his heart. Everyone else seems to think he might have turned over a new leaf since he came back, but they weren't there that day that he passed through the schism with me; they don't know what he was like, or how quick he was to almost kill me." He sighed. "Asher says that he must have fixed Isla's Foci deliberately, as some part of his overall strategy, but I just can't imagine how helping a random mage as ditsy as Isla would benefit him at all. You sort of knew him when he was still at school, Bonk—what do you think about all of this?"

Bonk rolled over on top of the sheets and burped loudly.

"An excellent point," Hayden muttered, rolling his eyes at Bonk and then closing them, covering his face with his arm to block out the moonlight as he tried to sort through his jumbled thoughts.

The next thing he knew, sunlight was streaming through the gaps between his arm and his face, and someone was shaking him roughly.

"Wake up, Hayden—I know you're not dead, or they would have laid your body to rest in a more dignified position."

Only the familiarity of that voice and the strangeness of hearing it in the Trout estate could shake Hayden from sleep so rapidly. Sitting up so fast that it made him dizzy, Hayden's mouth dropped open as his eyes confirmed what his ears had told him moments before.

"*Zane?*"

His best friend had a gash over his right eye and looked exhausted, but he grinned at Hayden's shock and said, "I'm starving. When do they serve breakfast in this place?"

7
A Battle of Wills

The shock of seeing Zane in his guest bedroom at the Trout estate was almost as great as if it had been Aleric Frost waking him up for breakfast. For a moment all Hayden could do was stare at his best friend in open-mouthed amazement. Eventually he got his wits together enough to ask, "How in the world did you get here?"

Delighting in Hayden's surprise, Zane sat down on the edge of the bed and said, "By magic. It's a harrowing tale, involving a lengthy battle with the Council of Mages, followed by days of living off the land and hiding in caves while they pursued me relentlessly—"

"Are you *serious!?*" Hayden exclaimed in horror.

"No, I totally made that up," Zane grinned. "In reality, one of the Council's goons showed up to interrogate me for the nine-hundredth time on your whereabouts, and for the nine-hundredth time I told them that I had no idea where you were, that we weren't really great friends to begin with, that you were probably vacationing in the northern continent with Bonk, things like that." He stopped and grinned again.

"The Masters said you and Tess would be badgered relentlessly by the Council about me, and that they would try to extract you both when it was safe," Hayden interrupted guiltily. "Sorry about that, by the way."

"Yeah, well you caused quite a stir when you disappeared from the middle of the dining hall at school, using magic so advanced that you didn't even have to look through your prism to cast it." Zane rolled his eyes. "You might have told your friends that you were planning to bail on us so we could prepare ourselves for the hailstorm of unpleasantness that followed."

"It wasn't exactly planned," Hayden explained. "Asher just busted into my head when those Council guys showed up and told me to grab hold of Bonk. It wasn't even my magic that took me away from there—Kilgore and Mrs. Trout did the translocation from here, using the sympathetic link between Bonk and Slasher to pull it off."

Zane's expression cleared and he said, "Ah, that makes more sense. I was wondering when you learned super-advanced translocation, since you had just that week told me you couldn't even properly pull off self-translocation within the castle itself."

"Get back to your story," Hayden changed the subject. "You said the Council showed up to interrogate you again…"

"Oh yeah, right," Zane shook his head to clear it. "I had instructions from Willow not to make any trouble with the Council or try to escape as long as they were just asking questions—it would make me look guilty or complicit or something like that." He shrugged. "Only this time, the Councilman said he was going to haul me off to the Crystal Tower to be magically-interrogated if I didn't give him any useful information."

"Magically-interrogated as in...tortured?" Hayden asked with a disbelieving wince.

"That's sort of the implication I got, though he never came out and said it—I guess it's only in stories that the bad guys stand around explaining all their evil plans in advance. Still, you always see people grimace when they hear about magical interrogation methods, so it didn't sound like something I wanted any part of." Zane shrugged. "I knew I needed to escape, and I didn't have a lot of time to come up with a plan. When the guy grabbed my arm to drag me off into the living room, I elbowed him in the face and broke his nose," he explained in a rush, face flushed. "While he was feeling around his face I grabbed his chalk and started drawing a translocation circle—"

"You broke a Councilman's *nose* and stole his weapon?" Hayden interrupted. "You're going to have your own Wanted poster beside mine before all this is over."

"Yeah, well, it's not like I had a long time to formulate a proper escape plan," Zane grumbled. "Anyway, Flory and Victoria—they're the only two sisters who are still at home—heard the noise and they jumped on the guy and held him down while I finished the circle."

"You let your *sisters* get involved in an attack on a Council member?" Hayden winced. "Aren't they going to get into trouble for that?"

Zane shrugged, though he looked a little guilty when he said, "They're older than me, and they knew what they were getting into. Besides, they hated that guy as much as I did; he haunted our family night-and-day for weeks."

"I didn't think you knew how to do translocations yet," Hayden interjected, changing the subject.

Zane looked a little green when he said, "I don't—or I didn't. I was never cleared to try it by Reede, but I've seen the circles often enough and I know the theory behind the magic. Desperate times call for desperate...desperateness," Zane continued with a shrug.

"And it worked on your first try?" Hayden asked, a little jealous.

"Thankfully, yes—well, mostly," his friend amended. "I didn't have a specific location in mind, which makes it harder. I just wanted it to bring me to Master Reede because I figured he would be able to tell me where to go afterwards to hide out. I was concentrating so hard on finding him, I didn't focus on sticking my landing, so I came out in the middle of the men's bathroom in the Crystal Tower, and fell from the ceiling."

"Wait, you transported yourself straight into the very place we've all been trying to avoid—in the *bathroom* of all places?" Hayden covered his mouth to prevent the burst of laughter that threatened to escape.

"Yes, the irony wasn't lost on me either, not that I had long to appreciate it." Zane made a face at him. "Like I said, I fell from the ceiling and nearly landed right on top of Reede, who was washing his hands at the sink and thankfully not in the middle of peeing." He grimaced at the thought. "I caught the sink with the side of my head as I fell, which is how I got this." He pointed to the gash on his forehead, which was bruising spectacularly.

"I was wondering how you came by that," Hayden admitted. "Usually when I imagine your face, it isn't pounded to a pulp."

"Nice to know you dream of my face," Zane teased flatly, earning him a punch in the arm from Hayden. "Anyway, Reede reacted so fast it was almost like he was expecting me to pop up in the bathroom at the Crystal Tower. He said, 'Sloppy execution, Laraby', and drew another circle so fast that my head was still ringing and my eyes hadn't even focused yet by the time he was done. Then he shoved me into it and sent me here just as the door opened and someone else was coming in to use the bathroom. When the world stopped spinning I realized I was in a mansion of some sort, but it wasn't until I saw Oliver that I knew exactly where."

Hayden made a noise of sympathy and said, "Yes, welcome to the palace that is the Trout estate." He gestured expansively around the guest room, nearly hitting Bonk in the head—who was no longer sleeping and had crept up beside him to listen to Zane's story. It was then that Hayden noticed Felix the Fox curled up on the foot of the bed, looking similarly exhausted.

"Yeah, magical creatures have their own means of travel—lucky for them," Zane scowled at Felix like this was all his fault.

"I like that you fell from the sky in the middle of the men's bathroom and the only thing Reede could think to say to you was that you executed your circle poorly," Hayden pointed out in amusement. "I swear, him and Willow are the most unflappable human beings I've ever met."

"I think it's a requirement for being a Master: never react to anything that happens or you'll be fired." Zane grinned. "It's probably part of their initiation or something."

Hayden's laugh turned to molten fear in his mouth, as a new thought struck him.

"Wait a minute—" he lurched out of bed and nearly knocked Zane to the floor. "If you're on the run from the Council and they think you're with me, what's going to happen to Tess?"

The smile slid off of Zane's face as he considered her fate as well.

"I don't know…I mean, surely they were monitoring her too. Maybe they won't do anything to her just because I left though. I mean, I haven't been in contact with her since we left school, so it's not like she had anything to do with me leaving. It wouldn't be fair to punish her."

"Sure, and the Council of Mages is nothing but fair." Hayden paced furiously in a circle. "Magdalene and Laris have been trying to destabilize Calahan for months because they both want his job, so now he's half-paranoid and hates anything to do with me. That is *not* who I want meting out justice to my friends, or my girlfriend."

Zane gestured towards the door. "Come on, let's go see if anyone knows what's going on with her. You live in the base of operations for the resistance; someone here must know what's going on. For all we know, Tess might be in another room in this museum right now."

It would make sense that the Masters would evacuate Tess as soon as Zane ran away, and Hayden felt mildly calmer as he left the bedroom and led Zane towards the informal dining room, where people were most likely to be at this time of day.

"Are you still wearing yesterday's clothes?" Zane asked pointedly as they walked, turning his head in all directions to take in the spacious hallways and opulent decorations as they hurried past them.

"Yeah, why?"

"Because they're ripped, dirty, and you kind of smell like a sweaty sock."

Hayden scowled and said, "I had a lot on my mind yesterday and didn't get to shower. I'll take care of it after we find out about Tess."

"Oh yeah, you can catch me up on what's really going on, since I doubt the Council of Mages is out there sharing the truth with the rest of the continent." Zane's eyes lifted in awe as they passed through the library. Hayden couldn't blame him; he had also been impressed with the collection of books during his first visit. "I can't imagine growing up in a place like this. No wonder Oliver and Lorn are such snobs."

Hayden didn't comment until they reached the dining room, where only Master Mandra was there to greet them. He was sitting at the table, reading a stack of papers while finishing his coffee, eyebrows furrowed as though what he was reading wasn't at all to his liking. He looked up at the sound of their arrival.

"Hayden, good morning," the Master greeted him tiredly. "Holy arcana, have you bathed at any time this week?" he wrinkled his nose.

"I know, I stink, I'm going to shower soon—but there's something more important I need to know first." He felt his cheeks flush and tried to ignore his embarrassment.

"Is this the friend that caused such a stir by showing up at the crack of dawn?" Mandra turned to Zane.

"Oh, right, I forgot you two didn't know each other." Hayden recovered his manners immediately. "Zane, this is Master Mandra—he teaches Wands at Valhalla; we met during the I.S.C. in my second year. Master Mandra, this is Zane Laraby, my best and sometimes only friend at Mizzenwald."

The two shook hands and Mandra said, "That's quite a gash on your forehead. Has anyone seen to it yet?"

"Not really," Zane admitted. "As you said, it was the crack of dawn when I made a break for it, and Reede barely had time to send me here before anyone saw me at the Crystal Tower, and Mrs. Trout only hung around long enough to tell one of her housekeepers to take me to Hayden's room."

"Then sit down, and I'll see what I can do for you," Mandra pointed him to the chair beside him, and

Zane sat obediently, though he looked a little nervous about letting a stranger work on his head wound. It was all Hayden could do not to jump up and down and shriek about Tess, but he forced himself to remain calm and patient until they were sure Zane would be alright.

The Master of Wands drew a birch wand from his belt and waved it a few times in front of Zane's face, casting a series of spells without speaking aloud. Hayden could see the wand shrink visibly, and knew that he must be using fairly powerful magic to consume a mastery-level wand so rapidly. The gash on Zane's forehead looked cleaner and less swollen when he was finished, and Zane seemed to relax as the man dabbed a blue elixir on the wound and wrapped an ethyl-infused bandage around his entire head.

"Your Mistress Razelle could do better, but at least it shouldn't get infected, and I've sped the healing up considerably," he said at last.

The mention of the Mistress of Healing raised a new question for Hayden.

"I've seen almost all of the other Masters here at some point or another, but not Sark or Razelle. Are they not on our side?"

Master Mandra looked at him in surprise.

"They're both contributing to our efforts in their own way, but we all have different assignments and some of them allow for less freedom of movement than others. You've also seen a few of our colleagues from the other Great Nine schools, but there are more that you haven't seen who are still doing their part behind the scenes."

"Oh," Hayden nodded thoughtfully. It was nice to know that they had even more allies than he had previously thought.

The more the better. It'll take everything we've got to get rid of my father and manage the Council of Mages at the same time.

"Master Mandra, I have to ask...do you know where Tess is right now?" Hayden blurted out.

The Master of Wands gave him a strange look and said, "Who?"

"Tess," he said with emphasis, his voice nearly cracking from strain. "She's my other friend—my girlfriend—and the Council has been watching her the way they've been watching Zane, only Zane's run away. They were threatening to magically-interrogate him about me, so what's going to happen to her now that he's gone? Have we done anything to get her out? Kilgore or Sark have to help her—she's a double-major in Powders and Elixirs, so if anyone would know, it should be—"

"You're rambling," Zane cut him off. "Stop talking for half a second so the man can answer."

Annoyed, Hayden shut his mouth and unclenched his fists. He felt taut as a bowstring and ready to snap at any moment.

She has to be okay...please, don't let her be suffering because of me...

"I wish I could tell you where she was, but I honestly don't know," Mandra admitted, and Hayden was pretty sure he felt his heart stop beating. "Magdalene only told me that something had happened and that I should make sure to keep you here and focused while the others try and sort things out, but there wasn't time for her to explain properly. The rest of them are in various meetings and appointments—Magdalene was late for hers just from the few minutes she stayed behind to update me. I'm sure we'll hear something more concrete when people start returning later in the day."

Hayden didn't want to hear that he would know later. He wanted to know *now*.

"Don't do anything stupid, like try to leave the estate," Mandra seemed to read his mind, or else his face was just that obvious. "I've been given explicit instructions by both Magdalene and Asher to keep you here by any means—the latter actually told me to 'beat the stuffing out of you' if necessary."

That sounds like my mentor.

"Asher told you keep me here too? Did he say anything else?" Hayden had often disagreed with what the Prism Master advised, but he had to admit that the man was rarely wrong and always had his best interests at heart. If anyone understood how important Tess was to him, it was Asher.

"He said to tell you to stay put and keep yourself occupied or he'd sic Kiresa on you." He shrugged. "The man's apparently been dying to exact his revenge on you for defeating him in battle."

"Whoa, you beat a Master in combat?" Zane looked impressed. "Wait, isn't Kiresa that Prism Master from Isenfall that hates you and creeps you out?"

"That's the one," Hayden agreed dully.

"Oh, weird, he's here too?"

"Sometimes."

Hayden exhaled heavily and tried to let go of his impatient desire to run from the room screaming and barge into the Crystal Tower with weapons blazing, demanding to know where Tess was. He didn't think that would bode well for their plans to convince the world he was really a good guy and that Cal needed to be fired.

"Alright, fine, I'll be a good boy and stay put," he conceded at last. "But if someone doesn't give me a proper update sometime today then you all are going to regret training me so well in magic, because it'll take every last one of you to keep me here."

Mandra inclined his head and said, "I'm sure we'll have some sort of information by tonight."

"Fine, then I'm going to shower. Zane, feel free to stay here and have some breakfast; I'll be back in a little while."

He stalked off, desperate to be alone with his thoughts for a little while, not caring that he'd rudely abandoned his friend with someone he hardly knew for company. He spent much longer in the shower than was normal, letting the hot water wash over him even after he was clean, as though it could burn away some of the feelings inside of him. It was all he could do not to imagine what sorts of horrible things might be happening to Tess right now: maybe she was alone and scared and crying somewhere, or maybe she was praying for him to come rescue her…

This isn't productive.

Hayden turned off the water, dried and dressed himself in clean clothes, and returned to the informal dining room in search of breakfast, properly hungry now. Master Mandra was nowhere to be seen, but Zane was still there, accompanied now by Master Laurren.

Zane looked like he felt awkward and out of place, casually dining in a mansion with one of their Masters, though that might be partly because he didn't take Abnormal Magic, and Laurren had that otherworldly aura about him that could make others uncomfortable even if you knew him well.

"Are you my first partner for the day?" Hayden greeted his instructor, sitting down across from him and Zane and motioning that he was ready to eat. The hand signal was read by a waiting staff member, who was standing unobtrusively in the corner, and she went to get him a plate of food. Less than a year ago, the concept of waving his hand and expecting adults to wait on him was hard to conceive of.

How times change.

"So it would seem," Laurren replied smoothly.

"I don't suppose *you* know where Tess is?" Hayden asked without any real hope of an answer.

"Nope, sorry kid. Try not to work yourself into a frenzy though; even Calahan isn't demented enough to harm innocents just for being your friend. It would start a wave of outrage throughout the magical community that would be impossible to contain."

"If people actually found out about it. Why would he tell them the truth when he can just lie and say whatever he wants?"

"Because some of us know the truth, and we would see justice done on her behalf," Laurren explained coolly. "No one wants to see the day where our leaders capture and abuse people without just cause."

Hayden did feel marginally better after that, but he would still worry horribly until he could verify for himself that Tess was alright.

She's tough, and far from defenseless, he assured himself. Remembering her knife skills, perhaps it was the Council members he should fear for.

"Hurry up and eat your breakfast; we're already late for our training as it is, and I actually have other things to do today," Laurren motioned Hayden along as soon as the plate was set in front of him.

Hayden shoveled food into his mouth as fast as possible without choking to make up for lost time, abandoning his plate when it was half-empty and asking Zane if he wanted to watch him get his butt kicked by Laurren.

"Sure, I haven't seen a really good fight in a while," he answered with enthusiasm, tagging along as they moved towards the back lawns.

"Don't be so pessimistic," the Master said fairly. "You may not get your butt kicked this time around; you're really getting much better these days."

"Don't be ridiculous," Hayden said with a raised eyebrow. "You're one of the strangest people I know, and weird people always win fights."

Laurren and Zane both laughed at that, though the former said, "Thank you for the compliment—I think. What about Asher?"

"He's also one of the weirdest people I know, which is probably why I'll never defeat him in a duel either," Hayden admitted.

Hayden checked his belt for weapons and then moved to the opposite side of the makeshift arena to prepare himself. He tried to push his worries to the back of the mind and ignore the fact that his best friend was going to watch him fight one of their teachers. He wanted to be impressive and instill confidence in everyone that he was going to be a real asset in the battle against his father, so he needed to be on top form at all times.

Ultimately he didn't do terribly against Master Laurren, though he did technically lose the bout. The Master of Abnormal Magic could no longer use prisms due to his color-blindness, but he was still deadly with the other arcana, and courtesy of his new area of expertise, he knew a lot of obscure magic that Hayden had never heard of or encountered before. Hayden limped over to the bench where Zane was sitting after their time was up, desperate for a drink of water and a short reprieve before his next bout with Master Kilgore—who was already here and waiting for him.

"Wow, you don't get much of a break between rounds, do you?" Zane remarked in sympathy, squinting against the brightness of the rising sun.

"Not until I'm done with fighting for the day. I've got Kilgore and then Mandra before I can take a break. Apparently it's supposed to help me build up stamina, on the off-chance I find myself dueling my father for three hours straight at some point."

He drained a glass of water and set it aside, getting back to his feet and preparing to meet the Master of Elixirs in battle.

"I don't suppose *you* can answer any of my questions about Tess?" Hayden greeted the gruff Master, who looked strange without his red Mastery robes on. Hayden had always been of the opinion that Master Kilgore looked more like a blacksmith than a Master of the arcana, and today the effect was highlighted, as the man was dressed entirely in black.

"As a matter of fact, I *do* know a little bit about her whereabouts," he explained evenly.

"What?!" Hayden perked up immediately, fresh energy flooding him. "Where is she? Is she okay? Is she coming here? Tell me!"

Kilgore held up a hand to silence him and said, "Knock me off of my feet and I'll tell you what I know."

Stunned with disbelief, Hayden said, "You're holding information about my girlfriend's wellbeing as *ransom?*"

That was the sort of petty behavior he expected from the Council of Mages, or Master Sark, perhaps, but he had always gotten along very well with Kilgore.

I must have done really badly on that Elixirs final for him to be this angry at me...

"I want to see how much willpower you can bring forth when the occasion calls for it," he explained easily. "Asher says you hold back as long as you don't feel you're actually in danger—or unless you have a reason to go all out. I want to see what you can do when you flex your willpower to its fullest."

Nettled, Hayden said, "I don't hold back on purpose. I've been giving it my all this entire time, just ask Kiresa."

"Your training with Kiresa is the one time I believe you actually *did* give it your all since you got here," Kilgore countered flatly. "And that only because you genuinely believed he was trying to hurt you. Since you know I have no intention of inflicting permanent damage upon you, I need something else to draw your power out. So, if you want to know how Tess is doing, show me what you've got."

Hayden attacked without warning, charging straight at the man—who probably outweighed him by double—and casting Push on himself as he lunged. The result was that he tackled Kilgore much harder than he would have been capable of unassisted, the Push spell giving him the force and momentum of a large boulder.

The Master of Elixirs was caught off guard by the physical attack, but managed to slap Hayden with a scripture as soon as they hit the ground together, which caused Hayden to soar up into the air like he had been shot out of a slingshot.

Weightlessness, of course.

He used one of his wands to slow his fall, watching the Master coughing and trying to catch his breath from having the wind knocked out of him.

You want to see how much willpower I have? Fine, let's play.

Hayden cast Bind, hoping to freeze Kilgore in place and win the fight early, but the Master reacted quickly and threw a cloud of powder at him as he fell, which not only made him choke as he fell through it and got a lungful of dust, it also exploded and changed his trajectory, launching him backwards through the air.

Hayden was deafened by the sound, only the ringing of his own ears echoing around his head as he flew backwards. Furious, he twisted his prisms around and compounded Stop to halt his fall. In his anger, the spell was so powerful that it dimpled the ground in a crater around him as he alit gently on the grass, turning his focus back to Kilgore, who consumed two elixirs in rapid succession from his belt.

Hayden cast Break at his remaining elixirs but the spell was deflected at the last second. He followed immediately with Stun, not waiting to see if the spell connected. He was already turning his prisms around to compound Pierce. Both of his spells were blocked, but he was casting so quickly that Kilgore didn't have time to retaliate; he was barely able to protect himself from Hayden's spells as is.

Determined to beat him and find out what happened to Tess, Hayden cast compound alignments as soon as he saw them, not even caring about strategy or planning. His Heat compound was so powerful that Kilgore was only able to partially-deflect it; his shirt began to smolder and the grass around him shriveled up and died. Kilgore threw another cloud of blue powder to absorb Hayden's next spell as he downed a third elixir and drew some scriptures from his robes.

Hayden tried freezing him, binding him, launching him through the air, and causing him unendurable pain within the next minute, but Kilgore managed to shield himself from the worst of the attacks.

Stupid Mastery Charm. If I get close enough I'm going to rip it off of his throat and then we'll see how good his defenses are.

Blind with rage, ears still ringing and possibly bleeding, Hayden looked through his compounded prisms and felt his eyes take a foreign path, scanning and interpreting and reacting to an alignment more complex than anything he had ever tried to use before, so complicated that he didn't even register what colors he was processing as the arrays entered his eye. With a burst of raw power, Hayden screamed and felt his body subtly transform, his skin becoming hard and unyielding, like diamond. The sun reflecting off of it caused a weird halo effect around him so that it looked like he was glowing, or on fire, and he felt invincible, impenetrable, like stone.

As soon as the feeling came it was gone, and a flash of light burst behind his eyes so intensely that it was like staring directly into the sun itself. Hayden cried out in pain as he went blind and his Foci burned, the correctors growing hot on both wrists as he fell to the ground.

He wasn't sure how long he lay there, rolling around on the grass in pain, clutching his eyes, but it couldn't have been more than a minute or two before the pain began to ease and the dancing spots of light disappeared from the inside of his closed lids. It was then that he realized Master Kilgore and Zane were leaning over him, shaking him by the arm and asking if he was alright. The Master of Elixirs looked whey-faced and worried, drawing a healing elixir from his belt and forcing it into Hayden's mouth.

He tried to ask, "Where's Tess?" while drinking, which made him cough and sputter. He felt tired and wrung out, like an overused sponge.

"Don't die, Hayden, you're going to be alright," Zane's anxious face was hovering above him now, blocking out most of the sunlight, for which he was grateful. Those two thoughts seemed sort of contradictory to one another—if Hayden was fine, then why was Zane telling him not to die?—but he didn't feel well enough to question it just yet.

"Get off me," Hayden insisted, forcing himself into a sitting position and ignoring his own slurred words. "We're not done fighting until I knock you on your butt so you can tell me where Tess is."

"Hayden, you knocked him over as soon as the fight started," Zane grabbed his arm to prevent him from reaching for a fresh prism—both of his had been consumed in that final spell. "Don't you remember?"

Stunned, Hayden finally let his brain wind down enough to process the fight itself. Now that he thought about it, he *had* tackled Kilgore right at the outset and knocked him onto the ground.

"You mean we could have stopped *there* and you would have told me?" he asked in disbelief.

"I would have said as much, but you knocked the wind out of me and then you never slowed down long enough to give me the chance," the Master explained in his usual gruff tone. "Well, I know I asked you to give me all the willpower you've got, but I didn't expect you to give yourself light-sickness."

"Light-sickness?" Hayden was momentarily diverted, reflecting on the feeling of all those colors and arrays shoving their way into his mind and how it felt like a sun bomb exploded behind his eyes afterwards. He looked down at his arms to check for obvious signs of damage, but his Focus-correctors were still intact, though his Foci tingled slightly.

"I thought you were trying to kill Master Kilgore," Zane said seriously, face still pale with worry. "You were throwing out spells like crazy and wrecking everything in sight, and then you did that crazy thing where you started glowing and turned into some kind of super-warrior…"

Hayden blinked a few times to clear his head.

"I don't know what that was. The alignments just hit me all at once—I don't even remember what bands of colors I saw, or how many. I felt weird though, like I was made out of something indestructible."

Kilgore scowled and said, "You're lucky you didn't cripple yourself—or worse. Messing with untested alignments that are powerful enough to cause light-sickness is no joke."

"I wasn't doing it on purpose," Hayden argued.

"Nevertheless," Kilgore cut him off, helping him to his feet. "You're not to do any more magic today, not until you've recovered. I'll tell Mandra that he'll have to reschedule your training for another day."

"You wanted to see willpower—well, you got it," Hayden told him, getting to his feet and steadying his balance before attempting to walk. He still felt a little queasy from the burst of light-sickness, and was relieved that he was excused from doing any more magic for the day. The last thing he needed was to warp his Foci even worse than they already were. At some point they would become damaged enough that he couldn't cast magic through them at all, and then he would be doomed.

Unless my father is feeling charitable and fixes them for me, like he did for Isla Strauss. His father's behavior on that day still bothered him.

"I was pleased with your level of willpower, but underwhelmed by your ability to control it and give it direction," Kilgore explained in response to his assertion. "If you really want to impress me, learn to come to every fight with that level of energy without letting it run away with you."

There's no pleasing some people.

"I did what you wanted—mostly," Hayden sighed. "Now tell me what you know about Tess."

The Master of Elixirs made a huffing noise and said, "She's under a sort of house arrest, guarded by one of the Council's lackeys at all times. Her father is less-than-pleased with the arrangement, but there's not a lot he can do about it without running amok of the law himself. She's been placed in Binders to prevent her from using magic—or from having it used on her—to escape."

Hayden's stomach lurched unpleasantly.

"They've got her in *Binders?*" he asked in horror, remembering how unpleasant it was being forced to wear them for two solid years, and that was even before he had known he had magic. It had somehow been even worse during his third year, when Fia Eldridge briefly forced him into the Binders and locked him in an empty classroom, to feel his magic shut away inside of himself, unable to access it even to save his life. The thought of Tess suffering the same thing on his behalf was horrible.

"It was the best arrangement we could manage for her, given that Calahan has been bleating about treachery and saying that he should have locked up all of your friends from the beginning so that they couldn't join you in your plot to join up with your father and overthrow the Council." Kilgore rolled his eyes at the notion.

"What about Conner, and Tamon, and my other friends?" Hayden asked belatedly, wondering how many people were going to be punished on his behalf.

"They're still being watched, but Tess has the worst of it so far. Binders aren't pleasant, but it's far better than being imprisoned or—otherwise harmed," Kilgore said cautiously.

Hayden nodded.

"I know, I just wish there was a way to get her out of there and bring her here where it's safe."

"We're working on it, but we have to be more careful than ever. If we could have gotten to her before the Council showed up, we would have, but we still have to be very careful about our own movements, as Calahan is looking everywhere for signs of traitors. Don't worry, Frost, we'll think of something. Now get inside and take it easy, or Asher will have my head on a platter."

Zane chuckled at the image that invoked, but Hayden still didn't feel well enough to be properly amused.

As soon as Master Kilgore left them, they settled into the library and Zane said, "Well, now that you've managed to score a day off…tell me what's been going on."

8
The Crumbling Alliance

Having Zane around made things more enjoyable for Hayden in the following days, once his friend learned that living in the headquarters for a secret resistance group wasn't nearly as exciting as it sounded like it should be. Since Hayden was under house arrest—lest the Council or his father get their hands on him—he now had another refugee to spend his time with while everyone else was away on their various assignments.

Due to its members frequently being unable to come together at the same time and place, Zane didn't get to attend his first actual meeting with most of the group for over a week after his arrival. He and Hayden had been researching a spell that would make an opponent's eyes cross in the library, but Hayden could tell that his friend hadn't been paying attention for the last quarter hour, constantly checking his chrono to see if it was time for their meeting.

When Hayden set his book aside and said, "Why don't we just give it up for today and go get good seats at the table?" Zane agreed enthusiastically.

"Lorn's probably furious that he's been kicked out of his own house for months so that you can live here instead," he pointed out cheerily as they made their way towards the formal dining room. Despite being forced to work together when the occasion called for it, there was no love lost between the two of them and Lorn Trout.

"I imagine so," Hayden agreed lightly, "and I feel a little bad for it, but he's probably safer staying far away from me anyway—everyone is."

Zane frowned at that, possibly realizing that he himself was in as much peril as Hayden at this point.

"I hope everyone has good news to report. It's going to be a huge letdown if we just go in there and everyone says, 'Nothing's happened.'"

Hayden nodded agreement.

"The last time we had a big meeting was when Mrs. Trout's friend came barging in to tell us my dad is actually a swell guy. Talk about a weird night, since we'd already spent weeks plotting out ways to kill him by that point."

Zane looked at him sideways and asked, "Are you okay with that?"

Hayden was surprised by the concern in his voice as much as by the question itself.

"Why wouldn't I be?"

"Well, I mean…the man *is* your father. Are you actually going to be okay with fighting him to the death when it comes down to that?"

"You know," Hayden raised his eyebrows with interest, "you might be the first person who has actually stopped to ask me that question." He smiled faintly. "Honestly, I'm not that upset about it—though the thought of fighting someone to the death doesn't appeal to me in general. He didn't raise me, he doesn't know me, he certainly doesn't care about me; in all the ways that matter, he isn't really my father at all."

Zane looked surprised by this pragmatic view on the matter, but said nothing as they entered the formal dining room. Predictably, they were the first to arrive, as they were still quite early for the meeting. Hayden took a seat near the head of the table without hesitation, while Zane covertly eyed a spot much further away.

"What are you doing?" the former asked curiously.

"Well, it's not like I'm important enough to take one of the *good* seats..." Zane answered uncertainly.

"If you're important enough to stand next to me when we're attacking the Dark Prism, you're important enough to sit wherever you want at the stupid table." Hayden pointed to the seat beside him and, reluctantly, Zane took it. "If anyone has a problem with it, they can show up early next time and claim whatever chair they want."

"You always did have a problem with authority figures," his friend chuckled, looking marginally more relaxed as he settled in.

"I'm told it's something the Frosts are known for," he joked.

It took another quarter hour for the others to begin filtering into the room, and twenty minutes after that before everyone was in full attendance. A few people eyed Hayden and Zane's prime spots at the table covetously before taking seats further down, but Hayden pretended not to notice or care.

"Alright, let's keep this as brief as possible," Magdalene began, sitting to Hayden's right at the head of the table. Up close, he could see how tired she looked, though her eyes were as alert and keen as ever.

"Where's Asher?" Hayden asked, scanning the table even though he knew his mentor wasn't there; he would have seen him come in.

"He wasn't able to make it tonight," Master Reede answered without looking at him.

"You don't need him to hold your hand during every meeting we have, do you?" Kiresa asked mockingly, leaning back in his chair and smirking.

"Enough," Magdalene raised a hand to call for silence before they could devolve into another brawl. "Elias, what news?"

Master Kilgore frowned, rubbed his red-grey beard thoughtfully, and said, "It's all very strange. I was inclined to believe that your friend Isla had taken leave of her senses when she made her report to us last week, but there have been five more confirmed cases of the same from around the Nine Lands."

Hayden leaned forward and said, "My father has actually been traveling the continent to heal people?"

The disbelief in his voice was mirrored on the faces of the other mages at the table.

"As strange as it sounds, it seems that he is." Master Kilgore shrugged. "All five of the people he has supposedly helped had long-standing damage to their

Foci that had rendered them completely unusable. All five can now cast magic normally, and reported that Aleric seemed quite normal during their interactions."

"Did any of them ask *why* Aleric was suddenly taking such a humanitarian view on things?" Master Mandra interjected.

"Not that I've heard. It's not surprising that none of his victims—if we can call them that—would be keen on questioning him too deeply. One wrong word could set the man off and be the end of their life, assuming that he is still prone to fits of instability."

Laris looked at Hayden and said, "Are you *certain* that you were telling the truth when you relayed your encounter with him outside of the schism?" the doubt was evident in his tone, which was a complete one-eighty from his feelings during their last meeting. "You're sure you didn't simply become frightened when you learned who the man was and embellish your encounter with him a bit?"

The collective group turned to stare at Hayden in eerie unison.

"You've got to be kidding me," he snarled, supremely annoyed. "You honestly think that after going through all sorts of hell inside the other realm, that I was so terrified of an unarmed man who barely regained his wits that I made the whole thing up?" He made no effort to keep the disgust from his tone. "Asher told you the same story I did, and he certainly has no reason to be afraid of anyone."

"He has more reason than anyone to fear the Dark Prism's return," Master Kiresa countered flatly. Hayden wondered if he'd dare question Asher's bravery if he was in the room with them. "Aleric is the reason that he lost his vaunted popularity and most of his prospects. He's spent the last six years recovering from the taint of that association, and he certainly doesn't want to be dragged back into the dirt again."

Hayden rolled his eyes.

"Yeah, Asher's always been *super* concerned with what other people think of him," he put in sardonically.

Surprisingly, his sarcasm seemed to convince some of his audience of the veracity of his story. Asher's eccentricity and complete lack of interest in the opinions of others was well-known.

"The fact still remains that Aleric is not behaving like an unstable, corrupted man, the way you two painted him to be at the end of last year," Laris continued doggedly.

Hayden shrugged. "I have no idea why he's doing what he's doing now; all I can tell you is what he was like when I last saw him. But as has already been pointed out tonight, Asher was the man's best friend, and he's convinced that my father hasn't had a sudden change of heart. Since he knows him better than anyone, I'd listen to whatever he says."

"If Hayden's dad is so innocent all of a sudden, why hasn't he turned himself in to the Council of Mages to prove he's all better?" Zane surprised them all by speaking up. "You can't tell me he's missed all the

Wanted posters spread across the entire continent, or the fact that every powerful mage is grouping up to hunt him down."

"A valid point," Master Reede acknowledged with a tilt of his head.

Magdalene Trout appeared to be lost in thought for a moment, eyes staring off at something that only she could see. She snapped out of it and said, "Speculating is fruitless; we need more data. Let us move on for the time being."

"How are things going on your end?" Master Kiresa addressed her directly. "I can't help but notice that Calahan is still the Chief Mage of the Council, despite your assurances that he wouldn't hold out for much longer some weeks ago."

Magdalene frowned and said, "He's not quite as stupid as I'd hoped. For some reason he refuses to publicly declare Hayden an enemy, despite stripping him of his honors. In fact, he seems to be backpedaling slightly."

"Are you sure someone isn't feeding him information about these meetings? If he had a spy amongst our number, it would certainly explain why he hasn't made that final, critical error yet."

Master Willow, who had been silent so far, said, "If he had an informant, he would already have Hayden in his custody and Magdalene and Laris sidelined. There's nothing to be gained by unfounded paranoia amongst us." At the last, he reprimanded the Prism Master of Isenfall with a glare.

Kiresa shrugged but didn't argue further.

"Every day that he is in power, we are losing ground against Aleric—if indeed Aleric is still a threat," Master Mandra put in. "Calahan's obsession with Hayden nearly rivals his desire to stop the Dark Prism. We've been slowed down enormously by having to keep Frost safely concealed here to prevent anyone from ascertaining his whereabouts."

Hayden could only silently agree. As lofty as the Trout estate was, it would be nice if he was allowed to leave sometime before he turned forty. He was also quite eager for Tess to be freed so that they could meet up and he could apologize for her being enslaved and interrogated on his behalf.

"I know that we need Calahan out of power, and believe me, Laris and I are doing everything we can to push him out the door without showing our hand," Magdalene snapped impatiently. "It isn't as easy as it looks."

"Well, keep trying. Until we get him out of the way, we're going to be running in place," Kiresa needled.

"Thank goodness we have you here to remind us of the obvious," Laris scowled.

Magdalene held up her hand again, calling for silence. Hayden was impressed that both her colleague and the Prism Master of Isenfall obeyed her.

"Have there been any reports of destruction, missing people, murders, or anything else that might suggest Aleric is up to his old tricks?" Master Mandra changed the subject.

"If so, word hasn't reached the Council yet," Magdalene conceded, deliberately avoiding Hayden's eyes.

"We haven't heard anything either," Master Willow reported, though he didn't look happy about the lack of information. "The High Mayor hasn't reported anything that matches Aleric's style—so if he *is* up to his old games, he is being remarkably subtle about it."

"More proof that his time in the other realm stabilized him and that his sanity may be restored," Laris put in unhelpfully. He seemed to have forgotten that he was the biggest opponent to this argument just last week.

"Even if that is the case, he still has to answer for crimes against humanity," Kilgore cut off Hayden's rant before he could start it. "I would be astounded if he avoided a death sentence for that alone; he's guilty of a list of crimes so long it would take hours just to read them all off at his trial."

"Come now," Laris made a sweeping gesture with one hand. "If he has truly been restored to sanity, it would be foolishness to murder the man for past crimes. Think of all that he could tell us about magic—all the potential he could open up for us."

Master Reede's voice was eerily neutral when he asked, "You would have us all dabble in corrupted magics?"

Laris looked like he'd just been punched in the gut.

"No, of course not! But you can't sit there and pretend that Aleric's knowledge only extends to banned magic. He must have discovered a few things using legitimate alignments during the course of his studies as well."

"It worries me that a prominent member of the Council of Mages—potentially it's future Chief—is so ready to ally himself with a mass murderer just to learn a few new magic tricks," Master Willow frowned across the table, as though suddenly seeing his colleague in a new light.

"Bear in mind that Laris does not speak for the entire Council," Magdalene put in softly, her tone dangerously low.

"It's more than 'a few magic tricks!' " Laris protested hotly. "Our progress on discovering new spells has waned significantly over the last decade or two. This could be the thing we need to revitalize that effort and give us some fresh perspective. You can't deny that the monster population is out of control right now!"

"And you would build that bright future on the corpses of all those that Aleric ruthlessly slaughtered over the course of a decade? You would call their deaths a cost of doing business?" Hayden had never heard Master Willow sound so undiplomatic before, or so angry.

"It would give their deaths more meaning than they have right now," Laris countered easily, not bothered by the opposition of the others. "Someone has to be thinking about the future of mage-kind, and we've become a stagnant group; spell-discovery is at an all-time low, mage-count is down as well, and the monsters are gaining the upper hand against us—everyone knows this."

Reede said, "The monster population goes in cycles; it always has. It's true that this is a particularly bad one for us, but that is largely because so many mages were killed by Aleric the last time he was powerful, so our fighting force has been greatly depleted. We will catch up in time. The same can be said of the reduction of our numbers and discovery of new spells."

"All I'm saying is that I'm not yet convinced we should kill the man on sight," Laris persevered. "I think we should see what he has to say and determine whether he can be of any use to us before we consider terminating his life."

"And that is why we will lose," Hayden said softly, but everyone at the table somehow seemed to hear him.

An uncomfortable silence fell in the wake of his words, but Hayden had heard enough. If his allies couldn't even agree that his father was evil and needed to be taken out, then their fight was over before it even began.

His chair scraped loudly on the floor as he pushed it backwards and stood up. Without another word to anyone, he turned and left the room. He could hear Zane following him by the time he entered the hallway, and the conversation resumed inside the meeting room once they were gone, though he was no longer interested in any of it.

"Well, that was awful," Zane summarized, catching up to him and matching his pace. "Always nice to have your allies bail on you."

Hayden scowled and said, "I'm starting to think poor decision-making skills and a general lack of morality are prerequisites for working on the Council of Mages."

"Well, there goes our career in politics," Zane sighed in a mockery of wistfulness. "To be fair, Mrs. Trout doesn't seem too bad, though I never thought I'd be defending anyone whose last name is 'Trout.' She'd make a decent Chief Mage."

"Assuming she can get rid of both Laris and Calahan, sure," Hayden agreed.

"Hey, I wouldn't put it past her. She seems like a pretty determined lady."

Hayden nodded weary agreement.

"I think I'm going to turn in early tonight. Watching our alliance begin to fall apart before the real work even begins kind of sapped the energy out of me."

"Well, don't go into a funk just because we've hit our first big roadblock. I'm sure this won't be the worst thing we have to face before it's all said and done, so we need to stay positive and focused."

Hayden turned to him outside the door of his bedroom and said, "You still believe that my father's evil?"

Zane looked at him like he was stupid.

"Of course I do. You and Asher said he is, and I trust you both—on this, at least." He smiled briefly. "Besides, it sounds like most of the others in there are still on your side as well. Don't lose heart just because we might have to kick Laris out of our little cabal."

"Too bad he knows where I've been hiding out, and he could walk into Calahan's office tonight and get Magdalene fired and me arrested all without lifting a finger. He'll look like a hero."

Zane grimaced at that unpleasant realization.

"Well, we'll just have to hide out somewhere else for the time being. Get some rest, and tomorrow morning we'll start fresh and work out a new plan, even if it's just you and me. If it isn't safe here anymore then we'll go somewhere else, and we can contact the others as we're able."

Hayden nodded, reassured by Zane's words and his determination not to give up. He wasn't sure what he would do if his friend hadn't been here tonight, but he didn't want to think about it.

Maybe along the way we can free Tess too. I know enough magic now to break through Binders, and I can probably take down whoever the Council has guarding her...

He bid Zane goodnight on that note and entered his bedroom. Bonk wasn't there, which meant he was probably still out hunting squirrels; there were alarmingly few to be found on the Trout lands, so he had to fly a bit further away to find his prey of choice.

Hayden changed into his pajamas and climbed into bed, dimming the magic-powered lamp on the end table.

His dreams that night were disturbing, filled with friends who turned into cobras and tried to bite him, and faceless strangers condemning him to death.

The sound of someone barging into his room and grabbing him by the arm abruptly woke him. Confused and groggy, Hayden looked around wildly and said, "Wuzzgoinon?"

He squinted, but the room was still dark and it was pitch-black outside. He couldn't even tell who was hauling him roughly out of bed until an unpleasantly familiar voice said, "Shut up and get moving, Frost."

"Master *Sark?*" Hayden asked in shock, stumbling to his feet and tripping over his shoes in the darkness. "What in the world are *you* doing here? I haven't seen you in—"

"Keep quiet and come with me," the Master of Powders commanded in the terse, annoyed tone he usually reserved just for Hayden.

"Hang on, let me change clothes…"

"There isn't time for that." He pulled Hayden roughly into the hallway. In his sleep-addled state, Hayden didn't immediately register that there was something off about this entire encounter, but as they padded through the library—Hayden still barefoot—his brain began to reengage.

"Wait a minute…" he spoke into the darkness as they continued towards the foyer. "What are you doing here in the middle of the night? Where are we going? Why do I have to keep quiet...?"

He dug in his heels and forced them to stop in the middle of the hallway. Apparently furious at being questioned, Sark tugged on his arms so hard that he nearly dislocated Hayden's shoulders. Reflexively, Hayden reached for his prism circlet to fight the man, but then realized that it had been left behind in his bedroom, along with all of his weaponry.

"HEL—!" Hayden screamed at the top of his lungs, but before he could finish the word 'help', Master Sark threw a pinch of powder into his face that caused him to choke and gasp for air.

While Hayden was desperately trying to breathe, Sark took advantage of the opportunity to drag him into the foyer, where they would be able to translocate away from the estate. Hayden struggled as hard as he could, but since he was still trying to recover from the effects of that awful powder, Master Sark was able to successfully pull him into the foyer, where he took hold of his Mastery Charm.

Lights were coming on in the house behind them. Someone had heard Hayden scream, they knew something was wrong, they were coming to help…

Between one blink and the next the Trout manor disappeared, and Hayden found himself standing outside in the cold, shivering as the full effects of winter hit him now that they were beyond the climate-controlled area surrounding the Trout estate. His bare feet sank into two inches of snow and immediately began to go numb. The only bright side was that the wintry air seemed to clear up his lungs, and suddenly he could breathe normally again.

Master Sark was still holding his arm as Hayden tried to take in his surroundings, but it was hard to see properly in the dark. All he could make out as the Powders Master shoved him forward was some kind of giant structure in front of them that glittered oddly in the moonlight. It was the tallest building he had ever seen—dozens of stories high, and also oddly shaped, like a giant needle....

The Crystal Tower. I'm at the Crystal Tower.

Remembering the numerous times he had been told that if he ever walked into this place he would never walk back out, he began fighting much harder, managing to elbow the Master of Powders in the nose. Sark cursed as his nose bled freely, but didn't release Hayden, instead shaking him hard enough to rattle his brain and make his head hurt.

"Pull another stunt like that and I'll have you vomiting yourself unconscious," he threatened furiously, pushing Hayden through a set of double-doors that opened when Sark put his hand against them.

"Why are you doing this?" Hayden demanded hotly. "I know we've never exactly liked each other, but I thought you were at least on the right side."

"You aren't nearly as clever as you think, Frost," the Master grumbled as they stepped inside the Crystal Tower. When the doors closed behind them Hayden thought, *Well, there goes my freedom.*

At least the interior of the building was still lit by mage-light, so for the first time since he'd been abducted, Hayden could properly see. From the outside, the Crystal Tower had looked like a giant glass needle, but from the interior the walls looked as opaque as any other building. It was odd to him that he couldn't see outside, knowing that the exterior walls were glass.

The Crystal Tower was also roomier on the inside than it looked, an effect that probably took a lot of magic to achieve on a place so large. Mage-lights in sconces dotted the wall along both sides of the narrow corridor that Master Sark was now towing him down.

"You of all people should want to see an end to my father," Hayden informed his least favorite Master quite calmly, accepting his fate. "How is locking me up going to help anyone achieve that?"

Sark didn't answer, though a muscle tensed in his jaw, and Hayden gave up on the man. They stopped in front of the first office they encountered, and Master Sark raised his fist and knocked firmly on the door, using his free hand to check his nose and verify that it had stopped bleeding. Hayden only wished he had hit him harder.

The door was answered by one of Hayden's least favorite people in the world a moment later.

"Hello, Hayden," Calahan greeted him with real delight, not bothering to conceal his surprise at having Hayden delivered to his door. "I've been looking for you."

"Yeah, I heard," Hayden answered flatly, allowing himself to be steered into the office. Master Sark shut the door behind them, giving Hayden the feeling that he was being entombed in here with the two men.

Calahan's office was circular and high-ceilinged, giving the illusion that they were standing in a large well. A floor-to-ceiling bookshelf lined the walls behind an enormous mahogany desk, which was mostly filled with neat stacks of paper or file folders. Two filing cabinets flanked the desk on either end, and Hayden didn't doubt that every folder inside was color-coded and in alphabetical order.

Hayden was shoved roughly into one of four padded chairs surrounding a small meeting table, also circular. Calahan sat down opposite him, but Master Sark remained standing near the door.

"Well, well, Kirius, fine work," the Chief Mage smiled tiredly, the flickering mage-light in his office casting ghostly shadows over his face. Up close, Hayden was surprised by how wrung out the man looked: his skin had a slackness that Hayden didn't remember seeing before, and there was something almost grey about him.

Paranoia—and his colleagues—have really done a number on him. If he wasn't about to be locked up by the man, he might feel sorry for him.

"I discovered his hideout and removed him before anyone could miss him," Sark drawled, almost sounding bored.

"And where was he hiding all this time?" Calahan asked with interest.

"With a friend," Sark shrugged, his eyes not meeting Hayden's. Hayden thought it was odd that he wasn't mentioning Magdalene Trout by name, but perhaps Sark had his own reasons for keeping silent about it. Whatever those reasons were, Hayden had no intention of selling out the woman who had given him shelter, so Sark's vagueness on the matter happened to suit him.

Calahan opened his mouth and looked like he was going to press for more detailed information, but Master Sark beat him to it by adding, "You said there was a reward involved?"

The Chief Mage actually looked surprised that the man would ask about such a thing, as though this was out of character. *Or maybe he just doesn't want to actually cough up any money for me.*

"Yes, of course. Once the guild banks open tomorrow, we can arrange the transfer."

"Do you seriously believe that I brought my father back from the other realm on purpose and turned him loose on a world that my friends live in?" Hayden asked Calahan, wishing he had something to cover his feet, because they were still freezing and wet from the snow outside.

"If you were innocent, you would have turned yourself in as soon as you returned to Mizzenwald and proven it."

"Oh sure, because you're nothing but fair. I learned an important lesson last year while I was studying up on estate law to get my inheritance back."

Calahan looked only vaguely interested as he said, "And what was that?"

"That the law cares nothing for morality. You can be on the right side and still lose."

Neither man made any attempt to deny the truth of this.

Switching tracks, Calahan turned to Master Sark and said, "I don't suppose you found any of your colleagues helping him conceal his whereabouts?"

Hayden tensed in preparation for having all of his other teachers thrown to the wolves, but all Sark said was, "Unfortunately, if any of them *were* helping him, I have found no proof of it."

It was all Hayden could do to keep his mouth from dropping open. He could have sworn that one of the others had told him that Sark was in on their plans from the beginning even though he didn't attend the meetings, which meant that he was lying to Calahan for seemingly no reason.

Maybe he still feels some allegiance to them, even if he's sold me out.

Calahan didn't look like he completely believed this testimony, because he added, "Are you certain, Kirius? You could earn yourself a substantial promotion if you were to give evidence against traitors."

"I know, and I wish that I could. But I cannot lie in good conscience, and I didn't see any of the others around him."

"I find it hard to believe that Asher Masters isn't up to his eyeballs in this. He has always sheltered the boy, stepping into his best friend's shoes as a surrogate father figure since the moment he laid eyes on him."

Master Sark shrugged and said, "He likely *has* been helping Hayden, but I can't prove it."

"Hmm...well, keep looking," Calahan relented at last. "I'll escort Hayden to a holding cell for the night, and we can begin the real work tomorrow morning."

That doesn't sound pleasant.

"Where are you putting him?" Sark sounded almost bored. "The fifth level?"

"No," a nasty smile played across Calahan's face, "the twentieth."

Master Sark, who was halfway to opening the door, stopped in place and turned around so fast it would have been comical under different circumstances.

"The *twentieth?*" He looked aghast, which did nothing to bolster Hayden's mood. "You're not putting him into one of the Boxes, are you?"

Hayden had no idea what the Boxes were, though somehow he didn't think it was the loose, plywood variety that he was imagining in his head.

"Why not? He is a criminal with dangerous powers, and the son of the most feared mage in the Nine Lands. It would be irresponsible to place him anywhere less secure."

"Sure, *I'm* the danger to the Nine Lands. Weren't you hanging a medal around my neck a few months ago?" Hayden asked sarcastically.

"You know I only did that to shame you into volunteering for a task you were clearly the only suitable candidate for, and if I had won the vote in Council that day we would have bodily thrown you into the schism with or without your consent."

Hayden's eyebrows lifted in surprise.

"You mean I have enough friends in the Council that they voted you down? Wow, Cal, not even your own people seem to like you very much."

"Don't address me so informally, you ungrateful whelp," Calahan snapped at him, red-faced. "And don't assume that anyone on my Council spared you out of affection or loyalty. They simply believed that the common people adored you so much that they would start trouble if they heard you were condemned to die against your will. But that love is fast evaporating since you've resurrected their worst nightmare and then disappeared these last few months."

Hayden had noticed the inflection on the word 'my' when Calahan was describing 'his Council'. *He really thinks these people belong to him...*

"You've been trying to get me banned from using magic, imprisoned, or killed since the day we met. I'll call you whatever I want, *Cal*," was all Hayden said in response.

"Get up," Calahan surged to his own feet and grabbed Hayden by the wrists, none-too-gently. "I'm going to enjoy the look on your face when I introduce you to your new home."

Master Sark was still watching the pair of them in silence, an oddly neutral look on his face. For a moment Hayden thought he saw sympathy there, but was sure that he had made it up, given what he knew of the man.

If he didn't want to see me suffer whatever Cal has planned for me, he wouldn't have dragged me out of bed in the dead of night to turn me over to him while everyone else was asleep.

He tried not to think of what the others would assume when they woke up and found him gone. They might think he lost his nerve and ran away, but Zane would know better.

Unless Zane thinks I left without him and struck out on my own...

He liked to think that Zane would know better, but if there were no signs of a struggle and Hayden had simply vanished from the Trout estate...

All of my things are still there, he realized with a wave of relief. *They'll know I wouldn't go anywhere without taking my circlet and weapons with me. Bonk will eventually come back from his hunt, and they might be able to use him to track me and find out what's happened...*

While he was thinking this, Calahan had pulled him out of the office and down a short corridor towards a strange set of doors that looked like iron gates on hinges. Behind the doors he could see a very small room, completely empty of furnishings.

Is that one of the Boxes? Hayden thought with wonder. *It's certainly small enough to qualify; it doesn't even have a toilet!*

With a wave of his wand, Calahan opened the iron gates in front of the room and pushed Hayden roughly inside. Hayden was surprised when the Chief Mage followed him in and shut the doors behind them.

"Oh lord, you're not staying in here *with* me, are you?" He'd rather be in utter solitude than have Cal for company.

Calahan looked at him like he was stupid and said, "Don't be ridiculous, Frost." He waved his wand in an agitated sweeping gesture and Hayden's knees buckled as the ground seemed to be pushing him upwards, fast.

"What's happening?" he asked, terrified. He braced his hands against the walls to steady himself, though there was nothing to hold onto if the floor dropped out from beneath him.

"It's an automated lift. You didn't think I was going to walk you up twenty flights of stairs, did you?" The Chief Mage smiled nastily at his fright, and Hayden forced himself to relax.

"Are there people waiting at the top who just sit around all day, waiting to cast the magic in case someone needs to move from one level to the next?" That sounded like the most boring job ever.

The question earned him another unpleasant look from his captor.

"Of course not; it's fully-automated."

Against his will, Hayden was impressed. He could appreciate the sheer amount of magic it must have taken to make such a thing possible.

In less than a minute the lift slowed to a stop, and Calahan waved the doors open again. Hayden had never been prone to claustrophobia, but he immediately began to feel the effects of the cramped space on this higher floor. They were at the top of the needle-shaped building, with the smallest amount of free space available, and there was much less lighting up here. In fact, it was completely dark when they stepped off of the lift until

Calahan activated a single torch along the wall, which cast light oddly through the circular foyer they had stepped into.

It took Hayden a few moments to realize that there was no magic on the interior walls on this level to make them appear opaque—in fact, there was probably magic in place to make them seem even more transparent, because the torchlight glinted off of crystal in all directions. It was still pitch-black outside, but Hayden could imagine what the view would look like during daylight, with a panoramic view of the world from the twentieth floor of the Tower.

Calahan didn't push him, but made a sweeping, *After you,* gesture that motioned Hayden forward. Upon closer inspection, there were five closed doors off of the circular foyer.

"Which one is mine?" Hayden asked without interest, trying to savor his last few moments of relative freedom.

"That one," Calahan pointed to the one directly in front of them, and Hayden walked slowly towards it. He considered putting up a fight, even now, but wasn't sure what the point would be. Calahan was armed and he wasn't, and even assuming he could overpower the man, what was he supposed to do—kill the Chief Mage and escape? Then he really *would* be a criminal.

Wondering what kind of horrible, cramped, smelly, torturous room he was about to enter, Hayden took a deep breath and opened the door in front of him. The room was dark, and Calahan did nothing to light it, so Hayden shuffled into the pitch blackness, feeling around carefully with his feet so he wouldn't trip over anything.

The moment he crossed the threshold of the room it felt like he was punched in the gut. He gasped and doubled over, trying to figure out what had hit him and how he hadn't sensed it coming. His Focus-correctors grew warm and heavy on his wrists, and Hayden dropped to his knees on the hard crystal floor and heard the sound of a door shutting loudly behind him.

The last thing he heard as he grabbed his stomach and fought the urge to be sick was the sound of callous laughter as Calahan got back on the lift and left him alone in the dark.

9
Unwelcome Surprises

Hayden was only able to mark the passage of time by the gradual progression of daylight filtering into his cell the following morning. The sharp pain in his body had faded to a dull ache, not enough to prevent him from moving around or thinking clearly, but enough to always be at the edge of his awareness, no matter what else he was focused on.

As the sun came up, Hayden pulled himself upright and slumped against a wall, little though he liked resting his body against a surface he could see through. His body was sore and sluggish after spending the entire night awake and in considerable discomfort, though he still hadn't figured out what exactly this place had done to him.

Now that he could see, he took the time to examine his new living quarters properly. The floor beneath him was the same clear crystal as the exterior of the building, and despite the fact that he knew there were nineteen other levels directly beneath him, there must have been some kind of magic on the floor to make it look as though his room was hovering unsupported, because he could see straight to the grassy ground far below.

Hayden had never exactly been afraid of heights, but between the transparent walls on all sides and the deceptive flooring, he had the sensation of sitting in the clouds, waiting to plummet to his death at any moment. Sunlight sparkled off of the exterior crystalline walls and refracted around the room, casting brilliant slices of colored light all around. The effect made him feel like he was sitting inside a prism, which wasn't nearly as enjoyable as he might have guessed prior to experiencing it. In fact, he was glad that he didn't have any actual prisms with him, because looking through them would probably just give him a screaming headache right now.

Other than himself, the only other thing in the room was a bucket and a rope that hung from the ceiling. The former was obviously for using the restroom, and after experimenting with pulling on the second, he discovered that it signaled someone down below to come and empty the bucket. Otherwise he was left alone for the entire day, with someone appearing at three separate intervals to bring him food and water. He tried interrogating these infrequent visitors, asking what was going to happen to him, when his trial would start, if anyone had shown up demanding to see him…but no one said a word to him or even looked at him in response. He might as well have been invisible for all the good it did to speak.

If he had ever lived through a longer, slower day he couldn't remember it. Whatever weird effect the room was having on him, it kept him feeling slightly nauseous and off-balance during every waking second. By evening, the sun glare in his room was so unpleasant that he just curled up with his face pressed against his knees, closed his eyes, and waited for it to get dark again.

That night he gave in to exhaustion and slept fitfully, feeling not-at-all refreshed when he woke up the following morning. It was another excruciating day of boredom and silence, though he tried to keep his mind sharp by mentally rehearsing all of the spells he could think of, first with prisms, then with wands, elixirs, conjuring chalk, and even powders—though the last was a short list. Around mid-day he finished his meager lunch of hard bread, cheese, tomatoes, and milk, and did a few experimental sit-ups, determined to keep himself in some kind of fighting shape on the off-chance he ever got out of here.

By the third day he felt himself falling into a routine. He wasn't sure if that was a good or a bad thing, but it gave him an anchor to sanity, which was something. He could still feel the discomfort that the room caused him, but found that he had grown accustomed to it and was able to ignore it at will. As the sun was setting that evening, he had abandoned hope of anything useful happening that day. He had already made a mental tick-mark to tally his third complete day of imprisonment when he heard the sound of the lift settling on the top floor.

Confused and a little tired, Hayden sat up straight and tried to recall whether he had received all three meals today. He thought he had, but maybe he was thinking of yesterday's dinner? It was hard to tell when all his dinners were the same…

The door to his cell opened abruptly, and two men stood framed in the doorway. The one on the left was one of Hayden's mute guards, who brought him food and took away his waste. The other was Master Asher, wearing his metallic red Mastery robes from Mizzenwald.

"You've got five minutes," the guard informed the Prism Master, who nodded and stepped across the threshold into the room, allowing the door to shut behind him.

Hayden surged to his feet unsteadily and said, "About time! I thought you all were never going to figure out where Calahan put me!"

Master Asher closed his eyes briefly and shuddered as the effect of the room washed over him. It was then that Hayden realized that his mentor wasn't wearing his circlet or any weapons on his belt. It might have been the first time he had ever seen the man completely unarmed.

"This place is wretched," he opened his eyes and made a disgusted face. "Also, you look horrible."

Hayden scowled and said, "Yeah, well if you'd been locked up here for three days without any decent food or a shower, you wouldn't look so perky either."

Asher raised an eyebrow and said, "They haven't let you bathe?" When Hayden shook his head he added, "I'll see to that. Even convicted criminals have basic human rights—and you are not yet convicted of anything."

"Oh good," Hayden said sarcastically. "I was hoping I hadn't missed my trial."

"No, it's scheduled to start in another week or so," Asher answered his sarcasm without amusement. "The Council is still finalizing its evidence against you and collecting witness testimony."

Hayden frowned at that and paced the small room.

"I don't suppose you all have caught up to Sark and kicked him in the teeth for turning traitor on me, have you?"

There was an odd inflection in his voice when Asher said, "Why would we attack our colleague for doing his duty to the Council of Mages and apprehending a Wanted man?"

"WHAT?" Hayden turned around angrily, unable to believe his ears.

"You were a fugitive of the law, and Kirius brought you in to face justice. What part of that would we punish him for?" Asher reiterated flatly, though he tapped his ear and pointed to the walls as he spoke, and Hayden suddenly understood.

The walls have ears. We're being monitored.

Asher still had to maintain his cover, or else he would be arrested too. Even though he understood it, it aggravated Hayden to no end that they couldn't even have a candid conversation right now. He had really been looking forward to someone being able to tell him what in the world was going on.

"If you say so," he answered neutrally. "Anyway, why are you wearing your Mastery robes? I thought you all were postponing the next school year indefinitely until my father is neutralized."

"The Council and the High Mayor's office—in a rare joint venture—made an executive override and determined that we should carry on with business as usual."

Surprised, Hayden asked, "Why would they do that with the Dark Prism still on the loose? Aren't they afraid that he's going to blow up the school with most of Junir's magically-inclined children conveniently penned up inside or something?"

Asher scowled and said, "The High Mayor wants his taxes, and Mizzenwald is the single largest source of revenue for him in that regard. The Council wants us to continue training up young mages in the major and minor arcana while your father is still being peaceable, with the thought that it might take every mage we can get to fight him properly if he becomes aggressive once more. The risk of putting most of our magical future in one well-known place has been pointed out and ignored—more than once."

Hayden was trying to think of something he could safely ask without giving away the fact that he had been in touch with the Prism Master since he left school.

"Is there any news on what my father has been up to since he came through the schism?" He already knew the answer, but since he wasn't supposed to have any inside information at this point, he couldn't ask any of his follow-up questions until they brought this out in the open.

"Actually, there have been reports of him helping injured mages with warped Foci. He has been reversing the damage that was done to them and enabling them to use magic again."

"Why would he do that?" Hayden asked, in case Asher had come up with some new theories since they last spoke about it.

The Prism Master shrugged and said, "No idea. I've been trying to explain to the Council that I don't think my old friend is up to anything good, no matter how pure his motives may seem right now, but they have been rather divided over the issue."

The guard opened the door behind Asher and said, "Your time is up, sir. Please return to the lobby and your weapons will be returned to you."

Master Asher sighed and gave Hayden one last cursory glance, his expression worried. Hayden was determined to look tough and unaffected, but inside he was screaming, *Help! Don't leave me here for another week in this horrible place! Take me with you— we can fight off the guards together and escape!*

"I'll see you when the trial begins," Asher said as he stepped back over the threshold and seemed to perk up immediately as the unpleasant magical effect of the room left him. "All of the schools will have representatives in the audience at a trial this important—at least one from each of the Great Nine."

"Thanks," Hayden fought against the wave of emotions that were welling up inside of him: the terror at being left alone here for another week, of losing the trial and being told he'd have to spend the rest of his life here, of never seeing his friends again. "I'll see you in a week then."

Asher nodded and then the door was closed between them. Once more, Hayden found himself utterly alone. The brief contact with another human being—the first time he had really used his voice in three days—was enough to sharpen the discomfort the room forced upon him so that he felt it more acutely. Now that Hayden knew he was being spied on, he was determined not to cry, beg, or betray any other sign of his emotions. Spiting Cal was all he had left at this point, the only control that was still left to him.

He curled up on the hard ground and closed his eyes, fidgeting with his Focus-correctors and waiting to fall asleep.

Things improved slightly the next day, courtesy of Master Asher's visit. Hayden had no idea what strings the man had pulled on his behalf, or if he had simply threatened to sue Calahan for some sort of human rights violation, but Hayden was allowed out of his cell long enough to bathe for the first time since his arrival. He was also given half an hour a day—heavily guarded—to exercise on a lower floor, and there was even a pillow waiting for him in his room when he returned to it.

In some ways leaving the room made things worse, because the horrible feeling of wrongness hit him even harder after a period of time without it. Still, he came to enjoy his brief moments of freedom from the discomfort, especially as it gave him a chance to see other human beings and to remember that he wasn't the only person left in the world, though no one else was allowed to speak to him. Even the pillow felt like a luxury, though his body still ached from sleeping on the hard crystalline floor.

Calahan must not think there's any danger of me suffocating myself before the trial, Hayden thought ruefully.

He spent the next several days composing a mental list of questions to ask the next person who visited him, on the off chance one of his other allies would stop by before the trial. First on his mind was Bonk, because the dragonling had not reacted well to Hayden's unexplained absences in the past, and he could imagine his familiar laying siege to the Crystal Tower in a furious attempt to get to him. Sometimes, in his darkest moments, he cheerfully imagined Bonk tearing this entire crystalline building to the ground; he didn't even care whether he was inside it when that happened.

But days went by without any other visitors, neither Bonk nor anyone else, and despite Hayden's constant determination not to betray any sign of weakness that Calahan might hear about, he couldn't help but feel forgotten and betrayed. All of these important mages had spent months—years, really—telling him that he was uniquely gifted, special, important to the world at large, that he was vital in the plans to bring down the Dark Prism once and for all. And now that he had been captured? 'Out of sight, out of mind' seemed to be the motto now.

Nearly two weeks had elapsed since Hayden began his imprisonment: two impossibly long, thoroughly depressing weeks. He was awoken early that morning by the sound of the cell door swinging open, as the sun was just beginning to herald the coming of dawn. A grim-faced guard was on the other side.

"You're to shower, dress, and eat breakfast before your trial begins," he said by way of greeting.

Hayden felt his heart sink into his stomach and suddenly he didn't feel terribly hungry or anxious to leave his confinement. He knew that his trial was supposed to start any day now, but after having weeks to dream up all of the horrible outcomes that were possible, he wasn't sure he really wanted to face the real thing. The only bright side was that he hadn't known last night, so he was able to sleep fairly well.

"Okay, how long do I have to get ready?" Hayden asked as he stood up and stretched his legs, wincing when his stiff muscles strained in protest. No matter how many days he slept on the hard crystalline floor, it seemed that his body never really got used to it.

"About forty-five minutes," the guard informed him, and Hayden picked up his pace, ignoring his aching muscles.

The two of them stepped into the lift, and Hayden watched the man activate the up-and-down control with his wand. Hayden tried to count the number of floors they passed to see how far down they were going, but it was impossible to keep track given how fast they were moving. The only thing he was certain of was that he hadn't been this far down in the building since the night he came in. Was it his imagination, or did the air smell fresher down here?

The floor they stopped on must have been somewhere near the base of the Crystal Tower, because the space was much wider than the upper levels. The walls no longer appeared transparent, which was a blessed relief after seeing nothing but glare from the sun all of this time. Hayden had long since concluded that his prison cell had been designed with the intention of keeping its occupants in the maximum level of discomfort imaginable without physically torturing them.

He was led down a corridor that curved in a wide circle, stopping about halfway around the arc. The guard directed him into one of the interior rooms, assuming a static position outside the door: back straight, legs shoulder-width apart, and hands folded together in front of him. Hayden wondered how much the man got paid to stand around looking decorative all day.

He entered the bathroom—a much nicer one than the one on the nineteenth level—and couldn't decide if it was a good thing or bad thing that they were treating him well on the morning of his hearing. Either it meant that they were going to find him innocent, and had decided he was entitled to a little common courtesy, or it meant that his fate was so horrible that they didn't mind showing him a little kindness before he met his doom.

The floor was tiled in smooth, white granite with black veins shooting through it in a series of concentric circles.

No question what the Council's favorite shape is, Hayden thought in mild amusement, eliciting a private smile. It was nice to know that he was still capable of dry humor these days, even if only with himself.

The walls were composed of much smaller tiles, and these were colored to depict a fantastical explosion of magic that wrapped around the room like a mural. A wand was shown disgorging a trail of red and blue smoke, a colored phial near the ceiling splashed green liquid towards the floor; they had even taken the time to arrange the tiles so that it showed the splash effect as the elixir hit the ground.

Hayden approached a shower head near what looked like an explosion of different colored powders, forming a cloud that in real life would almost certainly kill him if he were to encounter it. He pulled lightly on the chords for hot and cold water, adjusting the balance until it was just right and then stripping down to wash. Since he didn't know when his next decent shower would be, he tried to savor it as much as possible, keeping in mind that he didn't have much time to dress and eat.

Another surprise was waiting for him when he was finished showering. Instead of donning the same worn pants and T-shirt that he had been wearing for two straight weeks, he found his formal House robes waiting for him. Again, he couldn't decide if this was a good or a bad thing, but he did feel better once he had them on. He also hoped the Council burned his worn shirt and pants, because he never wanted to lay eyes on them again.

After a hurried breakfast of hardboiled eggs and sausage rolls, he was led to one of the exterior rooms on the same floor, where the guard chivvied him inside like an overbearing nanny and then departed.

He had stepped into a medium-sized room: smaller than the chamber where he had fought for his assets last year in Kargath, but larger than the one they had questioned him in when he was twelve and the Council was deciding whether or not to let him study magic.

There were two long tables angled towards each other in an inverted 'V' in the center of the room. All of the seats at the right-hand table were occupied by the ten members of the Council of Mages, wearing their formal gold-and-black robes, Calahan at the center. The other table was completely unoccupied at present, which seemed strange and made the room look unbalanced, but Hayden assumed it might be for witnesses or other people who could be called to testify later on.

Low benches lined the walls. There was probably only enough room for forty people to sit down, assuming they squeezed together fairly tightly—though it wasn't currently filled to capacity. A large black-and-gold banner hung from the ceiling with the symbols for the ten major and minor arcana on it, artistically intertwined around the

Council's insignia. Other than that, the room was completely unadorned.

All eyes turned to Hayden as he looked to the Council members for directions on where to go. Calahan pointed wordlessly to a seat in the center of the open space between the V-shaped table configuration, and Hayden sat down, looking out into the audience to see who he recognized.

It was either a weekend or else classes had been cancelled, because all ten Masters from Mizzenwald were in attendance, even Sark. The Master of Powders met his gaze neutrally before Hayden glanced at the others. Mistress Razelle looked like she wanted to whack the Council members over the head and whisk him off to the infirmary for a healing elixir, but most of the others simply looked neutral or slightly grim.

Well, that's encouraging...

Three of the Masters from Valhalla were there, including Mandra; four from Isenfall, though Kiresa was the only one Hayden remembered; two from Creston in Hazenvale; one from Branx, in Wynir. The other Masters were obviously from the western schools, because he had never seen their robes before and didn't recognize a one of them. More to give himself something to do than because he was actually interested, he tried to guess at who was who while the Council members finished preparing their notes.

Those three in the black robes must be from Vyra in Ryvale, because their colors are black and silver. The one in brown is probably from Sud-Benir, in Sudir; that robe looks like it was designed with a desert climate in mind.

He had no idea which of the remaining duos was from Irea in Osglen and which was from Redkamp in Norvale, knowing virtually nothing about either place, but it didn't matter much because by the time he started thinking about it the Council was ready to proceed.

"This is the first day of the trial Hayden Frost, who presently stands accused of returning his father, Aleric Frost—also known as the Dark Prism—back into power in the Nine Lands. He also stands accused of evading the law when he was called upon to report to the Crystal Tower to be tried for this violation," Calahan spoke loudly and clearly, addressing the room at large. A record-keeper was hurriedly taking notes, sitting on one of the benches beside the delegates from Isenfall.

Hayden let his eyes roam over the Council members, some of whom blinked and looked away from his gaze, while others met his eyes unflinchingly. Magdalene Trout was one of the latter, though, interestingly, Laris was one of those who looked away.

"During this preliminary hearing, the charges against Hayden Frost will be finalized before proceeding to the full trial tomorrow." Calahan turned to him now and said, "For the record, please state your name and major area of discipline for this assembly."

"Hayden Frost, prism-user," he answered calmly, determined not to look rattled.

"And do you understand the purpose of today's gathering?"

"Not entirely," he admitted. "You said you're finalizing charges…?"

Calahan pursed his lips as though annoyed that he had to explain things, which gave Hayden a fleeting moment of satisfaction.

"That is correct. The formal trial will begin tomorrow, or later in the day today if things progress rapidly. This morning we will determine, based on our questions and your answers, the severity of the charges against you and what penalties may be sought in recompense."

Ah, they're going to decide whether I brought my father back on purpose or on accident and whether they want to Bind me, leave me in jail to rot, or kill me…

"Do you understand?" Calahan addressed him evenly, and Hayden nodded. "A 'yes' or 'no' answer is required," the Chief Mage prompted.

"Yes, I understand," Hayden replied.

"Very well then, let us proceed with the questioning. Horace?"

The man at the far end of the table opened with an easy question, rather than getting right to the meat of things, and asked, "How old are you, Hayden Frost?"

"I recently turned sixteen," he answered in his most polite tone, determined not to give anyone a reason to punish him for sarcasm.

"Sixteen years old, yet you've already been involved in more dangerous situations than most mages encounter in a lifetime."

Hayden didn't respond, since he hadn't been asked a question, simply meeting Horace's gaze with an expression of polite interest.

"You participated in the Battle of Northern Aggression two years ago, did you not?"

"If that's what the war in the Forest of Illusions is being called, then yes, I was there."

"More recently, you entered the largest stable schism on the continent with two others in an attempt to close it from the inside, which you managed successfully?"

"Yes," Hayden confirmed once more.

Horace placed his chin on his folded hands when he asked, "But you were the only member of your original party to survive the other realm, is that correct?"

Frowning, Hayden nodded, then remembered he was required to answer out loud and said, "Yes."

Horace yielded the floor to the woman sitting beside him.

"How did your companions lose their lives inside the other realm, while you survived?"

Not liking this line of questioning, Hayden tried to remain calm and keep the emotion from his voice when he answered.

"Harold died after the three of us came to a fork in the road. The ley lines we were following split off in two different directions at that point: the left path went through a swamp, while the way on the right seemed clear. Tanner and I wanted to go left, but Harold refused and insisted on going right because it appeared safer. We couldn't reach an agreement on which route to take, and Harold announced that it was time to go our separate ways, and that he would meet us when the ley-lines came together again, assuming we all survived. He only made it a few yards away from us before quicksand got him and he was gone."

A few of the Council members raised their eyebrows at this, as well as a few of the various Masters in the audience.

"You claim that a member of your party was prepared to split away from the one mage in the group with the ability to seal the schism?"

Hayden frowned and said, "He wasn't terribly impressed with my leadership abilities when deprived of magic, and thought I was going insane and that we were all going to die there. He was grumbling a lot about how the Council pulled a fast one on him, talking me up beyond my abilities to convince him to even volunteer in the first place. I think by then he was planning on heading for the exit to the schism, whether I was there to seal it behind us or not."

A long moment of silence followed this, in which a few of the Council members had the grace to look guilty, though Calahan apparently felt nothing for tricking a man into volunteering for a suicide mission.

"Why would two of you want to walk through a swamp, when you yourself just said that the other path appeared clear?"

Hayden glanced at Master Laurren, unsure whether or not he was allowed to tell them about the

Master's warning to him, or if that would only make things worse. The Master wasn't looking at him, but gave a microscopic twitch of the head, which gave Hayden his answer.

"I just had a bad feeling about the other way. It seemed too easy, after everything we had already endured to get there. Tanner and I decided that if the other parties before us had gotten that far, they probably would have gone right, and it obviously hadn't worked out well or they would have come back through the schism and sealed it behind them."

That was vaguely true, and the most convincing excuse he could come up with on the spot.

"So, according to you, you and Tanner elected to wade through a swamp because you 'had a feeling', allowing your other party member to take a separate path on which he fell into quicksand and was killed."

"That's what happened," Hayden confirmed, not liking the woman's skeptical tone or the way they kept saying things like 'according to you' and 'you claim', as though he was lying through his teeth.

The next mage along the table asked, "You two couldn't assist Harold with breaking free of the quicksand before he was overcome?" in a tone of unflattering disbelief.

Are they really going to suggest I murdered my teammates in the middle of another realm while at a complete loss for magic and rapidly going nuts?

"It wasn't like quicksand in this realm. One minute he was walking, and in the time it takes to blink he had dropped straight through the ground and disappeared. We didn't even have time to call out to him before he was gone—he might as well have fallen into a hole, *that's* how fast he went down."

He didn't look around at the audience to see whether the other Masters appeared to believe him. This story wasn't new to the ones at Mizzenwald, but as far as he knew, everyone else was getting this account of his time in the schism for the first time, and it probably sounded a little far-fetched to anyone who wasn't there.

"So Harold was consumed by improbably-fast-acting quicksand," his interrogator continued, "and how did Tanner die?"

"We encountered an alligator—or a crocodile—I can never tell the difference," Hayden began. "Anyway, it had magic, and we fell into the water and had to fight it at close range. It took a good bite out of Tanner's leg before I could throw a flash bomb into its mouth and kill it. I gave Tanner the last of my healing tinctures after I dragged him out of the water, and we ultimately made it out of the swamp mostly-intact, but then we were attacked by hyenas. I got tackled by one, and Tanner put an arrow through its neck right before it could eat me, but another one got him before he could reload. I couldn't get there in time to save him."

"You want us to believe that he died saving you—this stranger who had only known you for a day or so gave up his life so that *you* could go on alone?" the mage did nothing to hide the disbelief in his voice.

This isn't going well at all.

"That's what happened," Hayden reiterated. "He knew that I was the only one who could do the magic we needed to seal the schism for good, or else he didn't see the other hyena coming at him until it was too late. I don't know for sure, and I didn't ask him because I was about to be eaten at the time," he added, nettled.

"Yet you survived even after Tanner was killed…"

"Yes," Hayden answered reluctantly, knowing how this next part would sound. "That was when my father showed up, though he introduced himself as Hunter."

Hayden could hear a few muffled whispers from the audience. Some of the Council members shifted in their seats.

The next mage at the table took his turn to question Hayden.

"And you didn't recognize your own father, despite having met him before?"

"No. Anyone can tell you that I don't remember what happened on the day he came to my mother's house, though I've spent years trying to recover that memory. I didn't remember anything about what he looked like, or why he was there."

"And you didn't notice the remarkable resemblance you bear to him?" Calahan interrupted his colleague, obviously deciding it was his turn to ask the questions—or else he was allowed to butt in whenever he wanted, being the Chief Mage.

Hayden frowned and said, "Honestly, I don't think we look that much alike. He's taller than me and built like a gladiator. He has blond hair and light eyes, while I have my mother's coloring. Maybe the shape of our faces, once I knew to look for it, but I wasn't expecting to run into the Dark Prism inside the other realm; he was supposed to be obliterated in the explosion that killed my mother."

"There is quite a bit of similarity in your facial expressions and mannerisms," Calahan informed him coolly.

"Well it's not like I stare at myself in the mirror every time I change facial expressions, so I have no idea what I look like when I'm making them," he pointed out, his temper getting the best of him.

"The accused will not speak unless spoken to," Calahan said with vindictive pleasure. Hayden was tempted to point out that Calahan *had* been speaking to him, but the Chief Mage seemed to read his mind and amended his statement. "—or not unless asked a direct question by a member of this governing body."

Hayden forced himself to remain silent, though he could feel his cheeks burning with anger.

"So what you're telling us is that both of your teammates died in the other realm: the first from not following a hunch of yours and the second while defending you. Then your father happened upon you when you were alone and in danger and saved you, assisting you for the remainder of your time inside the schism out of the kindness of his heart."

"Was that a question?" Hayden asked dryly after a moment of silence.

Calahan flattened his lips in displeasure and changed tracks.

"How is it that your father came to be on this side of the schism with you?"

Hayden knew better than to confess that he had encouraged the man he knew as Hunter to join him in this realm. They'd probably skip the trial and just send him straight back to his cell for that.

"I was overcome with the effects of the realm after I cast the Closing spell on the schism, and I wasn't going to make it back through before it shut. He carried me on his back and jumped through the opening with me."

Calahan looked like he'd struck gold.

"Why would he go to such extraordinary effort to help you every step of the way, even carrying you out of the realm on his own *back*, if not because you are his son and he was planning to ask you to join him in his return to power?"

Hayden nearly jumped out of his chair he was so angry.

Barely restraining himself, he said, "He didn't have a clue who he was in the other realm; he thought he was Hunter as much as I did. He was just being a nice guy, after I explained to him that the mighty Council of Mages sent a fifteen year old into almost certain death because they were afraid to risk their own sacred persons."

There was an outbreak of angry muttering from the Council members, like a buzzing of bees. Hayden didn't care. It was ridiculous to think that his father was waiting for him all this time in the other realm on purpose—when Hayden hadn't even been intending to go in the first place—then put on an elaborate show of amnesia to win his son's trust when he could have just taken his prism and left him behind.

Calahan's face flushed purple and he barked out, "Careful, Frost. You wouldn't want us to start wondering whether you purposely colluded with your father to restore him to power, so that you could overthrow this ruling body and exact vengeance upon its members."

"You're insane," Hayden responded to his threat with disgust, leaning back in his chair and folding his arms across his chest in contempt.

How is it legal for him to threaten me with more severe charges just because he doesn't like what I have to say?

"Do you remember the last words you said to me before you entered the schism?" Calahan asked in a level, unpleasant tone.

Unfortunately, Hayden *did* remember what he was talking about, and knew it wouldn't look good for him to have it shared with the collective group.

So naturally, that's exactly what Calahan did. "I believe your exact words were, 'Cal, you'd better hope I die in there. Because if I make it out of that schism in one piece, I'm going to make it my personal goal to get you ousted from your comfy position in the Crystal Tower. I'm sick of you making my life difficult, and I look forward to returning the favor.' One might think that those words suggest you *yourself* were planning to take action against this Council, so I suggest you be very careful in how you address us from now on."

Hayden had to hand it to the man, he had a fantastic memory, or maybe Hayden's words had just made that much of an impression on him.

"I wasn't revealing some secret, nefarious plot to bring my father back into play," Hayden explained as calmly as possible. "I was making a general threat about trying to get you fired because I think you're a terrible Chief Mage and you keep coming to me to solve all of your problems and trying to get me killed."

Calahan turned fuchsia again and said, "I've heard enough. Are there any more questions from the Council?" He looked around at his colleagues, who shook their heads, perhaps sensing danger from their leader.

"Do you have anything further you would like to say for yourself?" Calahan's voice was acid.

"I do," Hayden said immediately. "Please consider that I have absolutely no motive for bringing my father back into a position of power on purpose. I spent ten years fearing him before I even knew who he was, and during my only interaction with the man, he murdered my mother, nearly destroyed my Foci, and blew up our house. I spent two years in Binders and in an orphanage because of him. He's the reason I entered Mizzenwald with no friends and spent my entire first year getting stared at and attacked by people who hated me because of who my father was. He murdered my girlfriend's mother for crying out loud—why would I want to bring back the man who tore her family apart? It was an accident on my part and on his, and you all can't even agree that he's actually evil right now because he's fixed a few people's Foci. Yet you want to pretend like he had this elaborate plan plotted out on the off-chance I stumbled into a schism someday and met up with him, or to threaten me by saying I acted maliciously just because you think I'm more popular than you and you don't like it."

The look on Calahan's face could have curdled milk, but Hayden didn't care. His wasn't the only vote; there were nine other mages on the Council, and all he needed was six of them to agree that he was being wrongfully maligned.

After a long silence, during which Calahan looked like he was doing some rapid mental calculations, the Chief Mage said, "I call for Hayden to be tried for returning his father to this realm…unintentionally. I further call for him to be charged with malicious intent against this Council based on his threats against me, and evasion of the law when he was wanted for questioning. This delay in the matter of his guilt or innocence has set us back considerably in our strategic planning against his father."

Clearly Calahan isn't one of the mages who are conflicted over whether my father is still evil or not.

To his surprise, Magdalene Trout immediately said, "I second the charges."

Four more mages raised their hands after her, including Laris, and the motion passed. Thinking that things could have gone better, Hayden turned to look at the Masters of Mizzenwald, who looked absolutely blank. Had something happened in the last two weeks that he didn't know about? Was Magdalene Trout no longer an ally? Had the entire alliance fallen apart since he'd left and Laris cast doubt on his story?

"It appears we have a majority—" Calahan began, looking pleased, but Mrs. Trout interrupted him by stating, "Furthermore, I don't think that we're going far enough with these charges. I think that there is ample evidence to support a charge of malicious intent—that he brought his father back into this realm with a full understanding of who he was and what his goals were. We need to send a clear message to the magical and non-magical community that this kind of treachery will not be ignored, nor swept under the rug. A simple prison sentence isn't good enough for Frost. Justice must be served, and it must be seen to be served across the Nine Lands."

Hayden could only sit there with his mouth hanging open in shock as he watched his life fall to pieces around him. Strangely, Calahan was eyeing his colleague as though she was going scarily off-script, and Laris looked slightly perplexed.

"You want to *increase* the charges against Frost?" he asked softly, and when she nodded, added, "What—*exactly*—did you have in mind?" warily.

"I vote that we upgrade the charges to high treason against the Nine Lands."

Alarmed, Laris blurted out, "But that's for war crimes and crimes against humanity!"

"Can you deny that Hayden has committed both of those in bringing the Dark Prism back to power?" she scoffed. "We were at war with that monster for a decade: a decade in which he destroyed who-knows-how-many innocent people; entire towns perished at his hand. Hayden intended to resume that war—we all know this, even if no one else will say it out loud—and he should pay the ultimate price for his actions," Magdalene said forcefully, her voice carrying more authority than even Calahan's as it rang through the room.

"A charge of high treason comes with an automatic death sentence if he is found guilty," Laris pointed out to his colleague, as though she could have possibly not known that.

What?! Hayden thought in panic. *She can't be serious…this can't be happening!*

"Then justice would be served and the world would understand that we have no intention of letting a colluder off lightly just because of a few paltry medals he was once awarded."

"What?" Hayden meant to shout the word, but it came out barely a whisper. His voice seemed to fail him at this critical juncture. All he could keep thinking, over and over in his head was, *They're actually going to kill me. I never thought they'd really kill me…*

"I second the upgrade to high treason," the Councilwoman to her left said immediately, glaring hatefully at Hayden.

Ironically, it was Calahan who said, "Now, now, let's not be hasty..." only to be shouted down by three more Council members adding their approval to the mix.

"Magdalene, I really think we should reconsider whether Hayden's crime quite qualifies—" Calahan began desperately. For some reason he was acting like *he* was the one who had been tricked here and was about to be sentenced to die.

"You want to show leniency to a boy you just hinted might have malicious intent against the Nine Lands? If he means so much to his father's plans, let's remove him from the equation once and for all." There was no trace of warmth or emotion in her voice. It was like she had never met Hayden before in her life, cared nothing for him, and relished the thought of seeing him die.

How has it come to this? Hayden wondered hopelessly, mouth as dry as ashes.

"I agree," came the sixth and condemning vote from the Council, and just like that, Hayden was suddenly on trial for his life.

He was too numb with disbelief to even speak, but Calahan apparently didn't have that problem. The Chief Mage looked like he personally had been charged with high treason against the Nine Lands, standing up and glaring at Magdalene Trout like he finally saw her for the enemy that she was.

The setting and the large audience prevented him from venting his true feelings onto her, so he turned them towards the audience instead.

"Come now, this can't stand," he insisted. "The public will be outraged if we consider the death penalty for a boy who was their hero not two months ago. He still has higher approval ratings than this Council, despite everything."

Hayden felt a faint glimmer of hope. If the people really did support him more than they did the Council of Mages, even after all the slander Calahan had been spreading against him...maybe they would back off on their charges.

For a long moment no one in the audience spoke. Hayden wasn't even sure whether they were *allowed* to speak, or if Calahan was just appealing to anyone's common decency, since all of his colleagues seemed to be lacking it.

Wow, the day has really gone downhill when Calahan is my only ally.

"Normally his legal guardian would have the chance to dispute the charges and speak on his behalf," Magdalene explained lightly. "Since Hayden's mother is deceased and his father doesn't qualify for obvious reasons, he should be allowed to choose a guardian in this instance, and they may argue on his behalf if they elect to." Her tone suggested that she expected Hayden to jump out of his seat and praise her for her charitable consideration.

"Asher," he said without even needing to think about it, as soon as Calahan turned towards him. He doubted that anyone in the room would be surprised by his choice, as the Prism Master had been a teacher, mentor, friend, and father-substitute to him since he arrived at Mizzenwald.

Calahan grimaced but turned towards the group of seated Masters.

"Well, Asher Masters? Do you intend to contest the charge of high treason against Hayden?"

Looking perfectly relaxed, Asher opened his mouth and said, "No, I don't. Let the charges stand as they are."

"WHAT?!" This time Hayden did jump out of his seat and shout. He knew that the Prism Master enjoyed making people uncomfortable by being eccentric, but this hardly seemed like the time and place for it, not when Hayden's life was on the line.

Calahan looked similarly dismayed, clenching his fists tightly and not even bothering to tell Hayden to sit down and shut up. In fact, the only thing he said at all was, "This hearing is in recess," before storming out of the room.

Hayden walked towards the group of Masters during the general noise and movement while everyone prepared to break, but before he had closed half the distance between them, a guard grabbed him forcefully by the arm and steered him out of the room.

"Where are you taking me?" Hayden demanded, beyond caring about niceties.

He must have looked like he meant business, because the man answered his question for the first time since he was brought here.

"To a holding room until the trial resumes."

The holding room, as it turned out, was only a few doors down the hall, and it was much nicer than his first detainment cell. The room was almost entirely empty, save for a cot on the floor against one wall and a chair facing it.

As soon as the guard locked him inside and assumed his post outside the door, Hayden began to pace the room in a tearing fury. He had no idea what had changed in the short time he was locked up in the Crystal Tower, but it must have been something terrible in order to cause all of his allies to turn on him like this. They could have at least had the decency to warn him ahead of time so that he didn't go in there looking like a fool.

Hayden was so outraged with the lot of them that he kicked the wall as hard as he could, which did nothing but make his foot hurt.

I can't let them keep me here. I have to escape before they try to send me back up to the twentieth floor, or before they can officially sentence me to die.

He was determined on that much at least. He wouldn't sit here like a sheep, waiting to be led to the slaughter. He would die fighting if worse came to worse; at least then he would have his dignity.

Just as he began assessing the room he was in for weak points, he heard the click of the lock and the door swung open to reveal Master Willow. For once, he was thankful that it wasn't Asher coming to visit him. He might not possess the self-restraint to keep from attacking his mentor right now.

The door shut behind the Master of Wands and the lock clicked once more. Hayden immediately registered that the man was unarmed, as was Asher on the night he'd come to visit. It seemed that no one was allowed to bring weapons into Hayden's presence, on the off-chance Hayden could overpower them and make a break for it.

That's probably a smart move on Calahan's part, given what I'm currently planning...

"Hayden, I know how you must be feeling," Willow greeted him calmly. "Let me explain..."

"Explain what?" Hayden interrupted hotly, jaw clenched in fury. "Are you going to explain how the people who were supposed to be on my side just sold me out when I needed them the most? Even *Asher* is going to just let them convict me of treason!"

"I told them you would take this poorly, but it wasn't possible for us to warn you in advance or else Calahan wouldn't have played things the way he did just now and this would never have worked to our advantage."

Confused, Hayden stopped pacing and said, "What do you mean? This was somehow part of the *plan?*"

Master Willow nodded, and Hayden felt suddenly deflated, as if all of the energy had rushed out of him in a single moment. He felt relieved, drained, and more confused than ever in its wake.

He sat down shakily in the lone chair and said, "Okay, *now* you can explain."

10
The Midnight Visitor

Obviously relieved that he had settled down, Master Willow leaned back against the wall and said, "I'm sure you remember your last group meeting as well as I do, on the eve of your removal from the Trout estate."

"What, you mean the one where Laris said that maybe I was wrong about my father and he's actually a cool guy who we should get to share his magic with us?" He asked, surprised by the question.

"In a nutshell, yes," Willow confirmed. "You left the meeting before it came to its conclusion, but since we are short on time I'll just summarize and tell you that by the end of it, the rest of us were worried that Laris was about to switch sides."

"What do you mean?"

Master Willow frowned and said, "There was some concern that he would return to Calahan and tell him he found you at Magdalene's house, presenting himself as the hero who had no idea where you were all this time. He could name everyone who was involved in our planning, as well as alert Calahan that Magdalene was after his job and attempting to dethrone him."

Alarmed, Hayden looked around the room and said, "Aren't we being monitored in here, sir? Asher wouldn't speak plainly during his visit up in the Boxes because he said we were being spied on."

Willow shook his head, looking supremely unconcerned.

"The situation has changed. This room is not being monitored, though your cell upstairs certainly would have been."

Hayden would just have to take his word for it, though he was nowhere near as assured that their level of privacy was sufficient as Master Willow. Perhaps he was just becoming paranoid after two weeks in the topmost floor of the Crystal Tower.

"But why would Laris sell us all out to Calahan just because he wants to become buddies with my father and learn cool new magic that may or may not be a sin against nature?"

"Because Laris *also* wants to be the Chief Mage, and if he can get Magdalene and all the rest of us out of the way, there is much less competition. Learning that he'd been betrayed from one of his own Council members might have been the catalyst that drove Calahan to folly and ultimately got him deposed, and then Laris would be conveniently poised to rise to power. With him in charge, he could lift the manhunt for your father and request an open meeting to begin working with him—assuming Aleric was amenable and not on a killing spree by then."

"That would be a disaster," Hayden said in stunned disbelief, imagining how bad things would be if Laris's plans came to fruition.

"Indeed. We weren't sure if or when he was going to take action, so we needed to plan quickly in order to preempt him. We asked Kirius to stage an abduction that night, since he has been carefully avoiding any of our meetings at the Trout estate or with Laris."

"You mean Sark was actually doing me a *favor* by hauling me out of there in my pajamas?" he winced at the memory of how cold his feet were and how afraid he was. He still wasn't sorry for punching the man in the nose.

"We figured he would be the most convincing with Calahan, who would have been very suspicious of trickery if any of the rest of us had brought you to him; fortunately it is well known that you and Kirius haven't gotten along well in the past, to put it mildly."

I never thought my bad relationship with Master Sark would come in handy.

It was nice to know that four years of solid dislike was finally paying dividends for him.

"Why didn't he just explain himself as he was dragging me through the snow and into the Tower? Then I wouldn't have fought him so hard and I wouldn't have been going nuts for the past two weeks in that stupid Box upstairs, thinking you all had forgotten about me."

"We collectively agreed that in order to be convincing to Calahan, *you* also had to be kept in the dark for a period of time. If you didn't appear concerned with your fate, or if you didn't ask the right questions of him, he would have suspected something was amiss. Asher and Kilgore wanted to abandon the plan entirely and raid the Crystal Tower to liberate you when they heard where you were being kept."

That made Hayden feel slightly better about everything, knowing that he hadn't just been forgotten for those two miserable weeks.

"So it worked? Laris wasn't able to sell us out?"

"No, we managed to beat him to the punch. If he had come forward after the fact and claimed to know where you had been all this time, Calahan would have seen him ruined, even if he swore he was getting ready to bring you in and that he had only been a part of our group to gather information and act as a spy."

"Okay, so I guess I see why you all had me brought here without telling me anything ahead of time…but explain to me why me being charged with high treason is a good thing. I could have sworn that Mrs. Trout suddenly decided she hated me and was trying to get rid of me for good, except Calahan looked as angry as I was about it. You'd think he'd be thrilled for the chance to murder me legally, since there's no love lost between the two of us these days."

Master Willow frowned and said, "Magdalene showed her hand today when she upped the charges against you, though there was no getting around it at this point. Calahan now knows that she has betrayed him and is making a move against him, though it should be too late for him to do anything about it—or so we hope."

"I still don't get it," Hayden said bluntly.

"Calahan wanted to charge you with bringing your father back to this realm unintentionally, and with evading the law when you were wanted for questioning. Unfortunately, you are guilty of both of those crimes, such as they are, and there is no way any of us could get you out from under the sentencing for them."

Hayden narrowed his eyebrows pensively and nodded to show that he understood so far.

"If we left the charges at that, you would have certainly been convicted of them—possibly even of having malicious intent against the Council since you threatened Calahan before entering the schism. Depending on how generous the Council was feeling, you could have gotten any punishment from Binders for life to a simple prison sentence or even community service. That wasn't something we could risk happening."

"So she tried to up the charges against me because…"

"Because high treason happens to be a crime you are completely innocent of. They would need a mountain of evidence that I know they do not possess in order to successfully convict you, and as Calahan said, the people still love you and would never stand for it. Magdalene did an excellent job whipping her colleagues into a frenzy, and making them forget that they can't make the charges stick until she got the votes she needed to formalize them."

Hayden frowned thoughtfully.

"I get that they don't have evidence against me, but I don't think that they're above manufacturing some, and they've had a while to do it. What if they pull out something that I can't properly refute and convict me anyway? Magdalene is just one person, and you tell me we've lost Laris; there are eight other people besides them on the Council, and I need at least five of them to vote in my favor."

"Ah," Willow held up an index finger like he was about to lecture him on proper wand care. "You've touched upon an important point. I suppose you noticed the empty table that was opposite the Council members during the preliminary hearing?"

Not knowing where this was going, Hayden said, "Yes…"

"That table is always there but seldom used. The reason that Calahan didn't want a high treason charge—aside from the fact that you're innocent and you'll ultimately be set free without punishment—is because it is very difficult to convict someone of a crime that comes with a death sentence. The Council alone does not have the authority to make such a decision."

"Oh?"

"In the event such charges are set against a person, one representative from each of the Great Nine is called upon to participate as a voting member of the jury panel, thereby doubling the number of people that need to be convinced of your guilt—and half of them lack the Council's bias against you."

Hayden lifted his eyebrows in surprise at this new twist.

"That's convenient. But still, ten Council members against nine Masters...I would need every one of you *and* Magdalene to vote in my favor to get a majority, and I don't even know most of the Masters from the other schools."

"Not ten-to-nine, nine-to-nine." Master Willow gave him a genuinely pleased smile. "In order to prevent the Council from uniting and winning by simple majority in these matters, one member is required to excuse themselves from the proceedings. Specifically, the Chief Mage."

"Oh!" Hayden laughed out loud, suddenly understanding why Calahan was so furious with the more severe charge. "Not only does Calahan have to convince nine people who don't work for him that I'm guilty, but he's not even allowed to participate as a judge anymore?" He laughed again at the brilliance of it.

"Indeed. It was the best way we could assure your success in the trial, and while you may not know all of the Masters who will be acting as judges, let us just say that they will not be volunteering at random." He smiled again.

"You all called in some favors?" Hayden asked with a grin, hardly able to believe how much more cheerful he was than before Willow's visit.

And to think, I considered throwing him out of the room and refusing to hear what he had to say...or worse, attacking him for weapons and making a break for it.

"It's useful to be well-connected," the Master answered obscurely.

A knock on the door put an end to their candid conversation as the guard standing outside entered the room and said, "You're to be returned to your room upstairs while the Great Nine nominate their judges and assemble here. The trial will resume tomorrow morning."

Hayden grimaced at the prospect of spending another night in that horrible cell upstairs, even more now that there was hope of him being freed permanently in the near future.

"Okay," was all he said, since complaining would get him nowhere with these people. He allowed himself to be led out of the holding room by the guard, who simply looked relieved that he wasn't resisting.

"I'll see you when the trial recommences," Master Willow informed him, watching Hayden depart with his escort. "Try to get some rest."

"Thanks, sir, I will." Hayden nodded appreciatively, entering the lift ahead of the guard and watching the iron doors close in front of them. As the lift carried them rapidly up to the top floor, he made a personal vow to never enter one of these contraptions again if he ever made it out of the Crystal Tower. He had initially found them fascinating, but his stay here had rather ruined the effect.

The wrenching feeling of wrongness assailed him as soon as he entered his transparent cell, which still brought him to his knees, despite becoming accustomed to the sensation. He recovered after a few minutes and fought down a wave of nausea, fidgeting briefly with his Focus-correctors until he adjusted to the mild tingling of his wrists beneath them, as though tiny ants were crawling on his skin.

Now I just have to find a way to pass the rest of the day and night...

Lying on his back and closing his eyes, Hayden could only pray that this wouldn't be a long trial. He was running out of things to think about.

When Hayden reentered the room where his trial was being held the following morning, the first thing he noticed was that both tables of nine were now fully occupied, so that as he took his seat in the space between them he felt surrounded by a horde of mages. The second thing he noticed was that Calahan was sitting on one of the benches that lined the perimeter of the room, having been demoted to 'spectator' this time around.

Of the mages on his left, Hayden only recognized a few of them on sight: Master Willow was apparently the representative from Mizzenwald, Master Mandra from Valhalla, and the Conjury Master from Isenfall looked familiar—though Hayden couldn't remember his name right now. He wasn't surprised to see Willow there, since the Master of Wands was probably the most diplomatic person Hayden knew, and had an aura about him that radiated calmness and fairness.

I'm just glad they didn't pick Kiresa to be the judge from Isenfall.

No matter how many times people swore the Prism Master was on their side, Hayden still believed that given the chance, the man would knife him in the back and laugh himself stupid over it.

He also wasn't entirely surprised when it was Magdalene Trout who said, "Day two in the trial of Hayden Frost, formally charged with high treason," to the record-keeper who was sitting beside Calahan.

Guess she's in charge now.

She began by questioning him yet again about his motives while inside the schism, though her tone was much milder and more businesslike than the impassioned argument she had made yesterday. Even Hayden could tell that it was all for show, and some of her colleagues looked uncomfortable now that they had time to consider the charges properly. A few of them kept shooting glances back at Calahan as though expecting him to intervene, or explode.

It looked like the Chief Mage was sucking on a lemon, but apparently there was nothing he could do to alter the proceedings at this point, because for possibly the first time during Hayden's acquaintance with the man, he remained silent for the entire day.

"So you claim you don't harbor any ill feeling towards this Council," Magdalene summarized at the end of the afternoon, after making a long, circuitous point of annunciating all their past interactions at length.

"No, I don't," Hayden confirmed, exhausted and ready for the day to be over, even it meant returning to his horrible cell upstairs for another night. He had been holding his full bladder for the last two hours, hoping someone would call a break soon; it seemed wrong to interrupt a room full of powerful people to ask if he could run to the bathroom.

"And why should we believe you?" Laris asked for the third time that day. Master Mandra stifled a yawn.

"Because I hardly even know most of you, and certainly not well enough to hold a grudge against any of you—excepting Cal, perhaps." Hayden shrugged, not looking at the Chief Mage as he spoke. "He's the one who follows me around, making my life miserable for no good reason—the rest of you are just doing your jobs, as far as I can tell."

Wonder of wonders, this actually seemed to reach a few of them.

"We've run over on time," Magdalene Trout interrupted before Laris could ask his next question. "Let's leave it here for the day, and when we convene tomorrow morning we can continue with the discussion."

My bladder thanks you, Hayden thought gratefully.

He walked to the door as quickly as possible without actually running and alarming the guards. A whisper in the ear of the one charged with bringing him back upstairs led him to a bathroom on the second floor—or at least he *thought* it was the second floor—before they got back onto the accursed lift.

When he was finally alone in his nausea-inducing cell on the top floor, Hayden laid down on his back and stared up at the transparent ceiling; the sun had almost completely set, distorting his view of the sky in the crystal.

Surely they don't have another full day of questions left, Hayden thought to himself hopefully. *It even seemed like a few of the Council members might be on my side by the end of today, so maybe tomorrow they'll get the voting out of the way and I'll be cleared of all charges.*

If so, he personally vowed to himself that he would never again set foot inside the Crystal Tower as long as Calahan was in charge of the Council of Mages. If he never saw this building again, it would be too soon for his liking.

He drifted off to sleep with the comforting thought that this could very well be his last night here, and that everything would get better in the morning.

When Hayden snapped awake, it took him a minute to figure out exactly why. He blinked groggily and stared at the cell around him, which was pitch-black from the night sky outside—even the moon wasn't out tonight. He had no idea whether it was late at night or early in the morning, but either way, he had no desire to wake up just yet.

Yawning and feeling groggy, Hayden tried to ignore the frantic beating of his heart and relax himself.

I must've had a bad dream or something...

Just as he closed his eyes again he heard it, though it was so far away and faint that he couldn't be sure it wasn't his mind playing tricks on him.

Was that a scream?

Keeping his eyes shut, he listened more closely, straining his ears for all the good it would do him. He tilted his head to one side to try and pick up sound better, which was rendered pointless when an alarm bell activated a moment later, the horrible sound reverberating around the entire floor and startling him so badly that he shouted and scrambled upright.

For a few minutes all he could hear was the horrible klaxon-like alarm echoing around the cell and making his head hurt. He covered his ears with his hands and curled up into a ball in the darkness, resting his chin on his knees and waiting for the horrible noise to stop, all the while trying to figure out what was happening.

Surely they're not doing some sort of drill in the dead of night…

He wouldn't put it past Calahan to stage something like this just to annoy him, but he didn't think the Chief Mage would want to be woken violently from his own rest just to play along with Hayden's suffering. He didn't even know how many people lived at the Crystal Tower on the lower floors full-time, other than the guards and the night crew. Most of the Council members had probably already gone home for the day…

The alarm stopped as abruptly as it started, and Hayden dropped his hands from his ears in relief, though he could still hear the echo rattling around inside his head for a full minute afterwards.

Another minute or so of silence followed, and just when Hayden was beginning to calm down, he heard loud, banging sounds coming from somewhere below, accompanied by shouting. He had no idea how far away the noises were, or what was happening, but he became painfully aware of the fact that he was all alone in a cell, unarmed and unable to do magic, in the dead of night. Even if he had a prism in his hand, he couldn't see well enough to use it, and likely wouldn't be able to combat the effects of this horrible cell anyway.

Calm down, Hayden...this is the Crystal Tower, home-base of some of the most powerful magic-users in the Nine Lands. There are probably enough wards and protections on this place that nothing really bad could be happening...

He told himself this, over and over, even as the sounds of shouting, screaming, and fighting got progressively louder. He had no idea how many people were in the Tower right now, but he was surprised by the level of noise he could hear from the top floor.

The alarm probably brought people back to investigate...

His chest seemed to grow tighter and tighter as the sounds of chaos drew closer, until all at once there was complete silence, which was somehow even scarier than all the banging and screaming.

Silence is a good thing, it means that whatever happened, it's over now...

His feeble assurances did nothing to soothe his fears though, and he thought his heart was going to explode out of his chest when he heard the smooth sound of the lift settling into place on the top floor.

A single pair of footsteps was audible on the other side of the door, heavy and slow and deliberate. He heard a door open to one of the other cells on this floor, then another.

They're all empty except mine…the Council knows what room I'm in, so why would they be searching the others?

Before he could fully consider the implications of this, the door to his room was opened from the outside, illuminating a single figure in the blinding light of a prism, which was resting in the eyepiece on top of his head, pointed skywards.

Aleric Frost stood before him.

It wasn't supposed to be this way, Hayden thought in panic as his eyes widened. *I was supposed to face my father with a belt full of weapons, with my friends and allies at my side, not defenseless and alone in the Crystal Tower.*

Before he could even think of what to say or do, the Dark Prism opened his mouth and asked, "What are you doing here?" in a flat tone.

Since this had been the very question Hayden was about to ask of his father, he was completely derailed. Being caught off guard, he ended up telling the truth by default.

"I've been on trial for bringing you out of the schism with me," he admitted haltingly, swallowing hard. "They've kept me locked up until—"

"Yes, but why are you *here?*" His father gestured vaguely at the room around them, looking mildly annoyed with Hayden's slow uptake.

As he turned his head to take in the room, Hayden noticed with a pang of emotion that Cinder was perched on his father's shoulder, standing perfectly still and looking as regal as usual. He also noticed that his father was standing in the threshold of the room, not actually entering. Perhaps he could feel the effects of the room as well, and he wouldn't be able to use his magic if he came inside.

"In the Box, you mean?" Hayden asked, unsure of the question. His father nodded impatiently and he added, "Calahan hates me and wanted to see me suffer for a few weeks before the trial started."

The Dark Prism looked almost bored by the answer, but all he said was, "Calahan is dead, and you're wearing my House robes."

It took Hayden a long moment to process the first part of that sentence, forcibly reminded of all the shouting and fighting sounds from below. As much as he disliked the Chief Mage, he didn't think the man deserved to be violently murdered.

"Why did you kill him?" he asked softly, still trying to engage his brain and figure out if there was any chance at all of getting the upper hand against his father before the man could kill him where he sat.

"He got in my way," the Dark Prism answered simply, looking supremely unconcerned. Hayden glanced down at the floor and noticed a trail of dark red footprints in the foyer behind his father, where he had trailed blood behind him.

"How many others are dead?" he asked, wondering how long he could keep his father talking and whether it would ultimately do any good to delay the inevitable.

Aleric shrugged his broad shoulders and said, "I didn't count. Enough to convey the message that I am not to be trifled with."

The Black Prism continued to cast light around the room, perched on top of his father's head. He, Hayden, was completely unarmed, his powers dampened in this room, and nowhere near strong enough to take on his father in a physical fight. If everyone in the Crystal Tower was dead except the two of them, no one was going to come rescue him so he could fight another day. This was the end for him.

"Why did you come here tonight?" Hayden got to the point, seeing no reason for further delay. He wondered if it would hurt to die, or if it would be like falling unconscious—awake one minute, gone the next.

"I've come for you. Get up and follow me." He made an irritated gesture at Hayden as though he actually expected to be obeyed and was annoyed that it was taking so long.

"What do you want with me?" Hayden asked in alarm, getting to his feet but making no effort to approach his father. In fact, he backed up as far as he could go, until his back was pressed against the transparent wall behind him.

"Don't ask questions you already know the answer to. You can either walk out of here by my side like an adult, or you can resist like an insolent child and I can make you wish you hadn't."

Hayden didn't really like either of those options, and stood there for a minute, weighing the decision.

Apparently he took too long for his father's liking, because the Dark Prism sighed and then stepped across the threshold and into the room. The light from the Black Prism went out, plunging them into complete darkness, and before Hayden could say another word, his father grabbed him roughly by the hair and slammed his head into the crystalline wall with all of his considerable strength.

The first time Hayden's head hit the wall he cried out as stars exploded in front of his eyes, and the second time he thought he heard his skull crack. The third time everything went black.

11
A Changing of the Guard

Zane knew something was wrong long before Mrs. Trout returned home at the break of dawn; he'd been woken during the night by some kind of uproar in the house. He dashed into the hallway in his pajamas, conjury chalk equipped, stumbling into the foyer just in time to catch the end of Mrs. Trout's argument with her eldest son.

"—don't have time for this. As long as I draw breath, you will follow my orders, whether you like them or not," Magdalene was instructing Oliver in her no-nonsense voice, pulling a jacket on with the air of one who was doing things without conscious thought. "Stay here until you receive further instructions."

"Mother—" Oliver interrupted, but she had already vanished.

"What in the world is going on?" Zane asked the older boy, who startled at the sound of his voice and whirled around to face him, hand itching dangerously close to his belt full of powders.

"Go back to bed, Laraby. This doesn't concern you," Oliver vented his frustration on him, scowling and stalking back down the hallway.

"I beg to differ," Zane argued, matching his pace. "I'm as much a member of this team as you are, and if something is going on, I should know about it, so get off your high-horse and talk to me."

A few years ago, he would never have dreamed of talking to Oliver Trout like that—the older boy had terrified him during his earliest years of school. He was still a little terrified, because he'd seen Oliver in a fight, but that fear no longer ruled him.

To his surprise, as they rounded the corner into the library Oliver said, "Fine." He stopped walking quite abruptly, and Zane stopped a step ahead of him and turned around, trying to conceal his surprise at being taken seriously.

Probably because there are no other adults here who he can talk to instead.

"I woke up because I heard a ringing noise down the hall, coming from my mother's room. When I got there, she was already dressed and on her way out, saying that the alarms had been activated at the Crystal Tower."

Zane's eyebrows lifted in surprise.

"What does that mean?"

Oliver gave a noncommittal shrug and said, "Nothing good. I've never actually heard them go off before, except during drills—the sound is apparently tied in to all the Council members' homes so that they know if there's a problem at the Tower."

"So she went in to see what's going on?"

"No," Oliver shook his head, frowning. "She said she had a bad feeling about it and didn't want to charge in alone and unprepared, so she went to round up reinforcements first. She wants us to stay here and wait for news."

Zane frowned and fidgeted with the conjury chalk that was still in his hand. It left a remnant of pink powder on his skin where he touched it, and he rubbed two fingers together absentmindedly, taking comfort from the familiar sensation.

"What kind of thing is she expecting to find there that would require reinforcements?" he asked no one in particular, his mind flipping through several likely scenarios before settling on the most chilling. "You don't think…it can't be the Dark Prism, can it?"

Oliver's mouth tensed slightly as he said, "I don't know. It could be, though why he'd attack the Crystal Tower at night when most everyone has gone home is beyond me…"

"Unless he's after Hayden and finally figured out where he's being kept!" Zane clapped a hand to his forehead in horror, trying to convince himself it wasn't true the moment the thought struck him.

"It hasn't exactly been a secret where Hayden's been the last couple weeks. If the Dark Prism was so interested in finding him for…whatever he wants him for, why wait until now?" Oliver asked curiously.

"I don't pretend to know what Hayden's dad is thinking, but you're right; we shouldn't get ahead of ourselves trying to figure out what's going on. Your mom will come back in a few minutes and tell us that everything is fine...maybe it was a false alarm, or a simple break-in, or something like that."

He didn't believe the words even as he said them, and by the look on his face, neither did Oliver, but all the older boy said was, "Maybe. We'll just have to hang around here until we find out. We should probably get back to bed."

"I think I'll wait up a bit, just in case news comes quickly."

Oliver shrugged and said, "Suit yourself," before walking off in the direction of his own bedroom.

Zane had initially been optimistic that they would learn something within the hour, but as time went on and no one came for them, he became increasingly worried. He didn't want to go back to bed in case no one came to get him when someone arrived with information, so he ended up slouched over in an armchair in the library, which was sort of centrally located in the house and seemed as good a place to crash as any. Felix the fox was curled up in his lap, fast asleep, evidently not plagued by the worries that kept Zane awake. Stroking Felix's fur softly, he was forcibly reminded of Bonk, who hadn't been seen since Hayden was taken to the Crystal Tower—as far as Zane knew. Zane liked to think that the little dragon had found a way to infiltrate the place and was keeping Hayden company, despite Asher and Willow saying they hadn't seen him there.

He wouldn't just abandon Hayden in his hour of need. If Hayden's in real trouble, Bonk will be there.

There wasn't much he knew for certain about Hayden's weird familiar, but he did know that much—well, and that his favorite food was definitely squirrel.

Zane had no idea how long he stayed like that, slumped over in the chair, staring glassy-eyed at the spine of a random book in his direct line of sight without actually registering the title. For all he knew, he may have drifted into a muddled sort of sleep at some point. The first time he blinked in hours was when Master Reede crossed into his field of vision, obscuring the book with his metallic red Mastery robes and asked, "You're not dead, are you?"

Blinking rapidly to encourage moisture back into his eyes, Zane groaned and forced himself to sit upright, muscles aching in protest.

"Master Reede!—no, I'm alive...what's going on?" He tried to jog his brain back into action and look attentive, stifling a yawn with one hand and jostling Felix awake with the change in position.

The Master of Conjury gave him an unreadable look and said, "Come on, we're meeting at Mizzenwald."

Frowning at the non-answer, Zane got to his feet and continued asking questions as they walked towards the main foyer, leaving everything behind except for his belt of chalk and other weapons, which he had taken to wearing at all times ever since Hayden had been caught unaware in the dead of night and dragged off without his things.

"Oliver said there was something wrong at the Crystal Tower—that the alarms went off and Mrs. Trout went to get reinforcements. Is everything alright?"

Master Reede was either deliberately lengthening his stride, or else Zane was so tired that he had a difficult time keeping up with his mentor for a change. Either way, he began to feel a little winded as he half-jogged to keep up with the man.

"We'll talk at Mizzenwald, when everyone is together," he answered in a tone that did not invite more questions.

Zane pressed his luck anyway, taking a page out of Hayden's book, since his friend never seemed to know when to quit and none of the Masters had actually slapped him for it yet.

"What about the Dark—"

"Laraby, for the love of all things holy, please shut up," the Master of Conjury interrupted snappishly, touching his temples. "I've got a screaming headache that I haven't been able to address yet and your voice is the equivalent of etching glass with a cheese grater right now."

Zane clamped his jaw shut with effort, biting back a dozen more questions he wanted to ask now that he finally had someone to interrogate who knew what was going on.

There was one question that he thought couldn't wait, and he risked his mentor's wrath by asking it.

"Is it safe for me to go back to Mizzenwald, or is the Council still looking for me?"

Master Reede spared him a fleeting glance and said, "The Council is in disarray, and has bigger problems than you right now."

On that note, he grabbed Zane's arm with one hand, his Mastery Charm with the other, and they vanished from the Trout estate between one blink and the next. Zane found himself staring at his home away from home, the school where he spent most of the last four years. Until now, he had been wondering whether he'd ever see the place again.

They passed a few students on the front lawns, but not many, and even fewer once they entered the pentagonal foyer and made their way towards the eastern staircase—which led to the Wands classroom, among other things.

Zane frowned and said, "There don't seem to be a lot of people here…" to no one in particular.

Master Reede matched his expression and said, "Can you blame them? I *tried* telling the High Mayor that people weren't going to want to send their children to a place that might be attacked by the Dark Prism at a whim, but he wants his revenue." He scowled. "Attendance is barely half of the norm, and meanwhile we Masters have to spend our time teaching instead of dedicating ourselves solely to neutralizing the threat of the Dark Prism."

Zane wasn't used to hearing his mentor complain to him. It made him feel like a confidant…or an equal. It was a pleasant change of pace for him.

The place they were walking towards did indeed turn out to be the classroom where Wands was taught.

Zane was a little surprised to see Masters Willow, Asher, and Laurren already waiting for them, in addition to Magdalene Trout, Laris, another Council member Zane didn't know by name, and—most surprisingly—Tess.

"Tess!" Zane hurried towards her, looking her over and noting that she didn't appear any worse for wear. "Are you alright? How did you get out of the Binders and make it here?"

"Oh good, I was hoping you'd be here too," Tess greeted him warmly. Up close, he could see that she looked tired, but otherwise well. "Master Asher came and got me this morning. For some reason my guards abandoned their post late last night and no one really objected when he broke my Binders and said he was taking me away."

Zane raised an eyebrow at the Prism Master, impressed that he had thought to go collect Tess amid whatever other chaos had been going on all night. It was surprisingly thoughtful, and what Hayden would have wanted him to do.

"Are we all here?" Reede interrupted their reunion, glancing around the room.

"We're just waiting on Oliver," Magdalene had barely finished the words when her oldest son walked into the room and shut the door behind him. "*Now* we're all here."

"Where are the other Masters and Council members?" Tess asked before Zane could decide whether or not to raise the question himself.

"The other Masters are helping restore order after the events of last night," Mrs. Trout explained calmly. "Most of my fellow Council members are dead. The exceptions stand before you."

Zane felt his mouth drop open stupidly and hang there, but he made no effort to close it. Oliver blinked twice and raised his eyebrows fractionally, but otherwise gave no obvious reaction to this insane announcement.

"Uh...come again?" Zane forced his mouth shut, looking around at the others in the vague hope that it was just a really bad joke, only no one else was laughing.

"There was an attack on the Crystal Tower in the early hours of the morning," she explained more fully. "The alarms were activated, and each of the Council members responded as we were trained to—"

"Except for us," Laris interrupted softly, looking strangely diminished and rattled, no longer full of the arrogance Zane had seen from him on the eve of Hayden's abduction.

Magdalene pursed her lips at the interruption but agreed. "Yes, except for us. I thought that Aleric might be involved, and rounded up Laris and Wren before they left their homes. Together we began calling on others throughout the Nine Lands—some of you were included in that, and we went as a group to investigate the attack on the Tower. Unfortunately, by then it was too late."

Zane frowned and said, "What do you mean it was too late? What happened?" Worry was rapidly inflating inside of him like a balloon, but he didn't allow it to show on his face or in his tone just yet.

"It was a massacre," Laurren intoned solemnly, meeting Zane's gaze with those strange, purple-blue eyes that always gave him the creeps. There was something other-worldly about the man, which must have made him a good match for the subject he taught.

"So Hayden's father was there?" Tess asked softly, her face absolutely expressionless. Zane couldn't imagine what she was thinking right now, but she had to be wondering about Hayden even though she hadn't asked the question yet.

"He was there and gone by the time we arrived in force," Asher confirmed. "He left a trail of bodies in his wake—the night shift, and anyone who was unwise enough to show up on their own to investigate the alarms."

Zane shuddered inwardly at the image this invoked, bodies strewn about and bleeding on every level of the Crystal Tower. He hadn't really been in the place long enough to look around, so he had no idea if what he was imagining was even remotely accurate, but it was an image that wouldn't leave his head.

"And Calahan?" Oliver piped up from his position near the door, looking to his mother.

"Dead as well," she answered flatly, looking neither sorry nor relieved by the fact.

"Who's running the Council of Mages then?"

"I am," Magdalene said without hesitation. To Zane's surprise, neither of her colleagues argued the point. Oliver nodded as though expecting this and fell silent once more.

"Did anyone survive the attack that can confirm what happened?" Willow asked. He had apparently not been part of the initial investigation, or he would have already known the answer to his question.

Reede shook his head and said, "Not that we could find—and we did a fairly exhaustive search."

"It was Aleric. I know his magic," Asher spoke up, leaning against the wall as though propping it up.

A long moment of silence passed during which everyone just looked at each other, until Zane couldn't take it anymore.

"No one has said his name yet, which doesn't seem like a good sign," Zane spoke up loudly, "but I'll go ahead and ask the question. What about Hayden? Did you...did you find him dead too?"

Tess blinked and tensed slightly, which Zane only noticed because he was standing directly beside her. His own palms felt suddenly cold and sweaty.

"No, we did not," Asher said heavily. "He is currently the only thing unaccounted for in the Crystal Tower, and likely the reason for his father's visit."

Zane wasn't sure whether he felt better or worse upon hearing that. He was thrilled that Hayden wasn't dead—or probably wasn't, at least—but if the Dark Prism had him alone and unarmed, Hayden wasn't going to last for long.

"And you're certain you don't know why your old friend wanted to collect his son?" Laris looked pointedly at Asher when he asked the question, a bit of his old arrogance coming back to him.

"That's always been the question, hasn't it?" Asher answered seriously, which was surprising because Zane had expected him to be sarcastic.

"I still say he wants an ally and is planning to train Hayden on broken prisms as well."

Zane opened his mouth to interject but Asher beat him to it by saying, "Aleric has never needed allies before, and he feels no paternal affection towards Hayden."

"We don't even know that Hayden is still alive," Magdalene pointed out casually. "We did find blood in the room, and I doubt it came from Aleric."

Tess gasped, but Laurren shook his head and said, "Not enough blood to account for a corpse—unless it was a head wound. Besides, if he simply wanted to kill Hayden, why take his body away afterwards? No, he must be alive…for the moment, at least."

Zane didn't feel quite as confident as the Master of Abnormal Magic after hearing that there was blood in the room where Hayden was being kept, but he tried to keep a positive outlook.

He can't be hurt that badly…Laurren's right, the Dark Prism would never drag away a corpse.

"So if he's got Hayden, then where are they now?" Tess asked delicately, like she wasn't sure that she actually wanted to know the answer.

Asher shrugged and said, "My guess is the Frost estate. It's where he set up last time and he's bound to still have weapons and notes hidden away somewhere."

"I don't suppose we can just walk in and knock on the door?" Zane offered, sure that it was a dumb idea or someone else would have already suggested it.

"Not likely," Willow sighed. "In the past weeks we've already sent out scouting parties to see what the defenses look like. Whatever magic he has guarding the place must have come from his corrupt prism, because we've never seen anything like it. No one is getting into that house without being invited by its owner."

For a moment Zane was tempted to point out that Hayden was its legal owner, in which case they shouldn't have a problem getting an invitation, but he didn't think the humor would be appreciated right now.

Magdalene changed the subject by saying, "Down to what we can control...I'm in need of some new Council members. The government must continue to function, and the people must be protected to the best of our abilities. I've made several nominations already from around the Nine Lands, and I intend the last one to go to Kirius Sark."

A few eyebrows raised at the announcement. Zane was just amazed that the woman was able to worry about practical things like a working government after most of her colleagues were brutally murdered mere hours ago.

"A logical choice, and I'm sure he'll be pleased by the nomination," Willow said neutrally. "It leaves a hole in our staffing, but it shouldn't be too difficult to find a replacement."

"Actually, it shouldn't be difficult at all," Master Reede interjected, turning to Oliver. "Are you ready to step up and shoulder some responsibility?"

Oliver's lips parted in surprise and he said, "You want *me* to take over as Master of Powders?"

"Why not? You *are* a Powders major, and Kirius's most valued apprentice. This is why we have understudies in the first place, to groom the next generation of leaders."

Magdalene looked as though this wasn't part of her mental calculations.

"You can't take Oliver for the school; he's the heir to a Great House and has responsibilities that supersede—"

"We can select whoever we want to replace Kirius," Reede cut her off unrepentantly. "The Council has no voice in the selection of Masters."

"Besides," Asher interjected pleasantly, when it looked like Magdalene was getting ready to object, "He is only the *heir* to a Great House, not its ruling member. If you die, we promise to release him from his duties here if he requests it, otherwise Lorn can wear the mantle in Oliver's place."

She glowered at the group of them but could obviously brook no further argument. Zane was impressed that the Masters had obviously considered the possibility of Sark being taken by the Council and had this replacement planned out in advance. Oliver didn't look at his mother as he said, "If you're all sure about the nomination, then I accept."

"Good, now that that's settled…"

"Nothing has been settled yet," Tess interrupted Master Laurren, looking livid. "No one has said a thing about Hayden! Who cares who teaches Powders or takes orders from Mrs. Trout? What's the plan to get Hayden away from his father before something horrible happens to him?"

The room fell silent, probably because everyone was equally stunned at the typically soft-spoken Tess getting truly angry. It was like encountering a unicorn during a camping trip: it's theoretically possible, but you never really expect it to happen.

"We've just said we can't attack the Frost manor without all of us dying horrible deaths," Laris pointed out at last, annoyed with the interruption. "We might as well hurl ourselves off the cliffs behind Mizzenwald if that's all we're trying to accomplish."

"So that's it?" she countered hotly. "The scouts we've sent said it's too hard so we're just going to give up on Hayden and hope he finds a way to kill his father single-handed and escape the house?" When no one commented immediately she said, "You're all pathetic. Hayden worked his tail off doing everything you people asked of him to prepare himself to fight his father, and you all swore you'd be there to help, right up until things got hard and now you're just willing to write him off as a casualty and move on."

"No one's writing Hayden off for dead," Willow interrupted gently, before she could begin shouting at them, which she seemed very close to doing. "We're still working on a plan for extracting Hayden and defeating Aleric, but it is going to take time for us to unravel all the defensive magic around the place or we'll be throwing our lives away to no purpose. One failed attempt will set us back enormously, because he will fortify his defenses even further if he sees us break through any of them."

Tess calmed down and folded her arms across her chest, still glaring daggers at Laris.

"So until we can figure out everything guarding the estate, there's nothing we can do at all? There has to be some way to get to him—to send word to him that we're not abandoning him, if nothing else," she said a little desperately.

"Believe me," Magdalene began, "if there was any way for us—"

"Oh, I think there is a way to get Hayden some help on the inside," Master Asher interrupted, looking suddenly cheerful.

"What?" several of the others blurted out in unison, turning to face him. "Have you finally lost your marbles? No one can get inside that house or this would be much simpler!"

Still smiling and looking out the window, Asher said, "Oh, yes, I believe there *is* someone who can get in."

Zane moved a little to the side so that he could see what Asher was looking at, and then he too felt a smile tug at his face.

There may yet be hope.

12
The Lost Memory

Hayden groaned weakly as he returned to consciousness, shifting uncomfortably on the hard floor. At first he wasn't alarmed, because it felt like the same unyielding floor he'd been sleeping on for weeks in the Crystal Tower, though he wasn't sure where his pillow had gone. It wasn't until he blinked open his eyes and focused his vision that he felt a spike of adrenaline surge through him and lurched upright.

"Whoa, take it easy…" a girl he didn't know—maybe nineteen or twenty years old—was standing nearby, holding out her hands in a placating gesture. He noticed that upon sitting up, he had dislodged a blanket that had been draped over him, by her, presumably.

Now that he took in his surroundings, it became immediately apparent that he was no longer inside the Crystal Tower, though he wasn't entirely sure when he'd left or why he was lying on this disturbingly-familiar marble floor…

"Who are you, and why are we in a place that looks hauntingly similar to my family's estate?" he asked out loud, hoping upon wild hope that this stranger was about to tell him he was in a stunning replica of the Frost estate, which was actually a museum of some sort...

"I'm Harriet—Hattie, and you're, um, in the Frost family home..." she said in a lowered voice, eyes darting occasionally to the stairwell behind him as though expecting to see something horrible come down it at any moment.

Still not sure how he came to be here, Hayden reached up and touched the side of his head reflexively, hoping to conjure up the memory. There was something dry and flaky stuck to the side of his head and face, and he scraped a few fragments off with one fingernail, studying the brown-red flakes with interest.

"What is this stuff?"

"That's...that's your blood, sir. You were still bleeding a lot when he brought you here," she explained, still on edge. Hayden was afraid to make any sudden movements for fear that she might sprint away and leave him with no one to answer his questions.

"My *blood?* When was I bleeding from the head?"

It hit him even as he asked the question: the sound of alarms echoing through his cell in the Tower, his father trailing bloody footprints behind him as he entered the room, hearing that Calahan and however-many others were dead, having his head slammed against the wall over and over...

"Did he really bash my head against the wall until I passed out, without so much as a warning beforehand?" he asked himself out loud. "It's a miracle I'm still alive, let alone coherent..."

He shuddered at the casual brutality that his father was comfortable using on him, realizing that he had never encountered anyone so terrifyingly whimsical with their cruelty. It made his father frightening on a whole different level than he was accustomed to.

"I think he healed you once he brought you back here…" Hattie supplied helpfully, still nervously glancing towards the stairs. *My father must be up there somewhere, or else she just hates stairs.* "He carried you in and dumped you on the floor there, but then he did something with his prism and all the bleeding stopped. I wasn't sure what else to do, and he didn't leave instructions, so I put a blanket over you so you wouldn't get cold…"

Well, my father plainly cares nothing for me, but for some reason he wants me alive…

"Do you work here or something?" for the first time, Hayden registered the uniform of a housekeeper, and only because he had become accustomed to seeing them around the Trout estate.

Hattie frowned and looked down at her garb.

"Yes, me and about ten others; well, nine, ever since Jack tried to escape." She grimaced at some memory that Hayden could only guess at.

"Please don't tell me that you actually volunteered to work for the Dark Prism," he raised an eyebrow, suddenly wary of whether this was an ally or an enemy he was speaking to.

Hattie scowled and said, "Of course not; none of us did. He just showed up in town and grabbed a bunch of us one day. He said he needed servants to run his estate while he did his work." She frowned again. "He told us that there were defensive spells to keep people from crossing through the gates, but Jack tried anyway a few days ago. It was...horrible." She shuddered and grabbed her arms as though trying to warm herself.

"He died?" Hayden winced in sympathy when she nodded.

Well, so much for just walking out of here and calling the man's bluff...

"I'm a little surprised that he has so many people here," Hayden changed the subject. "I mean, I guess he needs to eat, so I understand a cook or two...but ten people? For living here by himself, that's almost a full crew."

Hattie nodded and said, "He's *very* serious about maintaining protocol, even though it's just him and you'd think he has more important things to worry about than whether the table is set properly for a formal dinner every night." She shrugged, relaxing as she grew more comfortable talking to him. "But everything has to be *just so*, and in line with how a Great House should run, or he gets furious and...bad things happen."

Hayden raised an eyebrow at that. It seemed an odd thing for his father to focus on, especially since he wasn't exactly entertaining friends and business partners, but reflecting on all the stories Asher had told him about Aleric's father and what a stickler for rules he was...maybe it made sense.

I wonder if that helps keep him from going totally insane, Hayden considered thoughtfully. *Keeping some of the fundamentals from his life before he became the Dark Prism must act as an anchor of sorts.*

He filed away that piece of information, along with every other scrap of knowledge he had been amassing about his father, in the hope that understanding him better would help him win the fight against him. He was suddenly thankful for all the time he'd spent at the Trout estate, having etiquette beaten into him by Magdalene.

I'd rather be lightly slapped by her than beaten to a pulp from my father for accidentally using the bread knife instead of the cheese knife.

Finally, Hayden forced himself to his feet.

"Well, I suppose I should go find him and see if he'll tell me anything useful, since apparently he doesn't want me dead just yet." He said this much more calmly than he felt for Hattie's benefit. "Is he upstairs?"

She nodded and then asked, "Are you going to fight against him and set us free?" very softly, not meeting his eyes. "The others—we were wondering...all that stuff we've heard about you these last few years, the medals you got for bravery and heroism and everything..."

Hayden felt an unpleasant tightening sensation in his chest at the thought of all these people counting on him and the knowledge that he was woefully overmatched and weaponless at present.

"Well, I certainly intend to try my best," he answered truthfully. "I've been training with some of the best mages in the Nine Lands to prepare me to fight him, but of course I can't promise I'll win."

Hattie nodded slowly, though she looked heartened.

"We all believe in you, and if there's anything we can do to help…even if it gets us in trouble or—or worse…" she trailed off, frightened but determined.

That's all I need, the deaths of ordinary people who shouldn't be involved in this at all on my hands…

"Thanks, I'll keep it in mind," was what he said out loud, though he privately decided that he wouldn't be asking anyone else to risk themselves unless he thought it was the only way to defeat his father once and for all.

Not sure whether he should report to his father immediately or get cleaned up first, he decided to err on the side of caution and check in before trying to do anything else. Trying not to let his fear rule him, he began walking up the stairs along the back wall of the foyer, winding gradually around to the upper level.

It wasn't supposed to be like this, he told himself for the second time as he walked. *All of that time and training, it was all so that I'd have a belt-full of prisms, wands, and anything else my heart desired, and about a dozen more skillful mages alongside me. It was never supposed to me alone and unarmed…*

Well, so much for well-laid plans.

From the sound of things, it didn't seem possible for anyone to escape the grounds without dying a horrible death, which probably also meant that no uninvited guests would be getting in either. Hayden was locked in a mansion with his super-powerful, mostly-psychotic father and ten—nine—unlucky victims who had been abducted from their homes to make sure the fires stayed lit.

He rounded the top of the stairwell and continued down the main hallway more slowly, peeking into every room he passed to see if the Dark Prism was inside. He wasn't sure what he'd do if the man was in the bathroom....Wait outside the door? Knock and announce himself? Leave and pretend to still be unconscious and come back later?

Fortunately, when he finally found his father, it was nowhere near a restroom. In fact, the man was in a large library-turned-workshop at the very end of the hall. The room was by far the largest on the floor—possibly in the entire house, with shelves of books that ran from about halfway through the room all the way to the back wall, lining three sides of the space, with free-standing bookshelves in between. The part of the room closest to the door was open floor space, and while Hayden suspected chairs and tables used to be set up here in the past, currently there was only a row of four tables put end-to-end. There were no chairs in the room at all, except for a pair of armchairs near the fireplace on the far end, and Aleric Frost stood in front of the worktables on the opposite side with his back to Hayden, making notes on a diagram of something Hayden couldn't see properly from where he was standing. The rest of the table space was filled with neat rows of prisms and organized stacks of notes and drawings.

Shame that none of my father's organizational skills rubbed off on Asher while they were friends. The Prism Master's office was regarded by most right-thinking human beings as a paper-filled fire hazard.

Taking a breath to calm himself, he raised a hand to knock on the open door to announce his presence, but his father said, "I wondered when you would awaken," without turning to look at him.

Frowning slightly, Hayden said, "How did you know I was behind you?"

"Blood calls to blood, especially at this proximity. Given sufficient time and energy, I could find you anywhere," he answered simply, still filling in an alignment with colored pencils without looking up.

"I'm not sure what that means," Hayden admitted, wondering how far he could push his luck before the man stopped answering his questions and knocked him unconscious again. "I don't feel your presence at all."

His father set down his red colored pencil and turned to face him at last. Hayden felt a lurch of fear when he saw the circlet on the man's head, the Black Prism currently tilted upwards so that it faced the ceiling. Of all the things his father couldn't remember, he had hoped that the location of the Black Prism was one of them...

Otherwise he looked much the same as when Hayden had met him inside the schism. The clothing was different, of course; he'd traded the leathers and animal hides from the schism for well-tailored slacks and a high-collared shirt that seemed less formal than his House robes but more formal than normal daywear. He was still muscular and handsome and didn't look the least bit insane or fatigued—actually, he looked more well-rested than Hayden had felt for months.

"I have a much more powerful connection with magic than you do," he answered Hayden's question at last, sounding completely matter-of-fact. It was strange hearing him sound so emotionless; Hunter had been much more animated.

Hayden didn't point out that a lot of his father's vaunted connections to the world had been grounded in corrupted magic and distortion, since it was something they both knew and he obviously was still reaping plenty of benefits from it. It didn't seem fair that there could be so many rewards for someone who used forbidden magic, like a sort of cosmic joke that punished the good and lauded the wicked.

No wonder he was tempted by broken prisms. He has powers that no other mage will ever have.

Hayden pushed that unproductive thought aside and said, "I wasn't sure whether to get cleaned up or come and see you first."

Without changing expression, his father asked, "Why would you think I needed to see you?"

Thrown by the question, Hayden said, "Uh, I don't know...I assumed there was a reason you brought me here, so it logically follows that you might want to speak to me now that I'm conscious."

"I didn't bring you here because I lack company and good conversation," the withering look he graced Hayden with let him know that his father thought he was a complete idiot.

"Since we're on the subject…" Hayden began hopefully, "why *did* you bring me here?"

"Don't ask questions you already know the answer to; I have no patience for it."

Hayden flinched at the tone of warning, remembering how much it hurt to have his brains bashed out…yesterday? The day before? He wasn't sure how long he had been unconscious in the foyer, just that it was now sometime during the day and he'd been knocked out sometime at night.

"I'm not," he explained. "I assume it's for the same reason you came after me when I was ten, but I don't remember much about that day and I never knew what you wanted with me back then."

For the first time, his father betrayed a microscopic amount of emotion, his surprise registering as nothing more than a momentary lift of the eyebrows.

"Is that so?" he asked with an almost academic sort of interest.

"Yes, and it's been driving me crazy for years." Upon reflection, that maybe wasn't the best choice of words, given the audience, but his father didn't seem bothered by it. "Whatever you did that blew up the house, it left me with a massive case of light-sickness and warped my Foci in some legendary way." He held up his wrists so that his Focus-correctors were visible for emphasis. "I've tried everything I can think of to get those memories back, but I still only have fragments."

The Dark Prism took a few measured steps towards him, and it was everything Hayden could do to keep himself rooted to the spot and not run away screaming. There was something inherently terrifying about Aleric Frost, something that Hunter had lacked.

His father took one of his hands and examined it as though looking for defects, before dropping it carelessly so that it fell back at Hayden's side.

"Why are you so eager to retrieve that memory?" he asked with mild curiosity.

"Are you kidding?" Hayden asked incredulously. "My entire life changed that day. You have no idea how frustrating it is not to be able to remember something so significant."

"Don't I?" he asked delicately, and again Hayden could have kicked himself for his choice of words. If there was anyone who understood giant, gaping holes in one's memory, it would be the man standing in front of him.

"Oh, sorry..."

"By all means," his father ignored his awkwardness entirely, "let me alleviate this particular concern of yours. It will make things less tedious in the weeks ahead."

For a moment Hayden thought the man was simply going to explain what had happened that day, but then he saw his father lower the Black Prism in front of his eye and twist it rapidly in search of an alignment.

Not sure what would happen if the Black Prism was used on him, but certain that he didn't want to find out, Hayden said, "Oh no, that's fine, you could maybe just tell me—"

Then his father found the right alignment, and Hayden watched the world shrink away from him as he was flung back into the recesses of his own mind. It felt like his eyes had rolled over backwards and he was staring into the depths of his memory, his new surroundings springing up out of the blackness.

Suddenly he was ten years old again, hiding behind the door to his bedroom in his mother's house. All of the things he had forgotten came rushing back to him: the sights and sounds, even the smell of bread baking in the kitchen....How had he ever forgotten that? He heard his mother's voice from somewhere in front of him, and he leaned closer to the door to listen.

"You!" she cried out in surprise, and Hayden heard the sound of a dish breaking against the floor. Risking a peek into the kitchen, he could see the shards of the yellow ceramic plate scattered across the floor.

"What—what do you want from me?" his mother's voice shook horribly this time. She looked like she was staring at a ghost, or a seven-headed hydra, but there was no one except for a handsome, youngish man standing in the kitchen. He had a strange circle of metal around his head, partially hidden by his hair, and a clear diamond glittered in an eyepiece on top of it, pointed towards the ceiling.

"You know why I am here," the man answered evenly, almost lazily. "I have come for the boy."

"I don't know what you're talking about," his mother lied terribly; she had always been bad at it. "There's no one here but me."

Is he talking about me? Hayden wondered in surprise. *But I've never seen that man before in my life. I would definitely remember someone with a giant diamond on their head...*

"He is in the house; I feel his presence. Call him here," the man replied calmly, as though there hadn't been anything unusual about his request.

"No, please. He's just a boy—he doesn't know anything about magic, or about you. Please, just leave us be..."

Magic? Hayden thought in alarm just as a loud slap caused him to jump. His jaw tensed in anger as he watched his mother's body hit the floor, reeling from the unexpected slap. Hayden was beginning to form a much more sinister guess of who this stranger was, because come to think of it, the man nicknamed the Dark Prism was supposed to have a black diamond of some kind, even though this one looked clear. But legendary villains didn't just show up in one's kitchen for no good reason...

"I will go when I have seen the boy. Bring him here or don't, but I will not leave without him."

Unable to stand being hidden any longer, Hayden darted out from behind the doorframe and ran into the kitchen. He pulled a knife off of the kitchen counter as he passed by, wielding it with shaking hands. It was still wet with pear juice, and smelled vaguely of the fruit his mother had recently been slicing with it.

"You leave us alone or I'll hurt you!" he shouted, though his voice pitched high with fear as he faced down this unknown foe.

A moment of silence and then, "Do you know who I am, boy?" The man didn't sound condescending when he asked it, merely curious, and suddenly Hayden knew who he was, though he wasn't sure how.

"You're the one everyone talks about..." he ventured carefully, "the one who wears the evil diamond on his head."

He spared a brief glance at the supposedly Black Prism, though it still looked perfectly normal to him, despite being the largest diamond he had ever seen in his entire life.

"Correct in essentials," Aleric Frost conceded mildly. "Do you really believe that you can hurt me with that knife?"

Ten-year old Hayden's hands gripped the hilt tighter. "I don't know, but I'm not going to let you hit my mom again."

"I do not discount the courage it takes to face me like this, knowing you cannot win. Many full-trained mages have not managed it as bravely as you, though you are obviously very frightened." He still sounded cool and almost bored, though the compliment seemed sincere. "Now put that toy down and come here. There is something I need to know about you."

Hayden stood frozen in place, unsure of what to do. Here he was, threatening this guy with a knife, and the man didn't look the least bit worried. If this was really the Dark Prism guy that everyone talked about, then he'd killed tons of people, and was probably perfectly capable of killing him too. And what did he even want with a ten-year old nobody in the first place? Hayden's mom had acted like she knew him when he came into the kitchen, or at least recognized him…

"What do you need to know about me?" he asked without lowering the knife, trying to buy himself time to think. There had to be some way for him to get his mom and run—maybe they could hide until he gave up and left them alone…

"I need to examine your Source."

This meant absolutely nothing to Hayden, but before he could ask the man to explain properly, his mother lurched up from the floor and said, "Hayden, stay away from him! Run and hide!"

"You cannot hide from me, boy; from others, perhaps, but never from me." The way he said it made Hayden absolutely certain it was true. It also gave him goose-bumps because it was such an eerie thing to say.

Hayden's mom tried to push him behind her, but the Dark Prism lowered his eyepiece so that the large diamond was directly in front of one eye. He adjusted it slightly, the monocle making a soft clicking sound as it rotated in place, and then he aimed it at Hayden's mother. Without warning, she screamed as though in terrible pain and fell back to the floor, writhing in agony long after the screaming ended.

Stunned, Hayden looked from his mother to the man who had somehow hurt her without even laying a hand her.

It's that diamond of his…it's magic, and evil.

"Now come here and let me examine your Source, or I will kill her while you watch."

Put like that, there was nothing Hayden could do but obey. He didn't think this man would hesitate to murder his mother, and that was something that Hayden couldn't live with. Silently, he lowered the paring knife and stepped closer.

The Dark Prism withdrew something from his pocket—two long, glass needles. For a moment Hayden worried that he was going to be skewered by them, but he relaxed when the man settled for touching one to his chest and the other to his forehead.

"What are you doing?" Hayden asked cautiously while the man stared at the needles through his Black Prism. His muscles tensed, preparing to be thrown to the ground like his mother, who was still twisting around in pain on the kitchen floor.

"Gauging your Source strength and compatibility," the Dark Prism answered flatly.

This still made virtually no sense to Hayden, but it was clearly the only explanation he was going to get. His captor spent a full minute staring at the needles through his diamond before he seemed satisfied, tucking them carefully back into his pocket.

He met Hayden's eyes briefly and then nodded.

"This will work," he said, seemingly to himself. He twisted the diamond slowly around into a new position. Hayden didn't know what the man was looking for, but he lost his courage and took a step backwards, stumbling over his mother and falling onto his butt on the kitchen floor.

She was still in pain, sobbing quietly but apparently determined not to give the man the satisfaction of seeing her scream and beg. She did mouth, *Run!* to Hayden over and over again, but his legs felt like lead, and it was all he could do just to scoot backwards until he was nearly to the door that led to the living room.

The Dark Prism stepped over his mother's twitching body and approached casually, dropping to a crouch when he caught up to Hayden so that they were at eye-level with each other.

"It is important that you hold still for this," he informed Hayden casually, as though there would be serious consequences if he didn't obey.

"What are you doing?"

"Removing your Source," the man explained calmly. Hayden didn't know what a Source was or why this guy wanted his so badly, but he'd do anything to get free of him at this point.

"Will it hurt?" he asked softly, voice quavering with fear.

"Terribly, I expect," the Dark Prism confirmed without emotion.

Hayden swallowed hard and then asked, "When you're done…will you leave my mom and I alone?"

One side of the man's mouth quirked upwards momentarily, as though faintly amused, and then he became expressionless once more.

"Yes, when I have finished with you, I will leave."

Steeling himself for the promised pain, Hayden asked, "What do I have to do?"

"Hold out your hands like this," the Dark Prism instructed, holding his own palm-out to demonstrate.

Hayden did as he was told, still sitting awkwardly on the floor, and the man pressed his own hands against Hayden's and interlocked their fingers so that their palms were touching. Hayden had no idea why they needed to hold hands, but maybe it was just to keep him from moving too much...

The Dark Prism stared at him through the diamond on his head, and from this close up Hayden could see little streaks of color in it from the light in the room. For some reason it made his head hurt, even though he'd seen the sun cast different colors through glass before and it had never bothered him.

Before he could think too much about it, the most hideous pain he had ever felt slammed into him like a wall of bricks. It felt like his entire body was burning up from the inside out, and he screamed as the pain exploded in his chest and shot down both arms. He was still screaming when the feeling changed from burning to tugging, as though something thick like molasses was being dragged from every part of his body and pulled into his protesting arms, which cramped terribly as the sensation moved from his shoulders down to his elbows and towards his wrists.

He could hear himself screaming, and his mother now as well, though both sounds seemed dim and faraway to his ears. It felt like his very heart was being ripped out of his chest, and he wanted to beg for it to stop—for the Dark Prism to just rip whatever he was pulling on out of his hands as fast as possible to make it all end—only he couldn't stop screaming long enough to form words.

The tugging sensation was all the way down to his wrists...to his hands...it was going to come out soon...

*Please hurry up...*Hayden prayed, staring into the pointy end of the diamond that was hovering over him. *Please just let it end...*

Inexplicably, something recoiled inside of his hands and the tugging sensation stopped quite abruptly. For a moment it felt like a rubber band that had been stretched as taut as it would go had been released and snapped back to its original form, and then instead of something being pulled out of his body, it felt like something was being dumped back in.

The thick, fluid feeling in his arms shot back into his body and seemed to flood him, and at an alarmed sound from the Dark Prism, Hayden looked into the eye that was uncovered and saw fear. The man tried releasing Hayden's hands and pulling away, but Hayden couldn't unclench his fingers as pain continued to shoot through him like knives, and then the burning sensation was back, this time moving in reverse. He had shouted himself hoarse but was still screaming silently, fingers locked tightly around the Dark Prism's as something bright and fluid surged through his hands and up his arms, streaming into him until he felt like he was overfilling and drowning inside himself. The burning sensation in his hands was agonizing and getting worse, and then all Hayden could see were explosions of light in front of his eyes, thousands and thousands of them flashing across his vision. It felt like his head was going to explode, like his brain was overheating and couldn't process anymore, and then everything went white and the last sound he heard was his mother's scream…

Hayden had no idea why he was lying on the floor in the library, but he lurched upright and leaned over a nearby potted plant, vomiting horribly. He could still feel the ghost of the light-sickness he'd just remembered, and his Foci tingled unpleasantly in an echo of the pain he'd endured back then. When he'd emptied every corner of his stomach into the poor potted plant, he blinked tears out of his eyes and stared down at his trembling hands to make sure that his Focus-correctors were still in place. The sight of the intact three-inch correctors was the most welcome sight in the world right now.

His entire body shaking horribly, Hayden stared up at his father—who was standing idly nearby, watching him suffer without emotion—and said, "You…you were trying to *take my Source?*" he now knew enough about magic to understand what that meant. The Source was the spark that was essential to life, that all living things possessed even if they lacked the Foci to channel magic with it. "You would have killed me."

Aleric Frost looked absolutely impassive when he said, "Obviously."

"You lied to a ten year old who knew nothing about magic," Hayden blurted out indignantly. "You told me you'd leave us alone once you had what you wanted."

"And so I would have," his father answered easily.

"You neglected to mention that you were trying to rip the very life from my body."

"That would not have made you any more cooperative."

Hayden still felt shaky and unsettled. He wasn't sure whether he felt better or worse for finally knowing what his father wanted from him all those years ago. He had deluded himself into thinking that maybe he had been seeking an ally, and even though Hayden would never have agreed to it, at least it would have made him feel somewhat valued by his own father...

"Why in the world were you trying to remove my Source?" Hayden suppressed a shudder at how close his father had come to succeeding. He knew what the heavy, liquid sensation being pulled through his Foci was now. It had gotten all the way to his hands before he'd somehow pulled it back inside of him.

The Dark Prism looked like he wasn't at all impressed with Hayden's inability to extrapolate, though Hayden was still reeling from what he had just learned and wasn't thinking very clearly at the moment.

"I intended to add it to my own to compound my power."

The simplicity of it made it no less breathtaking. Hayden stared up at his father for a long moment as he digested this.

"You found a way to remove my Source and add it to your own?" A normal prism would never have been capable of such a feat; why did broken prisms seem to have stupidly powerful alignments? Or was it just the Black Prism?

"I believed so at the time, though it obviously needs fine-tuning since you were able to break the spell by willpower alone," his father admitted.

"But why me? Of all people in the world you were planning to kill, why did you track me down specifically?"

"We are related by blood, which makes us similar in some ways. I believed—still believe—that it will be easier to merge with a Source that is more compatible with mine than a stranger's."

All this time, his only interest in me as a son was the fact that he could loot me for parts to make his own magic more powerful.

"There really isn't a scrap of human decency inside of you anymore, is there?" Hayden asked quietly. "I can't believe anyone ever thought you had been healed during your time in the schism and were one of the good guys now. Laris even wanted to approach you for a partnership…"

Aleric raised his eyebrows and asked, "Who?" with faint interest.

"Laris—he's on the Council of Mages, assuming you didn't kill him." He frowned at the thought, little though he liked Laris. "We kept getting reports that you were traveling the Nine Lands, healing people's warped Foci so they could do magic again, and he thought you'd gone humanitarian. He wanted to approach you openly and ask you to share some of your magical knowledge with the Council for the good of mage-kind, even though Asher insisted that whatever game you were playing, it wasn't for the good of mage-kind."

His father looked vaguely amused as he said, "They should have listened to my old friend. He may be a traitor, but he was never stupid."

Normally Hayden would argue that Asher wasn't the one who turned traitor, but he had other things on his mind right now and let it pass without comment.

"All of those people you helped—" he gasped and slapped a hand to his forehead as understanding washed over him. "You were healing their Foci to make sure it was possible. You were experimenting on them because of me…"

Making no attempt to deny this, Aleric tilted his head fractionally and said, "When I learned that you required heavy correction due to the damages you incurred during our first meeting, I knew that your Foci would need to be straightened before I tried again. I needed to be sure I had the right sequence of alignments before I attempted such a spell on you—I have never before had occasion to attempt to repair damaged conduits, and one misstep could have killed you at the outset. Better to practice on less valuable targets."

"You're still determined to pull my Source out, even after your disastrous last attempt?" Hayden had to admit, the man had nerve. He had been nearly blown up, thrown into a schism and forced to spend the last five years living inside the other realm without remembering anything about who he really was, and yet he was ready to give it another go as soon as he came back.

For a moment he worried that his father would strike him for questioning him like this, but the feeling passed when it became obvious that his father had his mind engaged elsewhere up until now. He finally turned his entire focus to Hayden—not necessarily a good thing—and seemed to size him up.

"While I do intend to extract your Source and merge it with my own, my more immediate concern is with regaining what you have taken from me."

Confused, and suddenly feeling like he was in terrible danger, Hayden cautiously asked, "What did *I* take from *you?*"

"Have you always been this unintelligent?" his father asked softly, though still in that dangerous tone of voice. "When the link was opened between us, you managed to siphon off a sizeable portion of my own Source before I was able to break contact with you." As the full implications of this hit Hayden for the first time, he added, "Did you honestly think you came by your power naturally? No one should be able to channel magic through such heavy Focus-correction under normal circumstances."

*Holy arcana...*Hayden thought numbly. *His spell backfired on him that day. I ended up with part of his Source added onto my own—that's why I have such a ridiculous amount of Source power, because I've got more than my share to work with.*

It all made perfect sense, and he wondered dimly how it had never occurred to anyone before now to think of it. Then again, he didn't even know it was theoretically possible to remove someone's Source and transfer it to another living host, or that it would merge successfully even then. He doubted that even Asher would have dreamt of such a thing, so maybe it wasn't so surprising that it hadn't occurred to them before now.

"Oh," was all he said in response to this amazing piece of information, because really, what else was there to say?

Now I know why my father wants me alive...he wants his power back.

He had no idea just how much of the man's Source he had siphoned off for himself, but it could only be a good thing that his father no longer had it to work with. That should make his spells weaker, or make him tire faster, shouldn't it? Maybe it was possible to beat him this time around after all...

"Is that what you've been working on since you got back to this realm?" he asked hesitantly.

"Yes."

Trying not to wince, Hayden added, "Are you, um, close to having your spell perfected?"

Without blinking, Aleric said, "I believe so, though I must be certain this time. It will take me a little longer before I am prepared to try again."

Right, so I have a little time to figure out how to destroy him, but not much...

"Um, may I be excused to shower?" He needed some time alone to process this enormous amount of information before his brain exploded, or worse, before he said anything to get him murdered preemptively.

His father waved him away like an irksome fly and turned back to his work without another word to him, as though Hayden had abruptly ceased to exist. Moving as quietly as possible to keep from drawing the man's unwanted attention, he fled the library and put as much distance between them as he could.

13
The Black Prism

Hayden spent such a long time in the shower that under normal circumstances someone probably would have checked up on him to make sure he hadn't drowned. As it was, his father didn't seem to care where he was or what he was doing—or how much hot water he used.

When he finally emerged from the bathroom, skin bright red from the heat, he chose one of the numerous spare bedrooms to claim as his own, trying to decide who might have owned it before him, back when the Frost family was in its heyday. If there were any clues within the room itself, they had long been purged, because there were no pictures on the walls or personal effects of any sort to be found. Mostly he chose the room because it was as far away as it was possible to get from his father's room on the second floor, and also because of the commanding view it had of the grounds, courtesy of the large bay windows. It almost gave the illusion of being free.

He dug through the closet until he found clothing to borrow. Judging by the size and fit, and the fact that the clothes didn't have that dated look that spoke to fashions of an earlier era, he concluded that these must have been his father's old things from his school days. He assumed the man wouldn't mind him borrowing them, since he didn't exactly give Hayden time to pack before abducting him.

Technically I own this house...so does it still count as abduction if I've been brought back to a place I legally own?

It seemed like a weak argument, but he didn't know what else to call it. Sure, under normal circumstances he might be living in this exact same room right now, but he would be free to come and go at will, not being held hostage by a man who was intent on draining the life from him and casting his discarded body aside. He tried to block out the mental image that invoked.

He was startled out of his brooding by a light knock on the door. He turned around with a knot of dread forming in his stomach, expecting his father, but was pleasantly surprised to find Hattie waiting for him.

Of course, my father would never run his own errands.

"It's time for dinner, sir," she informed him, still with that permanently on-edge look in her eyes.

"You can call me Hayden," he explained, hoping to put her at ease. Unfortunately, this only made her tense as though preparing to be slapped. "What?" he asked, wondering what he was missing.

"Sorry, sir, it's just that, if *he* heard me call you by name he might get angry..." Hattie trailed off, looking distinctly uncomfortable.

Oh right, my father's such a Great House snob that he makes Oliver Trout look humble.

Hayden sighed. "Alright then, lead the way."

He followed her down to the formal dining room, the one that was large enough to host large dinner parties of at least forty people, though there were currently only place settings for two. Hayden was unhappy to note that he had been placed at his father's left, which put him in close proximity to the man while eating.

Of course, because seating is done by rank, and the heir would sit on the left-hand side of the Head of House.

His father was already seated, and Hayden moved to take his place at the table, his eyes drawn to the patch of carpet that was slightly newer than the rest, where Asher had once told him he'd vomited and Aleric had taken the blame.

If Hayden had ever sat through a more awkward meal, he couldn't remember when. His father didn't speak a word to him during the entire four-course event, simply moving through each of the dishes with perfect etiquette and occasionally watching Hayden to see how he measured up. Hayden had never been so glad for all of the lessons from the Trouts.

For most of the meal, his father ignored him entirely. In fact, he appeared lost in thought, as though he wasn't even registering the meal in front of him, his gaze growing abstracted. Hayden did nothing to break his concentration, but he did study the man whenever he thought he could get away with it without drawing attention to himself. He wondered what his father was thinking about, or whether his thoughts even flowed in a coherent manner anymore or just appeared as disjointed fragments that he had to sift through. He could barely remember how it had felt inside the schism when he was suffering under the effects of distortion—odd how he could forget such a horrible thing so soon—but he remembered the feeling of losing control and being helpless to stop it.

Hayden ate as fast as he could in the hopes of ending the meal sooner, but in the end it didn't matter, since he couldn't be dismissed until his father finished eating as well. So it was nearly an hour later that Hayden was finally able to ask to be excused, squinting against the light of the setting sun that streamed in through a partially-open curtain.

His father seemed to snap out of his reverie and turned to look at him.

"May I be excused, Father?" Hayden asked politely.

Before he could even draw breath, his father's hand had shot out and clenched around his throat, jerking him out of the chair so that his knees crashed against the floor. Hayden coughed and tried to draw in more breath, but the hand at his throat was squeezing too tightly, and he could feel the blood pounding in his head as pressure built up rapidly.

He met his father's eyes, panicked by the unprovoked attack. There was something dangerous there—the insanity that people had spoken so often of but that Hayden had never really seen behind the veneer of self-control until now. Hayden clawed at the back of the hand that was holding his throat, trying to break his father's grip before he lost consciousness or died. Lights were swimming in front of his eyes and the edge of his vision was growing dark when he was abruptly released, shoved away so hard that his head struck the edge of his chair in passing before hitting the floor.

Dimly, he saw the source of his rescue: Cinder's little clawed feet were standing nearby on the floor, and it was the dragonling that Aleric Frost was now focused on.

Cinder must have warned him off of killing me. I guess it's not in his master's best interest to have done with me until he gets his Source back.

"Never call me that," his father's voice floated down to him from somewhere above, because Hayden was now staring at a patch of carpet as he struggled to catch his breath and massage his sore throat.

Hayden tried to ask what the man was talking about, but all that came out was another violent round of coughing and a few gasps. He tried to think back over what he had said that could have set the man off so abruptly.

All I said was, "May I be excused, Father?"

As breath returned to him, Hayden pushed his chair out of the way and sat up on the floor.

*He doesn't want me to call him 'Father'...*he realized, his brain finally speeding back up now that the imminent fear of death was passing. *He doesn't want to be reminded of the association between us, or maybe he just doesn't think of himself as my father? Maybe the word 'father' means something unpleasant to him...triggers unpleasant memories, maybe?*

From what Hayden had been told about his grandfather's parenting style, that seemed altogether possible.

When he thought he could speak again, Hayden asked, "What should I call you?" hoping that this didn't also set the man off in some way. He was so unpredictable it was hard to know what would trigger him into violence.

His father was staring down at him without apparent emotion, the mask of self-control pulled firmly back over his features once more. It was like nothing had happened at all, as if Hayden had simply flung himself to the ground during dinner and started to asphyxiate.

"If you must address me, 'sir' will suffice."

How very formal and impersonal...

"Then may I be excused from dinner, *sir?*" Hayden tried again, making an effort not to sound sarcastic because it would likely just earn him more punishment in the form of pain.

"Come with me," the Dark Prism instructed, ignoring his question entirely. He stood up and walked back towards the main foyer without offering any further explanation; he didn't even look back to see whether Hayden was actually following or not, simply expecting to be obeyed.

Feeling beleaguered, Hayden followed the Dark Prism back upstairs to the second floor, keeping several paces behind him so that he wasn't within arm's reach. Thoughts whirled around his head so fast that he felt dizzy as they approached the library-turned-workshop.

I have to find a way to kill him while he's still weak. I can't let him take his Source power back from me, or no one will be able to stop him.

That only gave him a finite window of time to work within, and unfortunately Hayden had no idea how close his father was to repairing his Foci and making another attempt on his life. That brought up another interesting thought.

Why hasn't he already straightened my Foci? He seems fairly confident that he's perfected that spell, so why wait…?

Did that mean that his father was afraid of him on some level, despite the total lack of emotion he displayed, or was he just being cautious?

Either way, he knows I'd be exponentially stronger if my Foci weren't warped so badly. If I managed to get my hands on a weapon he wouldn't stand a chance…

It was a shame that his father was still sane enough and crafty enough to recognize him as a threat, or this would be a lot easier. All he would have to do is get his hands on one of the prisms on that worktable…

I still need to get my hands on one of those prisms, if I'm to have any chance at all. I can't do anything against the Black Prism without being armed myself.

Surely his father wasn't ready to rip out his Source tonight—he had said as much just this morning—though maybe he had already forgotten that conversation. For the umpteenth time, Hayden wished he knew how his father's mind worked; it would make it much easier to predict his movements.

But why else would he want me to come to the library with him? Surely he doesn't want my opinion on his work...

He would find out soon enough. They were back in the library, and Aleric was standing in front of his worktable once more, though his eyes were now trained on Hayden.

Cognizant of being watched, Hayden walked slowly past his father and around the other side of the table, stopping in front of a large window and drawing back the curtains so he could watch the sunset.

"You wanted to see me?" he asked after a lengthy moment of silence, turning to face his father and deliberately not touching his sore—and probably bruised—throat. The end of the worktable that was covered in neat rows of mastery-level prisms was between them, no more than a few feet from where Hayden stood, and it took everything inside of him not to lunge at them and attack.

"You're thinking of fighting me in my own house?" his father asked with a note of condescending amusement, like an adult who humors a small child when they want to play some make-believe game.

"Technically, *my* house," Hayden corrected mildly, wondering how the man knew what he was thinking. "And yes, the thought has occurred to me." There didn't really seem to be a point in denying it. The man was evil, not stupid.

"You really believe that you can win against me in open combat?" there was nothing mocking in his tone now, just genuine curiosity.

Hayden frowned and said, "You asked me a very similar question during our first meeting, in my mother's kitchen. I don't suppose you remember?"

The Dark Prism looked momentarily thoughtful, his gaze growing abstracted as he retreated into his mind.

Now, while he's distracted, I should go for the table of prisms...

But before Hayden could do more than tense his muscles in preparation to move, his father's attention was focused on the present once more.

"You threatened me with a knife, acting out of ignorance of the disparities between our abilities."

Hayden was a little surprised that there were some things he could call up at will. He wondered if it only applied to certain pieces of information that he counted as important and could always access, or if his memories just floated around in some empty void, and it was only chance and coincidence when one moved into a place where he could access it. This didn't seem like the time to ask about the inner workings of his mind.

"I'm not a naïve little boy anymore," he explained calmly instead. "I now have a very clear understanding of what you're capable of, and of what *I* am capable of."

"And you still think you can overpower me, just because part of my Source currently resides inside you?" the hint of derision was back in his voice.

"With a decent prism in my circlet, yes," he asserted boldly. It was easy to make such statements when he knew there was no way he'd ever be permitted to test them out.

"Speaking of circlets, where is yours?" his father changed subjects abruptly. "I noticed when I removed you from the Crystal Tower that you lacked your circlet and your belt of weaponry."

Going with the change of subject, Hayden scowled and said, "I was caught off guard while I was sleeping, the night they brought me in. I didn't have my circlet or my weapons belt on me, and I haven't seen either since I went to the Tower."

The look his father gave him suggested that he was losing points for allowing himself to be caught unprepared. Hayden was tempted to ask if he was expected to sleep in his circlet and belt, armed to the teeth at all times despite the discomfort of having to sleep on prisms, wands, and phials of elixirs. He refrained from asking the mocking question only because he expected his father would answer, "Yes" in perfect sincerity.

"Learning that you possess some of my stolen Source power seems to have given you a sense of overconfidence," the Dark Prism returned to the previous topic. "Surely you were taught that Source power is not everything, especially when one does not know how to use it properly."

"Actually, I *have* been taught that," Hayden countered, betraying some of his annoyance. "I've also been training for years on just how to optimize my magic usage."

A brief silence fell between them as they stared at each other. Hayden was determined not to be the first to break eye contact, though he suspected that his father could stare intimidatingly at things for hours on end without even blinking. For all he knew, the man stood around doing just that whenever his thoughts grew too blurry.

Finally, Aleric blinked and broke eye contact, reaching into his pants pocket and extracting a wad of something thin and silvery. Before Hayden could ask what it was, his father tossed the ball of fabric to him one-handed, and Hayden caught it reflexively.

He glanced at his father, unsure what this was all about.

"Put them on," Aleric instructed. When Hayden actually looked down at the silky material he was holding, he realized what it was and became even more confused.

"Prism-handling gloves," he said softly, recalling other pairs he had seen before. The ultra-thin, close-fitting silk gloves were used by jewelers like the one at Mizzenwald, who needed to handle prisms extensively but didn't want to smear them with fingerprints. Hayden had even seen Asher use them a time or two during their research sessions together the year before. Hayden had never bothered having a pair made for himself yet, though he had been considering it at one point.

"Put them on," his father said once more, less patiently than the first time, and Hayden realized he was staring at them for too long.

Not knowing what his father was up to, Hayden pulled on the Dark Prism's custom-made gloves. As expected, the fit was a little loose, as he had smaller hands and a smaller frame than his father, but Hayden wiggled his fingers inside of the gloves anyway, appreciating how smooth and thin the material was.

Without explaining himself, Aleric reached up to his own circlet and began unscrewing the Black Prism from his eyepiece. Hayden could only stare in confusion and silent terror, because his last involvement with the Black Prism had resulted in his childhood home blowing up, his Foci warping, his brain nearly melting from light-sickness, and his mother becoming atomized in the explosion that nearly killed him.

Hayden felt his mouth drop open dumbly when his father tossed the prism to him. Again, Hayden caught it by sheer reflex, staring down at the sinister diamond in his hand.

This is the weapon that made my father nearly invincible, that killed thousands of people. This is the infamous Black Prism—the instrument that is so corrupt that it doesn't follow the laws of magic and is never consumed no matter what is cast through it, that allegedly shows every color in the spectrum, including black. This is what killed my mother, and Tess's mother, and most of Jasper Dout's family...the prism that warped Asher's left Focus and nearly killed him as well. The most notorious weapon the Nine Lands has ever seen, and I'm holding it in my hand.

On the surface it looked like any common prism. There were no distinguishing features visible to the naked eye. Hayden didn't know what he had been expecting, maybe a different tint? Or perhaps the words 'BLACK PRISM' etched into the glass, so that the world would know its terrible and awesome power?

It was fortunate that Hayden was wearing gloves, because his hands were becoming cold and clammy, sticking to the silken material.

An effect of the prism, or is it just that I'm terrified and fascinated to be holding it?

With effort, Hayden tore his gaze away from it and looked back at his father. Aleric Frost was watching him with no visible sense of interest, as though he was watching a newly-painted wall dry.

"You are now armed with the greatest weapon this world has likely ever seen, and I stand before you with nothing." He opened his hands as though to illustrate the point. "If you are indeed so powerful, then attack me."

Hayden just continued to stare at the closest living relative he had, wondering how a father and son could be so fundamentally different.

Is he joking? Did he really just give me his primary weapon and challenge me to use it against him?

Even in insanity, Hayden was fairly certain he would never have made such a bold move, but then again the Black Prism was supposed to be the most corrupt prism in existence. For Hayden to use it even once would probably ruin him beyond recovery.

This might be my only chance though. He's calling my bluff; he thinks I'm too scared to use it because he knows I don't want to be like him—if he remembers anything I told him inside the schism he'll know that much.

That raised another uncomfortable thought. Just how much *did* Aleric Frost remember from his time inside the schism with his son? Hayden had told him his life's story, including all of his less-than-charitable thoughts about his notorious father.

Stop avoiding the real issue.

He knew his mind was trying to put off the decision that was now before him: to use the Black Prism against his father or not. If he did, it would be the end of him; there could be no coming back from that kind of distortion. He would have to hope that he remained level-headed long enough to kill his father and then himself, or else he might simply replace his father as the Dark Prism. Well, he'd need a new name of course, there couldn't be *two* Dark Prisms….The memory of Oliver and Jasper jeering and calling him the Broken Prism—way back in his first year of school—came to him then.

Well, the name would still fit…

It meant certain death, but at least it would be an honorable death…wouldn't it? Asher would understand why he did it, that it was the only way to rid the world of the Frosts once and for all. Tess and Zane…would be less forgiving.

The hand that brought the prism up to eye-level was trembling slightly, but there was no helping that at this point. Even while confronting his impending death, he felt a strange fascination by the abhorrent thing in his hand. He had always idly wondered what it would be like to look through the Black Prism, what kind of alignments would open up to him—things that didn't exist in any other prism, or maybe they just weren't as easy to find…

He stopped with the Black Prism directly over his right eye, turned so that he was facing his father directly, and looked through it.

Colors and alignments burst to life before him, more than he could immediately process. He barely had time to register the alarming streaks of black that shot through the other bands of color before he was struck blind with a searing headache.

He cried out in unexpected pain and felt the Black Prism drop from his hand as he hit his knees, overcome with the wrongness of the alignments. He had looked through an imperfect prism once before, at the end of his first year, and recalled feeling a slight sense of unease—but that had been a prism with only mild distortion. Blinking tears from his eyes, he cursed himself as a fool for not having anticipated this: the Black Prism was a complete sin against nature, more distorted than anything he had ever attempted to look through; of course he couldn't see through it without the stupid thing making his brain hurt. It had probably taken his father years of working with increasingly distorted prisms before he was even able to build this monstrosity, let alone *use* it.

Even thinking of those alignments—red, blue, *black*, green—made him so sick that he clutched blindly for the nearest object and ended up vomiting into the bowl of a potted plant. He had no idea what his father was doing right now, other than watching the spectacle of his agony. Was the man pleased? Alarmed? Mildly amused? Angry that all of his potted plants were going to die now, since Hayden kept puking on them?

The sound of slow, deliberate footfalls approaching made Hayden aware that his father was coming towards him, and for a wild moment he thought his father was going to ask whether he was alright. But no, he was simply picking up the Black Prism where Hayden had so carelessly discarded it, casually returning it to the eyepiece of his own circlet.

When his brain stopped hurting and the urge to vomit finally passed, Hayden turned to face his father, expecting to see the man standing near the worktable. He almost shouted when he blinked and realized that his father was standing almost directly over him, staring down with pitiless blue eyes.

"It seems that you have overestimated your abilities," he said without emotion. "You had the greatest weapon of all time in your possession, and yet here you lie, in a heap on the floor."

Too annoyed to be properly frightened, Hayden snapped, "That's hardly a fair test and you know it. I doubt even *you* could have used that prism when you were my age. Give me one of those normal ones off of your table and then we'll see what happens."

Rather than get angry, his father simply tilted his head slightly, still staring down at him. Hayden wished he would step back a few feet so that he could at least sit up without knocking the man over; lying on the floor made him feel weak—but then, that was probably the point.

"All of the prisms on my worktable have some degree of distortion to them, though I suppose you could still use them, if you're willing to risk your principles," he allowed, gesturing back at them.

Dismay colored his tone when Hayden said, "You mean you *only* keep broken prims lying around the house? There aren't *any* normal ones here?"

"Oh, there are a few lying around, but you're a fool if you think I would allow them to come into your possession." His father frowned down at him now, finally openly acknowledging the threat that he posed.

"So you *are* afraid me," Hayden smiled, though nothing about the situation was humorous. If it was true that there were only imperfect prisms lying out the open, Hayden would either need to follow in his father's footsteps—something he swore he would never do—or find a way to strangle the man in his sleep.

The dangerous look flashed briefly across the Dark Prism's face once more, and Hayden braced himself for some sort of physical pain, tensing against his will. His father noticed, of course, and then the look was gone.

"I fear nothing—not even you," he informed Hayden coldly. "You may have latent power, but you are nothing to me. If you did not hold something important to me you would already be dead, and the carrion birds would have picked your corpse apart wherever I left it to rot." He said all of this without breaking eye contact with Hayden, voice growing lower and softer as more contempt crept into it.

Hayden clenched his teeth, biting back whatever stupid, unhelpful thing he was probably about to open his mouth and say out of sheer habit. How had he ever convinced himself that he was prepared to deal with this man? Somehow, in all the stories Asher had told him to prepare him for this, he had never managed to convey just how monstrous the Dark Prism had become.

Thankfully, his father seemed to think he'd made his point, because he finally backed away from Hayden and returned to his worktable, turning his back to him as though pronouncing him entirely unworthy of attention.

Fine by me.

Hayden got to his feet and was about to leave the room when he realized that it would be an admission of defeat, a sign of weakness. Even if he was simply returning to his room to regroup, it would be a loss of face, and appearances were clearly extremely important where Aleric Frost was concerned.

So instead he stayed, swallowing the cowardly voice in his head that was screaming, *You idiot! Run and hide while you still can, and smother the man with a pillow when he sleeps!*

He returned to his position by the window, unlatching the panes and swinging them open to let the cool air blow across his face. In another hour the sun would set completely behind the mountains in the distance, but for now the orange and pink light still cascaded across the land, as if the world were a giant prism.

In a way, I suppose it is.

"Why are you still here?" his father asked without looking up from his worktable, looking through a magnifying glass while making bold slashes of color with a red pencil. Even in a moment like this, Hayden could envy his ability to sketch alignments so rapidly and precisely, without need of a ruler.

"You never told me why you wanted to see me."

Aleric waited until he had finished his work with the red pencil before answering. Hayden was beginning to understand that this was one of the many tactics he employed to control a conversation—forcing others to conform to his sense of timing.

"I've concluded that one of the primary reasons my last attempt at extracting your Source failed was because of your active opposition."

A little surprised by the topic, Hayden forced his expression to remain neutral, focusing on the feel of the breeze across his face. Having a connection with the outside world helped remind him that there was actually something worth living for outside of this ornate dungeon.

"That makes sense," he conceded. "I hope you aren't expecting me to apologize for struggling to stay alive."

The Dark Prism ignored the jab completely, as though he hadn't even registered the words. For all Hayden knew, he hadn't. It was hard to tell when his father was actually paying attention to him and when he was simply talking out loud to himself while Hayden happened to be present in the room.

"Your physical struggles I had planned for, but your magical opposition—"

"I didn't fight you with magic," Hayden interrupted. "I didn't even know I could use magic."

"—posed an unexpected problem," his father continued speaking despite the interruption, with the result that they ended up talking over each other and Hayden could barely hear the last part of his father's sentence.

I might as well be a cactus for all the respect he shows me.

Biting back frustration, Hayden tried again.

"But I didn't have a weapon, so how could I have resisted you magically?"

His father selected a blue colored pencil, still not honoring him by paying proper attention, adjusting his magnifying glass and glancing through the Black Prism to confirm something before he returned to coloring.

"You had an affinity for prisms even then, whether you were aware of it or not," he answered at last, exchanging his blue pencil for a black one without looking up. Hayden grimaced as he saw the large black band that his father filled in on the sheet of paper in front of him, suppressing the urge to hurl at the memory of that unnatural hue.

"That doesn't change the fact that I was prismless at the time," Hayden countered lightly, still watching the man carefully. Normally he would love to treat his father to the same contemptuous treatment that he himself was receiving, but in this case he couldn't afford the luxury of petty revenge. He needed to know everything he could about the way his father thought, worked, and conducted himself, which meant studying him as closely as possible at all times.

"But *I* was not," Aleric answered simply, still shading in an area of black in his notes.

It took a second for the implication to set in, and then Hayden didn't have to feign surprise when he blurted out, "You think I used *your* prism to fight you off? I had never attempted magic in my life, and I somehow managed to look through the Black Prism—inverted, I might add—and find some alignment to stop you from leeching out my Source without my brain exploding?"

Well, I suppose my brain did *nearly explode, come to think of it.*

He had always assumed that the light-sickness that gave him amnesia and nearly killed him was a side effect of whatever magic his father had been using on him at the time, but what if it wasn't? What if Hayden himself had caused it by using a distorted prism?

That would mean that I've already used a broken prism, even before I started school! Even inverted, it's a miracle that it didn't screw me up completely or alter my mind!

Then a more sinister thought.

But what if it did? *How do I know that it didn't have some effect on my mind, and it was just so subtle that I didn't notice? Does that mean there's something evil inside of me, festering, waiting to come out? Or is it like Asher said...sometimes people don't start to change until they've been dabbling with broken prisms for a while, so maybe I was lucky...*

His father didn't seem to be aware of the internal debate raging inside of him, or perhaps he just didn't care, because he kept speaking under the assumption that Hayden was hanging onto his every word, so he was forced out of his dark thoughts to avoid missing anything.

"—not a conscious decision," he explained coolly, still focused on his research. "Under threat of death, your mind likely reached out and found a successful pathway without any intent on your part. It has been known to happen when magic-users are under extreme pressure."

Hayden thought about that for a minute. It was true that he had discovered alignments that even Asher had never seen before, during moments of intense stress or when he was about to die. He thought back to his second year at school, during the I.S.C., when he had managed to bend light around him and repel all magical attacks. He had been trying to escape the horrible burns of that violet web, and had no idea what spell his mind latched onto. And only recently, when fighting Kilgore for information about Tess, he had panicked and found some spell that nearly made his skin turn to diamond.

"Huh," Hayden said out loud, having new respect for his ten-year old self. "That's good to know."

"When I am finished making adjustments to the spell itself, your opposition may still create difficulties—though not of the magnitude we experienced previously." His father said this as though it was bad news for Hayden in some way.

"You mean because if I was able to shut you out when I was ten and uneducated, I'm almost certainly able to do so now that I know what I'm on about?" He smiled to himself. "Seems like a valid concern."

"I thought you would make the childish, insolent decision, and you have proven me correct."

Unnervingly, his father didn't look upset when he said this. Hayden could see no reason why he should still be cool and collected right now, knowing that Hayden could muck up his plans time and again.

"Look at this from my point of view," Hayden explained. "There's really no reason for me *not* to resist you. You want to drain the very life from me and leave me dead for the carrion birds to pick at, while you boost your own power immensely. Why would I want to go along with this plan?"

Aleric set down his colored pencils and closed his eyes pensively. He looked like he was searching his memory for something, though Hayden had no idea what that might be. Still, he was worried when his father finally opened his eyes and leveled his gaze at him, because nothing good ever happened when he had the man's full attention.

"Tess?" he asked softly, as though plucking the name from thin air.

Hayden felt his face blanch, as all the blood in his body seemed to drain towards his feet. The sensation was so abrupt that he swayed a little and had to lean against the window ledge for support.

Of all things he could remember from the schism...

He wanted to kick himself for telling Hunter his life's story, especially all about Tess.

"Yes, that was her name," Aleric confirmed after seeing the look on Hayden's face. "I seem to recall you speaking about her...at length. One might infer that she has special value to you."

I'll kill him, I have to kill him, he cannot leave this house alive, Hayden chanted inside his head, seeing red.

"Leave her out of this," he said out loud, voice shaking with barely-controlled rage.

"Someone *very* special, then," his father continued. "Perhaps I should bring her here as a means of encouraging your good behavior. If you become insolent, I could punish her instead of you—you know that I need you intact until I've removed your Source and the part of mine that you hold. If you attack me, she would be punished accordingly. Were you to resist my attempts to reclaim what is mine, well..." he let that thought trail off, the silence spiraling horribly between them.

Hayden clenched his fists and his jaw so hard that his teeth hurt. He knew he was not in a position to fling himself at his father and beat the man to death, but that's exactly what his back-brain was screaming at him to do at this very moment.

"You've already killed her mother, and if you so much as glance sideways at her, I will make you wish you had never threatened me with her," Hayden informed him, scarily calm.

"You are not in a position to make good on that threat," his father explained, looking unimpressed. He turned back to his work. "I believe I will go to her tonight."

Hayden punched the glass of the open window pane beside him, wincing as his hand scraped against the broken fragments and began to bleed. He grabbed a particularly large shard and held it up triumphantly.

His father looked mildly annoyed.

"You think I care that you broke a window? Glass can be replaced."

"Try again," Hayden held the shard of glass against his own throat, over the spot where only a few months ago, his father had pressed a knife. The irony wasn't lost on him now.

The Dark Prism's eyebrows lifted.

I've finally managed to surprise the man.

"If you go anywhere near Tess, I'll end my own life and rob you of both my Source and yours. Study all you want, but you will *never* be able to recover what I took from you."

His father gave him a look of grudging respect, which was both annoying and gratifying.

"But you will be dead."

"I'll be dead whether you get my Source or I end things myself," Hayden shrugged, still clutching the shard of glass.

"I could stun you while your guard is down and keep you immobilized until I am ready to recover my Source from you."

Hayden called his bluff.

"You need me awake and my Foci clear to work your magic. You can't leave me immobilized, and I'll only make trouble for you the moment I can move again."

His father continued to stare at him.

"What do you propose?" he asked lightly.

"You leave Tess and all my other friends out of this, and I'll give you what you want. When the time comes, I won't struggle at all, and then I'll be dead and you'll have your power back and I won't care what happens to the world anymore."

He wondered if his father knew him well enough to realize that he was lying. Hayden's entire threat hinged on the fact that he didn't.

The Dark Prism considered him thoughtfully for a moment, and Hayden tried not to show any visible sign of emotion. If this didn't work, he would have to take his life now, because that was the only thing he could do to deprive his father of the extra power. Besides, Aleric would have no reason to pursue Tess or any of the others once he was dead.

After a tense moment, his father said, "We have an agreement."

Hayden exhaled and lowered the shard of glass, dropping it to the floor and finally acknowledging that his hand hurt really badly; there were still bits of glass poking out of the skin in three places, and he began working to extract them.

The deal struck, the Dark Prism immediately lost interest in him once more, and was about to turn back to his work when suddenly he whirled around to stare at Hayden once more. He was completely alert and focused, and Hayden had no idea what he'd done to rivet the man's attention just now.

Then he realized that his father wasn't staring at him. He was staring out the window that was just behind him.

"What is it?" Hayden asked curiously, wondering what could command so much of his father's attention as to make him seem almost human again.

"Something is coming," Aleric answered simply.

Intrigued, Hayden raised an eyebrow and asked, "What kind of something?"

"Something powerful."

Powerful enough to get my father's attention from a distance? Maybe Asher and the others are about to storm the place...but they don't know the details of the defensive wards!

"Powerful enough to get through your barriers?" Hayden solicited mildly, heart hammering with fear and hope.

"Yes."

Hayden tried not to let the relief show on his face.

They've found a way through and they're coming to rescue me! Together we'll take down my father while he's still comparatively weak and this nightmare will all be over with.

But then Hayden saw the small figure that soared over the gates and through a ripple of magic as though it wasn't even there, approaching the window at speed, and he understood.

Bonk perched on the window ledge and looked at Hayden's bleeding hand as though to say, *What am I going to do with you?*

14
Masters and Companions

Hayden had never been happier to see Bonk in his entire life. His familiar looked him over as though checking for signs of damage, before perching on Hayden's shoulder. The weight of the dragonling was a welcome relief; he hadn't realized just how badly he'd missed his familiar until they were parted at the Trout estate. He also noticed a scrap of paper tied to the dragonling's leg, but for the moment he left it alone.

The Dark Prism was watching the scene with a mildly interested look on his face. Hayden didn't think the man was faking surprise when he said, "Bonk?" as though greeting an old colleague. Then, looking at Hayden, he added, "Bonk is your familiar?"

Not seeing what the big deal was, Hayden said, "Yeah, why?"

His father and Bonk seemed to be in some sort of battle of wills, each staring the other down and refusing to blink or look away. Hayden knew that Bonk had been at Mizzenwald for fifty years before choosing to become his familiar, and that that meant he knew Hayden's father on some level from his old school days, but that was also true of nearly every student to pass through Mizzenwald in the last fifty years as far as Hayden knew.

It was Aleric who finally broke the silence and said, "All that time, and you were waiting for him?"

He seemed to be speaking to the dragon, not Hayden, and by the slight emphasis he placed on the word 'him', Hayden finally understood that his father was jealous.

My father wanted Bonk *to be his familiar?*

He had no idea why the Dark Prism would have been after such an oddball dragonling, even before he corrupted himself. Cinder was the very definition of a proper dragon: regal, haughty, a slick killer, mighty hunter, and generally not a creature to be trifled with. Bonk was pretty much the opposite of all of those things except in very rare circumstances, in which case he could drum up some dragonish pride. Even his name was dumb.

Then it hit him. *Bonk is powerful. How many people have said he's the me of dragons—that he's extremely powerful for no apparent reason.*

Of course his father would have learned about that while at school, and since he'd already proven that power was his weakness, naturally he would want such a creature to become his ally.

The Dark Prism is actually jealous of me.

That probably didn't bode well for him, but since Hayden already knew that his father was planning to kill him in the most painful way possible, the thought didn't frighten him nearly as much as it might normally. What was his father going to do, kill him twice?

Bonk turned away from Aleric—a feat few humans could survive—and looked instead at Cinder, who returned his gaze steadily. Hayden felt uncomfortable on their behalf, knowing that they were now enemies by virtue of their alliances. If either dragon felt awkward, they didn't show it, though the only emotion Cinder usually showed was contempt, and Bonk was being unusually stern right now.

"Where has he been all this time?" Hayden's father drew his attention once more. "He was not with you in the Crystal Tower."

"He was out hunting when I got nabbed from where I was staying," Hayden explained.

"And he did not follow on to assist you during your captivity?" his father asked with some surprise. Hayden couldn't entirely blame him, as he had—more than once—had the same thought.

"He must not have thought I was in any real danger, or that him being there would only make things worse," Hayden defended his familiar out of habit, and because he didn't need to annoy his one ally at a time like this. "Familiars always serve the best interest of their companion."

The look his father bestowed upon him was laced with derision. "You don't think of yourself as his master?"

"I think of us as partners. Only a fool would forget that his familiar is more powerful than him."

His father tilted his head in acknowledgment of this without conceding the point.

"Then as your partner, he has a choice to make." It didn't escape Hayden's notice that his father was now looking at Bonk through the Black Prism. He had no idea what would happen if his father attacked, or whether Bonk was more powerful than the Black Prism.

"Oh?" Hayden asked mildly, shifting his body weight so that he would be in a position to tackle his father if he needed to buy Bonk time. The movement didn't escape Cinder's notice, and his father's dragonling fixed his eyes on Hayden and tensed.

"I have no personal objection to him keeping you company—creatures of power will always be honored guests of the Frost estate—but neither can I have him coming and going, running letters to my enemies." He gestured to the scrap of paper still tied to Bonk's leg, calling attention to it for the first time since Bonk's arrival. "Nor do I underestimate the power your familiar commands; as you said, only a fool would be so blind."

And sadly, you are no fool, Father.

"What are you saying?" Hayden felt his muscles go taut, preparing to pounce. The moment seemed very close now; he could see his father's prism-eye idly scanning for alignments while he spoke.

"He can leave now and resolve to stay away, or he can accept Binders and be deprived of all magical power." He looked almost uneasy as he said, "An embarrassment, I realize, for such a distinguished creature, but the alternative is even less unpleasant for all parties involved."

Hayden could see the alternative clearly enough. *My father and Cinder against me and Bonk. Normally that might be even odds, but I'm completely unarmed. I'd be battling the Dark Prism with my fists and whatever blunt objects I can grab onto before he slays me.*

But the choice wasn't Hayden's, it was Bonk's, and if his familiar decided that he would rather fight than suffer the indignity of being cut off from his magic, then Hayden would do his best to occupy his father long enough for Bonk to bring down Cinder.

All three of them seemed to wait with bated breath until Bonk stuck out one leg in surrender. Hayden exhaled heavily, feeling a little lightheaded and unsure of how long he was actually holding his breath. His father and Cinder both relaxed marginally.

The Dark Prism turned his back on them and crossed to the other side of the library, stopping at the end of a seemingly random bookshelf and drawing a knife from a sheath at his waist. He nicked his thumb and smeared the drop of blood against the grain of the wood, and Hayden heard the sound of a latch release as a square panel opened up. The wood of the bookshelf didn't seem thick enough to contain anything—it was less than an inch thick—but the compartment his father reached into seemed much deeper so he assumed it was magically-enhanced.

His father withdrew a set of Binders that were large enough to fit on Hayden's wrists and shut the compartment. As the panel swung shut, Hayden noticed that the blood on the outside of it was gone.

I'll bet you haven't realized that I can access all your little hidey-holes too, Hayden thought with grim satisfaction. *By all means, keep showing me your secrets.*

The Binders were much too large for Bonk's legs—nearly large enough to circle his chest—but his father approached anyway and Hayden watched silently. The Dark Prism detached the scrap of paper from Bonk's leg and set it aside without looking at it, before fastening one of the ridiculously-oversized Binders around each of Bonk's legs.

As soon as the second one was closed, the lead contracted until the miniature cuffs fit snugly just above Bonk's feet.

I'm an idiot, Hayden shook himself out of his stupor. *Why did I let Bonk sacrifice his magic just to stay with me? Now we're both useless and we'll never be able to fight!*

Well, Bonk still had his poison glands, but Cinder could cure the effects so it seemed like a useless tactic to employ.

Still, Hayden couldn't bring himself to be upset with his familiar. He was ashamed by his cowardice, but mostly he was just glad to have company during his final days of life. He didn't want to spend his remaining time alone and friendless in his father's house.

Finally, his father picked up the scrap of paper, unfolded it, and briefly scanned the words on it. Hayden had no idea who it was from or what it said, and his father's face gave no clue beyond a slight compression of the lips.

"What does it say?" Hayden asked when he thought his father was finished reading, wondering if the man would tell him.

In response, the Dark Prism tossed the scrap carelessly at him and turned back to his worktable, apparently finished with him for the evening. Curious, Hayden looked down at the note, written in the instantly-recognizable handwriting of Master Asher.

Let Hayden go, or I'll bring the fight to you. This time I will win.

Hayden clenched the piece of paper in his fist, crumpling it in his hand. The last thing he wanted was for any of his friends or allies to die trying to save him, especially now that he knew that he wasn't just here for his father's amusement. The Dark Prism would never let him walk out of here alive; even if Hayden escaped, his father would hunt him down to the ends of the earth, because he was bound and determined to recover his Source.

"Are you going to write back and tell him 'no?' " Hayden asked hopefully. Maybe if his father explained why he wouldn't let him go, Asher would see the futility in trying to rescue him and would do the sensible thing.

Right, Hayden almost snorted in amusement, *because Asher always does the sensible thing.*

"He knows I will not," his father replied without turning around. "Leave me."

Deciding not to push his luck, Hayden backed out of the library, mostly because he didn't like the idea of turning his back on a man who intended to kill him, even if he didn't expect it to happen for some days or weeks—possibly months, if he got really lucky.

Bonk remained on his shoulder, looking around the house without interest as Hayden returned to the room he had claimed for himself, shutting and locking the door behind him. He knew that a locked door wasn't going to stop his father from getting in if he decided to do so, but it still made him feel more secure.

"I'm glad you're here," he said to Bonk, "even if it was dumb to give up your magic just so you can sit around and wait for me to die." He began changing into some borrowed pajamas, climbing into bed and propping a few pillows beneath his head so he was semi-reclined.

Bonk hopped onto the other side of the bed and examined his Binders with obvious distaste.

"I guess I should tell you about my father's plan for me...and why he tried to kill me when I was ten. I've learned a lot since I came here, which is about the only good thing that can be said about this whole ordeal."

Bonk listened patiently as Hayden relayed everything that had happened since encountering his father at the Crystal Tower. It was nice to have someone to share it all with, even if Bonk couldn't really answer back or ask any follow-up questions. On the other hand, he couldn't be entirely sorry that none of his friends were here to talk to. At least he had managed to keep them out of this—especially Tess.

Despite his inability to speak, Bonk let his sentiments be known, looking angry or pacing from one end of the bed to the other whenever Hayden described his various near-death encounters with his father over the last couple days.

"Even Hattie and the others are counting on me to finish off my father so that they can go home free—assuming I can find a way past the barriers around this place once he's gone," Hayden frowned as a new thought struck him. "Hang on—what happens to a person's spells when they die? Will his defenses still be active around the house or will they end too?"

Bonk didn't answer, not that he really expected his familiar to have the answer. He couldn't believe that in four years of magical education he had never thought to ask the question, but he hadn't really planned on encountering this sort of thing until now.

I'm getting ahead of myself.

"Of course, none of this will matter unless I can overcome the minor problem of defeating the most powerful prism-user in the Nine Lands with nothing but my wit." Hayden sighed. "At least if I had a decent prism I'd stand a chance—not a good one, mind you, but it would be better than trying to smother the man in his sleep with a pillow."

Now it was Hayden's turn to get out of bed and pace the room, burning off his pent-up energy, though he knew that as soon as he stopped moving he would probably collapse; exhaustion was hovering just behind the manic energy that was keeping him animated.

"Because I *will* die fighting, even if the only thing I can do is take my own life before he can pull my Source out of me," Hayden continued, fueled with the conviction of someone who knew that his death was inevitable and necessary. "I won't sit there like a scared little boy while he reclaims the rest of his power and all of mine. If my Foci weren't damaged beyond imagination, I would be terrifyingly powerful as is. I can't imagine what kind of horror the Dark Prism would be capable of with all of that power added to his own—and without warped Foci."

Bonk gave a little shudder to echo the sentiment.

"Then again, maybe trying to absorb someone else's power—or so *much* power—is unnatural, and would warp his Foci no matter what. Surely no human is capable of channeling *that* much power uninhibited."

Though my father says my Foci were only warped because of whatever inverse alignment I pulled out of the Black Prism when I was on the brink of death...

"Heck, getting my Foci nearly destroyed was probably the luckiest thing that ever happened to me," Hayden mused thoughtfully, finally seeing the event in a new light. "I never would have been allowed to learn magic if I had that much power at my command at the age of ten, so I'd probably still be in Binders in the orphanage right now. And if my father caught up to me there somehow, it would be that much easier for him to pull the Source back out of me. At least this time he had to waste time figuring out how to correct warped Foci first, giving time for the others to prepare for fighting him."

If I can just get a message out to the others somehow, I could tell them that he's at a disadvantage this time. Sure, he's still miserably powerful and skillful with and without his Black Prism, but he has much less Source power than last time. He'll wear down easier, have less kick behind his attacks…

It would be easy to write a note and send it off with Bonk, except that his familiar had lost the ability to cross the defensive barriers because he knew Hayden was lonely and wanted company. He wanted to kick himself all over again for letting Bonk hinder himself in such a way.

"But I guess things would have been worse if you had stayed but refused the Binders," he conceded with a sigh. "He was about half a second from attacking you with the Black Prism, and I have no idea whether you're strong enough to take him on with him using that thing or not. Even if you are, there's no way you could have fought off him and Cinder at the same time, though I was prepared to launch myself into harm's way if you were determined to try."

Hayden sat back down on the side of the bed, and Bonk waddled over to him and head-bumped his arm as a show of solidarity. Hayden smiled and patted his familiar on the head.

"I'll write a letter tomorrow anyway, just in case there's ever an opportunity to get word out; I'd actually kick myself if I missed out on a chance to report on what I've learned since coming here."

Frowning, he added, "What do you think the others are doing right now? Do you think they know about the slaughter at the Council yet?" he rubbed his eyes and answered his own question. "They must, it's been at least a day, and they hadn't finished my trial yet. The Masters would show up to a place full of dead bodies and known something was horribly wrong." He scowled and added, "I hope none of them were there when my father came to get me. I know he got Cal, but maybe Mrs. Trout and the others managed to escape..."

The alternative was too depressing to contemplate right now.

"They must have searched the place thoroughly and saw that I was missing, and from there it probably didn't take long to guess where I ended up. Now they know where to attack, though that doesn't help with the problem of getting through the defensive perimeter. It might help if I knew what some of the defenses actually *were*, then I could tell them in this fictitious letting I pretend I'll be able to send."

Bonk became a distraction at this point when he began making coughing, retching noises, as though he was a cat who was about to hock up a huge hairball.

"What did you eat this time?" Hayden frowned down at his familiar. "Don't tell me you swallowed another monstrously-fat squirrel without chewing before you came here...you should remember what happened last time."

Bonk paid him no mind, but continued making the retching noises, leaning right over Hayden's lap.

"Seriously, Bonk? This entire room is at your disposal—there's a trash can right over there, in fact—

and you're going to hurl in my lap?" Hayden asked in disbelief, making no effort to move. It wouldn't be the first time he'd gotten dragon-vomit all over him. "What did I do to offend you this time?"

Bonk gave no answer, his entire body heaving with the effort of coughing up whatever was stuck in his stomach. Hayden sighed and patted him on the back soothingly, formulating the apology he would have to give the housekeeping staff—slaves—around here when he asked them to wash his puke-covered sleep pants.

Finally, whatever was upsetting Bonk's stomach began sliding up his throat, creating a noticeable bulge that Hayden was not at all looking forward to seeing up close.

"Whoa, Bonk, that thing is huge..." he recoiled in revulsion. "What the heck did you take on...a badger?"

In response, Bonk coughed the mass into Hayden's lap, and all Hayden could do was stare at the thing in utter shock.

Even covered in slime, muck, and bits of whatever else occupied the inside of Bonk's stomach, the object was immediately recognizable as a prism. Hayden pulled off one of his socks and began cleaning the thing as best as he could, wishing he had a pair of prism-handler gloves like his father's to keep from getting his fingerprints all over the thing.

It took both of his socks and the corner of his bed sheet to get the thing shined up properly, and Hayden held it by the very edges as he turned towards the light and put it in front of his right eye.

It was a mastery-level violet prism, which made up for the fact that it still smelled a little like dragon puke.

Looks like I'm not unarmed after all, Hayden thought with glee, a smile creeping onto his face as he patted Bonk on the head.

Then, on the heels of that thought he added, *Thanks, Asher.*

15
Modified Alignments

Hayden slept late the next morning, since there wasn't really any place he needed to be. In fact, if not for the realization that he was wasting valuable time that would be better served strategizing, he might have stayed in bed all day.

After Bonk had coughed up his mentor's gift to him, Hayden had promptly become paranoid that his father would somehow sense the prism in the house and come searching for it. That had prompted him to hide it in the most secure place he could find inside of his bedroom, which happened to be in his pillowcase. He knew it was a pretty poor hiding place for anyone who was actively searching for something, but since the room was sparsely furnished it was either the pillowcase, the desk-drawer, the closet, or under the mattress. Of all the options, the pillowcase seemed like the best bet—plus it would be readily accessible to him if he happened to be attacked inside his bedroom.

Again, Hayden thought mulishly, still angry about being caught off guard by Master Sark in the dead of night at the Trout estate.

"Well, Bonk, let's go get something to eat and see if we can find out anything useful about this place's defenses."

The little dragon perked up at the promise of food and took flight, coasting out of the bedroom behind Hayden and gliding overhead as they made their way towards the first floor.

It took Hayden a few attempts to find the kitchen, as he still hadn't spent an appreciable amount of time in the Frost estate until now.

I guess that's one good thing about my captivity: plenty of time to explore my house.

As nice as the mansion was, he wasn't particularly looking forward to dying here.

I wonder if I'll even want this place when all this is over with, making the large assumption that I actually find a way to defeat my father in combat.

The bad memories alone might drive him to sell it, though no one else would probably want to live in it either, unless they were a strange Frost-family enthusiast. Maybe it could be a museum of some sort...

It was eventually Bonk who found the kitchen, following his superior nose and leading the way. They had to descend a partial flight of stairs to get inside, as the kitchen was recessed into the ground, making it feel almost like a basement.

Six people were sitting around a wooden table in the center of the room, in various stages of eating breakfast. The rest of the space was lined with countertops and islands. One entire wall was devoted to ice boxes, gas-fired burners and ovens.

Apparently the poor souls who worked here weren't used to being visited in the kitchen, because most of them blanched at the sight of Hayden and Bonk and leapt to their feet.

"Sir!" a man who looked old enough to be Hayden's grandfather greeted him reflexively, obviously terrified.

"Whoa, relax," Hayden held up his hands in a gesture of surrender. "I'm the sane Frost, remember?" His eyes went to Hattie, and she was the first to take her seat and give him a small smile. "I was just looking for breakfast for Bonk and I."

A middle-aged woman with frizzy brown hair went over to one of the ice boxes and withdrew a plate of raw meats that had been covered in foil, which she placed on the table for Bonk. Hayden was tempted to tell her that his familiar would have been just as happy with a soap cake or a mouse, but remembered that his father insisted on Things Being Done Properly.

Bonk descended on the plate with indecent fervor, startling those nearest into scooting back in their chairs.

"It's alright, he won't hurt you," Hayden explained. "He just acts like every meal is his last. Actually, he's quite friendly, for a dragon."

Hayden noted that no one was scurrying about to get him any food, and finally added, "Uh, I don't suppose there's anything left for me?"

The other six people were all finishing cereal or buttered toast, which looked really good right about now.

Looking mildly uncomfortable, Hattie said, "Sorry, sir, but when you missed breakfast your—the Dark Prism—said that you obviously didn't need to eat this morning. He had us throw your portion away."

"Ah." Hayden supposed he should have seen that coming. "Out of curiosity, what was on the menu?"

The others began to relax when they saw that he wasn't angry with them. He'd never seen such a skittish group of people in his entire life. *Then again, they were kidnapped from their homes by the bogeyman of their nightmares and made to serve him in his fortress under threat of death. I guess I might be skittish too under those conditions.*

Technically, Hayden supposed he was in the same situation—worse, probably—but since he had been living with his association to the Dark Prism for five years now it wasn't nearly as surprising or paralyzing as it would have been at the age of ten.

"Ham and bacon, spiced potatoes, rye toast with jam, poached eggs and juice," Hattie rattled off.

"Wow, sounds delicious, though ham and bacon together seems a bit excessive." He smiled. "I'd settle for some of that lovely-looking cereal right now if there's any more of it to be had."

"Would you like it in the formal dining room?" the man who had first greeted him asked as he went to pour Hayden a bowl.

"Good heavens, no. It's weird enough eating in that room when there's only one other person; I can't imagine how awkward I'd feel eating in there alone." He shuddered at the thought.

It would also remind me constantly of how my father almost strangled me to death last night for making the mistake of addressing him as 'Father.'

Despite his assurances, the others still looked surprised when he joined them at the table in the kitchen, though Bonk smoothed things over by making himself endearing and allowing the others to pat him.

An all-purpose companion, Hayden thought cheerfully.

"Where are the rest of you?" he asked after taking another mental headcount. "I thought you told me yesterday there were still nine of you here," he addressed the last to Hattie, who nodded.

"The others are already out working. We have to get going soon as well or we'll get in trouble."

"I see," Hayden said at the same time as one of the others blurted out, "Are you really going to take down your father and free us all?"

An awkward moment of silence fell over the table, and then Hayden said, "Well, that's my plan. If I die, you can assume it didn't work out for me, though eventually the team of mastery-level mages I was working with will figure out how to bust in here and then they'll try to take him down too. You might be able to escape during all the fighting once the defenses are down."

The middle-aged woman with the frizzy hair frowned and said, "You seem very cavalier about the thought of dying here."

Hayden shrugged and said, "I was a little less casual about it when I first found out that that is my father's eventual plan for me no matter what, but I've had a night to sleep on it. Now the only thing it means is that I have to think of a way to defeat him sooner rather than later, but the price of failure is the same as the price of doing nothing, which is strangely freeing," he elaborated around a mouthful of cereal. "It means I don't have to worry about holding back."

The others looked at him like he was either crazy or heroic, maybe a touch of both. Hayden certainly didn't feel terribly heroic sitting in the kitchen right now, with no real plan and only one prism to fight with.

Still, yesterday I had no plan and no prisms to fight with, so things are looking up every day. Maybe tomorrow I'll stumble upon an entire cache.

"Speaking of the defenses around this heap of stone...what can you tell me about them?" Hayden polled the others. "I know you recently lost one of your friends, and I'm sorry for bringing it up, but anything you can tell me about what happened to him would be helpful."

A few of the others exchanged grimaces or looked down at the table in front of them, but finally someone answered.

"Jack got fed up with being held here; he said no man was going to keep him cooped up forever, and that he was going to get out or die trying. Obviously, you know how that turned out for him."

Hayden nodded but didn't speak, silently urging him on.

"A few of us were watching when he said he was making a break for it. He looked around to make sure the Dark Prism wasn't watching—though he almost never does, he's always cooped up in his workshop. Then he ran for it."

"Just like that?" Hayden interrupted. "He ran for the main gates?"

The man nodded confirmation.

"For a minute we thought he might make it. He got to the gates and flipped the lever on this side that lets them open. He slipped through and made it maybe three feet before he died."

Hayden raised an eyebrow even as he processed the fact that all of the defenses appeared to be on the outside of the gated wall. If someone with no magical prowess whatsoever could walk out the front door, it made him feel better about his ability to roam the front yard without getting his head lobbed off.

"What exactly happened to him?" Hayden pressed apologetically.

"I don't know," the man snapped, "it's not like I understand all that magic business you people do."

Hayden backtracked.

"I know you won't know the spells that are up, but if you could tell me what you saw, and—sorry—what it looked like when Jack died, it might help me and my friends break through them."

"You don't even know when your friends are coming," the man eyed Hayden skeptically. "Besides, it's not like you can send them a letter and tell them whatever we tell you, so what's the point?"

Hayden frowned and said, "I'm working on a way to contact my friends, so don't worry about that part." Well, that was sort of true, and if they inferred that he had some kind of elite magic that could get a message through those walls and across however-much distance then Hayden wasn't going to relieve them of their ignorance.

Hattie looked impressed with him, and he tried not to feel guilty for pretending to be further along than he was with his plan. He resolved to spend the rest of the afternoon trying to research a way to get a letter out of this place.

"There wasn't a lot to see," the man admitted at last. "At first we thought he was having a stroke or something, since he just stopped in his tracks and started screaming."

"He put his hands over his eyes," the woman with frizzy hair added softly. "Like his eyes were hurting him really badly all of a sudden. He just fell on the ground and screamed and screamed until he didn't move anymore."

What in the world?

Hayden was at a loss for what sort of spell would make a person's eyes hurt so badly they died from it. Their description had raised more questions than it had answered. Had Jack been paralyzed, or was he just in too much pain to think of moving? If he had been able to move, could he have pressed on and eventually broken through all the invisible barriers, or would something else have prevented it? Just how many different defensive spells were in place around the perimeter of this place, anyway? Obviously enough that they could stop both magical and non-magical people, which implied that the spells didn't rely on entering through the Foci—or at least, not all of them did.

"Does that help you?" Hattie interrupted his train of thought. "Do you know what got him and how to get around it?"

Hayden didn't want to give them false hope, but he also didn't want to reveal just how bleak things were looking right now.

I'm in way over my head.

"Yes, it helps. I don't know exactly what that spell is yet, but it narrows down my search a lot, so I might be able to figure it out with some research in the library."

"The library where the Dark Prism does his work?" one of the others asked in alarm. "Do you think he's just going to let you sit there and dig through his library for a way out of here while he stands ten feet away from you?"

Hayden shrugged and said, "Why not? I've gotten the impression that my father doesn't feel terribly threatened by me, which is all to the good. He doesn't consider me an enemy worthy of close scrutiny, so he may not care what I'm doing as long as it doesn't threaten to kill me before he can do it himself." He stood up and said, "Come on, Bonk. Let's go ask Father if I can do some reading."

Frost Prisms

The others watched him go, their expressions leaving no doubt in Hayden's mind that they didn't necessarily consider him to be 'the sane Frost' anymore.

Hayden stopped outside the door to the library and took a deep breath for courage. He entered without knocking, trying to look purposeful and unafraid. His father was staring out the broken window with an abstracted look on his face, and Hayden wondered what he was seeing with his mind's eye. He could tell the exact moment that his father registered his presence in the room; there was a subtle focusing of his eyes and a tightening of his features that would have been imperceptible if he hadn't been looking for it.

"Good morning, sir," Hayden greeted deferentially, hedging on the side of courtesy for now.

"Closer to noon," the Dark Prism answered without looking at him. It was amazing how many of the things the man did were subtle power-plays, intended to put him in a position of dominance and intimidate everyone else. It was even more amazing—to Hayden at least—that he recognized these gestures for what they were, and wasn't falling for them. Well, maybe a little, but he was growing more comfortable dealing with his father as he got more experienced at it.

"Breakfast sounded delicious," Hayden added pleasantly. This didn't rate any kind of response from his father. Switching subjects abruptly he asked, "Do you mind if I use the library?"

"For what purpose?" the Dark Prism asked without any sign of surprise, or any other obvious emotion.

"If I'm just sitting around, passing time until you're ready to leach the life out of me, I'd rather do some studying to keep my mind occupied." Well, that was true enough. "I'm supposed to be in my fifth year of school right now at Mizzenwald, and it feels weird not to be up to my eyeballs in homework."

Now his father did look at him, though Hayden had no idea what he had said that was particularly attention-grabbing. It was hard to tell what the man saw value in.

"What level were you at in your schooling?" he asked with idle curiosity.

Whoa, is my evil father showing an interest in how I'm doing in school? It was probably just because he was curious as to Hayden's strengths and weaknesses—magically-speaking—but it was still odd to be asked.

"Last year I hit mastery-level prisms and started helping Asher with his research," Hayden watched the man's face closely for signs of anger at the mention of his old friend's name, but there was nothing. "I was hoping to start the last round of Abnormal Magic and mastery-Wands as well. I'm pretty good at Charms and Healing, less good at Elixirs and Conjury, and was declared a menace against humanity in Powders during my first term."

His father considered him for a moment and then said, "I was always quite adept at Powders."

"Yeah, I heard. Master Sark—Kirius, to you—was still teaching there the last I saw him. He spent years trying to get me expelled, but I saw a chapter in Te—in my friend's Powders book, where you and he discovered something together."

He had almost said Tess's name, and while he assumed his father could guess who he was talking about if he cared to try, he wasn't going to bring her to his attention any more than necessary.

"You said you began prism-based research in the last year," Aleric gave him a measured look, as though appraising his value.

"With Asher, yes. I started working on mapping a new alignment back in my third year, but only because the Fias were running the school during the war and they were slave-driving us for profit."

"Excuse me?" his father asked softly, as though this was brand new information to him.

Of course, he probably doesn't remember much of our conversations inside the schism, otherwise he might not be planning to murder me.

"The northern sorcerers invaded the Forest of Illusions when it was on the coast and set up base there. They had most of the Masters and Council members trapped inside, draining their Source power continuously with these spikes that were linked to Suppressors, which they used to dampen magical power in the area so no one could attack."

The Dark Prism lifted his eyebrows in mild appreciation of this, and Hayden was forcibly reminded of his meeting with the Magistra, who had claimed an acquaintance with his father and thought he would like her tactics. It seemed she was correct.

"An elegant solution," Aleric allowed judiciously. "If memory serves me correctly," *and it may not,* was implied, "the Magistra was both intelligent and merciless."

Too true, Hayden mentally agreed, before adding, "She was overconfident, and it led to her downfall."

"You've met her?" his father waited for him to nod before continuing. "Does she still live?"

"No, she died in the Forest while trying to bring in reinforcements," Hayden replied. "By then we'd broken everyone out of their cages and people were fighting back, and she needed the help."

"How did she die?"

"I killed her," Hayden said flatly, before considering that it might be a bad idea to give his father a reason to fear him. If the Dark Prism took him seriously as a threat, his movements would be a lot more restricted, and he'd be more closely watched. "Not on purpose," Hayden added hastily. "My Focus-correctors had shattered by then and my magic is very unstable without them. I was trying to set fire to her ships, but I accidentally blew them up instead, and her along with."

His father listened patiently, and some of the interest faded from behind his eyes as he downgraded Hayden's importance once more.

"What were you doing in the Forest of Illusions? Don't tell me that the Masters and Council members have become so weak and ineffectual that they were drafting third-year mages?"

"No," Hayden grimaced. "But Asher had gone down with the last wave, and we didn't hear from anyone for months. Bonk started getting sick almost as soon as he left with Cinder, and after a while Torin and I figured out that Bonk was suffering because Cinder was being drained, so a few of us went to find them."

Something about what he said genuinely surprised his father, because the man looked properly stunned for the first time in their acquaintance.

"Cinder went with Asher?"

"Well, yeah. Horace—Asher's falcon—went too, but ever since you disappeared, Asher kind of adopted Cinder as well. He and I were the only ones Cinder much cared for."

Hayden hadn't even seen his father's familiar enter the room, but suddenly the dragonling was perched on the top edge of a bookshelf, his shadow in the sunlight looming over them. The Dark Prism looked up at him and they exchanged a long look that could have meant anything. Eventually Cinder made a noise and tilted his head, which apparently meant something to his master because Aleric said, "I see," and turned back to Hayden.

Maybe being driven mad by magic means he can understand magical creatures or something. An interesting thought.

"So, F—sir," Hayden caught himself immediately, though he saw a flicker of that dangerous anger behind the Dark Prism's eyes at the hint of being called 'Father', "would it be alright if I did some reading? I'll keep quiet and not bother you…"

"Come here," his father ignored him entirely, finally leaving his place at the window and approaching his work table. Wary of a trap, Hayden followed, thankful for Bonk's presence on his shoulder, even though he knew the dragon couldn't do a lot to help him without magic.

When they were standing beside each other—uncomfortably close, as Hayden didn't like to put himself in arm's reach of his father—the Dark Prism gestured to his research notes and said, "What do you make of this?"

Is he asking my opinion of his research, or is he stuck and wondering if I have any ideas?

Hayden would never cease to be surprised by the man standing next to him. Either way, he thought it was galling to be asked to contribute to something that was intended to kill him.

This is a test of some sort, he reminded himself. With his father, it was always a test, though he had no idea what he was being evaluated for this time. He was slightly ashamed of the part of himself that wanted to pass and be worthy of the man's regard.

Silently, Hayden looked down at the notes in front of him. Unlike Asher's handwriting, which was long and loopy and ended with flourishes that usually left ink marks all over the table as much as the paper, his father's handwriting was very neat and precise. Block letters—all capitalized—were written in even, perfectly legible rows, so that the contrast between the two men was even more apparent.

How were they ever friends?

Hayden's eyes scanned the mathematical models and the notes in the margins, but it was way beyond his level. He was lucky to understand a quarter of it, as it seemed to be a totally different kind of formulation than what he was accustomed to, as though his father had even managed to discover corrupted math. Then again, Hayden had always privately suspected that all math was corrupt and that no sane person could enjoy doing it, so perhaps he shouldn't be surprised by this.

"I don't really understand it," he admitted, not sure whether this was the right or wrong answer. Perhaps his father was just trying to impress his authority and intelligence upon him again, and he intended for Hayden to be cowed.

"At all?" the Dark Prism prompted neutrally.

"Well, maybe this part…a little," Hayden amended, pointing at the passage in the middle. "It looks like some sort of inverse triangulation between four alignments, but I've never seen it done that way, and I'm not even sure what alignments would orient themselves like that."

He couldn't tell if the man was impressed with his intelligence or not. If he hadn't seen his father look surprised when they were discussing Cinder's friendship with Asher, he would have thought his facial muscles were paralyzed in that neutral expression.

"If you have never used a modified prism, it is unsurprising that you don't recognize the orientation," his father explained, pointing to one of the drawings he had been working on in colored pencil. Hayden noticed how he used the term 'modified' instead of 'broken' or 'imperfect' when describing his work.

One glance at the drawing told him why he hadn't recognized the alignments initially. For one thing, all of them contained a streak of black, a horrendous abomination that made Hayden queasy even though the colored pencil held no power. For another thing, his father was correct: no alignments in a regular prism would ever be positioned like that in relation to each other. On paper like this, it became glaringly apparent just how severe the distortion in the Black Prism truly was, and Hayden marveled again at how anyone could look through it without their brain melting.

His father stared contemplatively at the page for a long moment, and Hayden was just beginning to relax and let his guard down when the man suddenly pushed him away so forcefully that he tripped over his feet and crashed into the table before falling to the floor. Bonk took flight to avoid the fall, and went to perch on a green armchair a safe distance away, glaring at the Dark Prism.

Having banged his elbow on the edge of the table on his way down, Hayden winced and worked his arm a few times, scooting backwards a few feet on the floor before getting to his feet.

Apparently their father-son moment was over, and Hayden was reminded once more to never relax while within striking distance of the Dark Prism. He was tempted to ask why his father had suddenly turned on him, but that would only invite more unpleasantness. The man's entire demeanor had changed, from his stance to the level of tension in his jaw, to the burning insanity behind his eyes. It was like a switch had flipped somewhere in his head, and the comparatively-relaxed persona had been buried once more.

Without saying a word, Hayden walked over to the bookshelves and began browsing for prism-related books, anything that looked like it might help him get out of here. He had asked for permission twice, and he wasn't asking again. If his father wanted him out of the library then he could just kick him out, an experience the man would likely take joy from.

When he had a pile of likely-looking books, Hayden sat down in the armchair that Bonk was perched on and began to read. There was one thing he hadn't confessed to his father while reading his notes: if Hayden was following the general flow of the research correctly, and he believed he was, then it may only be a matter of weeks before his father was finished remapping the alignments needed to rip out Hayden's Source.

Before spring has turned to summer, I'll either be victorious or dead.

He turned his focus back to the book in his hands, determined to study until he had a plan.

16
Dragon Delivery Service

Hayden spent the next six days in the library, sometimes staying in there so long that his father had to order him out of the room at the end of the evening, when he himself was planning on retiring to bed. Apparently he didn't want Hayden inside the room with his notes and experimental prisms while he was asleep, because he locked and warded the door every night upon leaving.

Hayden went to bed each night with his head stuffed so full of theories, new alignments, and abstract math that his brain felt saturated with knowledge. In fact, his dreams were often riddled with the things he read during the day, so that he woke up feeling like he hadn't had a break in studying at all.

Bonk often grew bored and flew around the house and the grounds. Hayden had watched him from the still-broken window in the library before, soaring to the limits of where his Binders would allow him to pass without magic. Hayden kept careful mental notes of where the defensive spells began, intending to put all of it into his letter as soon as he had enough information to send something useful to his friends. He still hadn't worked out the problem of how he was going to accomplish this feat, and often found himself sitting up late into the night with Bonk in their bedroom, running through ideas with his familiar and asking the dragonling's opinion.

He was beginning to wonder if Bonk was shaking his head 'no' at all of his ideas just to mess with him, or perhaps he had just forgotten how to nod 'yes'. Either way, Hayden was desperately dreaming up wilder and more dangerous ideas in the stubborn determination that there must be *some* way to get a message out. No wall was impenetrable, not even one made out of magic.

On the seventh day since his studies began, Hayden was eating dinner with his father when a reckless idea seized him.

"Sir," he set down his fork and pushed his plate to the side, "How did Jack die?"

His father waited until he was finished chewing and swallowing the food in his mouth before he asked, "Who?"

"One of the servants—" *slaves,* Hayden substituted in his head, "—that you have here. He died a few weeks ago trying to escape. I asked the others and they said that he made it to the other side of the gate before he grabbed his eyes and started screaming until he died."

His father continued to eat while Hayden talked, somehow managing to sip wine without breaking his measured gaze.

"Still imagining you can escape?" he asked mildly, and Hayden scowled.

"Sadly, no, I abandoned hope of that some time ago. I was mostly just wondering what spell you'd managed to discover in your Black Prism that caused people to scream to death," Hayden lied easily. He was becoming much more practiced at dealing with his father these days.

"The screaming isn't what killed him," the Dark Prism explained without emotion. "It was the agonizing pain that caused the screaming that killed him."

Hayden raised an eyebrow in mild interest, realizing that he was copying the gesture from his father. He told himself that adopting his father's mannerisms was simply a means of getting information out of the man, but vowed to dedicate himself to unlearning everything he'd picked up here if he ever got free. He didn't want to carry anything from this monster away with him.

"Then it's only a simple pain spell?" Hayden frowned in mock-disappointment. "Hmm, I'd expected something more glamorous."

Touching on his father's pride—*ha! I knew I spotted his weakness!*—was a risky thing to do, but the Dark Prism didn't seem to be in a physically violent mood at the moment. Then again, that could change in the blink of an eye.

Oh well, Hayden sighed inwardly. *If he hits me, he hits me. Cinder will stop him from beating me to death for a few more weeks at least.*

"It is more than a simple pain spell," Aleric answered dryly, his annoyance becoming evident. "It is the most impenetrable part of all of the defenses surrounding this estate. Nothing can get through that barrier."

"Except Bonk," Hayden pointed out. "And presumably Cinder as well, since I've seen him flying outside the gates."

His father narrowed his focus on him and said, "Dragonlings are arguably the most powerful creatures on the planet. There is little that they cannot do when they exert themselves."

So if any dragon can cross the border, except Bonk now that he's wearing Binders...

Hayden shelved that thought for later.

"So not a pain spell," he brought the subject back to the thing that mattered most. "Or at least, not *just* a pain spell. Still," Hayden pressed lightly, "I haven't been able to figure out how you made it affect even non-magical people. Most magic travels through the Foci, which a normal person doesn't have—else we'd all be able to use magic."

His father looked almost amused as he said, "Oh, it does enter the body via the Foci."

Hayden was about to open his mouth and insist that there must be a secondary mode of entry for it to affect normal people, but something in his father's tone of voice stopped him. The Dark Prism had sounded amused, like he was posing a riddle and wanted to see if Hayden was smart enough to figure it out on his own. His posture was even relaxed, the back of one hand resting under his chin as he watched Hayden closely.

Okay...so it enters through the Foci, but somehow it still affects normal people...

Hayden racked his brain for ideas, but it seemed completely contradictory to everything he had ever learned about magic. The only Foci that non-magical people had was in their—

"The eyes," Hayden widened his own as understanding dawned on him, leaning forward in his chair so that his elbows were resting on the table. "That spell doesn't just go through the Foci in our arms, it can go through the eyes as well. That's why Jack was grabbing at his!"

He was so excited at having figured it out all by himself that it took him a moment to realize that he was enthusiastically recounting an innocent man's gruesome death. The reminder had a sobering effect, dampening his joy so that he was able to compose himself once more.

"The Frosts have been accused of many things, but stupidity was never one of them."

It was the first time his father had ever really associated him with the Frost family. Hayden tried not to be too pleased that the man had tangentially acknowledged their relation.

"So it's some sort of pain spell that can go in through any Focus," he summarized. "That still doesn't really explain what it does." Hayden frowned. "I mean, shouldn't shutting his eyes have blocked whatever effect it was having on him?"

His father looked like he was changing his mind about none of the Frosts ever being considered stupid. Hayden realized his mistake even as the man said, "Does closing your fists prevent magic from traversing your magical Foci?"

"No, of course not, I wasn't thinking," Hayden chided himself. He couldn't afford to make careless mistakes when he was dealing with his father, especially not when he was actually manipulating the man into telling him what he needed to know.

"You should be familiar with the effects of the spell," Aleric continued, "having experienced them yourself."

Now Hayden narrowed his eyes thoughtfully, thinking back through anything that made his eyes and Foci hurt like that. It wasn't at all hard to figure it out.

"Light-sickness?" he asked cautiously, not wanting to be wrong. "You've put something in place to channel light-sickness into whoever passes through?"

The edge of a smirk at his father's lips confirmed the horrible truth. Knowing just how terrible the pain was for Jack, stuck in a haze of light-sickness, dying on the lawn, made it all the worse somehow. It was a fate he wouldn't wish on anyone—well, present company excluded.

"Ouch," he said lamely, trying to sound unaffected. "I don't suppose there's any good way of getting past that," he admitted, miserable at the invincibility of it all. Sure, maybe someone who was completely blind and not magically-inclined could stumble through that particular spell, but then the other spells would certainly take him out. Besides, even if a blind, non-magic person got through everything perfectly, he wouldn't stand a chance in a fight against the Dark Prism.

"That is the general idea," his father confirmed neutrally. "My old friend can make all the idle threats he wants, but he is not fool enough to risk his neck for you. And if he is, well..." he trailed off with an unpleasant smirk, and Hayden suppressed a shudder at the thought of his mentor writhing on the ground, dying of light-sickness.

He doesn't know Asher as well as he thinks—not anymore at least. Hayden knew that the Prism Master was stubborn enough and honorable enough to risk his own life to rescue Hayden, if he thought there was even a slim chance of success.

I have to warn him not to try. That letter is more important now than ever.

"May I be excused?" Hayden asked abruptly, itching to get to work.

His father waved him away with a careless gesture and Hayden left without another word. He waited until he was in the foyer to break into a run, taking the stairs to the second level in twos and threes, so that he was winded by the time he made it to his room and shut and locked the door behind him.

Bonk was already buried somewhere beneath the covers on Hayden's bed, settling in for the night, but when Hayden said, "Get up, quick, I've had an idea," the dragonling popped his head up and looked alert.

Hayden sat down on the edge of the bed, feeling around the underside of his pillow for the reassuring lump that told him the violet prism was still in place. He turned to his familiar.

"The barrier that no one can cross, the one he doesn't think anyone can break, it causes light-sickness," Hayden summarized rapidly, still breathless from running upstairs and from anticipation at this next phase.

Bonk nodded as though he wasn't surprised by this bit of news, and Hayden wished that his familiar could talk to humans, because then he would have known all of this weeks ago.

Maybe I'll try to teach him to write. Hayden imagined Bonk trying to wield a pencil and suppressed a laugh.

"But dragons can cross the barrier because they're more powerful than anything even my father can come up with," he continued hurriedly, lowering his voice conspiratorially.

Bonk tilted his head in provisional agreement, perhaps uncertain whether dragons were stronger than *anything* the Dark Prism could come up with, but acknowledging that they could pass through the defensive barriers.

"I don't suppose you can cross through with Binders on?" Hayden asked without real hope. If it had been that simple, Bonk would have volunteered before now.

His familiar spared him a flat stare at the stupidity of that question, and Hayden moved on.

"Sorry, but I had to ask. But even if you can't pass through, another dragon should be able to, like Slasher?"

Bonk paused thoughtfully to consider this, and then slowly nodded.

Finally I get a nod out of him!

It felt like the greatest achievement Hayden had ever accomplished, including getting kicked out of Powders during his first term at school because he'd loosed poisonous gas on his classmates.

"And you have a connection with Slasher," he continued enthusiastically. "It's not as strong as your link to Cinder is—was," Hayden amended, feeling awkward at the reminder that Cinder was now their enemy. "But you used it to get me away from the Council at the end of last term, when they wanted to arrest me in the dining hall for bringing my father back into this realm; you two transported me to the Trout estate."

Bonk nodded once more.

"Can you call on him in some way and tell him to come here? If we could get him across the boundaries then you could give him the letter to take back with him. Isn't there some way you can get in touch with him?"

The look Bonk gave him seemed to say, *Sure there is, with magic...*

"There has to be some way, even though you can't use magic," Hayden insisted. "Just...just please, think it through and give it a try. I'll write my letter so that it's all ready to go, and you work on getting Slasher to figure out he needs to come here."

Bonk looked a little uncertain, which wasn't very reassuring, but Hayden ignored it and turned his back on his familiar, rummaging around the room for something to write with. The only thing that kept him from giving up was the belief that there was still something useful he could do for the mages on the other side of the barrier, the truly powerful people who had been trying to train him and make him better for years now: information. He could give them as much useful information as possible about the defenses around the estate and his father's plans, so that even if—when—he died, better mages than him would be in a position to take down the Dark Prism for good.

But all of these plans hinged on Hayden's ability to communicate with the outside world, which is why he had to remain positive and believe that Bonk would somehow come through for him and find a way to pull on his bond with Slasher.

So he turned to his part of the task, which was to sit down and write. Sitting up in bed with his legs bent, he propped a worn accounting ledger book against his thighs and began thinking. The first question he had to answer was who he would address the letter to.

Tess?

That seemed like a bad idea, given that he planned on telling the recipient that he was likely going to die here and ask that no one do something stupid like try to brave the light-sickness defense just to try and rescue him. Tess was likely to ignore his request and come charging in with her hunting knife, and if there was one thing Hayden didn't want, it was for Tess to come within a hundred yards of the Dark Prism.

Zane?

But that was almost as good as sending the letter to Tess directly. Zane would be tempted to mount a rescue operation as well, though at least he would probably realize from Hayden's letter that it was pointless. He would tell the Masters, as Hayden intended, but there was no way he would keep it from Tess.

There was really only one good choice, only one person who could be trusted to do what was needed with the information while also respecting his wishes.

Asher it is, then.

Hayden wrote the salutation on the top line and then paused with his pencil above the blank paper. It was hard to organize everything he needed to say into an efficient order in his head, but eventually he managed it. It took him over an hour to complete the letter, and several sheets of paper, but finally he was done.

It was very late at night, and Hayden's writing hand was cramping so badly that he might have just finished one of his final exams. He wiped the pencil smudges off of the side of his hand from where he had tracked it across the paper, rolled over, and went to sleep.

Hayden was plagued with bizarre dreams that night, dreams that made him wonder if he was hovering somewhere between consciousness and sleep. He kept imagining that he saw Bonk perched beside him on the bed, eyes closed and face focused as though in deep meditation. Occasionally he dreamed that Bonk was pacing the room in obvious frustration, or flying quiet circles around the space, venting his displeasure. Then Hayden would sink back into restful oblivion until some variation of the scene reformed in his mind. Several times he was aware of hovering in that obnoxious in-between state, not fully asleep but not truly awake, feeling his body struggle to transition from one state to the other with limited success.

At one point he must have truly fallen asleep, because he dreamed that he opened his eyes and saw Cinder and Bonk communicating quietly near the door. He couldn't hear what they were saying from his bed, as the dragonlings kept the noise down, but they looked like they were having an engrossing discussion. Hayden knew he had to be imagining things, because Cinder and Bonk were officially enemies now, each bound to serve their respective masters, who happened to be trying to murder each other. Besides, the whole thing was ridiculous anyway, since Hayden had locked the door before going to bed, so Cinder shouldn't even be able to get into the room with him.

Hayden woke the next morning feeling as tired as when he went to bed. He cursed his overactive mind for keeping him from sleeping properly, and then forced himself to get up and shower before breakfast. His father would probably knock his teeth out if he turned up in the formal dining room looking groggy and disheveled.

It became quickly apparent that the Dark Prism was having an off day, cognitively-speaking. One thought never seemed to track the next, and he would go from staring blankly into the distance to violently angry for no apparent reason. Hayden had seen shorter periods of this behavior in his father before, and knew by now to stay well clear of the man until his mind returned to whatever shaky equilibrium it normally maintained.

He gobbled down breakfast as fast as he could and decided not to go to the library today, since at some point he would inevitably draw his father's attention and that could only turn out badly for him. Instead he joined Bonk on the front lawns, walking around the neatly trimmed grass and watching his familiar soar overhead.

He saw one of the imprisoned groundskeepers and nodded politely in greeting, before turning the opposite direction to avoid conversation. It wasn't that he was trying to be rude, or that he didn't want to talk to the others—though he had been avoiding their company since that morning in the kitchen. His self-appointed solitude was mostly due to the fact that he was constantly researching ways to bring down the magical barriers around the place or take down his father, though if he was being completely honest with himself, it was also because he didn't want to face any more hopeful questions about his progress. He could focus on his work better if he could ignore the fact that nine other people were eagerly counting on his success.

After flying around within the limits of the barriers, Bonk alit on a stone statue in the middle of a small fountain, landing gracefully on the tip of the angel's wing and watching the water trickle gently through her outturned stone hands.

"Did you have any luck contacting Slasher last night?" Hayden asked his familiar, stifling a yawn and trying to enjoy the sunlight.

Bonk made a noncommittal gesture and looked like he regretted landing near Hayden at all.

"Come on, don't be like that; this is important," Hayden insisted. "I spent all night dreaming that I was watching you try to call out through the bond you have, which is why I'm dead-tired this morning. If I had to lose an entire night of sleep over it, the least you could do is tell me whether you actually managed to make contact with him."

Bonk hesitated for a moment, as though there was something he wasn't sure whether to reveal. Finally he came to some internal decision, and shook his head 'no'. Hayden didn't bother concealing his frown as his breakfast seemed to curdle in his stomach.

"Okay, well, that's a bummer…but promise me you'll keep trying, okay? This is the most important thing we need to do right now, and it'll all fall apart if we can't get Slasher to show up and take our letter for us. You're the only one here with a bond to him that can summon him, or I'd do it myself."

Bonk made a slight negating gesture, flapping his wings a few times for reasons best known to him.

"Well, okay," Hayden amended, "you're technically not the *only* one who can communicate with Slasher, but I doubt Cinder is going to help us since we're working against his master's best interests."

He remembered a fragment of his strange dream, where he had been watching Cinder and Bonk discussing something quietly near the door to his bedroom, but pushed the thought aside once more. There was one thing he knew for certain, and that was that familiars didn't ever side against their masters.

Bonk took flight again and resumed his circling of the Frost estate, and Hayden sighed and left him to it, instead approaching the gates cautiously and staring through them. Freedom was deceptively close; it looked like all he had to do was open the gate and walk about three feet, and he'd be free to go wherever his heart desired, but he knew it was all a ruse. He had no desire to have different colors of light burn through every receptor in his eyes—again. He had survived it once, by some miracle, but was pretty sure that this time his brain would turn to jelly and he would die, just like every other poor fool who tried to cross through the barrier.

Instead he closed his eyes and tried to sense any of the other defensive spells that separated him from freedom. His father seemed to think that they were not infallible, which was mildly reassuring, but all that meant was that the Dark Prism would have found a series of alignments that could bypass them in his Black Prism— which had a host of alignments not available in normal prisms. Still, the fact remained that of all his defenses, the only one his father was relying on to prove absolutely impenetrable was the light-sickness curtain.

That meant there was a slight chance that Hayden could discover and unravel the other defenses, assuming he took down his father and still had enough of his violet prism remaining that he could cast the magic needed to bring down the defenses. It wouldn't get him and the other nine captives out, but it would make it much easier for his other allies to focus on the light-sickness spell in the hopes that someday they would break it.

Hayden had seen the Masters ferret out magical spells just by standing nearby and focusing on them with their eyes closed, though admittedly, they often gripped their Mastery Charms while doing this. Hayden didn't know whether they used the Mastery Charms to amplify their own senses, or if there was something critical inside the Charms that actually enabled them to detect magic. If the former, then Hayden still had some kind of chance; if the latter, then he was wasting his time.

Still, he had to try, if only to be thorough. He stood there and bent all of his concentration towards the gates, trying to let himself slip away from his consciousness and become one with the world around him. It was a similar process to getting earth-based magic to work: he had to train his brain to almost leave the physical world behind in order to connect to the living world around him.

He tried for over an hour, but no matter how hard he focused, he felt nothing. Well, that wasn't entirely true, he could feel the magic readily enough, standing before him like an impenetrable fortress with razor-glass all along the walls, lava pouring down from the top, and a few sorcerers standing nearby waiting to hurl spells at him just to add insult to injury. That wasn't truly how the magic looked to his mind's eye, but it was fairly representative of how difficult it would be to get around or through the wall without dying.

He mentally cursed himself for never asking any of his Masters how they sensed specific spells and unraveled them during the entirely of his magical education at Mizzenwald. Why did he ever bother wasting time on things like petty grudges against the Trouts when he should have been preparing day and night for this?

Maybe if I had known that my dead father wasn't quite dead enough, I would have taken more effort to prepare for disassembling his magic.

Frustrated, he went back inside and looked for something else to do.

His father never came downstairs to lunch, which didn't bother Hayden in the slightest—it was nice to eat a meal without worrying about setting off the human time-bomb beside him.

Afterwards he roamed the upper floor, reading through a few old ledger books in the office he passed and generally killing time, wondering whether it was safe to go back into the library yet. Before dinner was scheduled to begin, he happened to glance out the window and catch sight of something that made his spirits soar.

Slasher.

Bonk was hovering in mid-air with Hayden's folded-up letter clenched in his talons, communicating with a sleek, black dragonling who could only be Slasher. Hayden had never been so happy to see anyone affiliated with the Trout family in his entire life, and vowed to buy the dragon a lifetime supply of whatever meat he wanted if he made it out of this mess alive.

Slasher passed easily through the barriers, though he didn't look happy about it, and Bonk passed him the letter.

Now go, Hayden prayed inwardly, hands clasped so hard against the windowsill that his knuckles were turning white. *Go before my father can look out the window and see you, before he can find a way to stop you!*

He wanted to shout, but that would only draw attention, and Hayden thought his fingers were going to snap from clenching the windowsill so hard, until finally Slasher turned and flew back the way he came, disappearing into the distance until Hayden could no longer see him.

He felt light as a feather inside. If he accomplished nothing else in the fight against his father, at least he did this one good thing to help the others continue the battle. His father would go down, whether or not he was still around to see it; with part of his Source missing and the secret of his defensive barriers known, Asher would see to it. Somehow.

He was so pleased he was tempted to skip down the hallway, and might have except for the roar of rage, followed by the ear-splitting sound of something heavy being knocked over.

He knows.

A thrill of terror went through Hayden as another crash sounded from further down the hall. Hattie, who had been changing the sheets in the bedrooms, came running down the hall and flew down the stairs so fast that Hayden was afraid she would fall. He couldn't blame her from trying to get as far away as possible from the Dark Prism's wrath.

Well, he can rage and kill me all he wants. The letter is already gone and there's nothing he can do about it.

Hayden was sorely tempted to take off running like Hattie, but thought he ought to show a little more grit. The others would probably lose confidence in him if he was hiding behind sacks of flour in the kitchen alongside them. So he did the brave—or stupid—thing and began walking towards the sounds of mayhem coming from the library.

17
Things to Burn

The door to the library was already ajar when he approached, which in itself was unusual. He pushed the door open and entered without knocking, since his father obviously knew what he had done by now and tiptoeing around wasn't going to save him. Even as he steeled his courage, he wondered why the Dark Prism was reacting so badly to a simple letter.

The library was a mess.

His father's worktable had been knocked over, drawings and notes scattered all over the floor wherever they landed. More than one window was missing glass now, the remaining shards dangling dangerously in the panes. Two entire bookshelves had been knocked over, which accounted for the loud crashing noises, and Hayden found his father pacing furiously back and forth across the length of the room, artfully stepping around broken bits of wood or fallen books as though he didn't even see them in his path.

"—will not, you cretinous old man," his father was muttering to himself while he paced, occasionally stopping long enough to slam one closed fist into his open palm, or to kick something out of his way. "You never could see past your own ego," he continued, seething.

Confused, Hayden paused in place at the threshold, wondering if he had missed something. He had no idea who his father was talking to—or ranting about—but it didn't seem to have anything to do with his sending a message. Besides, the more Hayden thought about it, the less certain he was that the Dark Prism would get this upset about anything Hayden did. Most of the time he didn't even think his only son was worth the time of day, let alone getting riled up over. Besides, even though Hayden confided everything he had learned about both his father's motives and defenses in his letter, that didn't make the barriers any easier to get past, or the man any easier to defeat.

Maybe the timing of this outburst was coincidental?

If so, that was a relief, because it meant that his father probably didn't know what Hayden had done, and was therefore much less likely to punish him for it. On the other hand, it made Hayden walking into the library during the Dark Prism's psychotic break from reality all the more dangerous, and stupid, as it drew unnecessary attention to him. Belatedly, Hayden realized that he hadn't even stopped by his bedroom to get his prism, and Bonk was still flying around somewhere outside, so he was completely defenseless. He had no idea where Cinder was, but the dragonling didn't appear to be in the library with them, which was a shame since his father's familiar was the only living thing that could ever talk some sense into him.

Hayden tried to back out of the room quietly and pass unnoticed, but of course his father chose that moment to wheel around and face him. His face was a mask of rage, and there was something demented and inhuman in his eyes, like a wild animal that had lost all control over itself. Hayden had never been so afraid of the man.

"You," the Dark Prism said coldly, eyes scanning Hayden's face. "Are you one of his puppets too? Come to check on me and see how I'm getting along?" he snarled hatefully, clenching and unclenching his fists with rage. Hayden was uncomfortably aware of the Black Prism perched in his father's circlet, currently pointing upwards at the ceiling.

Not knowing why his father didn't recognize him or who he thought Hayden was working for, he tread as carefully as possible.

"No, sir...I hate him just like you do," he said in his most soothing tone, afraid to break eye contact or even blink. He felt like he was alone in the woods, facing down a chimaera, and that the slightest wrong move would spur it to action and be the end of him.

The Dark Prism leaned back slightly and gave him a scrutinizing look. Hayden prayed he had said the right thing, or his lifeless corpse would be the next thing his father kicked out of the way to make room for his pacing.

"He thinks I can't do it, just because Ash beat me those first two rounds for the I.S.C.," he snarled, drawing himself up so that he was the epitome of arrogance. "I was hardly even serious about things back then. This time

I *will* win, and Ash's project on light-bending through water is going to look ridiculous by comparison." Now he looked almost smug as he confided in Hayden. "I've had Maralynn spying on him for weeks, though he thinks she's just finally returning his interest in her. His work doesn't hold a candle to mine, and maybe when I've left him in the dust, that unfeeling old man will acknowledge my value."

Hayden knew enough about his father's teenage years to form a picture of what was happening now. Aleric thought he was back at Mizzenwald, working on his mastery-level research project and competing with Asher for the glory of the next big discovery in prisms. Asher had told him about this time in their lives, when his best friend had been driven to cut-throat competitiveness by his overbearing father and, having greatly overestimated Asher's progress on his own project, turned to imperfect prisms in an effort to out-shine him once and for all.

The 'old man' my father is seething over right now is my grandfather.

The realization left Hayden feeling depressed. Apparently the horrible man couldn't find it in himself to bestow a shred of praise upon his only son, who was desperate to please him in any way he could and live up to the Frost family name. In a way, all of this was *his* fault. A young Aleric Frost had even been driven to recruit his best friend's crush as a spy to report on how his research was progressing. He wasn't even sure if Asher knew that part of the story, or what had happened to the mysterious

Maralynn since then, as Asher certainly wasn't married to her and Hayden had never even heard of her until this moment. Perhaps she had run away from Junir once she saw what Aleric was becoming, or maybe she had been caught up in the eventual fight between the two former best friends and was killed.

"I think I can safely say that your research will be far more impressive than Asher's project on light-bending through water," Hayden assured him gently, because whatever else his father had become, his discoveries and powers were certainly impressive.

"What would you know of it?" the Dark Prism sneered, before his expression became wary and he asked, "Who are you?"

Deciding that honesty was the best policy, Hayden replied, "I'm Hayden."

He might as well have said, "I'm a sea cucumber," for all the recognition he received in response. His father narrowed his eyes like he was trying to place the name and failing, grabbed the eyepiece of his circlet containing the Black Prism, and brought it down over his eye.

Hayden dove to the side without even stopping to think about it, and a wave of magic rippled past him, blasting a dent in the stone wall where it hit. Part of the carpet smoldered, though the embers burned out quickly and left only the smell of singed carpet behind.

Apparently my father has decided to simplify things by killing me instead of wasting more time on pesky questions.

Before the Dark Prism could attack again, a small dark-purple dragonling flew through one of the broken windows and hovered in the space between them.

About time Cinder got in here. What was he doing, playing lawn tennis with Bonk out front?

Cinder kept himself positioned directly between Hayden and his father, meeting the Dark Prism's gaze for a long moment. He must have been silently trying to communicate something like, "Hey, don't kill this kid yet, you still have to rip out his Source."

Then the dragonling opened his mouth and let out a shriek. Hayden clapped his hands over his ears reflexively, because he had seen the dragonling's cry rupture the eardrums of nearby sorcerers and break steel cages, but to his surprise, the scream was almost entirely silent. Removing his hands from his ears, Hayden wondered if the dragon had gone for a higher pitch than he could actually achieve, or if he had lost his voice, but Aleric crumpled to his knees and covered his ears as though in terrible pain, so it must have been doing something.

Hayden watched for a minute until Cinder stopped his weird, silent shriek, and then the Dark Prism stirred and pulled himself back to his feet, shaking his head a little to clear it. The scary rage was gone, and mostly the man just looked confused. He looked around the room at the destruction and then at his familiar.

"Again?" he asked casually, as though this sort of thing was perfectly normal and could happen to anyone.

Cinder made a noise that could have meant anything, but the Dark Prism nodded curtly and said, "Thank you." Then he turned to Hayden. "What do you want?"

Hayden wasn't sure whether his father remembered anything that had happened since Hayden came into the library, but he thought not.

"I only came to tell you that dinner was ready, but I'm not hungry, so I'm just going to go to bed," he lied on the spot, praying that the servants had indeed prepared dinner in case their insane host decided he was feeling peckish.

His father said nothing, though his eyes never left Hayden's face as he retreated from the room with as much composure as he could muster. He could feel the Dark Prism's eyes following him until he had turned into his bedroom and shut and locked the door behind him. Bonk was already waiting for him.

"Some help you were," Hayden grumbled, his hands shaking now that he was relatively safe and could afford to emote properly.

Bonk pulled a face and held up one Binder-wrapped leg as though to say, "What did you want me to do about it?"

"I know, and I'm sorry," Hayden sighed, rubbing his face with the palms of his hands. "I'm not mad at you, just kind of on edge. Actually, I wanted to tell you you're the best familiar in the entire world; I saw you hand off that letter to Slasher. I knew you'd find a way to get in touch with him if you put your mind to it."

Bonk made a noncommittal gesture, as though he didn't really want to take credit, which was odd since Bonk normally loved being praised.

"Anyway," Hayden continued, "I don't think either of us should go out in the hallway, no matter how hungry we get. My father completely lost it in there, and if Cinder hadn't shown up when he did and cured him, I'd be a smoldering pile of ash on the carpet right now." He shuddered at the near miss.

Bonk didn't argue with him, though he didn't look overjoyed at being stuck inside the bedroom this early in the evening. Hayden supposed his familiar could always leave via the window and hunt around the yard for a vole to eat if he got desperate, but Hayden would be stuck inside until breakfast.

He had no idea how long he spent in his room that evening, watching the sunset through his window and listening for sounds of further devastation from the library. Fortunately, whatever magic Cinder had used to snap his master out of his insanity, it seemed to be holding, because Hayden didn't hear any unusual sounds in the hours that followed.

Harder to ignore were the pangs of hunger assailing his stomach as the evening progressed. He made a mental note to hurry up and eat dinner before going to investigate any more dangerous situations involving his father in the future.

Also, next time bring a weapon. It would have been embarrassing to have Bonk bring him a mastery-level violet prism to defend himself with, only to leave it in his pillowcase when he actually needed it to fight.

And so dies Hayden Frost, an idiot until the end. He could imagine the epitaph on his tombstone.

After changing into his sleep pants and preparing to turn off the gas lamps, Hayden had relaxed to the point that the knock on the door nearly sent his heart flying into his throat.

Now?! he thought wildly, racing to his pillowcase and withdrawing the violet prism. *I thought he was safe again—or as safe as he can ever really be! He's been quiet for hours!*

This was it, the moment he had been dreading. His father was on the other side of that door, waiting to tell him that he had worked the kinks out of his spells a little ahead of schedule and was ready to drain the life from him now. Hayden would never let that happen, but one way or another, he knew he was going to die tonight…

Another knock.

Now Hayden actually stopped to think, still grasping the edges of the violet prism with sweaty fingers.

Wait a minute, that knock was way too quiet and timid to be my father, he realized, a wave of relief flooding him as Hayden remembered that there were nine other people in this house as well. *Besides,* he added further, *Father would never knock twice.*

Despite his returning sensibilities, Hayden still maintained his grip on the violet prism, though he held it with his left hand and opened the door with his right, so that he was leaned casually against the frame and had his left hand and the prism concealed behind the open door.

"Holy arcana, Hattie, you about scared me to death!" he greeted her, a little annoyed by the fact that he had to worry about dying twice in one afternoon.

Hattie looked so nervous that Hayden began to wonder if the Dark Prism was actually hiding just out of sight in the hallway, waiting for her to lure him outside so he could kill them both. That was stupid, of course, since the room wasn't barred against him in any way, and even if it was, his father was certainly capable of breaking down a simple door, locked or not. Hayden wasn't going to waste any of his violet prism on putting more extensive protections around the door, as his father would know how to break through them anyway.

"I'm sorry to bother you, sir," Hattie's voice was barely a whisper, and Hayden felt bad for the poor girl. It wasn't easy for Hayden, living under the threat of death in his father's—his—house, but it had to be even harder for her and the others, knowing they weren't magically-inclined and couldn't do much of anything to fight back or escape.

"It's fine, sorry, I'm just a little jumpy tonight," Hayden apologized, forcing a smile and trying to put her at ease.

It worked, sort of, or at least she returned his smile briefly before saying, "He wants to see you in the library."

No need to ask who 'he' was. Hayden's father was the only one around here that none of the others would call by name. They either weren't sure whether to use Aleric, the Dark Prism, or whatever other pompous agnomen the man had dreamed up for himself. Or maybe they were just afraid of saying his name, as though he were a monster who could be summoned by name alone.

Hayden focused on the more important part of the message.

"He sent you to get me? *Why?*" he asked in alarm, trying to think of any reason for his father to want to see him that didn't end badly. He was drawing a blank.

"I don't think he wanted to come get you himself," Hattie explained, taking the wrong meaning from his question. "He doesn't like doing servant work, like looking for people, when he can have them brought to him and—"

"No, that isn't what I meant," Hayden interrupted. "I know he's too arrogant to do something like going to find someone he wants to see or knocking on a door; what I meant was, do you know why he wants to see me?"

Maybe he's embarrassed that I saw him lose all control of himself and wants to threaten me until he feels like he's reasserted dominance.

That didn't seem to fit his persona though. If he felt he'd been humiliated irreparably, he would just kill Hayden and have done with it. Otherwise he probably didn't even care that Hayden had seen such a display of weakness, since Hayden wasn't even really a person to him.

"I'm sorry, sir, he didn't say."

"Of course. Thanks for telling me," Hayden waved her away with his empty hand. "You can go on back to whatever else you were doing; I'll go see him in just a second."

He shut the door as she turned away and stuffed the violet prism back into his pillowcase, withdrawing it and then returning it twice more before deciding to leave it behind. If he walked into the library with it, his father would either see it or sense it on him and it would be taken away from him. Hayden was betting that if the Dark Prism was really in a killing mood right now, he would have come barging into Hayden's bedroom himself, rather than sending someone to calmly retrieve him.

For the second time that day, Hayden found himself walking into the library, and he was no gladder to see it this time around. The doors were closed, so he knocked before entering to announce his presence.

When he opened and shut the doors behind him, he was a little surprised by how dark the room was. Even at night, the library usually had the gas lamps lit, until Aleric was ready to call it a night on his research. Currently, the only light in the entire room was coming from a fireplace on the far side, where Hayden sometimes sat reading books if he was trying to get as far away from his father as possible when they were both in the room.

The firelight threw eerie shadows around the space, and Hayden shivered a little and stepped further into the room, telling himself that it hadn't actually gotten colder since he was last here, that it was just a side-effect of his fear.

Aleric Frost was sitting on a hand-woven oval shaped rug on the floor, just in front of the grate. He was staring thoughtfully into the flames, feeding the fire scraps of something Hayden couldn't immediately identify. Not sure if the man had even heard him enter the room, Hayden approached warily and brought himself into his father's line of sight.

"You wanted to see me?" he asked softly, because something about the entire situation seemed to warrant a quiet, almost reverent tone.

Without turning his eyes from the flames, the Dark Prism said, "Sit down," though there was no malice in his voice, and for once it sounded more like a request than a command.

Curious despite his underlying worry, Hayden sat.

He knew he was inside his father's reach if the man decided to go nuts and start physically attacking him again, but it would be painfully obvious that he was scared and trying to avoid punishment if he backed up any further, and sitting in one of the chairs while his father was on the floor was out of the question.

For a moment Hayden studied the Dark Prism at close range, who in turn studied the fire, still steadily feeding scraps into the flames. From up close, Hayden realized that the scraps of paper were actually pages from books. There were half a dozen empty bindings scattered around them, where his father had clearly already pulled out each page and fed it to the flames, like the tome he was now calmly ripping apart, page by page. The slow tearing was loud in the otherwise quiet space, and it became like nails on a chalkboard to Hayden after a few minutes.

He wanted to snatch the book out of his father's hand and tell the man that books were expensive and that there was no good reason to disrespect a vessel of knowledge, but somehow he didn't think the interference would be appreciated.

Instead he asked, "What book is that?" into the silence.

It took his father a moment to answer, but for once Hayden didn't think he was being ignored or manipulated. Then again, wasn't that the mark of a master manipulator, to make the victim not even think they were being messed with? But his father really did look tired and somehow more human and approachable than usual.

"I neither know nor care," the Dark Prism answered calmly, still tearing off one sheet at a time and feeding it into the flames.

*Okay...*Hayden was kind of at a loss for what to say next. After all, his father had been the one to summon him, not the other way around. Yet here he was, not even telling Hayden why he had called him here.

Maybe he wants to show me how truly horrifying he can be to innocent books? Hayden suppressed a snort.

"You once told me that Asher was the only father you'd ever known," Aleric said at last, apropos of nothing.

The completely unexpected topic nearly stunned Hayden stupid. He had no idea why the Dark Prism was bringing this up right now, and had to rack his brain to even remember *when* he had ever made such a comment to the man sitting beside him. Not here, certainly.

When we were inside the schism, he realized at last, and immediately became more alert.

"Yes..." Hayden began invitingly. When no other comment was forthcoming, he added, "Do you remember much of that conversation?" *At the moment, I mean.* His father's memories were more fluid and fleeting than anything.

"Some of it," the man answered at last, still staring at the fire without blinking. Hayden wondered how he managed that without his eyes watering, and wondered whether he'd be temporarily blinded in the darkness of the library when he finally looked away. Somehow he just couldn't imagine the legendary Dark Prism stumbling around in the dark while his eyes adjusted to ambient lighting.

If he remembers that, then he probably remembers all of the horrible things I said about him and his path towards evil. This could get awkward...

"I suppose he took an interest in you, being one of the few prism-wielders at Mizzenwald during your time," his father continued thoughtfully.

"I was the only Prism major there, actually," Hayden corrected, still unsure as to why they were having this conversation or what state of mind his father was in right now. It was always difficult to tell, but it was impossible tonight to determine whether he was about to be tricked, murdered, or if they were having their first semi-normal discussion.

"Not entirely surprising; natural prism-users are quite rare. It takes a unique level of awareness to be able to interpret light as magic."

Hayden said nothing in response to this. He didn't know what the man wanted him to say.

Finally, because the silence was becoming unbearable, Hayden blurted out, "I don't think that was the only reason he watched out for me. I mean, I think he would have still had my back even if I wasn't a Prism major," addressing his father's earlier point.

For the first time since he'd entered the room, the Dark Prism turned to face him. Hayden had no idea if he could actually make out the features of his face after staring into the fire for so long, but the man's gaze was steady and he didn't act like he was trying to blink his surroundings into focus.

One more mystical power my father possesses.

"And why is that?"

Now it was Hayden's turn to break eye contact and stare into the fire, because it was easier to speak freely when he wasn't watching his father watch him.

"He always felt partly responsible for what you became, even after most people stopped publicly shaming him over it. He thought he should have recognized what was happening to you and found a way to save you before you were too far gone to recognize friend from foe." Hayden's eyes began to water from the warmth of the fire and he blinked the moisture from his eyes. "He told me once that if you were still..." –*sane*— 'like you were back then, you would have wanted him to look after me if you weren't able to. He said you would have been proud to have me as a son."

Well, there we go, I've just said about ten different things that are all triggers for him to go nuts and strangle me. Let's see just how effective Cinder's magic really was this afternoon.

He waited to feel some sort of pain, but it never came. Finally, he turned to look at his father again, only to find that the man was staring at him as though finally seeing him for what he was. It was an odd feeling.

"I never wanted a son," the Dark Prism said at last. "I don't even remember your mother's name, or her face. She was nothing to me but a passing whim." He didn't say the words cruelly, just matter-of-factly. It still hurt to have himself and his mother marginalized like that.

"You were too busy trying to impress your own father," Hayden answered instead.

And how much of this could have been avoided if that stupid, over-bearing jerk had just sprinkled some praise upon you?

A hint of the familiar danger flickered behind Aleric's eyes, but it winked out so fast that Hayden wasn't sure if it was really there, or just a trick of the light. Still, when his father spoke again, he said, "Do not speak of him again or you will regret it," in a tone that brooked no argument.

Casting for a maybe-safer subject, Hayden said, "Asher never betrayed you, you know. He didn't turn his back on you until he had no other choice. He abandoned his other research projects when you started working with broken prisms and has been working on finding a way to reverse the distortion in your mind ever since."

Rather than acknowledge the spirit of this, his father said, "You call them 'broken prisms.'"

Oh right, I probably should have said 'modified prisms' since he finds the term less offensive, Hayden realized in retrospect. The term had come to him out of habit.

"Yes?" he asked cautiously.

"Since returning to this realm, I've heard whispers that you have earned that title for yourself somehow: the Broken Prism. And yet, I don't believe you have ever used them."

At first all Hayden could think was, *Wow, that nickname actually stuck?* Then he explained, "It's nothing to do with actual imperfect prisms, other than as a play on words. A couple of bullies who kept picking fights with me during my first year at Mizzenwald gave me the name because of my enormous Focus-correctors, implying that I'm defective in some way. The broken prism-user, you see?"

His father tilted his head slightly in acknowledgement.

"Most notable mages do not receive a secondary name until middle-age is upon them. I was considered quite young at nineteen, when others began referring to me as the Dark Prism."

Hayden was a little surprised that people had used that name within his father's hearing, as it had a negative connotation. Then again, he had no idea how the man actually felt about the name—perhaps he liked it.

"And yet you've received your name even before me," his father finished without emotion.

"Not by design," Hayden explained. "People only noticed me at all because of your legacy and the fact that I was the last surviving member of the Frost family—until you returned from the schism, obviously," he amended. "Most of the attention I got was negative, and I kept getting thrown into stupid situations and blundering through them with talented friends and dumb luck. Somehow things snowballed and here we sit."

They sat in silence for a few minutes longer. Hayden's exposed arms were beginning to get very warm from sitting so close to the fire, but he didn't dare move. His father had finished burning the book he had been tearing pages from, and hadn't reached for another, much to Hayden's relief.

"What did Cinder do earlier when he did that silent screaming thing?" he asked, since he might as well try to get as much information as possible while his father was feeling forthcoming.

"Occasionally I attempt alignments that cause my mind to scatter. Cinder refocused it."

Oh great, he was probably practicing one of those lovely alignments that will help him wrench out my Source.

"It seems to have worked pretty well..." Hayden offered cautiously. "You seem a lot more like how you were when we met inside the schism." *And I liked you a lot better as Hunter.*

"You think I am unaware of the price I pay for the magic I have learned?" His father asked evenly. "I know that my thoughts and memories are no longer linear, and occasionally those connections become frayed or sever altogether. I understood what the cost would be before I ever started using modified prisms."

Astounded, Hayden asked, "Then why did you do it? Was making someone else proud really so important that you would throw your whole life away for it?"

"You have no idea the amount of magic I have discovered since I began working with alternate prisms," his father said flatly. "The Frost family has always been amongst the greatest in the Nine Lands, and new magical discoveries have become a rarity in the last generation. I have forgotten more new magic than you will ever know."

Hayden didn't doubt that for one second, and it also wasn't the first time he'd heard that people were discovering fewer and fewer new spells in recent years. It still didn't seem a goal worth giving up one's sanity and becoming a mass murderer for.

"I don't deny that you probably know more ridiculously-complex, powerful magic than all ten Council members combined," *assuming they've managed to replace the ones you killed back at the Crystal Tower and have ten again...* "But do you ever wonder whether you made the right decision?"

His father's gaze turned unexpectedly sharp and he said, "No, never." He paused before continuing. "It does no good to question one's decisions after they are made. There is nothing to do but keep forward momentum at all times, because to look back is to see the sand crumbling beneath one's feet. It is one thing you would have learned, had you grown up in this house: there is only one direction to move in, and that is forward."

Hayden raised his eyebrows and gave this some serious consideration. To never doubt his decisions, to never second-guess himself and just accept that he was on the path he was meant to be on...there was something freeing about the idea of abandoning his worries. And in some ways, this is what made great leaders and revolutionaries what they were, the ability to always look ahead and not behind.

By the same token, there was no one rule that could be adhered to all of the time, including this. There are times when a person has to be able to reflect on their decisions, acknowledge they were wrong, and change directions before too much damage is done. His father was a prime example of what total inflexibility in this regard could lead to.

"You know, I've seen a bit of Asher's research," Hayden said cautiously. "The stuff he was working on for reversing the effects of distortion on your mind. It looks promising, though it's still incomplete."

His father said nothing, turning back to stare at the fire while Hayden spoke.

"If you agreed to work with us...if you added the weight of all the things you've discovered that no one else knows, we might be able to finish it and use it to help undo some of what's been done."

"No," his father answered definitively. "I chose my path years ago, and he chose his. To remove the distortion is to remove all of the things I have sacrificed and discovered; I doubt my old friend's spell will let me select which parts of my memory I retain and which I lose. Even you should know enough of me by now to realize that I would not ever want to be less than what I am; I will never go back."

Well, it was worth a shot.

Another heavy moment of silence passed between them, until finally Hayden got up the nerve to ask, "Sir, why did you want to see me tonight?" He only just realized that they had never really gotten to the point of him being summoned here.

There was something undefinable in his father's expression when he turned to Hayden and said, perfectly deadpan, "I don't remember."

18
Asher

Asher Masters paced his office, which was hard to do in the cramped quarters. His feet automatically bypassed stacks of papers that littered parts of the floor space, though they were nowhere near as large as they were before his office was blown up and his research scattered to the wind. As it was, he could probably step over the piles if he wanted to, but he had already trained himself to simply walk around them while crossing the room in three long strides, first one way, then the other. If he moved fast enough he could make himself dizzy.

If I never stop running, I can outpace time itself…

Pacing gave his brain the false impression that he was actually accomplishing something, even though he was about as useless as a drying spell in a desert. Sitting made him feel stagnant, defeated. Moving made it seem like he was going towards something, progress of a sort.

He missed a step and accidentally kicked over a pile of mathematical notes—he didn't even remember which project they were associated with anymore. Papers scattered all over the floor beneath his worktable and chairs, but he made no move to bend down and retrieve them. If Hayden were here, he'd make some dry, pointed comment about the merits of a tidy office.

Well, he isn't here. For all I know, Aleric has already disposed of him.

Asher paused and glanced down at his worktable. It looked exactly the way he and Hayden had left it during their last meeting, several months ago now. It wasn't that he left the space untouched on purpose—well, not exactly. Soon after their last meeting, Hayden had ventured into the schism, returned with his father in tow, and all hell had broken loose. There hadn't been time for either of them to resume work on their projects, even had they been inclined to do so. Then that useless sack of oxygen, Laris, had let his career objectives outweigh his good sense, and they'd had to have Hayden arrested while they still controlled the situation. He, Asher, certainly didn't have time to work on his projects with Aleric loose, Hayden on trial for his life, and the Council spying on his every move.

Then the boy went and got himself kidnapped from the heart of the Crystal Tower.

No, it wasn't fair to blame Hayden for that. What else could he have done when his father came to get him? The boy was weaponless and alone, weakened from his time in the oppressive cells that were typically used to contain only the vilest of criminals.

He must have been terrified.

So there really hadn't been time for Asher to sit down and sort through his and Hayden's research notes, much less to decide which ones to shelve for later and which to throw away. All of that made perfect, rational sense, and yet he knew it wasn't the real reason he had left things intact at all. The true reason wasn't rational or logical, but emotional. If he shelved Hayden's notes, he was acknowledging that his protégé might never come back. And if he admitted that, he might not work as hard to find a solution to the insolvable problem of getting through Aleric's unassailable defenses, overpowering the most magically-skillful man on the continent, and rescuing his son before all was lost.

Aleric's son, not mine.

Sometimes it was hard to forget that fact, after all the time and energy he'd invested in the boy.

His thoughts turned back to the defenses around the Frost estate. Most of his colleagues and a few of the Council members had probed them experimentally, testing to see what they could unravel magically without raising any alarms. Some of it was surprisingly straightforward, probably aimed at barring non-magical interlopers rather than trained mages. Aleric had always been contemptuous of those who couldn't interact directly with the world's magic, often speaking of them as though they were second-rate humans.

Why did it take me so long to realize what he was becoming?

He waved away the unproductive thought and made another pass across the room. Between a couple dozen of the most powerful mages in the Nine Lands, they had been able to work together and map out a surprising number of the Frost estate defenses. Even better, they were fairly certain they could break through them given sufficient time and coordination, though it would all have to be done at once to prevent Aleric from discovering their attempt until it was too late to put up new defenses.

But then they had hit a barrier of magic so foreign, so powerful, that none of them knew what to make of it. Normally a mage—especially one who possessed a Mastery Charm—could close his eyes and open his Foci, allowing any nearby magical constructs to filter into his awareness. Eventually a person could become good at unraveling what magic they were sensing, and thus derive a workaround.

But this spell had nothing. Any time he stood before the wall and stretched his senses, he could only soak in magic until he hit that bear of a spell, at which point he would feel a stab of pain behind his eyes and then nothing. It didn't help that the other, more trivial spells were blocking his path, and he had to sort through them in his mind before even attempting to comprehend The Beast—as they'd hatefully dubbed it.

At times like this it felt like a cosmic joke was being played on them all. Corrupted, distorted magic had proven itself enormously more powerful and diverse than what mankind had been able to collectively glean through legitimate sources. Why did the dark, evil magic have to be the most powerful? How were they supposed to fight such a thing without succumbing to it themselves?

"I don't suppose you have any bright ideas, do you, Cinder?" he asked out loud without thinking.

There was no answer, neither the soft fluttering of wings, nor the screech of a dragonling.

Idiot, he chided himself for the dozenth time. He had grown so used to the dragonling's company that he forgotten that Cinder wasn't here with him anymore. He'd gone back to his real master and was probably helping Aleric keep Hayden in line.

If he's even still alive.

Kicking over another stack of papers just because he could, Asher stopped pacing and left his office, feeling suddenly claustrophobic in the confined space. He threw open the door more forcefully than he'd intended, startling a passing group of level-three students when the door banged against the wall. The children jumped out of his way and cast frightened looks at him, and he blew past them without apology, his metallic red Mastery robes billowing behind him.

They weren't the only students who seemed afraid of him these days, not that it much mattered to him what others thought. Some of them were doubtless wondering if he was going to join up with his old friend and start slaughtering the innocent; most of them could probably just sense what a bad mood he had been in since term started, and were trying to stay out of his way, which suited him just fine.

He was passing through the Pentagon when someone did finally get up the nerve to speak to him.

"Sir—Asher, wait!"

Oliver Trout still hadn't gotten used to treating the other Masters as his peers. Not surprising, as he hadn't been elevated to their status for terribly long, and was trying to overcome years of conditioning to view the others as his superiors.

Then why didn't I have that problem when I became a Master?

Asher had been calling the Masters by first name since his fifth year of school—countless detentions hadn't been able to break him of the habit.

I've always been arrogant enough to believe myself equal to or better than everyone else.

Another unflattering admission to himself, though most of his recent revelations were. Since Aleric made his grand reappearance at Mizzenwald at the end of last year, all of his normal emotions had taken a back seat to his anger, which burned through everything in its path.

He wasn't even sure what he was angry at, truth be told. Himself, for failing to be good enough to rescue Hayden when it counted the most? Hayden, for foolishly believing in him and relying on him all these years? Aleric, for getting them all into this mess in the first place?

"What?" he stopped walking and addressed Oliver, who still looked uncomfortable in his Mastery robes. He didn't move with the same easy, self-assured gait as the rest of them, rather, he seemed like a boy who had stolen his parent's robes to play dress-up and was hoping not to get caught.

Go easy on the kid, he reminded himself, inhaling sharply and trying to release his anger as he exhaled. *You were that age once, and also in over your head.*

Yes, his inner voice added, *but when I was his age I was trying to come up with a way to destroy my former best friend, who was murdering every decent human being we knew. All he has to do is teach Powders and let us heavy-weights plot out revenge on Aleric.*

"Sorry to bother you," Oliver interrupted his internal debate, ignoring a passing group of students on their way towards the dining hall. "I was wondering if you've seen Slasher recently."

Caught off-guard by the unexpected question, Asher's anger fell away for a moment, replaced by genuine interest.

"No, why? Is he missing?"

That would be a terrible blow, as Slasher was the only magically-inclined dragon they had to assist them right now. Asher had sent Bonk back to Hayden with a violet prism so that the boy wouldn't be completely alone and defenseless, and Cinder had rejoined Aleric at the end of last year.

"I don't know," Oliver frowned, trying to act less worried than he actually was. "I haven't seen him since yesterday morning, not even at meals. I've searched the grounds and Torin's cabin, but no one has seen him. I'm beginning to worry that something has happened to him."

"Not a lot can bring down a dragonling," Asher pointed out, trying to imagine where Slasher would be if he wasn't injured or in some other way physically prevented from returning to Oliver. "He could be in the Forest of Illusions, I suppose."

Surprised, Oliver asked, "Why would he be there? I thought we'd all gotten enough of the place after the sorcerers attacked two years ago."

Asher could almost feel the golden spike being hammered into his chest all over again, the unpleasant sensation of his Source power trickling out of him through the spigot while he slumped in a semi-comatose state for months on end. He blinked the memory away and refocused.

"Magical creatures are at their most powerful in the Forest. Perhaps Slasher wanted to return there to boost his power, or to speak with the other animals who live there, or for some other reason I can only guess at." He shrugged.

Oliver looked obscurely relieved.

"I hadn't thought of that," he sounded reassured. "You really think he's there?" The look on the young Master's face made Asher's throat constrict with suppressed emotion. The fear only partly-concealed behind a veneer of frantic hope, it was a look Asher had seen on Hayden's face during his most desperate times, when he was counting on his mentor to reassure him that everything would somehow be alright.

Why do these children keep relying on me to help them? Haven't they realized that I'm more lost than anyone?

No, of course not. They took his casual arrogance for self-assurance, his eccentricity for brilliance, his apparent apathy for the regard of others as humility. After the entire continent had turned against him for being the best friend of a monster, he had gone out of his way to throw it in their faces, tossing social graces to the wind and welcoming whatever punishment came with that decision. Strangely, the expected punishment had never come. Instead he had gained an ethereal quality that only made people respect and admire him more—a consequence he had never anticipated and was now stuck with.

He'd kept up the charade long enough it had almost become true, so he forced a lopsided smile and said, "There's every chance he's in the Forest, using his own methods to try and help us. Who knows, maybe Slasher will come back with the answer to our prayers, and we'll be able to break down Aleric's wall and storm his house at last."

Wouldn't that be nice.

Oliver nodded, allowing himself to be persuaded. Asher felt a stab of guilt for giving young Trout false hope, but truly, he had no idea where Slasher was or whether he was in danger. For all he knew, the dragonling *was* in the Forest of Illusions trying to beef up his magical repository, so it's not like he was lying.

Sure. I'll keep that in mind when Oliver's sobbing over Slasher's corpse once we eventually find him.

Mentally cursing himself for always going to the darkest explanation, Asher walked outside, deciding on a whim that fresh air was what he needed right now. He was only a little surprised when Oliver followed him, but neither of them made an attempt at further conversation until they were standing near the obstacle courses that familiars trained on.

Aleric and I convinced Jonah to crawl through that tube during fourth year, he remembered while staring at it. *He got stuck halfway through it and the masters had to cut it open to get him out of there.*

He and Aleric had to collect obsidian needles from the thorn prairies as punishment. They'd both come back with so many scratches and cuts that it had taken weeks to heal, even with the aid of elixirs.

"I don't think Hayden's dead," Oliver said at last, apropos of nothing as far as Asher could tell.

Asher glanced sideways at his newest colleague only to find him staring out into the distance, as though hoping to see Slasher approaching at any moment.

"Because you think Aleric has been cured of his distortion and decided to become a loving father all of a sudden?" he returned dryly. He could almost believe it, if not for that time he threatened to slit Hayden's throat, or the time he murdered everyone in the Crystal Tower to kidnap the boy, or the fact that he was holding his son captive at his estate even now…

"No, I mean because he doesn't really have a reason to kill him," Oliver continued vaguely.

"Yes, and Aleric has always needed an excuse to commit murder…" Asher countered with even more sarcasm, letting the bitterness wash over him once more.

"Well, no, but he went out of his way to raid the Crystal Tower to get Hayden. As far as we know, he hasn't killed anyone since then—he hasn't even really left his estate, unless he's found a new way to sneak around without us finding out. Why go to all the effort of collecting him if he just meant to kill him?"

Asher had had the same internal argument for weeks, though it had rapidly become circular with no further information incoming. It was true that they hadn't had any reported sightings of Aleric recently, not since he abducted Hayden, really. That either meant he was being incredibly stealthy, or that he hadn't left the estate. If he was staying home, *why?* Everything about Aleric's behavior had been different this time around, like there was some critical piece of information that the man had and no one else possessed. As soon as he returned to the realm, everyone waited for him to begin killing, but instead he began healing people. Then came the attack on the Crystal Tower, which they were sure heralded the start of his new murdering spree, but everything had been quiet since then. Now Asher wondered if Aleric had only committed those murders necessary to get to Hayden.

But what does he want with his son?

Asher had been trying to unravel the answer to that question since the day he met Hayden. Nothing about the man was making sense anymore, and it was driving him crazy. Everyone expected him to have some hidden insight because he used to be friends with the monster they were trying to kill, and no matter how many times Asher tried to explain the truth, it never did any good.

I was friends with Aleric. I barely knew the Dark Prism.

Indeed, his only real interaction with the Dark Prism had been during their memorable battle, when public pressure had finally gotten so great that Asher had been convinced to throw away his life in a last desperate attempt to stop his old friend. He had known he would lose that fight before it even started. The only surprise had been that he had been left alive at the end of it; perhaps some shadow of the friend he once knew had some reservation about killing him.

I doubt I can count on that mercy a second time.

"Asher?" Oliver asked hesitantly, and Asher just remembered that he hadn't answered his colleague's last statement.

"Maybe he hasn't killed him, but he can't have anything good in mind for Hayden," he allowed. "I wish I knew why he's hiding inside his estate; it isn't like him at all."

"Maybe Hayden's already found a way to stop him, and he's just trying to figure out how to get through the barriers around the place like we are?"

Now there was a wild thought. Everything would be so much simpler if Hayden had disposed of his father for the world and was just waiting for someone to help him break down the barriers around the place.

It would explain why Aleric hasn't been seen in weeks.

"A nice thought," Asher sighed, "but I doubt we can count on it."

"Why not?" Oliver pressed on boldly. "They each have a dragon, and they each have a prism. You've said yourself that they're about evenly matched...Hayden's more powerful but the Dark Prism is faster, and so forth. Why couldn't Hayden win?"

Because speed is more important than raw power, except in very rare circumstances, and Aleric has forgotten more spells than Hayden will ever learn.

"Hayden has one prism, which will be consumed as he uses it; Aleric has the Black Prism, which will never be consumed, and gives him a host of spells Hayden has never encountered before. Besides, Aleric would be a fool to leave Bonk free, and Aleric is no fool. He has always held dragonlings in the highest esteem, and would never underestimate the threat that Bonk could pose to him."

Oliver frowned and said, "I'm going back inside. The others are having a meeting later tonight. Kilgore told me to tell you that you should stop throwing a tantrum and join us this time." He said the last part nervously, and Asher couldn't blame him, though he could tell the words were Elias's.

"I'll think about it," he replied noncommittally, relieved when Oliver walked back towards the castle and left him alone.

For a few minutes he stood there and stared across the grounds, the wind blowing through his hair. The weather was mild—as always—and he was struck with the desire to make it storm and thunder, so that the outside would match his feelings. He wanted it to rain down hail and lightning, scorching everything in sight until he felt better. But he had promised Willow after the last horrendous storm he'd caused that he would keep his weather magic better contained in future. Apparently they didn't have time to go around fixing all the damage he caused to the grounds—though since they weren't making any progress on the problem of taking down Aleric Frost, he wasn't sure why they didn't have time for other menial work.

It took a moment for his brain to process what his eyes were seeing while lost in thought: something in the distance was flying towards the grounds, too small to make out properly from here.

Someone's familiar, no doubt.

Maybe a hawk or a falcon…perhaps a raven, but probably not—

"Is that Slasher?" Asher asked out loud, despite being alone. Well, there were a few students sitting in the main courtyard, working on homework, but for the most part people kept indoors these days.

As if it would make a difference whether one was inside the school or outside if Aleric showed up with murder on his mind.

He watched the small flying shape in the distance grow steadily closer until he was able to confirm that it was indeed Slasher, returning to the school at last.

Huh, Asher thought with mild satisfaction, *maybe he was in the Forest of Illusions after all.*

It would be nice to be right about something for a change.

Asher expected Slasher to fly past him and into the castle in search of Oliver, so he was truly perplexed when the dragonling soared towards him and hovered at eye-level, extending a rolled sheet of paper that was clutched in his talons.

"For me?" Asher raised an interested eyebrow, reaching out to accept the paper. "Who in the world would use you to deliver a message to me?"

His lips parted in surprise when he saw his own name scrawled across the outside of the letter in very familiar handwriting. In fact, he had just seen similar penmanship while pacing his office, studying his worktable.

"Hayden," he said softly, staring at the outside of the letter for a full minute, even as Slasher continued his flight towards the school.

How in the world had Hayden managed to get a note to him using Slasher? Come to think of it, how had Slasher even known to go to the Frost estate in the first place?

Only the first of a dozen questions I'll need to think about after I read this...

Standing in the falling light of sunset, Asher opened the letter and began reading.

Asher,

Hey, it's Hayden. Well, you probably knew that when you saw the handwriting, but I don't write a lot of letters so I never know how to start them. Anyway, first off, I'm still alive, so if you've been worrying about that then you can relax a bit. Well, not really, but I'll explain in a minute.

I know what my father wanted from me when I was ten; he used the Black Prism to unlock that memory. He came to my mother's house because he was experimenting with removing someone's Source. He wanted to steal mine and merge it with his to boost his power; he figured since we're related that our Sources would be more compatible and it would be easier than trying with a stranger.

Asher looked away from the letter as the impact of those words hit him.

Holy arcana... he thought dumbly, dazzled by the audacity and the simplicity of it all. *Why didn't I think of that sooner?*

The truth was, not even he had dreamed that Aleric was arrogant enough and brilliant enough to attempt such outrageous magic. To remove someone's Source—the very essence of life itself...it shouldn't even be possible. It was utter madness.

But Aleric has long since proven himself a madman.

Turning back to the letter, he continued reading.

You're not going to believe what happened when he tried to take my Source; I'm not even sure I believe it. He says that I must have found an inverse alignment in the Black Prism and used it to block him at the last second. I don't remember doing it on purpose, but I do remember looking at the prism and feeling the horrible tugging feeling stop right before it got pulled through my hands. But that's what gave me the light-sickness—I did it to myself by using the Black Prism on accident. Both of us casting through it at the same time was apparently too much for it to handle, and it blew up my house and knocked my father into a schism. I don't know what to think about having used the Black Prism....Does that mean I'm distorted too? Should I even be using magic, or am I okay since it's been years and nothing bad has happened? I don't feel evil or messed up, for whatever that's worth…but my father probably didn't either until it was too late.

Anyway, that's not all. The reason he took me from the Crystal Tower is because I didn't just stop him from taking my Source when I was ten; I accidentally broke off part of his and merged it with my own. That's why my Source seems stupidly powerful, even with three-inch correctors on each wrist.

"Great and holy gods…" Asher said out loud, eyes wide as everything began to make sense.

It had always bothered him that no one had known Hayden possessed magic until his mother's house exploded, because with the largest Source the Nine Lands had ever seen, it would have been impossible to keep magic from streaming out of him at random. Magic would have burst from his hands as he walked down the street when his powers were still forming and he was too young to control them.

Except he didn't have an unnaturally-large Source until the day he encountered Aleric, and he managed to warp his own Foci almost beyond repair in the same moment that he gained all that power.

He wasn't sure whether to laugh or cry as wave upon wave of understanding crashed over him. Aleric wasn't leaving the Frost estate to continue his reign of terror because he wasn't ready to face hordes of skilled mages yet. He was missing a sizable chunk of his Source power, and until he got it back, he was vulnerable. He would bend all of his considerable intellect towards figuring out what went wrong with his spells and preparing for another attempt…

"That's why he was healing them!" Asher actually smacked himself in the forehead with the palm of one hand at this. Of course it hadn't been out of the goodness of his heart, or even in the pursuit of discovery. He wouldn't be able to pull his Source back from Hayden through warped Foci; he needed Hayden's channels to be straightened perfectly, or it would be a worse disaster than the first time around. So he was practicing on other mages that he tracked down with damaged Foci to make sure he had the spell right.

Asher looked back to the letter.

He's going to try again—to take back the part of his Source I have, as well as the entirety of mine. I think he's only a few weeks away, maybe less—it's hard to tell since I don't get very close to his notes that often. But don't worry, I won't let him make himself powerful again. I'm either going to bring him down or die trying, and then at least he'll be weaker than last time when you all fight him. That's partly why I wrote this to you instead of Zane or Tess—they won't understand that I have to keep him from reclaiming his Source at all costs.

But you understand, don't you? You know the price of failure better than anyone, and you know how much I don't want to become like my father (by the way, don't ever call him that where he can hear or he'll choke the living daylights out of you). You probably already know this, but I've always thought of you as the father I never had. You didn't have to go out of your way to be nice to me five years ago, or to keep an eye out for me after what your best friend turned into, so thank you for everything you've done for me. I'm not sure I've ever said that to you in person, which was stupid, so this letter is the best I can do.

Tell the others not to come after me here; you'll never make it inside. One of the other hostages here tried to escape and ran into a light barrier of some sort. Father says it's impenetrable, and I believe him. Anyone who tries to cross it gets hit with light sickness from all directions—through the Foci in their arms or their eyes, so even non-magic people can't get in or out. I've been researching ways to bring it down, but I can't find anything. He's got a lot of other variously-distorted prisms lying around the library, and I think that's what they're for—he's using them to support the light barrier. To break it, you'd have to have someone working the spell from both sides, so it's a moot point, as I'm the only one on this side of the wall and I have no idea how to break it.

I hope you can use what I've told you to bring an end to my father for good. When it's all over, please make sure everyone knows that the Broken Prism died as one of the good guys; I've always hated that people assume I'm going to morph into my father.

Hayden

Asher stared down at the paper for several minutes, unfocusing his eyes and blinking hard several times to make sure they were clear of standing moisture. He'd been wishing to have all the answers magically appear to him for years, but now that he held them, he wasn't sure he wanted the letter after all. The casual way that Hayden wrote about his imminent death or his father's abusiveness—the reference to getting the daylights choked out of him couldn't have come from nowhere—was heartbreaking.

He scanned the letter again.

But you understand, don't you?

Another sentiment aimed at his heart. Of course he understood Hayden's plight; he knew exactly how it felt to be associated with the Dark Prism and to have the entire world doubt him when he hadn't actually done anything wrong. He understood being so determined to do the right thing that he was willing to die a horrible death just to inconvenience his enemy.

Hayden only addressed this to me because he thinks I'll be reasonable enough to not let emotion override good sense and come charging in after him. He thinks I'll accept his chosen death and only share the parts of his letter that are essential to the fight with the others.

A grim smile lit his face as Asher crumpled the letter in his hand.

Hayden doesn't know me as well as he thinks.

He turned back towards the castle with purposeful strides to find the others. They had a fortress to storm.

19
A Meeting of the Minds

Zane scarfed down his dinner in record time and bolted from the dining hall before anyone could speak to him, determined not to miss the meeting tonight, though he wasn't sure why he bothered going; they hadn't really accomplished anything useful in weeks. Still, for as long as his best friend was being held captive—and hopefully alive—at the Frost estate, he was going to do everything he could think of to be even mildly useful in planning his rescue, even if it meant attending a hundred frustrating meetings where nothing really got done.

The problem was that they had little new information to work with, so they were forced to work through the same theories and assumptions they'd been operating with from the beginning, and they were running low on fresh inspiration. Conner, Tamon, and his other friends knew that he and Tess had been brought into the inner circle, and often expressed their regret that they never had time to spend relaxing or socializing anymore.

Zane lamented the loss of his carefree childhood, but at the same time realized that he was nearly an adult and that it was time to stop sitting around and letting others shape the future of the Nine Lands while he played card games. He picked up his pace as he strode down the corridor that connected the dining hall with the Pentagon, not wanting to be late for the meeting.

Tess would already be there. She rarely appeared at mealtimes for longer than it took to grab something off of the table and walk away with it, most of the time without even looking at it. Zane had been amused once to watch her snatch up a head of lettuce without even glancing at it and walk out of the room. She hadn't returned that night to get more food, so he assumed she just ate the whole thing and went hungry until breakfast, a rare touch of pride she seemed to have picked up from her time with Hayden.

Zane crossed through the empty pentagonal foyer to the eastern stairwell and took the stairs two at a time to the second floor. Most of their meetings that only involved Mizzenwald Masters were held in Master Willow's classroom, because it was the largest of the teaching rooms and was out of the way of casual passerby at this time of evening.

He entered the room just before Oliver—*Master Trout, yuck*—could close the door. As expected, all of the Masters were present with the exception of Asher, who had begun skipping most of their meetings about a week ago. It irked the others to no end, but the Prism Master said he could think better on his own than while listening to a bunch of grown men squabble like children over minutia. Asher had always been kind of an odd man out amongst the Masters though, and had surely taken

Hayden's disappearance much harder than the rest of them.

It was still strange seeing Oliver Trout in red Mastery robes, even weirder having to address him in public as Master Trout. Thankfully, Zane no longer took Powders, so at least he didn't have to suffer being taught by one of his least favorite people. Weirdly, Lorn—who had returned to school for the spring term—was also a Powders major, and was therefore being taught by his own brother. For some reason no one was concerned about the potential conflict of interest, or maybe the others had counseled Oliver in private and Zane just didn't know about it.

"Laraby," Master Reede beckoned, and Zane crossed the room to join his mentor, who had sort of adopted him as an apprentice since term began, though he didn't officially have any open slots for new apprentices and had turned down a number of other applicants. "Did you make any headway on the tunneling idea last night?"

Zane frowned, hating to deliver bad news.

"Yes, but you won't like it." He was aware of the others ceasing their conversations to listen with interest. Zane couldn't blame them. Their most recent wild idea for breaking through the barriers at the Frost estate hadn't been to go through them—it had been to go *under* them. He and Reede, as their resident conjurers, had been given the task of determining whether a summoning/sending circle could get them under the walls and out the other side without killing them.

"Yes?" Reede prompted him, looking weary.

"I think the magic itself is sound...at least what you and I figured out yesterday is. I made some adjustments and went out onto the grounds to try it out—"

"You tried sending yourself underground without a spotter, using an experimental spell in the middle of the night?" Master Willow asked with a touch of reproach in his voice.

"Uh, yeah," Zane admitted abashedly.

Master Laurren gave him a small smile, eyeing him as though appraising his value as a future crazy-brilliant trailblazer like Asher and himself.

I've obviously done something stupid and/or amazing if Laurren approves.

He made a mental note to be more cautious in the future.

"Anyway, it was possible to dig a tunnel with magic that would get me underground, but I still couldn't bypass the wards Mizzenwald has placed around it, and I figure the Dark Prism's spells have to be at least as strong as ours."

"So the defensive barriers will still hold, even below ground," Master Reede sighed as though expecting this.

"Perhaps someone else should try, to make sure the problem isn't with the caster," Oliver said without making eye contact with him.

Zane scowled and snapped, "My magic was good, it's just not a viable solution in this case. If you want to draw your own circles, then be my guest. I tried so many times that I almost banished my legs at one point."

Oliver opened his mouth to press the point but Master Reede held up a hand and said, "I have confidence in Laraby's magic, or I wouldn't have put him to the task of sorting it out. If he says it won't work, it won't work; to be honest, I had only put our odds of success at around twenty-percent anyway."

Zane tried not to look too pleased with his mentor's level of faith in him. He'd been doing everything he could think of to stand out since he came to Mizzenwald at the age of ten, and finally his work was showing results. Of course, being the best friend of the guy who was critical to the fight against the Dark Prism didn't hurt either.

"Well great, then what do we do now?" Oliver tossed his hands up in frustration. Zane couldn't blame him; it seemed that all they did these days was hit one roadblock after another.

How is it possible for one man to outsmart the brightest minds in the Nine Lands?

Last he heard, the newly-formed Council of Mages wasn't making much headway either, though they also had the monumental task of handling emergency preparations throughout the Nine Lands and preventing a full-scale panic. Since they—weirdly—hadn't picked up any reports of the Dark Prism terrorizing towns since his return to power, they actually had some time to prepare for the eventuality before people started dying.

"Why isn't he killing anyone or conquering any towns?" Zane asked out loud, forgetting that he was in a room full of people. Since everyone had been silently contemplating their options, everyone heard his question.

"If I knew, I'd tell you," Master Willow grimaced, looking older than usual. "The only one who was ever any good at unraveling Aleric's motivations is Asher, but the more warped Aleric has become, the more reluctant even Asher is to guess at what drives him."

Kilgore rolled his eyes and said, "That's no reason to sulk about on his own. He should be here with the rest of us, strategizing."

"Though admittedly, we haven't made much progress as of late," Laurren intoned regretfully.

"Nevertheless," Kilgore grunted in annoyance.

"I'm sure he's still working on the problem on his own," Tess surprised them all by speaking up. "He cares about Hayden as much as anyone." *And more than most*, went unsaid. "He's not going to give up on him until we know for sure that he's dead."

Zane could tell that she was trying to sound even-keeled and unaffected, but on the word 'dead' her voice pitched slightly higher. A few of the others looked away, as though her emotions were indecent.

"Tess is right," Zane put in loudly, mostly to take the attention away from the awkward moment. "Asher's crazy-brilliant—"

"You're half-correct," Reede muttered so that only he could hear.

Trying not to laugh, Zane continued. "He's not going to show up for one of these meetings until he's got all the answers, and then he'll dazzle us as usual."

"We're all very talented, Laraby," Oliver huffed in displeasure, "but you're giving the man supernatural powers. Not even Asher can just waltz in here with all the answers in the palm of his hand."

At that exact moment, the door opened and Master Asher walked in saying, "Oh good, you're all here. I've finally got all the answers to our most burning questions." He waved a crumpled sheet of paper with one hand for emphasis.

Every eye in the room turned and froze on him in comical and never-to-be-repeated unison.

"What?" Asher came to an abrupt halt, looking mildly unnerved by the reaction.

Holy arcana, Zane thought appreciatively. *The man is superhuman!*

He had no idea whether the Prism Master had been lurking outside with his ear pressed against the door, waiting for the right moment to enter the room and stun them all, or if the timing was a total coincidence, but either way it was amazing.

Willow recovered first.

"Asher, this is not the time to play jokes with us, no matter how much it may entertain you."

"I'm not joking," his colleague said with a lopsided grin that was much more reminiscent of his usual personality. "I know why Aleric has Hayden and what he's planning to do with him. I also know that we don't have much time left to stop him before he becomes nearly invincible."

"And how in the world would you know any of these things?" Reede raised a skeptical eyebrow. "I don't suppose he wrote you a letter, kindly explaining it all for your convenience?"

"Don't be ridiculous," Asher waved an airy hand, the one still holding the crumpled piece of paper. "Aleric wrote his last letter to me years ago."

"Well, then—"

"Hayden is the one who wrote me," he continued cheerfully.

Eleven people said, "WHAT?" at roughly the same time. The combined volume was probably loud enough to be heard from the basement.

"Am I being unusually inarticulate today, or are you all just having a hard time understanding?" Asher raised his eyebrows curiously. "I said, Hayden wrote me—which reminds me: Oliver, Slasher was playing courier; that's why he's been missing."

Oliver swiveled his head around to look at his familiar, who was perched regally in front of the window overlooking the grounds.

"*Slasher* was at the Frost house, working for Hayden?" he asked in unflattering disbelief. "How is that even possible? He has no way to contact Slasher directly, and it's not like we're close friends or anything. Besides, there are two other dragonlings living with him who could have carried messages for him."

"I doubt Cinder would have been up for the task," Kilgore corrected mildly.

"Yes, and Aleric is an absolute fool if he leaves Bonk unconfined inside of his estate," Laurren added. "There are few things the Dark Prism holds any reverence or respect for, but the power of dragonlings is one of them."

"He would never allow Bonk to remain unbound," Asher confirmed with a nod. "We knew that when we sent him to Hayden, that it would be a choice between Binders or a fight to the death."

"If Bonk can't use his magic, then how is Hayden supposed to have summoned Slasher to him?" Mistress Razelle spoke up for the first time. "Don't tell me you think Hayden managed to work magic that penetrated that defensive barrier with only the violet prism you sent him. The boy is talented, but he's not smarter than the eleven of us collectively."

Asher shrugged and said, "As to that, I have no idea. We'll have to ask him when we next see him."

"You said you had answers," Willow changed the subject abruptly, eyeing the crumpled paper in Asher's hand. "Enlighten us."

"The reason Aleric hasn't been slaughtering the masses this time around is because he's weaker this time—for a little while longer, at least," Asher began. "When he came after Hayden the first time, he was attempting to remove his Source power and merge it with his own."

A riot of loud objections and exclamations prevented him from saying anything further. Zane felt the blood drain from his face as he contemplated the horror of having one's Source ripped out of the body. He hadn't even considered it as a possibility; he didn't even think magic that strong existed—not for humans, at least.

Willow waved one of his wands and a sound like the snapping of fingers rang through the room, amplified so loudly that it made Zane's ears ring. Everyone fell silent once more.

Asher continued talking as though there had been no interruption. "His spell backfired, and Hayden ended up absorbing part of his father's Source instead—a fair bit of it, given how much latent power we know he possesses."

"Heavens..." Mistress Razelle murmured softly, touching her fingers to her lips. Zane thought that was a colossal under-reaction to the news that his best friend had not just his own powerful Source to work with, but part of a notorious mass-murderer's as well. He'd always known that Hayden had an unusual amount of Source power—that had been readily apparent ever since he got three-inch Focus-correctors on each hand and still overpowered most of his opponents. But he'd never really considered the idea that Hayden was *that* formidable...

"How much does of Aleric's Source does he hold?" Laurren asked with frustratingly academic interest. "Half?" he added optimistically.

Asher shrugged and said, "I have no idea. If I knew the extent of Aleric's Source since he became the Dark Prism and did whatever tampering he's done to himself to boost his power, then I might be able to estimate how much Hayden holds based on what I've seen him do…"

"It doesn't matter how much he has," Master Graus interrupted. "Even if he only holds a fraction of his father's Source as hostage, it is the best chance we will have of overpowering the Dark Prism once and for all."

"Yes," Asher agreed heartily. "We have to get in there and bring him down before he can work out the details of reclaiming his power from Hayden—along with his own. At that point I'm not sure whether it would even be possible to stop him."

"And how long before that happens?" Tess asked, eyes blazing with resolve and with something else Zane had a hard time identifying. "Did he happen to mention that in his letter?"

Now Zane knew what emotion lay beneath her clipped tone: hurt. As glad as she doubtlessly was to hear news that Hayden was alive, when he had to choose who to write, he didn't choose her.

Come to think of it, he didn't write to me either. Zane frowned thoughtfully but wasn't really upset—or at least, he could understand Hayden's logic in writing his mentor. The Prism Master would be in the thick of things and have access to the rest of his allies that Zane and Tess might not be able to reach.

He could have written more than one letter though...a note, even, for the rest of us...

He shook the thought from his head. For all he knew, Hayden had been frantically scribbling a letter to Asher as fast as he could in fear of getting caught by his father and murdered. It was unreasonable to expect he had all the leisure time in the world to pen missives to everyone he knew.

"From what he's able to gather, he's only got a couple weeks left before Aleric is ready to give it another shot," Asher frowned, some of the cheerfulness evaporating from his face. Zane had the impression there was something else the Prism Master wasn't saying, but it probably wouldn't do any good to call him out on it. Asher always kept his own council, and if he wasn't telling them something, it must not be important, because he would never withhold information that would hurt Hayden.

"Then it doesn't really matter that we finally know what has been driving Aleric's motives all this time," Master Reede frowned. "Aside from assuaging our personal curiosity, we're no closer to getting through his barriers than we were before."

Asher surprised them all by saying, "Hayden's helped us there as well. He's identified what the impenetrable wall of magic is made of, which is more than we've been able to manage."

Now the level of interest in the room was palpable, and Zane felt a surge of hope flare up inside him.

Maybe we'll be able to save him after all...

"Well don't keep us in suspense," Kilgore said with his usual gruff tone. "What is the blasted thing made of?"

"It's a light curtain," Asher responded, for all the world like it explained everything. Zane waited for the others to say something like, "Of course!" or, "That was my next guess!" but instead the group seemed to share in his confusion.

"A light curtain..." Asher repeated, as though not sure everyone else had heard him properly. "You know...a curtain of light..."

"We're not all prism-users, Masters," Reede said flatly. "Most of us don't deal in light magic."

"Okay, maybe I should back up a few steps," the Prism Master tried again. "You all *do* know that our eyes' ability to receive and interpret light is what allows us to *see*..."

"We're not idiots, Asher," Willow interrupted, mildly annoyed.

"You told me to dumb it down."

"Dumb it down *less*," the Master of Wands said through clenched teeth.

It was Master Laurren who explained, for some reason.

"Prism-users work their magic exclusively through light, as you all are well aware—translating alignments and arrays is the bread and butter of Prisms. Without the ability to distinguish colors, a Prime Trifecta would look the same as a Broad Triple. The other majors use other conduits to exert magic on the world, but in an indirect way you also rely on light perception for most of it."

Zane was surprised to find that the Master of Abnormal Magic had a thorough knowledge of prism-based magic, which caused him to wonder about how Laurren came to be the Master of Abnormal Magic, when surely he must have had other skills within the major arcana. For all Zane knew, the man could have also been a prism-user, though that hardly made sense, or else he'd still wear a circlet.

"Hayden says that Aleric has created a barrier of light around the compound," Asher took it up from there, "using a myriad of variously-distorted prisms to maintain it. It explains why I wasn't able to tell it was a light curtain of some sort on my own—if he's using distorted prisms then it wouldn't look like anything Kiresa and I have ever seen before."

Zane couldn't help but note the admiring note in the Prism Master's voice, like he was giving his old friend points for cleverness.

"If it's something that only affects prism-users though," Kilgore asked, "why can't the rest of us break it down or simply walk through it?"

It wasn't the first time the others had speculated at what would happen if one of them attempted to simply pass through whatever barrier there was, just to see what would happen. Asher had been able to convince them that while he had no idea what magic was on the place, he was positive that Aleric would ensure it killed whoever tried passing through it.

"Oh you would certainly die," Asher said easily. "I was right about that much, even not knowing what we were facing until now. It doesn't matter whether you can use prisms or not," he paused while Master Laurren walked unobtrusively closer and gestured for him to pass over Hayden's crumpled letter. Asher hesitated for a fraction of a second before coming to a snap decision and handing it to his colleague, who smoothed it out and began to read it silently.

"The very fact that your brain can interpret light and color properly guarantees that the curtain would work against you," he finished answering Kilgore's question. "Hayden says that he saw someone die horribly attempting to pass through it—someone non-magical, which means that his spell can pass through either set of Foci: the magical conduits or the eyes."

"And what exactly happens to someone who gets hit with this light curtain?" Oliver asked skeptically.

"From the sound of it, it gives you a severe dose of light-sickness. It overwhelms the part of your brain that registers colors and burns you up."

"So we have to send someone both non-magical and blind if we wanted to pass through that particular barrier," Willow acknowledged with a frown. "Which would be effectively sending them to their death as soon as they encountered Aleric on the other side, assuming the rest of the defenses didn't prevent them from crossing through."

Asher nodded to concede the point.

"I hadn't worked out how to get past that little wrinkle just yet," he admitted. "Knowing what it is, Kiresa and I can probably come up with some spells to bring it down in a matter of days, but that still leaves us with a big problem. If the light curtain can only be brought down from both sides at once—and Hayden believes that it will need to be—then we would need someone magical on the inside working the counterspells at the same time as we are, and we have no way to coordinate with Hayden."

"We don't even know if he's free to move about on his own or if Aleric is keeping a close eye on him," Master Graus put in. "We have to assume that he only has the one prism you sent him, and with Bonk chained, he's going to need to use it to defend himself, especially at the speed at which he can burn through a mastery-level prism."

"I know," Asher nodded. "As I said, even if Kiresa and I can work out some sort of counterspell—which I am cautiously optimistic about now that we know what to look for—there's still that minor hurdle to overcome."

"Hardly a *minor* hurdle," Kilgore rolled his eyes.

"Well, we either need to find a way to get our people inside to bring down the light curtain, or we need to work on getting Hayden more prisms and instructions on when, where, and how to use them."

"And we only have a few weeks, at best, to figure it all out before Hayden gets the life ripped out of him,"

Tess pointed out softly, staring off into space as she spoke. "Or none of this means anything."

Master Potts said, "Agreed. If we wait too long, Aleric will be effectively invincible and we'll never manage to bring him down."

That isn't what she meant, Zane thought with a glance at Tess. *She meant that Hayden will be dead and nothing else will matter.*

"First things first," Master Willow interjected. "Asher, you need to seek out Kiresa and anyone else who might be able to help you figure out how to breach the light curtain."

"I'll do that as soon as we finish here," Asher nodded.

Master Laurren handed him back the letter from Hayden, which Asher crumpled again and stuffed into his pocket without offering anyone else the chance to read it. Zane noticed how Tess's eyes followed its trajectory and seemed to stay fixated on the pocket of Asher's Mastery robes even after it vanished from sight, but she didn't ask to read its contents.

Asher and Laurren exchanged a look that could have meant anything, and Zane began to wonder if there *was* something in that letter that the Prism Master was holding back about, but whatever it was, Laurren didn't call attention to it by asking. Instead, he walked calmly over to the window where Slasher was still perched, standing beside the dragonling and staring out across the grounds as he seemed to process whatever he had just read.

"Still seems like a wasted effort if we can't get someone from inside the Frost compound to work the spells at the same time as Asher on the outside," Master Potts observed, and the room fell silent.

For about five minutes they all stood there, not speaking, each absorbed in deep thought about how they might circumvent the insurmountable problem before them. Zane, who knew much less magic than the Masters, felt especially useless as he stood around watching the others, trying to look pensive but unable to think of anything helpful. He glanced at Tess and saw that she also appeared lost in thought, though he suspected she was dwelling on thoughts of Hayden and of how little time he had left to live if they couldn't find a way to get to him soon, rather than on ways to solve an unsolvable problem.

Just when Zane's legs were beginning to get tired of all this standing in place and he was wondering whether it was okay for him to move to a chair, the most exhilarating and terrifying thing imaginable happened.

Asher and Laurren both snapped back into focus and said, "I have an idea!" from opposite ends of the room in perfect unison.

Every other face in the room mirrored the thought that flashed through Zane's mind.

We're all going to die…

20
Bending and Breaking

The morning after his strange heart-to-heart talk with his father, Hayden woke up later than usual and spent a long time just lying in bed, staring at the ceiling. He wondered how much of the night before his father remembered by now, or if the moment had ended as soon as he'd left, never to be thought of again by the Dark Prism.

If only I could have said the right thing to reach him, maybe I could have talked my way out of here...

There were moments when he had felt so close to success, so sure that he was finally about to breach the wall of distortion surrounding the man's brain and actually get through to him that he was on the wrong path and needed to stop.

I wonder how many times Asher felt that way before he finally realized there was nothing to do but kill him.

Hayden frowned thoughtfully, thinking back to his letter and wondering if he had put everything that needed to be said into it. As much time as he had spent drafting it, he still had nightmares that he left out some crucial piece of information—like the existence of the light curtain, or that his father was currently operating without his entire Source available to him.

Not that it mattered, at this point. The letter was gone, and though he had asked Bonk whether it would be possible to call Slasher back in the future to send and receive more messages, his familiar had made it quite clear that that option was not on the table.

His thoughts strayed to Tess. Would she be angry with him because he didn't write to her when he had the chance? He had considered sending a note to her along with the longer, more informative one to Asher, but hadn't been able to think of what he would say. A farewell would only make her angry because he would be accepting death, and "See you soon!" seemed way too optimistic, knowing what he knew of the days to come. Since he couldn't very well lie to her, and the truth was too unpleasant to bear, in the end he had decided that it was best not to say anything at all.

Once they find a way to stop my father, at least she'll be free. She won't have to think about anyone with the last name Frost ever again, or the devastation we seem to bring upon her life.

That was a depressing thought—that Tess might be better off without him in her life. He tried to imagine what the future might hold for her. She would probably marry and have children—maybe with Conner, now that Hayden was removed as competition. They'd have a nice house in the country, and Conner would go to work doing something perfectly normal, like making mage-lamps or fixing broken carriage axels with magic, nothing dangerous that was likely to get him killed—like monster-hunting. The thought made Hayden quietly furious and propelled him out of bed.

"I'm not dead yet," he growled to Bonk, who flapped his wings as though to say, "That's the spirit!"

Hayden dressed quickly and made his way towards the library to do more research, determined to do his very best to find a way out of here before his time was up. He ignored the growling of his stomach, resigned to the fact that he had missed breakfast.

He strode into the library, half-expecting to find that his father had ripped the pages out of every book in the room and burned them one-by-one the night before. For all he knew, the man had done it on purpose to deprive Hayden of the chance to find the knowledge he needed to escape.

Fortunately his fears were baseless; there were plenty of books left in the library. Strangely, the only thing visibly missing from the workroom was the Dark Prism.

Hayden stopped at the threshold in surprise, trying to recall if he had ever really been in here without his father before. Usually he kept the double doors locked when he wasn't in here, probably so that Hayden couldn't wander around and mess with his stuff.

Wondering if it was a trap of some sort, Hayden moved inside and said, "Sir? Are you in here?" looking around the room to make sure he hadn't missed his father crouching behind a bookshelf or something. Then again, it was hard to imagine the great and fearsome Aleric Frost doing anything as mundane as hiding behind a bookshelf for the soul purpose of testing Hayden. He usually regarded his only son with little more respect than a hat rack.

Convinced that he really was alone in the room, Hayden hurried over to his father's worktable and began to scan his notes, taking care not to touch any of the pages. His father was perceptive enough to notice if anything was out of place, and the only way to truly make sure that didn't happen was not to touch anything at all.

A few prisms were arranged neatly on the far end of the table, and Hayden did risk future punishment by handling these. He picked them up one at a time, careful to touch only the edges and holding each up in front of the light from the windows to see if it was useable. Unfortunately his father hadn't been lying when he said that they all had varying levels of distortion, even the mastery-level orange prism, which was a shame because he had never actually looked through a mastery-level orange prism before until now and would have been interested to see what alignments it had.

He returned the prisms to their places on the table, hoping his father didn't notice or care that he had handled them. He also realized that there were a lot fewer prisms here than there had been when he first arrived at the Frost house.

He's probably had to replace a few of the ones that are maintaining the light barrier around this place, especially since Jack activated it and probably consumed a lot of the prisms' magic. It must take a huge bite out of a prism to force that much light through a person's mind.

He turned to the notes again, scanning them without really understanding most of it. His father did research in a very different way than Asher, and until recently Hayden hadn't realized how much personal preferences and style mattered in research. Then there was the fact that his father was working with alignments and colors that were so unnatural Hayden could barely look at the colored pencil sketches without wanting to hurl, let alone understand how they were being used. His written notes were hardly more helpful, as he used a form of shorthand that only he understood clearly, and only wrote one or two words at a time, just enough to prompt his memory if he forgot something. It was like trying to read a book where only one word on each line was visible.

Well, that was a waste.

Hayden moved away from the workstation before his father could come in and catch him spying, because he didn't feel like getting strangled for no good reason this morning. He contemplated searching the library for a promising-looking title and sitting down to read like he did every other day during his captivity, but then he realized that there was a chance his father had left the property entirely, and that this might be a good time to search the house and the grounds in more detail for ways to escape.

Wishing he hadn't wasted time in bed feeling sorry for himself, Hayden turned and hurried out of the library, walking briskly down the second floor corridor and slowing only to peek into the various rooms he passed to make sure his father wasn't in any of them before continuing down the main stairwell to the ground level.

He was considering which end of the main level to search first when he heard an alarming sound from outside—a sort of screeching that seemed vaguely familiar and made his blood run cold.

Hayden wondered briefly whether it was worth running back upstairs and getting his prism, just in case he needed to fight off anything perilous, but then realized that his father probably wouldn't go to the effort of keeping Hayden alive if he was going to be careless enough to let him be eaten by something in the yard.

Trying to hold onto that bolstering thought, he proceeded out the front door and into the front yard. It wasn't immediately apparent where the noise had come from, as everything looked normal and his father was nowhere to be found.

Maybe I just heard a random monster approaching the barriers around the estate and got worked up over nothing.

Before he could convince himself this was the truth of things, he heard the worrisome screeching again, and this time he realized it was coming from around the side of the house, which explained why he didn't see anything through the library windows when he was upstairs.

Owing to the size of the property, Hayden had to jog to make decent time in rounding the side of the house and turning towards the back yard. He had just turned the corner to the side of the property when he stopped in his tracks.

Three chimaeras had somehow breached the barriers and made it onto the property, which explained the source of the screeching. They were deceptively small and innocent looking, which meant that they were horrendously dangerous, as the smaller chimaeras were the more powerful. Standing calmly in front of them was the Dark Prism.

Hayden reached reflexively for the circlet he wasn't wearing, itching to draw down his eyepiece and attack the collective group of them. He was momentarily tempted to call out a warning to his father, but then realized that it would make things a lot simpler for him if the man was eaten by chimaeras. Sure, Hayden would have to avoid them until he could go get his prism and fight them one at a time, but it would still be better than having his father to contend with.

Unfortunately the Dark Prism didn't seem concerned by the appearance of deadly monsters on his property; in fact, he seemed to expect them. Beginning to suspect he was missing something, Hayden approached slowly, calling out when he was within hailing distance because his father didn't like surprises.

"Why are those things on our lawn?" he asked as casually as possible, though his heart was racing with fear of being poisoned and ripped to shreds.

"I've summoned them," his father answered without turning around, showing no sign of surprise at encountering Hayden outside. Hayden wondered if the Dark Prism had known he was standing there all along.

Hayden moved closer upon realizing that the chimaeras weren't attacking, though they looked like nothing would please them more. It wasn't until he got within a few feet of them that he saw the strange swirling blackness in their eyes, something he'd never seen before on any creature.

"What's wrong with them?" he asked with interest, glancing sideways at his father, who was still staring at the chimaeras through the Black Prism. He turned it fractionally to the right, and Hayden realized that he was using magic on them, which perhaps explained the strange black mist in their eyes.

"They are being subdued," his father explained after he was finished casting, lifting his eyepiece so that the Black Prism pointed up at the sky. "They will now serve me if necessary."

Alarmed, Hayden asked, "Uh, serve you in what way?"

Instead of answering, his father lowered the Black Prism back in front of his eye again and cast silently. All three chimaeras vanished.

A simple banishing spell?

The Dark Prism began walking around the side of the house and towards the back yard, and Hayden followed wordlessly, since he hadn't been expressly told to go away yet. From his father's mood, it didn't seem as though he remembered much of their discussion the night before.

More's the pity, Hayden thought ruefully.

He didn't speak again until they stopped about a hundred feet away from where they were before, and his father began summoning more creatures to him—this time a yeti and a warg.

Hayden jumped and moved rapidly behind him to shield himself from harm, because in the moment before the Dark Prism subdued them, both animals roared and began to charge, and Hayden was unarmed.

Annoyingly, his father didn't even flinch at the sight of deadly monsters coming to kill him, simply twisting the Black Prism back and forth with unerring precision as he cast the spells to bring the creatures under his will. Hayden saw the black mist swirl into the creatures' eyes and felt a stab of pity for them.

Once the danger seemed to pass, Hayden stepped away from his father and asked again, "Sorry, why are you summoning monsters and bending them to your will?"

Up close, the Dark Prism looked like he hadn't slept the night before. Dark circles framed his eyes and there was a waxy quality to his skin that Hayden usually only noticed on himself after extreme fatigue.

The weariness in his features didn't seem to carry over to the rest of him, because he moved with the same sort of energy and purpose as usual when he said, "It seemed prudent to install additional defenses around the grounds."

Surprised, Hayden asked, "Why? Are you expecting to be attacked?" His heartbeat pounded in his ears as it occurred to him that maybe his father *did* know that he'd gotten a message out…

"I am always expecting to be attacked by those less talented than myself—mages who lack scope and vision," he replied easily, continuing into the back yard with Hayden in tow.

*It doesn't sound like he's angry with me, or like he knows about the letter…*Hayden considered. *Surely he would have said or done something by now to show he was wise to my tricks and didn't feel threatened by them.*

"I thought your light barrier was supposed to be impenetrable," he trolled for information, thinking that something must have changed to bring his father outside to augment the defenses.

The Dark Prism stopped in place and whirled around, grabbing Hayden's arm so tightly that he cried out and sank to his knees in the grass. The madness danced behind his father's eyes as he asked, in cold fury, "Who told you about the light curtain?"

Struggling against the pain to free his arm, Hayden gasped out, "You did, sir!"

His father didn't release him, nor did he appear to believe him.

"Do not lie to me, boy." He moved behind him without loosening his grip on Hayden's arm, and Hayden didn't know what was coming until it was too late, and his father had wrenched his arm backwards so hard that he felt his shoulder dislocate and screamed in pain.

"Who have you been communicating with about the defenses around this estate?" he asked again, still in that deadly tone.

"No one!" Hayden lied, blinking through tears of pain, still twisted around awkwardly on his knees in the grass.

"You will tell me all you know before this is over. They always do," his father informed him with chilling certainty, releasing his injured arm and grabbing the other one in his vice-like grip, bending it slightly backwards at the elbow as a threat of what was to come.

Don't tell him anything, Hayden closed his eyes and braced for more pain. *No matter what happens, I won't give him any information about my friends and allies.*

"Who are you and how did you breach the defenses around my estate?" his father continued quietly, transferring some of his weight to the arm holding Hayden's so that he could feel the pain build in his elbow from being bent backwards.

He's so far gone that he doesn't even remember who I am?

"I'm Hayden!" Hayden answered immediately. "I didn't break into anywhere and I don't know anything; you brought me here and I wish you'd let me leave."

A dark shadow blinked between him and the sun, but Hayden's eyes were still closed in anticipation of pain so he didn't see what it was until he heard Bonk screech. He opened his eyes and blinked rapidly to clear them of tears since he couldn't raise his hands to wipe at them, and saw that both Bonk and Cinder had joined them on the lawn.

Cinder perched on his master's shoulder and began making a strange, guttural noise that must have been some attempt at communication, while Bonk hovered in front of the Dark Prism's face and began buffeting his wings furiously.

Being whipped in the face by dragon wings was no small thing, and it forced Hayden's father to release him and step backwards, which was probably Bonk's plan all along.

Using his good arm to cradle his bad one, Hayden scrambled to his feet and staggered well out of reach, walking backwards to avoid turning his back on an enemy. Cinder was still making those strange noises, and his father had his head inclined to one side as though listening intently, while his gaze remained fixed on Hayden like a predator evaluating his prey before attacking.

Bonk remained in front of the Dark Prism long enough to shriek furiously a few times—Hayden wondered if dragons had their own curse words—and then returned to Hayden, graciously not perching on his dislocated shoulder. He seemed to be motioning Hayden back towards the house, and at this point Hayden was only too willing to comply.

He walked backwards a few more feet and then trusted that Cinder had things under control, turning his back and hurrying to the main entrance as fast as he could without jostling his arm too badly. Bonk flew low circles around him like a small planetoid, acting as his personal defensive barrier.

"Would have been great to see you about two minutes earlier," Hayden grunted against the pain, entering the foyer and turning towards the servants' quarters.

Bonk didn't dignify that with a response, and Hayden eventually said, "Sorry, buddy. I know you got there as soon as you could—my arm just hurts really badly."

His familiar stopped orbiting and preceded him into the smallest sitting room in the house, where several of the other captives were currently relaxing on stiff, uncomfortable-looking sofas that were nonetheless very expensive. They jumped to their feet at the sight of Hayden barging in with a dragonling.

"Can one of you shove my dislocated arm back into its socket?" he asked without preamble, still cradling it with his other hand.

"What happened?" two of them asked in unison, sounding shocked and curious. Hayden had no patience for it right now.

"What happened is I got my shoulder dislocated and now I'm trying to get it reset," he retorted snappishly, and a door on the other end of the room opened as Hattie swept in.

"What's all the noi—sir! What happened to you?" she asked, dropping the basket full of neatly-rolled washcloths she had been holding so that it spilled its contents all over the floor.

Feeling obscurely bad for her because she was going to have to reroll all those washcloths on his behalf,

Hayden forced himself back to politeness and said, "Small disagreement with my father. I'm trying to find someone to help me set it properly before I lose the arm." His fingers had been numb for almost five minutes now.

"Well of course," Hattie stepped over the fallen basket and approached him, feeling gingerly around his shoulder. "I'm no doctor, but I've done some midwifery, and the doctor said I had a good demeanor, so I was starting to apprentice with her. I only did little things, mind, but I think I can fix this."

Not the ringing endorsement I'd like to hear from someone who is about to try and shove my bones back together...

But it wasn't like there were a lot of other options, so Hayden nodded and said, "I trust you."

His faith seemed to galvanize her, because her cheeks flushed and she looked to one of the others and said, "Thom, help me get Mr. Frost settled on the couch where he can be more comfortable. Carlotta, fetch me some of those washcloths from the floor."

Hayden allowed himself to be steered to the sofa, which was every bit as uncomfortable as he feared, though he kept his opinion to himself because the others were doing their best to be kind to him. Bonk perched on the arm of the sofa beside him and watched Hattie move about, his gaze flickering to Hayden at one point as though to say, "You see what this is, right?"

She doesn't really like me, Hayden assured himself, trying to communicate the message to Bonk with a flat-lipped glare. *She's just pinned her hopes on me getting her out of this alive is all.*

He had to tell himself that, because it would make things even harder if he had to start feeling awkward around the one person around here who would actually speak to him somewhat normally.

Hattie's cheeks were still pink when she said, "Here now, open your mouth so I can put a few of these cloths in for you to bite on."

Oh right, so I don't bite my tongue off. Hayden had been wondering what the washcloths were supposed to accomplish. Even in his mother's care, they had always been able to afford basic medical supplies, and he had never been subjected to the more archaic healing practices.

Well, this should be a nice educational experience then...

He opened his mouth and tried not to feel like an idiot while she carefully stuffed cloths in there until he feared he would choke on them.

"Alright, now I'm sorry, sir, but this is going to hurt..." Hattie informed him needlessly, motioning for Thom to hold his torso in place while she grabbed his arm with both hands at the place his father had been gripping before, which hurt even worse.

Hayden groaned and bit down on the cloths in his mouth so hard that his ears popped, no wanting to cry in front of the people who were counting on him to be their savior.

It took her two attempts to reset his arm, which Hayden supposed was better than ten, but still felt like one try too many. He could feel the bones grind against each other the first time as Hattie missed the mark, and nearly broke his teeth biting down to keep from screaming. The second time he nearly passed out, the world wavering dangerously in front of him as patches of light exploded in his eyes. He must have swayed to one side, because Bonk was suddenly much closer than he had been before, and he didn't remember resting his head on the armrest of the sofa.

Sensation immediately began to return to his arm once it was set in place, and Hattie was pulling the cloths from his mouth and using fresh ones with cool water on them to dab at the sweat on his forehead.

"Thanks," he mumbled, pushing himself upright once more.

"Of course, sir. I'm only sorry I didn't get it the first time," Hattie looked furious with herself and Hayden felt compelled to try and cheer her up.

"It's a lot better than I would have done if the situation was reversed, trust me," he assured her. "I'm glad you were here to help—" he realized the implication and said, "—well, not that you were taken from your home, of course. Darn it, I'm making a mess of this."

She was back to blushing, which Hayden pointedly ignored as he watched her and Thom bind his arm in tight linens to keep it near his body while it healed. He could already see bruises forming where his father's fingers had grabbed him.

Well great, when it comes time to fight, I've got one prism, a dragon that can't use magic, and a useless arm. My odds are just getting better and better…

"I know what you meant, sir, and I appreciate it."

"I wish you all would just call me Hayden," he sighed. "It feels very weird being called 'sir' by people who are older than me, especially since I didn't hire you to work for me and we're all technically captives here."

"Hayden," Hattie whispered softly, meeting his eyes.

Oh lords and ladies, I don't need this right now.

He should find some way to cannily mention Tess and his unwavering devotion to her even though he would likely never see her again, but he didn't have the energy to tackle that problem right now.

Tomorrow, he assured himself. *I'll deal with this tomorrow.*

He stood up and looked at Bonk.

"Well, we'd better get going if we want to make it back out there before he's finished with his summoning."

"Sir?" Thom asked in surprise, apparently unable to bring himself to address Hayden by name.

"You're not going back out there with *him,* are you?" Hattie asked in horror. "Not after what he did to you!"

"He snapped before I was able to get him to tell me why he's summoning all these extra monsters to defend the place," Hayden explained more calmly than he felt. "I need to know how many he's got serving him now, and if he's doing this because he knows something I don't and is expecting someone to break through his other defenses, or if he's just being paranoid because it suits him. If I need to be patched up again, I'll have Bonk bring me back here."

He gave them a confident smile he wasn't feeling and added, "Really, I'll be fine." Then he hurried off with Bonk before Hattie could make him feel even worse about himself for taking advantage of her kindness.

It was the last thing he wanted to do, but he hadn't been lying when he said he needed to know why his father was beefing up the defenses around the estate. Asher should have gotten his letter by now, and if he and the others had been able to do what Hayden couldn't and find a way through the light barrier—the light curtain, as his father called it—then he needed to know as soon as possible to prepare himself.

"What do you think, Bonk? Are they coming to get us?" he asked as they left through the rear entrance, placing them directly into the backyard, where two more of the captive servants were busy tending to the freshly mown grass and trimming the shrubbery.

Bonk made a noncommittal noise like he honestly had no idea. It was disconcerting, remembering that his familiar had no access to his magic, and could no longer sense things like this. Then again, he had somehow managed to call out to Slasher, which should have required a magical connection, so there was something weird about that...

He saw his father rounding the corner towards the opposite side of the house from where he'd last seen him. Hayden walked purposefully after him with Bonk resting on his good shoulder and caught up to him when he stopped to summon the next round of monsters: a pair of cockatrices this time.

His father spared him a careless glance and asked, "What happened to your arm?" without real interest.

He's already forgotten? Hayden wondered in amazement, unhappily registering that Cinder was nowhere to be seen.

"Tripped on the stairs coming down this morning," Hayden lied automatically, not wanting to draw him back into insanity. He gestured to the recently-subdued cockatrices. "I see you're summoning monsters to boost the defenses around this place. Do you have a reason to believe that someone is going to make it through all the other barriers?"

His father banished the subdued cockatrices and resumed walking.

"I woke up this morning with an unsettling feeling and decided to act on it," he explained flatly, not looking at Hayden.

"Really?" he asked in surprise. "All this effort just because of a weird feeling?"

His father rounded on him and for a moment Hayden was terrified that he was about to be attacked again, but his father looked perfectly sane and controlled as he said, "I always trust my instincts, even without knowing the reason for them." Hayden's heart was still hammering furiously as his father added, "I have never had occasion to regret following my intuition, and nothing but regret from failing to do so."

That actually seemed like sound advice, and Hayden filed it away for later as his father continued walking to their next destination along the side of the house.

Figures that my father would get a magical heads-up about my letter through the distortion in his brain.

Some people had all the luck.

"How come we're walking all along the inside perimeter, summoning them in small groups?" Hayden asked curiously. "Why not just summon them all and subdue them at once?"

His father didn't seem to find anything unusual about his interest in magic. Then again, why would he? Hayden had already shown a love of learning and some native talent for the craft.

"There are limits to how many creatures even I can overpower at one time," he allowed, though he glanced briefly at Hayden in a way that made it plain that he was thinking about how much less restricted he would be once he absorbed Hayden's Source. "Additionally, when the defenses are activated, each of the creatures will be summoned back to the spot where I first called upon them to fight my enemies. If they were all clustered in the same spot, most of the estate would go unguarded."

"Ah, I see."

They walked in silence for a little longer, and Hayden watched quietly as he brought forth a few more wargs.

I wish there was a nice big rock out here that I could bash him in the back of the head with...

Of course, with only one functional arm right now that would be even more difficult, and besides, he would be astounded if his father didn't have some kind of basic magical sense for when he was about to be attacked. He seemed to always know when Hayden was behind him, even if he didn't make a sound during the approach.

"So anyone who miraculously breaks through all the other defenses around this place will still have to contend with dozens of monsters who are all bent on murdering anyone who isn't supposed to be here?" Hayden asked, just for confirmation.

"That is correct," his father responded with a ghost of a smile.

Hayden wished he had held off sending his letter for another day or two so he could have mentioned the hordes of slavering monsters his friends would encounter if they found a way onto the grounds, but it was far too late. The estate had never felt more like a tomb, but now Hayden was certain that he was going to die here.

21
A Meeting of Friends

Despite knowing that the Frost estate was virtually unassailable, Hayden still got his hopes up in the following days that someone would make a rescue attempt. It was hard not to let himself believe in the possibility that his father had sensed danger was coming and had amped up his security to meet it. It was then easy to deduce that since he was adding protection to the grounds themselves, that he expected his light curtain and the other exterior defenses might fail him. Add all of that to the timing of Hayden's letter to Asher—and the fact that the alternative for him was a horrible death in the imminent future—and Hayden was desperate to believe that anything was possible.

But in the four days that followed, nothing remotely interesting happened. If people were gathered outside of the compound, hacking away at the defenses, they obviously weren't making any progress, because he didn't even hear the sounds of powerful magic clashing.

His father also seemed to have satisfied his momentary paranoia, because he made no additional efforts at increasing security from what Hayden could tell, nor did he appear evenly remotely worried. In fact, the man seemed to have gotten a few decent nights of sleep recently; the dark circles were gone from around his eyes and he looked more energetic than ever.

Hayden was occupying his usual chair in the library, reading the umpteenth book since he came to the Frost estate and trying to estimate how long it would take him to get through the entire library, when suddenly his father looked up from his work, glanced through the Black Prism and said, "Excellent."

Figuring that anything his father considered excellent was a sure sign of doom for Hayden, he nonetheless asked, "Sir?" to indicate his interest.

His father turned his head as though just realizing Hayden was in the room with him. "I've overcome one of the few remaining obstacles that prevent me from reclaiming my Source from you."

And also from reclaiming the entirety of mine, thus killing me. Funny, how his father liked to gloss over that part whenever they discussed the matter.

"Oh," he said aloud. Hayden wasn't really sure whether to congratulate the man to prove that he wasn't afraid of death, or whether to be snarky in the face of defeat. Since he couldn't decide which would be more impressive, he did neither, instead asking, "So what does this do to your timeline for fixing my Foci and having another go at the Source removal?"

He was proud of himself for sounding unaffected and only casually interested in the answer. He was determined not to die begging and crying on hands and knees, like so many other innocent people his father had murdered in the last decade.

"The issue of melding was my greatest concern," the Dark Prism explained vaguely, "and now that I have addressed that particular issue, it will probably take no longer than a week to resolve everything else."

Six more days to live. The countdown begins.

"I see," Hayden replied evenly, turning pointedly back to his book to feign disinterest, though his eyes weren't taking in any of the words or diagrams on the page in front of him. He wanted to get up and run from the room until he found Bonk, whom he could plead with to help him find some way to escape. There had to be something they hadn't thought of yet, some glitch in his father's defenses that would let them get away unharmed. He was only sixteen; no one should have to die that young.

But he knew, even as his mind conjured wild images of him chewing through the Binders on Bonk's legs so he could unleash his magic and somehow get them both out of there, that there was no escape. If Bonk knew a way to get them out, he would have already volunteered it by now. The fact that they were still here only proved that there was no way out. He'd even tried using the violet prism to break the Binders on Bonk's legs to no avail, wasting a precious fraction of his only weapon only to learn that the Binders used on a magical creature were not the same as the Binders used on humans.

I should just try to appreciate the last few days of my life as much as possible.

But how was he supposed to do that, when he was trapped inside his own house with a madman who was taciturn at best and psychotically homicidal on a whim? Sure, he could try to avoid his father for the next few days, but his only other sources of companionship were the other nine captives, eight of whom were wary of him and one of whom might have a mad crush on him.

No, there's no time for fun. I need to make sure I'm as prepared as possible for ending my own life before he can get a chance at taking my Source.

It seemed like it should be easy, ending his own life before his father could, but there were several complicating factors: primarily, that Hayden was determined to try to defeat his father with the violet prism he possessed before he just resigned himself to death. That would make things much more difficult for him, because if (and when) he engaged his father in combat, the Dark Prism would do everything in his power to incapacitate him early, making it impossible for Hayden to take his own life even if he wanted to.

He had done nothing but study magic for weeks, but he still felt woefully unprepared. From what he had seen of his father's abilities, the man obviously knew much more magic than he did, and had a monumental advantage with the Black Prism. Ideally, Hayden would find some way to get the Black Prism away from him and hide it, but he suspected that would be more difficult than beating his father to death with a tissue, since the man never removed his circlet from what Hayden could tell.

Setting down his book, Hayden watched his father from across the library. He was visible in profile, leaning over his worktable and peering through the Black Prism with one eye, sketching something in green pencil on the paper in front of him. He looked relaxed and focused, and if he noticed Hayden watching him he didn't give any indication of it. With his features relaxed, the resemblance between them was quite striking.

I can't do this right now.

Hayden stood up and walked calmly from the library without speaking. His father ignored him completely. When the door closed behind him, he picked up his pace and hurried down the second floor hallway, taking the stairs downward two at a time. He threw the front door open as he approached it and burst out onto the grounds, inhaling deeply and relaxing marginally in the fresh air and sunlight. Standing out here like this, basking in the mid-day sun and listening to the gentle trickle of water running down the nearest fountain, he was almost able to convince himself that he was free, and that all of his problems had been locked away in the overbearing mansion behind him.

Walking idly around the garden paths, winding his way around topiary and fountains, he let his thoughts turn inward once more.

What would my life be like now if my father had never realized he had a son?

It was hard to imagine. First of all, his mother would likely still be alive, and there was a chance that Hayden would never even learn that he was magically-inclined. If that happened, he would never have ended up at Mizzenwald, would never have met Zane and his other friends, or Asher and the other Masters.

I'd never have met Tess.

That was painful to even consider, undoing some of the best (and worst) years of his life just to preserve his childhood memories. If someone had asked him when he was ten, he would have said without hesitation that he'd sacrifice anything and everything to get his mother back and return to the way things were. But now? Even if he could go back in time and make it so he never encountered his father that day and absorbed part of his Source, he wasn't at all sure that that's what he would do.

Somehow it was calming to know that he would still choose this fate, even though it meant a very short life expectancy in the end. There was something freeing about having it be a choice, rather than something forced upon him.

He rounded a stone bench and found Cinder perched on the head of a statue carved in the image of a dragon.

Surprised, Hayden stopped short and said, "Cinder?" feeling distinctly awkward. He remembered years past, playing fetch with Cinder and Bonk, confiding his problems to them when it didn't seem there was anyone else for him to talk to. Now they were supposed to be enemies, but he couldn't muster any bad feelings for his father's familiar, even now, at the end.

Cinder regarded him neutrally, looking as regal and self-contained as ever while he surveyed Hayden from his perch.

"Well, this is a bit of a mess, isn't it?" Hayden asked with a sad smile, sitting down on the stone bench and regarding the dragonling. "I didn't really think things would end up this way for me."

Cinder, naturally, said nothing to this.

"Did you know, all this time, that he was still alive somewhere?" Hayden asked. "Or did you think he was dead too?"

That was an interesting thought, and one that had just occurred to him. Had Cinder known that his master was locked away in the other realm, and was just biding his time at Mizzenwald until he returned, or had he believed his master to be dead and was just spending time at the place he chose to call home? There were still many unknowns regarding the limits of a dragonling's power, so it was hard to say whether their magical senses could transcend realms. But if Cinder *had* known where the Dark Prism was waiting all that time, had he subtly guided events so that Hayden was fated to end up inside the schism and encounter his father? That was a chilling thought.

Unfortunately, while Bonk's expressions were usually easy for Hayden to interpret, Cinder was quite opaque, and Hayden had no idea what the look he received right now meant.

That dragon could out-stare the statue he's perched upon.

"Well, I guess it doesn't matter anymore," Hayden conceded. "I'll just let my father rip out my Source, and that'll be the ignominious end of Hayden Frost."

This time Cinder vented what was unmistakably a derisive snort, and Hayden smiled.

"Alright, so I was lying, but it's hard to get a reaction out of you sometimes," he said. "I'll still get my Source ripped out soon, but I won't go quietly."

Cinder didn't look at all surprised by this piece of information. And why should he? He had spent years observing Hayden and learning to understand his motivations and his temperament. He knew Hayden infinitely better than his own father did.

I wonder how much insight he has shared with my dear Father.

If his father knew he was going to go back on his word and fight at the end, then things could get interesting very soon. On the heels of that thought he realized something else.

My father can't know that I plan on fighting him, or he would have captured Tess and brought her here to threaten me with. He would want everything to be in place when he's ready to try his spell again to make sure I'm compliant.

There was always the chance that he was just waiting until he was done perfecting his alignments before he brought her here, but Hayden forced himself to believe that Cinder hadn't told on him and that the Dark Prism simply assumed he was young and too frightened to do anything but keep his word.

"Will you promise me something?" Hayden asked the dragonling, who was still watching him silently. "It shouldn't interfere with your mandate not to act against my father's best interests."

Cinder inclined his head, cautiously willing him to go on.

"Please don't kill Bonk." Hayden had to pause here at an unexpected tightness in his chest that choked off the last word. He swallowed the emotion down and continued. "When he sees me fighting my father, I'm sure he'll try to help in some way, and I know that you'll have to interfere on my father's behalf. But Bonk's in Binders and he doesn't stand a chance against you in a fight, so he's not a real threat. But you know how he is; he won't care that there's no point in him trying to save me, and I know you all were friends and that you can't actually want to hurt him, even if you think he's ridiculous most of the time."

Hayden paused to calm himself once again before continuing. "Just…just knock him out or something until it's all over, and then there'll be no reason for him to keep fighting. He can go back to Asher or Tess and they can look after him and vice versa. Please, Cinder. Bonk's been the best companion I could have asked for, and I didn't always appreciate him properly, but he doesn't deserve to die just because he's loyal to me."

Cinder considered him for a long moment, his expression as unreadable as ever, though there was something else behind it that Hayden couldn't quite interpret. Finally, the dragonling gave a curt nod, and Hayden exhaled in relief.

One less thing to worry about.

It was the only loose end he could really tie-up from where he was at, so it would have to do. He thanked Cinder and stood up, turning back towards the house with new resolve.

I need to keep studying.

He retraced his steps back to the library on the second floor, entering the room quietly and returning to his seat by the fireplace, though it wasn't currently lit. His father gave no indication that he had noticed Hayden's absence or his return, though Hayden knew that was all an act by now. He picked up his book and continued reading about an alignment that could melt metal.

An hour and a half later, he heard an explosion.

Hayden dropped his book in surprise, and Aleric snapped his attention away from his work and looked through the window. Hayden had no idea what had blown up; it sounded like something large, but the sound had also had an odd, muffled quality to it.

Another crash followed, less muted, and the distorted prisms that his father kept on the worktable shuddered slightly, along with the crystals on the chandelier.

The Dark Prism hurried to the window for a better look, and his eyes widened in surprise—one of the few times Hayden had seen that much expression on his face. Before he could ask what was going on, Bonk soared in through the still-broken window beside his father, clutching the violet prism in his talons.

Hayden and Aleric both watched his flight in unison, as Bonk coasted over to Hayden and dropped the prism in his waiting hands.

For a moment that seemed to stop time, Hayden and his father made eye-contact. The dangerous flicker of insanity flared to life in the latter's eyes as they came to an understanding.

The Dark Prism brought down the eyepiece of his circlet just as Hayden dove out of his chair and rolled across the floor behind a bookshelf. A moment after he'd left his seat, it burst into bright green flames that consumed the entirety of it and burned out within a few seconds, leaving only ash in its wake.

Guess he's too crazy to remember that he wants me alive.

Hayden scooted back from the bookshelf as it exploded towards him, deluging him in heavy books, which slammed into him hard enough to leave bruises. He frantically turned the violet prism in front of his eye before the dust settled and cast Clone on himself three times in rapid succession, watching the copies of himself fan out.

Run around and cause confusion! he mentally commanded, leaping to his feet and doing the same so that it wasn't immediately apparent which Hayden was the real one.

The ruse worked. Four Haydens were running around the room in different directions, and the Dark Prism had to pause for a moment to consider which to attack first. Fortunately, he turned towards the Hayden on the opposite side of the room from the real one, putting his back to him.

Hayden cast Pierce at his father's back just as he heard a roar from the grounds that could only mean the magically-enslaved monsters had been called into play.

That means they've made it through the light curtain!

His heart soared at the thought that help might be coming, but he didn't have long to celebrate, as his father whirled around so fast that he might have been waiting for Hayden to attack from behind, rebounding the spell and causing Hayden to cast Shield on himself just to block it.

"You can't defeat me," his father said calmly, twisting the Black Prism and silently casting something that shattered Hayden's shield. "I always know when magic is being used against me. It is a spell that you could never hope to replicate."

Awesome, Hayden thought ruefully, dispersing his clones and casting Break at the Black Prism.

His father didn't even bother blocking the attack, and somehow the Black Prism absorbed the spell without any visible sign of damage. Hayden targeted his father's heart and cast Stop, trying not to dwell on the consequence if he was successful; he had told everyone that he was willing to do what was necessary to win, and now it was time to step up.

In a way, this was better than having the extra week to dwell on the inevitable, slowly counting down the hours of his life. The abruptness of the fight prevented him from thinking about anything except the battle, before his courage could fail him.

His father blocked the spell and fired back something that Hayden tried to shield himself against. The shield was only half-formed when the spell shattered it, the magic grazing one arm and making it feel like he was being burned alive from the inside out.

Somewhere outside was the unmistakable hunting cry of a magically-inclined dragon, but there was no time to figure out which of the three dragonlings it was. Praying that Bonk was alright, Hayden dove behind the worktable and knocked it onto its side so he could hide behind it. He threw himself into his magic with reckless abandon, peeking out from behind the table and casting faster than he had ever cast in his life.

He started with Sear, which was deflected, and then followed with Stun, Blind, Break, and Pierce in rapid succession, before ducking behind the table again.

His father avoided the first three spells—barely—but Hayden's piercing spell caught him in the shoulder and Hayden saw his father wince.

I wonder how long it's been since anyone actually landed a spell against the Dark Prism? Hayden twisted the violet prism rapidly in front of his eye, seeking fresh inspiration. *If I survive long enough to see Asher, I'll have to tell him about my accomplishment.*

His father was clearly furious at being wounded, and returned with a volley of magic that seemed to explode out of him at random. The first spell slammed into the table and knocked it into Hayden so hard that he got thrown into a backward roll. The second spell caused the table to break into dozens of wooden fragments, which flew at Hayden like spears. He tried to roll out of the way but was only partially successful, and one of the fragments of wood sliced through his pant leg, drawing blood as it flew past.

In a rush of adrenaline, Hayden cast Clone again even as he was rolling out of the way, over and over until half a dozen copies of himself were attempting to right themselves alongside him.

"Not this time," the Dark Prism said coldly, twisting the Black Prism in his eyepiece and casting some sort of magical net that seemed to rush past Hayden, banishing all of the copies as it made contact. "Where did you get that prism?" he demanded, as Hayden dodged another spell and was almost crushed by a falling bookshelf.

"You shouldn't have underestimated me, Father!" Hayden yelled back from beneath the detritus of books and splintered wood. "I'm as much a Frost as you are."

He was still sitting on the floor, but there was no time to get up. Hayden's sweaty palm almost caused him to drop the remaining prism fragment—now half its original size—as he turned it in front of his eye.

This is going to get terrifying when my prism is spent.

He started to cast Break, but his father cast his own spell at Hayden's prism, and Hayden was barely able to throw it away from him before it exploded in brilliant white light, which surely would have blinded him or forced some kind of hideous light-sickness upon him if he had still been looking through it. The effect of the dark magic being used on it caused the violet prism to shudder violently and then shatter into a mist of fine powder.

Well, I gave it a good try...

He hoped his father's shoulder was really hurting him. It would be some small consolation to cause the man any amount of inconvenience.

Aleric bestowed a condescending smirk upon him at last, twisting the Black Prism slowly in front of his eye as though deliberating over which spell would be the best one to kill his only son with. Hayden was ashamed at the momentary spike of fear that surged through him, that made him want to cry out that he was supposed to be kept alive long enough to have his Source drained, because it would buy him another few minutes of precious life, if nothing else. He mastered the impulse and took a deep breath, determined to face death like a man, not like a scared little boy.

His last, wild prayer as the Dark Prism prepared to cast was that hopefully whoever had brought down the defenses around the estate would be better armed than he was.

Something that looked like black lightning burst out of the Black Prism and streaked towards him so rapidly that Hayden didn't even have time to do anything other than close his eyes and prepare for death.

The unexpected crash that heralded powerful magic colliding set off a shockwave so forceful that it knocked him flat on his back. Wondering why he wasn't dead yet, Hayden opened his eyes and saw the remnants of light dissipating from around some sort of shield that had been cast in front of him.

Eyes widening in surprise, Hayden struggled back to a sitting position and saw who had shielded him from death at the last second.

Asher.

The Prism Master was at the door of the library, panting as though he'd sprinted the whole way there from Mizzenwald, his combat circlet around his head and fully-loaded with prisms. A violet prism was in his primary eyepiece, with a clear one in the compounding slot in front of it.

Hayden couldn't help but feel a wild surge of relief at the sight of Master Asher, because his presence had always meant safety in the past.

His father noticed Asher at the same moment as Hayden had and said, "How did you get past the light curtain?" in a tone of cold disbelief.

Asher smirked and said, "Your son isn't the only one you seem to have underestimated, Aleric. You'll be unhappy to hear that I've brought quite a few friends with me."

"You seem to have lost them along the way," the Dark Prism observed flatly.

"Some are battling monsters, and some of them scattered to search the house for you." Asher shrugged. "But I knew where you'd be, Aleric; even in madness, you're too predictable."

Hayden's father scowled at that and attacked his old friend with the Black Prism, casting so many spells in rapid succession that Hayden marveled at anyone being able to look for alignments that quickly.

Asher was no novice though, and met the attacks head-on, twirling his primary and secondary prisms around in their eyepieces so fast that Hayden almost got a headache just watching it. Unfortunately, with the speed of the Dark Prism's casting, Asher was barely able to keep up with defending himself, let alone go on the offense. Hayden saw his mentor cast shielding spells more powerful than he had ever seen before, reflecting and dispelling the attacks against him over and over again. The clash of magic as their spells collided sent scattered beams of light splitting off in all directions and occasionally toppled more furniture as shockwaves rippled through the library.

If Asher slows down for even a second, my father will have him.

Hayden forced himself out of his stupor and pulled himself to his feet, finally feeling the pain from where his father's spells had hit him but doing his best to ignore it. He could still hear shouts and the roaring of monsters outside, as well as the sounds of magic being unleashed around the grounds. He wondered how many people had come to help fight, and sincerely prayed that his mentor had the good sense to leave Tess and Zane at school where it was safe.

Hayden looked around wildly, sifting through debris and the ruins of the library in the desperate hope that there would be a weapon he could use to help Asher fight. Preferably a prism or a wand, though he doubted he would get so lucky. More likely, he'd have to settle for a splintered table leg.

It would be nice if Asher would toss me one of his spare prisms...

Hayden didn't dare raise his voice to ask, because if he broke the man's concentration for even a second, he would likely die.

He seized the sharpest looking fragment of wood he could find and tried to approach his father slowly from behind, in the hopes of passing unnoticed. Unfortunately, his father blasted Asher off of his feet with an Incendiary spell at that moment and turned in time to see Hayden approaching.

The Prism Master flew backwards and slammed into the closed doors before falling to the floor and rolling back to his feet as though unfazed by the entire ordeal.

"Hayden, RUN!" he called out as the Dark Prism turned his eyepiece to find a new alignment.

Not waiting to see what spell his father chose, Hayden threw the table leg at him and dove to the floor just as a ripple of heat passed directly overhead. More books flew off of the shelves behind him and nearly buried him once more.

"Just go!" Asher commanded, spinning his secondary circlet around to put a fresh prism in front of him. "Leave him to me!"

There was nothing Hayden wanted to do more than follow directions right now, but he knew what happened the last time Asher had fought his father alone, and he didn't think the Dark Prism would feel terribly forgiving towards his old friend a second time.

His father's attention was diverted again by the more immediate threat of Master Asher as he began casting, this time taking the offensive and forcing Aleric to defend himself.

*We just need to hold out long enough for more help to come...*Hayden thought desperately. *Once the others clear out the monsters, my father will be outnumbered.*

Just as Hayden began to wonder why his father hadn't simply translocated himself to a safe location, he realized he already knew the answer. Even as the Dark Prism shielded himself against Asher's attacks, he was moving steadily closer to Hayden, as though positioning himself for something.

He won't leave without me. He either wants to kidnap me again or kill me, but he won't risk me being rescued, because if I am armed, I am dangerous to him—I showed my hand when I managed to injure him.

It seemed that his father acknowledged him as a threat at last, especially after fighting him when Hayden was armed with only a single prism. Still, that didn't bode well for his chances of survival...no wonder Asher was telling him to run away.

His father took advantage of a momentary pause in Asher's attacks to turn to Hayden and cast some sort of squeezing spell. Hayden only knew it was a squeezing spell because in his father's haste, his aim was off, and the upside-down armchair beside him cinched in at the middle like an hourglass and then ripped itself apart completely.

"Hayden, GO!" Asher shouted, sweat pouring down his face as he dodged attacks and switched prisms a third time. Half of the prisms in his secondary circlet had been consumed completely; he was going to have to reload soon, which would make him vulnerable to attack.

Deciding that his presence here really wasn't helping anything, Hayden made for the door. He was only halfway across the room when he felt something slam into his back and cause him to pitch forward so hard that the air was knocked out of his lungs when he hit the ground. Coughing and gasping for breath, Hayden spit out a mouthful of blood, only then realizing that he'd cut his lip with his teeth in the fall. He also realized he couldn't feel his legs.

A paralyzing spell! he thought furiously. He had read about this just days ago, and if he had a clear prism on him he could actually dispel it. As it was, he was forced to pull himself forward with his arms, scraping his lower half over bits of wood, glass, and the remains of hundreds of books that were in his way.

It was as he was belly-crawling towards the door that he realized Bonk and Cinder were perched side-by-side at the exit to the second floor hallway, turned towards each other and engaged in some sort of conversation that consisted of low squeaks and clicking sounds that Hayden didn't understand.

Well, at least Bonk is alright...

Of course, it would be nice if his familiar would stir himself to bring Hayden another prism, but at least Cinder was keeping out of the fight as well so far. Hayden hoped whatever they were talking about was really important, because they were ignoring the battle completely, thoroughly engrossed in their discussion.

Bonk's probably asking where the nearest squirrel can be found now that the light curtain is down.

"AH!" the sound of Asher crying out in pain caused Hayden to turn his head in terror. Fearing the worst, it was actually a relief to see that the Prism Master had sustained a burn to one arm that caused the skin to bubble and turn black and not something worse, though normally a necrotic burn was about as bad as things could get.

Another spell from the Black Prism sent Asher toppling backward end-over-end, slamming his head against the wall and becoming still.

Without thinking, Hayden used all the might in his arms to fling himself towards his mentor, determined to get to him before his father could kill him, even if he was only delaying the inevitable by a few seconds. His fingers bled from clawing himself forward across the wooden floor so hard, but he flung himself close enough to grab the last prism from the circlet around Asher's head as his father approached them both.

"Asher is dead," his father greeted him coldly, "and you haven't a hope of defeating me in the condition you're in."

"Probably not," Hayden panted, out of breath as he held onto the prism in his hand as though it was the only thing that mattered in this world, willing himself to believe that his father was wrong about the Prism Master being dead. "But I'd rather die fighting than spend another minute in your company, and I intend to take your Source and mine with me when I go."

A moment of hesitation while sanity flashed across his father's features, remembering why he had been trying to keep Hayden alive all this time. Knowing this was the best opening he would ever get, Hayden cast Stop at his father's heart once again.

And once again, his father reacted in time to shield himself from the spell.

"Damn it, Hayden," Asher muttered weakly, still lying crumpled on the floor. "I told you to get out."

Hayden was so relieved to hear his mentor's voice right now that he said, "Yeah, well I told you not to bother rescuing me, so I guess we're both terrible at following directions."

This moment of camaraderie between them seemed to infuriate the Dark Prism more than anything else that had happened so far. The insanity burned back into life behind his eyes as rage transformed his features so that he looked like an avenging demon from a scary story.

With an inarticulate sound of raw hatred, his father turned the Black Prism once more in his eyepiece, and time seemed to slow down all around Hayden as his vision suddenly sharpened. In that moment their eyes met, and without knowing how he knew, Hayden understood exactly what his father was about to do.

He isn't going to kill me right now. He's going to blind me.

And not just a simple Blinding spell, which was a difficult compound of violet-violet and was only temporary. His father was going to use a corrupted version through the Black Prism, which would rip away his sight for the rest of his life, burning through the foci in his eyes as well as his magical conduits, robbing him of the ability to do any magic or even to perceive light for the rest of his short, miserable life. Somehow he had brought his father from a place of wild rage straight to bitter, spiteful hatred.

Hayden didn't even remember looking through the prism in his hand, or what alignment he was seeking, but abruptly he found himself casting in time to intercept the Blinding spell, which stopped in front of him and sheared off into brilliant arrays of light with black streaks coiled throughout. For the second time in his life, Hayden seemed to have found the spell that made magic scatter and part around him.

He felt it tug on his Source, but he was stronger and more skillful than in his second year, and it didn't fatigue him as rapidly this time around. The prism began to fractionally shrink in his hand as the spell continued to burn through him, making him momentarily impervious to magical harm.

Hayden dispelled the paralysis from his legs and cast a simple healing spell on himself, giving him the energy to get to his feet and face his father on equal terms. The Dark Prism cast black lightning at him, and Hayden made no effort to block it, letting the light bounce off of him and veer off at an angle, shattering the glass from one of the remaining intact windows in the room.

For the first time, his father looked worried.

"What have you done?" he asked in alarm, taking a step backwards.

"I told you, Father," Hayden said calmly, "I'm a Frost. You should never have underestimated me." He aimed at his father and cast Pierce, followed by Stun, Fire, and a spell that was intended to deplete the oxygen from his lungs and make him lose consciousness.

Now it was his father's turn to be on defense, because Hayden had the upper hand. He might still be a slower caster than the Dark Prism, but for the time being, he was immune to magical attacks, so he didn't have to worry about defending himself until the prism ran out, at which point he would be weaponless and soon-to-be murdered anyway.

His father blocked the first three spells, but the fourth caught him off-guard and he fell to his knees and gasped for breath in the moment before he was able to dispel the effects. Hayden cast a Blinding spell at him next, giving him a dose of his own medicine, but it was also blocked.

The prism in Hayden's hand was shrinking more rapidly now, a side-effect of maintaining his invulnerability as well as channeling powerful magic. He probably only had enough time for four or five more spells before it vanished completely.

"That prism won't last forever," his father pointed out coolly. "Then you will be utterly at my mercy."

And I've never met a more merciless man in my entire life...

A spell shot past Hayden, but not from the direction he was expecting, and it took him a moment to realize that Asher must have brought spare prisms along with him and had just reequipped his combat circlet while Hayden distracted his father.

The Dark Prism slapped the spell away in annoyance, still on his knees on the floor, and said, "I've told you both before: you can't outsmart me. I always know when magic is being used against me," in his haughtiest voice.

Then he pitched forward so that he had to catch himself with his hands to avoid falling flat on his face, as though he had been pushed hard from behind.

"Shame the same can't be said for arrows," Tess said coldly, standing behind him with her empty bow still raised in position to fire.

Hayden hadn't even seen her come into the room, and had no idea how she managed to get in the back of the library without coming through the main doors, unless she had somehow translocated directly into the room with them. It was then that Hayden saw the arrow sticking straight through his father's back, the head poking out through the front of his shirt. A scripture note was wrapped around the shaft of the arrow, which could be the only explanation for how Tess had managed enough power behind her shot to go straight through a man that muscularly built.

Aleric Frost gasped and touched the tip of the arrow that protruded through his shirt, before reaching up with one hand to adjust the Black Prism.

Of course, Hayden thought ruefully. *Asher said that broken prisms had even better healing spells than normal ones, way back in my first year at Mizzenwald.*

He raised his own prism back to dueling height and looked for anything that would prevent his father from healing himself, when a small shadow passed overhead and distracted him.

Cinder coasted gracefully to his master, alighting only long enough to snatch the Black Prism from its eyepiece and then dropping it in front of Hayden, who was probably meant to catch it, but was so stunned by the turn of events that he let it fall to the floor in front of him.

His father stared at his familiar with wide eyes as Cinder landed beside him, regarding him silently. The Dark Prism looked shocked, hurt, and like he suddenly realized he had made a horrible mistake.

"Cinder…" he choked out, as blood continued to pump out through the hole in his chest and back.

Then he looked at Hayden, who had no idea what emotion he saw pass behind his father's eyes before the infamous Dark Prism fell to the floor, dead.

22

The Last Frost

For almost a full minute the room was utterly still. No one moved, no one spoke, and for all Hayden could tell, no one even breathed. It was as though they were all waiting for confirmation that the Dark Prism was really gone, half-expecting him to spring back to his feet and murder them all. Hayden still couldn't wrap his mind around what had just happened.

Finally Tess said, "That was for my mother," to the corpse of Hayden's father, dropping her bow and stepping around the body to face Hayden. Upon closer inspection, she was covered in scrapes and bruises, clearly having been in the battle against the monsters outside. Now that Hayden listened for it, he couldn't hear the sounds of fighting on the grounds anymore, though he had no idea if the fighting had been over for a long time, or just since his father's magic ceased working on the magical creatures he'd subdued.

"Tess," Hayden said dumbly, not knowing how he intended to follow that one word. "You should have stayed where it was safe," he blurted out without thinking.

She pursed her lips at him and said, "I've lost enough people I care about to that man," she gestured to the body on the floor with distaste. "I refuse to lose any more." Turning her scowl on Hayden she added, "You should have written me instead of Asher."

"I wasn't planning on making it out of here alive," he said defensively. "I, uh, didn't think you'd be okay with that."

Tess approached him and said, "I figured it was something stupid and noble like that."

And then they were kissing, and Hayden's arms were wrapped around her so tightly he worried that he might crush her against him. As far as he was concerned, they were the only two people in the world right now and he could go on like this forever.

Then Asher said, "Forgive me if I don't greet you with quite the same level of enthusiasm," ruining the moment.

Hayden released Tess and turned to his mentor.

"Oh, are you alright? I forgot you were here."

"Thanks," Asher grumbled, getting to his feet and checking himself for obvious signs of damage, casting a few healing spells on himself for good measure.

"Sorry, that isn't what I—"

"I know what you meant," Asher waved down his apology before he could give it. "How did you even get in here?" he asked Tess with academic interest.

"I managed to find a clear spot through the fighting and climbed the outer wall," she replied as though this was the most obvious thing in the world. "I came in through that broken window," she pointed to it for good measure.

"You scaled a two-story mansion from the outside while carrying a bow and arrow, and didn't fall to your death?" Asher looked genuinely impressed with her.

"My father has been teaching me survival skills for my entire life," she remarked casually.

Asher turned to Hayden and said, "This one's definitely a keeper."

"Yeah, I thought so too," he agreed immediately.

"And here I thought Aleric would be defeated by the might of another prism-user," Asher continued, now glancing around at the damage in the room. "I never would have thought of shooting him with a bow and arrow."

Tess shrugged and said, "No one ever thinks of the non-magical solution, but you heard what he said: he could detect magic being used against him, but not ordinary weapons."

Hayden frowned and pointed out that she had used a scripture on her arrow to give it more piercing power.

"Yes, but that magic was being applied to the arrow, not to your father directly."

My girlfriend is much smarter than me, Hayden realized in that moment. He had long suspected it to be true, but now he had actual confirmation.

"Do you realize, Tess, that you just defeated the infamous Dark Prism?" Asher observed mildly. "You'll be a hero for the ages."

To Hayden's surprise, Tess blanched at this and said, "No—I don't want that." She hurried to the body of Hayden's father and pulled the arrow roughly out of it, breaking it into pieces with her bare hands and tossing the fragments into the debris that was already scattered around the library.

"What? Why not?" Hayden asked, stunned by her reaction.

"When have I ever wanted to be famous?" she pursed her lips, wiping her bloodstained hands on the back of her pants. "I don't like being the center of attention and I don't want all the fanfare of being people's mascot; that's *your* job."

Hayden had to admit that it wasn't always very fun having strangers recognize him on sight, and dealing with all of their preconceived notions about him. And Tess *had* always been rather shy...

"Just say that you two did it," she pleaded. "You all did most of the fighting anyway. If you weren't distracting him when I showed up my arrow never would have worked against him," she explained rapidly, as they heard footsteps ascending the stairs from the ground floor.

"Are you sure you want to give away the credit for this great victory?" Asher asked, a sympathetic look on his face. Hayden noticed that his mentor avoided looking at his old friend's body as much as possible.

"Yes, please," Tess insisted. "Besides, this way there won't be any doubt in people's minds that you two aren't evil like him. No one can say anything against you now."

The others began bursting into the room at that point, ending their conversation. Kilgore and Willow were there, along with Oliver and Magdalene Trout. Hayden was surprised to see Master Kiresa alongside them, looking a little worse-for-wear from the fight outside, though Hayden had never felt more warmly towards the man in his life.

Kilgore stopped at the threshold, took in the scene inside the library and said, "He's dead," in mild surprise, returning an elixir and a wand to his belt.

"Yes," Asher agreed, "we got him."

There were some cheers at that and exclamations of relief, as most of the group turned back the way they came to help with the remaining monsters on the grounds. Apparently there were people outside that were still fighting monsters, but these five had broken through to help take down the Dark Prism.

Only Master Willow and Magdalene Trout stayed behind, now entering the library and taking in the scene more fully.

"What happened?" the latter asked thoughtfully, stepping carefully around the body of Hayden's father and looking around at the signs of magical damage to the room.

"Hayden and I took turns fighting him until we scored a lucky hit," Asher explained without looking at Tess, who exhaled in relief against Hayden at this summary of events. "He might have been able to heal himself, but Cinder came in at the last minute and took the Black Prism away from him. I don't think it was until then that Aleric realized he was in the wrong all this time."

Master Willow raised his eyebrows and said, "*Cinder?* His own familiar took away his prism and condemned him to death?" he didn't look like he believed this for a minute.

"I know it sounds impossible," Hayden interjected. "But it's true; we all saw it. I don't know how he managed to betray his master like that, but—"

"He didn't betray his master," Asher put in quietly, meeting the dragonling's gaze. "He chose to ally himself with Aleric Frost all those years ago, not the Dark Prism. His master died years ago, for all intents and purposes," he explained, still maintaining eye contact with the familiar. "I suppose he finally decided that no trace of his old master could be salvaged, and intervened to protect the memory of the boy he served from any further desecration from the monster he had become."

They were all silent after that, and Hayden finally thought he understood what Bonk and Cinder had been discussing while he was fighting for his life. He also thought back to the night he had asked Bonk to find a way to contact Slasher, and how he had dreamed he'd seen Cinder in the room with him then. He hadn't been dreaming after all; it wasn't Bonk who had found a way to contact Slasher and summon him. It was Cinder.

"I know you didn't do it just for me," Hayden said to the dark purple dragonling, who was so unlike his own familiar and yet somehow just as much a part of his family. "But thank you."

Cinder inclined his head slightly in acknowledgement of this and then took flight, soaring through a broken window and disappearing over the grounds.

"Where's he going?" Tess asked in alarm. "Do you think he's going to leave for good?"

Asher followed the dragonling's progression with a tired smile and said, "Oh, I expect he'll reappear at Mizzenwald sometime. He always comes home eventually."

Hayden hoped he was right about that, because he didn't like the thought of Cinder going to live somewhere all alone for the rest of his years, probably in the Forest of Illusions, which was still the creepiest place he had ever been.

"Is that the Black Prism?" Master Willow asked softly, pointing to the floor at Hayden's feet.

Hayden looked down and saw it lying there in front of him. He had completely forgotten about it in the wake of his father's death, and he also realized that the prism fragment he had been holding in his hand had vanished at some point as well, and that the light-scattering spell he had cast upon himself had dissipated.

"Yeah, it is." He leaned down and picked it up, ignoring the soft gasps from the others as he held it out in front of him. "Trust me, I have no desire to use this thing. My father made me look through it one day to prove a point, and just glancing at the corrupted alignments made me vomit spectacularly."

"May I?" Asher held out his hand, and Hayden passed the Black Prism to him gently, noticing the wary looks pass over Magdalene Trout and Master Willow's faces.

Asher held it up in front of him gingerly, as though it was fragile, closing his right eye and looking through it with his left. Almost immediately, he pulled back from it and clamped his mouth shut. Hayden recognized the look of a man who was trying desperately not to hurl.

"Mother of magic," Asher groaned. "This thing is horrible. It's astounding that Aleric was able to use it without his brain liquefying."

"That's what I thought when I looked through it, too," Hayden observed.

"We'll have to destroy it, but it's going to take some planning," Asher continued. "I suspect that this thing is going to unleash an unholy amount of magic once we break it apart, and the last thing we need is to blow a crater in the middle of the continent and inadvertently kill more innocent people."

Hayden hadn't even considered that, but it made sense.

"I want to help destroy it," he put in. "After all the time I spent with my father, seeing what he was inside the schism and in this realm…it feels like something I have to do."

Asher nodded as though this made perfect sense.

"Come," Master Willow interrupted at this point. "We should make sure the others are alright. Further discussion about the future will have to wait."

The others nodded, and though Hayden was so tired and sore that nothing seemed less appealing than going outside to look for more monsters to battle, he went along with the group as they walked down the stairs.

"Oh, that reminds me," Hayden remembered as he glanced in the general direction of the kitchen. "Have you found the nine other captives my father had here? I promised them I'd do everything I could to set them free, and it seems that—thanks to you all—I may actually be able to keep my promise on this one."

"I didn't see anyone else," Asher said, "but then again I was in quite a hurry to get upstairs to help you, so I could have walked right past them for all I know."

"We certainly didn't attack any people out on the grounds," Magdalene added helpfully. "As long as they kept away from the monsters, they should be fine."

Hayden exhaled in relief, following the others out onto the grounds. He noticed that Asher had tucked the Black Prism into one of his pockets and out of sight.

"Hayden, you're alive!" Zane called out from across the lawn, limping towards him around the ruin of statuary.

I'll have to get those rebuilt, Hayden thought automatically, beginning to mentally add up how many house repairs he was going to have to do before he could live here again…assuming he could bring himself to drown out all the bad memories.

The library is going to have to be completely destroyed and turned into something totally different.

"Zane!" he dredged up a short burst of energy to hurry forward and meet his friend.

"They said you did it, that the Dark Prism is gone for good this time!"

"Yeah, he is," Hayden confirmed, glossing over who exactly cast the final blow. "How did you all even get in through the light curtain? I didn't think it was possible to bring that thing down, even knowing what it was."

Zane pointed across the lawn to where Mistress Razelle and Councilman Sark were leaned over Master Laurren, working powerful healing magic.

"It was brilliant—and insane," he explained enigmatically. "Asher and Laurren had this idea at the same time, which meant it was either going to be awesome or tragic."

"Thanks for the vote of confidence," Master Asher put in brightly, looking much more like his normal cheerful self.

Zane turned red in the face but continued. "Anyway, they worked out how to bring it down with magic, but the problem was they needed someone on both sides of the curtain casting the spell at the same time, which seemed impossible."

"Yeah, I'd gotten that far on my own," Hayden waved a hand impatiently, willing his friend to get to the point.

"Well, since you said in your letter that the light curtain would use the light-translating cones in your eyes to burn up your brain and melt your Foci, they had an idea that maybe Master Laurren—"

"Oh," Hayden interrupted, suddenly understanding. "Laurren is completely colorblind—I'd forgotten." He almost laughed at the chink in his father's defenses, the one thing he had never considered. After all, how many magically-inclined people in the world had been stricken colorblind by a spell gone wrong but were still able to use other forms of magic?

"So he was able to just walk right through?" he asked with interest.

"Well, not exactly," Asher winced. "There was still some damage to him—we knew there would be, since he isn't completely blind, so obviously he can still perceive at least white and shades of grey. Our only hope was that the light-sickness was mild enough that he would be still be able to use magic once he got through the wall so that we could bring down the curtain and get the rest of us inside the compound."

"Oh lord, is he alright?" Hayden looked over at the slumped form of Master Laurren with fresh alarm, wondering just how much he had sacrificed to save Hayden and defeat the Dark Prism.

Well, at least his sacrifice paid off. It would have been a hundred times worse if my father was still alive after all this.

"I think so…or, well, I *hope* he will be once Razelle and Sark are finished working their magic on him," Asher amended.

"He remained conscious long enough to help bring down the light curtain, but by the time we encountered the monsters on the grounds he was in poor condition and the others had to peel away from the fighting to begin working on him," Master Willow added grimly.

"Speaking of the monsters," Zane scowled at Hayden, "you might have mentioned them in your letter. About scared the daylights out of us when we made it all the way through the defenses only to be greeted by about fifty monsters who were bent on eating us all."

"Sorry," Hayden frowned apologetically. "I would have if I had known, but the monsters didn't come until after I sent the letter. He got paranoid one day and started summoning them and subduing them; he also dislocated my shoulder that day and was getting ready to torture me to death before Cinder intervened."

The others looked at him in horror, but Hayden waved it away and said, "My shoulder still hurts like crazy, but Hattie shoved it back into place so it should heal eventually. Maybe Kilgore has an elixir that will help speed things up."

"Aleric was going to torture you to death?" Asher asked in a low voice, and Hayden nodded.

"Sometimes he was in perfect control of himself, but then at random he would go nuts and forget who I was or that he was trying to keep me alive long enough to rip my Source out, and he would attack me. Cinder and Bonk both had to save me on more than one occasion, until I got better at keeping out of arms' reach when talking to him."

They were walking while talking, and had finally reached the place where Master Laurren was slouched against the gate, resting in the shade of an oak tree while the Mistress of Healing continued casting magic on him.

"Hi sir," Hayden greeted him first. "How are you feeling?"

"Ah, Frost, it's good to know you survived," Laurren greeted him brightly. "I feel terrible, but thanks to the ministrations of my capable colleagues, I'm recovering. I'll probably get my sight back in a few days—or weeks."

He's blind?!

Hayden could tell it was true as soon as he looked at the Master of Abnormal Magic's purple-blue eyes, which were staring off vaguely and out of focus.

Seeing the look on his face, Mistress Razelle said, "We don't think it's permanent, Hayden. He's just suffered a huge shock to his system, and the light curtain did quite a bit of damage even with the limited impact it had on him."

"I'll be alright," Laurren seconded, looking annoyed at the others for worrying about him.

"Oh yeah," Zane recaptured Hayden's attention. "We found some other people that were being held captive here while we were fighting the monsters. Once we had things mostly under control, we set them free, but this girl—she said her name was Hattie—asked me to tell you that she always believed in you and said you should stop by her house and see her sometime."

Hayden felt his face turn beet red and knew that his friend had chosen this moment to reveal that information to cause him maximum embarrassment. Tess arched her eyebrows at him in surprise.

"I'm going to kill you later," Hayden muttered to his friend. "She had a bit of a crush on me, I think," he added to Tess. "I should visit her at some point, if only to say goodbye and make sure she's not permanently traumatized from this entire ordeal."

Zane made a low-voiced comment about how she'd likely express her gratitude, and Tess helpfully punched him in the arm as hard as she could, which was very effective at quelling any further teasing.

"Ouch," Zane grumbled to Hayden. "Has anyone ever told you that your girlfriend does *not* hit like a girl?"

Thinking of the steely look in her eyes as she put a bolt through his father's heart, Hayden said, "Yes, I've noticed."

EPILOGUE

It took the better part of a week to decide how to get rid of the Black Prism so that no one could ever find it and use it for corrupted magic again. In the end, Asher and Hayden boated out into the Yrani Sea, which separated the northern and southern continent at the place where the Forest of Illusions used to border the coast. Asher suspended it as high as he could hold it over their heads with magic while still keeping it in his line of sight, and Hayden had the honor of casting the magic that broke it.

His mentor had been correct when he'd guessed that the Black Prism would not go quietly, and the resulting magical explosion had capsized their boat and created a sort of magical vortex in the middle of the sea. It had taken a combination of magic, luck, and Bonk to save them and haul their freezing, drenched bodies back to shore where it was safe.

"Well," Asher had said as soon as his teeth stopped chattering. "That giant magical vortex will probably discourage the sorcerers from approaching us from that direction for a few years at least."

That's my mentor, Hayden thought, *always looking on the bright side of things.*

Hayden had once sworn never to return to the Crystal Tower, but it didn't seem that the Council was going to let him keep his promise. At least he returned as a hero this time around, greeted by the thunderous applause from the crowds of people who had showed up to see him—and everyone else who helped fight—receive their medals. Tess should have been the one getting all the praise instead of him, but she seemed quite content to get her slightly-less-prestigious medal for participating in the battle. Zane was soaking up the attention and enjoying every minute of it, and Hayden knew he had always hated being overshadowed by his famous descendant and being the only boy in a family with five sisters.

After the accolades were awarded and the crowds dispersed, there were a lot of boring Council meetings, which Hayden was expected to attend as the ruling member of a Great House. The first few were mostly formalities, confirming the newly appointed Council members into their permanent posts. Sark looked pleased and a little smug to be in his new position, but Hayden didn't begrudge the man his joy to be free of teaching, though he suspected that the two of them would never become friends.

It was another week before he had any free time to himself, and he spent it walking around the perimeter of his estate with Zane and Tess, directing the work crews on the repairs and improvements that were to be made on the property.

Someday this place might just be livable again.

If he was honest with himself, the very thought of living in the Frost estate gave him chills—there were too many bad memories right now for anything else. But Hayden was nothing if not stubborn, and had decided that to be driven out of his rightful home by his father's memory was to accept defeat, and he had no intention of giving the Dark Prism any posthumous power over him.

Eventually I'll get over my discomfort and this place will feel like home.

"So," Zane broke his train of thought. "I thought I should tell you that Master Reede fired one of his apprentices and offered me the open position." He grinned smugly. "All I had to do to get his attention was befriend the most famous kid on the continent, get into all sorts of trouble with him without dying, and then battle about a million monsters for the honor of throwing my life away at the feet of your evil father. Easy as pie."

Hayden snorted in amusement and Tess rolled her eyes.

"I thought you wanted to be a famous monster-hunter," she said to him.

"I do," Zane countered. "But I might as well take the opportunity to learn as much as I can from Reede so that I have a better chance of not being eaten by the monsters I'm hunting in the future."

Tess conceded the point and turned to Hayden.

"What are you going to do?" she watched him carefully for a reaction. "Are you going to drop out and reestablish your Great House, or rally for a spot on the

Council of Mages while everyone is in love with you and they might be willing to actually let you in?"

Ah, so she also heard the rumors about why the tenth Council position is still vacant.

Hayden frowned thoughtfully, though he had given the matter a lot of thought already. It seemed that everyone was pulling him in different directions, supremely confident that they knew what his best interests were better than he did. He'd been quietly offered a place on the Council of Mages—as the youngest member in its history—by Magdalene Trout, who was eager to keep their business interests aligned and the public in her favor. He'd been offered a position in Kargath, working for the High Mayor, who had expended considerable effort explaining why it would be a good thing for him to take a more active role in the local government.

"I should warn you," Zane interrupted his train of thought, "Oliver says that if you come back to Mizzenwald, you're never to come into direct contact with any sort of powder ever again or he'll have you arrested. Apparently he remembers the evacuation from first year quite vividly."

Hayden rolled his eyes and said, "Fine, but if he thinks I'm going to call him 'Master Trout'—which sounds ridiculous, by the way—then he's got another thing coming."

In truth, Hayden didn't harbor any ill will towards his former nemesis. After everything they had been through together, it seemed silly to hold onto a childhood grudge that he barely remembered the reason for. They may never be best friends, but Hayden didn't forget that Oliver had helped him out on numerous occasions—grudgingly, sometimes—and that he had joined the raiding party that stormed the Frost estate to rescue him.

"Hayden, have you noticed that Bonk is fighting a squirrel?" Tess interjected, pointing into the distance.

"Bonk's always fighting squirrels," he answered immediately, not seeing why this was something she considered noteworthy.

"Yes, but I think this time he's losing."

Hayden and Zane turned to see that Tess was correct. Bonk could be seen in the distance, rolling around the grounds with a fat squirrel, which appeared to be getting the better of him.

"Behold the dragonling," Hayden sighed. "Noblest and mightiest of creatures…"

The others laughed and Hayden turned his back on his familiar, trusting that Bonk would eventually triumph over his prey.

"You should replace some of these broken statues with new ones of us, looking dashing and heroic," Zane grinned, pointing to the crumbled bits of plaster and dust that were being hauled away by work crews.

"Sure, because nothing conveys humility like sprinkling enormous sculptures of myself around the lawn of my own house," Hayden snorted in amusement, before turning to Tess. "I don't suppose, once the place gets fixed up, that you would consider stopping by more often? I'll even invite your dad, if you promise that he won't try to glare me to death over dinner."

Tess smiled and said, "He's actually starting to warm up to you, especially now that you've defeated the Dark Prism," she replied smoothly, keeping up the ruse because Zane was with them.

"Oh sure, invite *Tess* to come and stay with you. Never mind your *best friend*..." Zane trilled annoyingly.

"Don't pout, honey dearest, you can stay over as well—Heaven knows I've got enough spare bedrooms."

Zane made a swooning gesture and threw himself at Hayden so that he found himself carrying his friend across the threshold like a new bride, while Tess muttered about boys being idiots as she followed on.

It felt nice to relax and laugh with his friends. After everything they had gone through in the last year, there were times when it felt like Hayden would never be able to enjoy himself again. Days like these gave him hope that everything would turn out okay.

"I think I'm going to go back to school," he said at last, addressing Tess's earlier question. "Everyone else is pressuring me to grow up overnight: run a Great House, attend Council meetings, settle on a career...but I'm sixteen, and with the threat of my father safely removed, I'll probably even live to be seventeen. I want to finish what I started at Mizzenwald, and I've got another year before I hit mastery level in my other classes of interest, plus the apprenticeship with Asher to finish up. After that, who knows where I'll end up?"

His friends accepted his decision without argument, though Zane grumbled about the massive salary he was passing up by skipping out on the Council of Mages' last open position. Hayden pointed out that with the income of a Great House at his disposal, it wasn't like he'd be forced to live off the land and fight Bonk for squirrels at each meal. It just meant he would only be able to afford to staff the Frost estate by half, instead of in full, until he got a job.

Not bad for a kid who spent two years in an orphanage without a single piece of clothing to his name.

He hadn't told anyone at Mizzenwald to expect him back, so Hayden expected Master Asher to be surprised when he returned to school and presented himself for lessons.

What he actually found was that his research notes were waiting for him on the desk in Asher's tragically-cluttered office, along with a mug of hot chocolate that was miraculously still warm.

"How did you know I'd come back?" Hayden asked, still struck by his mentor's ability to surprise him, even now.

"Have you forgotten who you're dealing with? I'm amazingly intelligent," the Prism Master explained easily.

"I see you haven't bothered tidying up the place in my absence," Hayden said flatly, tossing his book bag onto a rare bit of unoccupied floor space.

"If I cleaned up, you'd think you came to the wrong place."

After taking two more steps into the office, Hayden was struck by something else, something horrible, and wrinkled his nose reflexively.

"Uh, sir? What's that terrible smell?"

"Ah, yes," Asher acknowledged cheerfully. "Well, I think I left a bologna sandwich in here a few weeks ago, and it seems to have gotten lost amongst my stacks of paper and gone bad. Your first assignment as my apprentice is to help me locate and remove the odious thing before maggots infest my office."

Well, Hayden thought in amusement, *at least I can't say I didn't know what I was getting into...*